Michael Larsen was born in (published in 1992, followed by U̶N̶C̶E̶R̶T̶A̶I̶N̶T̶Y̶ ̶i̶n̶ ̶1̶9̶9̶4̶ (Sceptre 1997), which was a bestseller in Denmark and published in translation in over twenty countries. THE SNAKE IN SYDNEY is his third novel, and has also been a runaway bestseller in Denmark.

Also by Michael Larsen

Uncertainty

The Snake in Sydney

Michael Larsen

Translated by Anne Born

SCEPTRE

Hodder and Stoughton would like to acknowledge the kind support of
the Danish Literature Information Centre in this publication.

Copyright © by Michael Larsen 1997
English translation copyright © Anne Born 2000

First published as *Slangen I Sydney* in 1997 by Forlaget Centrum A/S, Denmark
This English translation first published in Great Britain in 2000
by Hodder and Stoughton
A division of Hodder Headline
A Sceptre Paperback

The right of Michael Larsen to be identified as the Author of
the Work has been asserted by him in accordance with the
Copyright, Designs and Patents Act 1988.

10 9 8 7 6 5 4 3 2 1

All rights reserved. No part of this publication may be
reproduced, stored in a retrieval system, or transmitted,
in any form or by any means without the prior written
permission of the publisher, nor be otherwise circulated
in any form of binding or cover other than that in which
it is published and without a similar condition being
imposed on the subsequent purchaser.

All characters in this publication are fictitious
and any resemblance to real persons,
living or dead is purely coincidental.

A CIP catalogue record for this title
is available from the British Library

ISBN 0 340 74884 2

Typeset by Palimpsest Book Production Limited,
Polmont, Stirlingshire
Printed and bound in Great Britain by
Clays Ltd, St Ives plc

Hodder and Stoughton
A division of Hodder Headline
338 Euston Road
London NW1 3BH

To my family

I

Saliva ran from her mouth and she gasped desperately for breath, slumped between the shocked elderly couple who had supported her in through the door of Sydney's Prince of Wales Hospital. A tall, younger man Annika assumed to be with them had come on ahead to open the door.

The girl's legs were giving way under her, her head flopped from side to side, and Annika noted she was clutching her hand. Then she collapsed.

Annika was already on her way towards them after alerting Intensive Care. She had been through to Anaesthetics and asked them to make ready, and accompanied by the ward sister and a porter she rushed to meet the little group, with the porter pushing a hospital bed in front of him.

'Take care,' said Annika, as together they lifted the girl on to the bed. 'Has she been drinking?'

The shaken couple looked at her. Then the man, tall, tourist-white in a sun hat, shorts and khaki-coloured socks in white lace-up plimsolls, pulled himself together. He was battling with a thick black canvas bag that hung over his shoulder, which Annika thought must belong to the girl. Then he said:

'We . . . we are tourists. From Sweden. We don't know . . .'

'I can speak a bit of Swedish,' said Annika.

'Oh,' the man said. 'Yes, we don't know the girl . . . we just happened to come across her.'

'Is she breathing?' asked Annika, and without waiting for an answer she bent down towards the girl's face, and felt a faint warm breath on her cheek. There was no trace of alcohol. With her hand she localised a feeble, irregular pulse.

Annika quickly examined the hand the girl had been clutching, and at once caught sight of two bites. One was obvious. The other only showed as a small thin line on the skin. She was no longer in doubt about what had caused the girl's condition. *Bapi*, a snake. Or the ominous *yirritja*, the term used by Kookillo Dhamarandji, John Farrow's assistant at the reptile park in Brisbane, in his work with poisonous snakes.

She took a sterilised tissue from her pocket, bit off the packaging and pressed it to the back of the wounded hand. Then she carefully pulled clear the girl's arm, allowed it to fall loosely down along the side of the bed and locked her own hand in a firm grip around the upper arm.

The small company half ran beside the bed the porter was steering along the corridor. Annika examined the girl as far as the awkward position allowed. The impressions of the snake's teeth were quite far apart, and Annika noticed there was no noticeable swelling around the bite, unfortunately not necessarily a good sign. She cautiously turned the girl's hand and saw two microscopic marks which, to be on the safe side, she also ascribed to the snake. Half running, trying to find more signs of bites, her brain was working at high speed.

'Does she have any allergies?'

'We don't know her,' the elderly Swede replied.

'Where did you find her?'

'She was in a car. Out at Quarantine Head.'

Annika directed a hail of questions at the two old people, asked about proof of health insurance and vaccination cards, but it was clear that they knew hardly anything about the girl. Neither did the young man contribute any helpful details. Later on, Annika could not in fact remember whether he had actually said anything or talked to the others or had just stayed in the background the whole time, and the only thing she had noticed about him, apart from his height, was a scar winding down his right cheek.

The couple had not known the girl had been bitten, they had no idea how it had happened, nor what kind of snake had attacked her. Annika studied the bite again. The distance between the perforations. A large snake. No doubt about that. The bites on the underside of her wrist were more like scratches. Slight grazes that had left a little dry veil of blood like a superficial scrape on the skin.

'What happened out there?'

'We were beside her. In our car. Parked. Suddenly the door of her car opened. And she came staggering out.'

'She's hardly breathing now,' said the nurse.

'Hurry. I daren't let go of her arm,' said Annika, pushing the couple out of the way. 'Please would you wait out in reception?'

Annika, the nurse and the porter ran as fast as they could beside the bed for the last stretch down to Room 2, and when the porter swung it in through the door the anaesthetist and the anaesthetics nurse were finalising their preparations. The electrocardiograph, the defibrillator, medicaments.

Together they lifted the girl carefully on to the table.

Next Annika sent the nurse off to the laboratory for a test of the poison she had wiped on to the tissue.

'Freeze the poison and blood. But take a quick test first.'

Annika glanced at the anaesthetist.

'Why didn't they call an ambulance? Or drive to Manly hospital?'

'Tourists!' he said.

All the same Annika was forced to wonder bitterly whether their chances would have been any better if the couple had called an ambulance so that treatment of the girl could have been started earlier. Or if they had just given her some elementary first aid. Neither she nor the other doctors at the Prince of Wales Hospital ever passed up the chance of drawing attention to Sutherland's method. Pressure Immobilisation. A tight compress around the bite and as far up the stricken part of the body as possible. Followed by binding the limb to keep it completely immobile. That and nothing else. No incisions or sucking out the poison and no pressure on arteries, which at worst could necessitate amputation resulting from lack of oxygen.

To avoid moving the patient about too much they left her in her clothes. They did not even touch the black nylon belt bag she wore round her waist.

A drip was attached to the girl's left arm, and at the same time Annika gave her an adrenalin injection, while she ordered the preparation of promethazin HCl and diluted antidote.

Snakebites always came as a surprise. They never became routine, even though they happened at regular intervals, and each case felt like an emergency. Given the virulence of Australian snakebites, this meant that the situation when it occurred was always one that demanded the highest degree of crisis preparation. Annika swiftly calculated that it must have taken the couple at least half an hour to get to the hospital, so she knew they had already lost precious minutes.

Normally adrenalin was given to prevent any possible allergic reaction, since there is always a potential risk of the patient going into anaphylactic shock. As a rule, an allergic reaction causes the blood pressure to crash-dive, while adrenalin makes the blood vessels contract so the pressure rises again.

The antidote was infused slowly and intravenously for a period of twenty minutes, diluted ten times. Yet another precaution against serum sickness. Before all this the identity of the snake was if possible swiftly identified in order to make use of a monovalent serum, which always considerably reduced the risk of an allergic reaction.

The scanty information provided by the couple was of no help. Annika's experience told her – as did that of other Australian doctors – that unless herpetologists or other experts from zoos were brought in people could not tell the difference between snakes. In ninety per cent of the cases of snakebite they were confronted with, the snake remained unidentified. In reality, time – seconds, minutes – was the only factor she reckoned with.

Annika came to a decision. The girl's condition was critical. She had no idea how long she had been sitting in the car, or how long the poison had been in the girl's body, and she had no idea what kind of snake had bitten her. It could have been a tiger snake. But it could also have been a brown snake. A mulga or a black snake. Annika decided on polyvalent serum.

She stood for a moment studying the attractive, dark-haired girl under the blue woollen hospital blanket. She often asked herself whether she would ever get used to the fact that decisions in the profession she had chosen not only often had to be made quickly, they also had to be right. Every time.

In any case, she had not been in her job long enough not to worry and ponder over the consequences of her decisions. In a few moments they could lose the girl. They could keep her. It was impossible to say. She alone had to decide on the course of action, and there was a large margin of uncertainty in a case like this. She knew nothing about the girl. She did not know if she had allergies, if she suffered from asthma, or if she had received horse proteins before. There was no way of knowing. And there was no time to find out. She asked for the bag, but no one knew who had it. Annika threw a glance at the girl's stomach belt and considered whether it should be examined. But even if and when the contents of the bag or the belt were revealed, there was no guarantee that they would be any the wiser.

The anaesthetics nurse drew her attention to the fact that the girl was hardly breathing and had only a very weak pulse.

'Ninety over sixty,' she said.

'We'll put in a tube,' said the anaesthetist.

As they inserted the tube into the airway, to ensure a free air passage through the larynx, Annika observed the girl, and thought she was growing paler and paler. Almost as white now as the sheet she lay on. Annika took her eyes away, looked at the green lines being drawn across the electrocardiograph against the dark background. The pulsar-like bleeps on the screen like a sign of life. When she again looked at the girl she noticed a difference. The colour had slowly come back to her cheeks.

The anaesthetics nurse looked up.

'A hundred and ten over seventy. It has adjusted itself. We've got her.'

Michael Larsen

Annika felt almost maternal feelings well up in her at the sight of the girl, who had to be at most in her mid-twenties, and she reminded herself that they would have to contact her family as quickly as possible.

'Twelve thousand units intravenously,' said Annika to the nurse. 'If there is no allergic reaction we'll give her the same dose a little later.'

The nurse gave Annika a glance full of unspoken objections. Annika ignored these reservations.

'No one is too ill to receive serum,' she said.

At heart she realised they had only just started to save the life of the young girl. As long as the identity of the snake remained unknown there was an uncertainty factor. She might wake up, go home, then later suffer a delayed reaction and collapse on the lavatory floor, with the black urine in the bowl showing for certain that she had acute kidney failure. The snake might have been an inland tiger snake and their efforts would have been in vain.

By far the greatest number of snakebite victims, apart from a few cases of people who died of blood loss or kidney failure, die of suffocation. And where Australian snakes are concerned, the victims die quickly. Seven of the world's ten most poisonous snakes are Australian, thirteen out of twenty. As a comparison, the poison of the most dangerous Australian snake is 850 times stronger than that of the American rattlesnake. For obvious reasons, it is therefore vitally important for bite victims to receive medical treatment as soon as possible. But because of the huge distances in Australia, for equally obvious reasons this is often impossible. Annika herself had only a few times experienced giving the antidote within the prescribed ideal of half an hour. She looked at the girl again. There was no apparent rejection of the serum but she knew that any reaction would not be likely to occur until later, taking into account the use of a polyvalent serum and the high dosage. Again she thought of the time factor. Of how long the girl had been in the car. Of how much she had moved, and of how little had been done for her before they reached hospital.

When one is working within a timeframe of only half an hour, perhaps a whole hour, possibly two, perhaps less, it stands to reason that the most effective counter-action is taken by the victim's themselves, or those who come to the rescue. And Annika often felt impotent in the face of the enormous faith people exhibited when confronted by a snakebite. It seemed as if they thought of hospital as somewhere they merely had to reach for all to be well. Occurrences of snakebite were infrequent in a sparsely populated country like Australia. And neither was the tally of deaths alarming. But with the huge body of knowledge available, developed precisely because of the extreme venomousness of the snakes, it still amazed Annika that people showed no interest in absorbing this knowledge. It seemed that most of them were completely ignorant of the land they lived in. As if they were all uninformed tourists; they did not adapt and made no attempt to do so, did not grow up as a part of the country but in opposition to it. From her house up at Whale Beach she still watched the rich neighbouring housewives gardening without gloves, she still heard of people walking around barefoot out in the bush, there were still surfers who went out where there were no helicopters on guard, still people who took it into their heads to swim in the rivers, and still people who went swimming north of Brisbane in the summer when the water was a thick soupy anarchy of poisonous jellyfish tentacles. Perhaps it was Annika Niebuhr's Danish-Swedish past that caused her bemusement even if that seemed so remote. The in-built common sense of the Scandinavians. Perhaps it was her wrecked marriage to Jay Morgan. Her meeting with Australian man. Whatever it was, she felt many were heedless to the point of irresponsibility.

The men were the worst. They tried to latch on to the power of the country. Tried to transform its harsh characteristics into a virile attitude that on the face of it stood out like an antiquated macho hybrid, a crude blunted persona, tough, beer-swilling and muscular. But which in reality was pretty pathetic and completely helpless when faced with what it ostensibly stemmed from – the country itself. No more than a month ago a colleague of Annika's in Perth had admitted a young backpacker up from Darwin, who 'while mucking about', as he had expressed it, had been bitten by a dugite. The bite was in his hand, and he had put a tight tourniquet on his arm so that it had lost all feeling owing to a lack of oxygen. 'But don't worry,' he said, 'I've sucked most of it out.' Next moment he lay bleeding on the hospital floor, unaware that he had probably absorbed far more poison and far more quickly via the mucous membranes of his mouth and scratches on his palate. She had also heard from colleagues up in Cairns that they still encountered patients who had risked secondary infection because in their panic they had cut into the bite even though it was well known that now and then snakes struck without injecting poison. There were also stories of people cutting off a finger or toe even though there was a considerable chance that the poison had already spread through the body. It was as if information would not penetrate. As if a snakebite continued to trigger the panicked reaction of a new settler. As if the inhabitants were still ill-adapted guests in their own country.

Annika cast a last glance at the monitor, the saline solution and the intravenous drip, and when she was sure everything had been put in motion to save the girl's life, tore herself away after giving a couple of further instructions.

'She must be kept under continual close observation, until we know whether her circulation is stable. I'll be back in a moment.'

The medical secretary busily sorting accident files loosened her shirt and leaned towards the rotating fan on the table. As Annika walked past she held up some papers and slapped them to indicate she had obtained all the relevant personal data from the elderly couple.

They were waiting in reception.

'I'll come back later,' she told them. 'I just need to know: were either of you near the girl's car?'

'I helped her,' said the man, 'to get out of the car. She could barely stand up, but she wanted to take her bag with her.'

'Are you sure you didn't see the snake?'

They glanced at each other and shook their heads.

'And neither of you has been feeling ill?'

They looked at each other a little uneasily, then the man wrinkled his forehead and looked at her.

'Why should we feel ill?'

'You often don't feel it. Where is the other man?'

'What man?'

'There was a young man here before. Wasn't he with you?'

Both of them shook their heads.

'Oh, I had the impression you were all together. But you are all right? No apparent scratches? No tenderness in your limbs?'

'There was no snake. At least, we didn't see one,' the man said.

'It may have been in the car. It may still be there,' said Annika. 'You said the car door opened suddenly. Was she there for long before the door opened? Was anyone else in the carpark before you arrived?'

The man looked at her in confusion. There was a curl on his forehead beneath the brim of his sunhat.

'It was the girl who came. We had parked there. She came on foot. Went over and unlocked the car. Got into it.'

'And how long was it before she opened the door?'

The man looked at his wife again. Now she was the one who answered.

'Ten minutes. She arrived precisely ten minutes before the sun went down, and at that point she seemed perfectly normal. We were sitting enjoying the view when it happened. She got into the car and leaned forward. As if to switch on the radio, it seemed. Then she threw up her arms. It looked as if she had turned up the volume too high. Then she just went on sitting up straight for . . . yes, for ten minutes, because when she opened the door the sun had just gone down.'

'Did you hear any music?' said Annika.

'We're a bit hard of hearing. Did you hear anything, dear?' the man asked his wife, who shook her head.

'Her bag?' said Annika, and looked at the man appealingly. 'Her papers. We need to know more about her.'

The man pointed across the vestibule.

'I gave it to a man out there.'

'What man?'

The nurse appeared in the doorway behind Annika.

'Have you got a moment?' she asked, drawing Annika away with her.

Annika turned to the couple.

'Can you wait just a bit longer? I'd like to talk to you later.'

Annika and the nurse walked a little way along the corridor.

'Annika, I think you ought to look at this.'

She held up the result of the quick test.

Annika looked at the sample, saw the mauve colour, saw the control colour, also mauve.

'Impossible,' she said, walking on. 'Get a diluted blood sample and try again.'

The nurse stayed where she was.

I've done that. It showed the same thing.'

Annika turned.

'Then call the police.'

Annika knew about the carpark on the point at Quarantine Head just by the entrance to Sydney Harbour. She knew it to be a favourite place for young lovers' meetings and one of the preferred launch sites for potential suicides.

The Swedish couple had parked there just beside the girl's car, at that time empty, and quite near the end facing outwards on to Clarke Island and Bradley's Head, close to the patch of bush from where the point ended in a precipitous fall of about a hundred metres. Annika was familiar enough with the place to know it was not crawling with snakes.

Sometimes there were errors in the results, even when cross-checked, in the packages they received from Melbourne. But they were extremely rare. The girl had been bitten on the left hand only, which indicated that the snake must have been on her left, on the seat or perhaps on the floor, assuming, as the old people had asserted, that she had been sitting in the driver's seat. It had happened before that snakes had crawled into cars in and around Sydney. Annika recalled a couple of episodes in the suburbs when people had left their cars parked for longer periods. Both times it had been red-bellied black snakes that had found their way into the vehicles. Fortunately this species is very unlikely to strike. In one case a woman had almost grasped the snake as she pulled what she thought to be the seat belt across her body. The great majority of snakebites in and around Sydney are from tiger snakes or eastern brown snakes. When the eastern brown, which is widespread over most of eastern Australia, attacks, it spreads out its neck like a collar

13

and lifts a third of its body above the ground in its characteristic S position. For this reason it bears the name of pseudonaja – the false cobra. The neurotoxic component of this snake's venom is the most powerful yet measured in a land snake, stronger even than the nerve venom in the fierce snake, which has the strongest snake venom known. The neurotoxin in a bite from an eastern brown constitutes only three per cent of the poison, but seventy per cent of the cause of death. The venom is unusually swift-working, and the first symptoms – vomiting, stomach pains and dizziness – show after only a few minutes. After this the relay stations of the brain are inactivated one by one, a darkness falls as fast and dense as the real darkness around the equator, lit places are switched off, main and side channels in the interior of the brain laid waste, in a few minutes over 100 billion nerve connections are cut, the most advanced unit in the world is on its way to total meltdown, and finally all is in darkness, the last sporadic signals flare up one last time in a primitive distress rocket, and then all light is definitively extinguished.

The actual discharge of venom is inconsiderable, but the eastern brown tries to compensate for this by clamping on hard so that it can thus, through contractions of its jaw, pump additional doses of venom into its victim. That would have left different bite marks on the girl. Also, the snake would probably have been found coiled around the girl's neck, because, like the others in the brown snake family, when the eastern brown attacks large prey it does something quite exceptional to the genus Elapse, which is to try to strangle its victim in the same manner as boa constrictors and pythons.

These were the considerations that, along with the result of the test, convinced Annika Niebuhr that the girl had not been bitten by an eastern brown but, however strange it seemed to her, by a taipan. Her wounds, four in all, when Annika had been able to study the hand more closely, revealed the appearance of scratches, and only one, on the back of the hand, showed an actual toothmark.

The taipan is an intelligent snake. And nervous. Like most other Australian snakes it only attacks when it has been provoked or surprised, but then it is with terrifying ferocity. In Annika Niebuhr's circles it was generally accepted that in almost all cases snakebites were the result of human factors. Investigations had shown that in eighty per cent of cases people had been bitten because they had tried either to catch or kill a snake. Nearly all other snakebites were caused by the snake having been surprised. By far the majority of snakes will retreat when they sense vibrations in the ground and seek to avoid a confrontation. The only exception to this rule is the death adder. This lethargic snake allows a person to get quite close, but if it is trodden on it comes streaking along the ground like a rocket with its triangular head, its oval nocturnal eyes and a phallic discharge of venom, which, if it misses its target, a rare occurrence, will be hurled several metres through the air. The taipan, on the other hand, like most other Australian snakes, and in fact snakes as a whole, is evasive. Only when it is trodden on or cornered, and when all else is impossible, will its shy nature be changed in a schizophrenic shift of character from quivering nervousness to an explosion of violence no other snake can match, not the eastern brown, the gwardar or the invariably aggressive roughscaled snake. Again and again, often five or six times, it will attack with uncontrollable savagery, and because of its size, two to three metres, it is able to strike high up on the body, close to vital organs. All in all these inconvenient traits, added to a violent venom discharge and a devilish concentration of potency, give the taipan its status as the world's most dangerous snake.

'The police will arrive shortly,' said Annika to the Swedish couple. 'I'd like you to stay on for a little while to explain to them what you have told me.'

'Does it make any difference what it was that bit her? Why is this snake so important?'

'It's the temperature,' said Annika. 'It is too cold here.'

'I don't understand . . .'

'The taipan isn't native to Sydney. In fact it is only found in the far north of New South Wales.'

Annika stood up as her personal bleeper sounded. She hurried down the corridor and into the small cubicle in Room 2.

It was already full of people, in a state of some confusion, as she found on entering.

'Annika. Relapse.'

'Ready.'

The girl's body jerked up from the bed, but no life showed in her. Annika brought the electrical stimulators together to remove static electricity and then replaced them on the girl's chest.

Again the girl was jolted upwards. But nothing happened.

'Wasn't she stable?'

'As good as.'

Annika felt the sweat trickle down her temples and behind her ears. She wiped her forehead with the back of her hand.

'Again.'

But no life returned. Heart massage, more shocks, nothing helped.

'Allergic reaction?'

'Could be a blood clot. Who fetched the girl's papers?'

'They weren't there.'

'Pulse?'

'None.'

'Ready.'

Seconds passed. Minutes passed. More shocks. But nothing helped. A kind of apathy filled the room. No one could think of anything else to do. And finally all that seemed left was resignation. That and the straight line of the electrocardiograph. Death's irreversible semiotics.

'What do you mean, the papers aren't out there?' asked Annika.

'He can't remember who he gave them to, the Swede.'

The group stood around the girl's bed. The nurse, the anaesthetist and Annika herself. She still worked on the girl's chest, but with each minute that passed oxygen would be seeping out of her organs, and her brain would began to suffer damage.

'Where is the younger man?' asked Annika, and went across to the electrocardiograph. She gave the apparatus a shake. There was no response, and instead of asking more questions she began to think.

'We know it was a taipan ... she has had ... how many times? ... Twice? ... twelve thousand units. That's enough. That *has* to be enough.'

'Perhaps it's shock. A blood clot in the coronary artery?'

'Why can't we get it going? Vasoconstricting medication? What ... ?'

Annika was about to put her hands on the girl again when she suddenly stopped and moved slightly back. The others stared open-mouthed. Slowly at first, but then quickly, the green curves denoting a heart under pressure ran across the screen.

'Impossible.'

'It's going too fast,' said Annika.

'Ninety over seventy. It's rising. Rising.'

'What's happening?'

Suddenly the girl opened her eyes, sat up in bed and looked around her. She stared at them as if terrified by all the equipment that not only surrounded her but was directly attached to her. The electrocardiograph, the oxygen machines. Then it seemed as if her eyes suddenly popped out of her head, and protruded for a second or two before falling back into place.

'Back off.'

She began to tear off plasters and lines. Annika approached her cautiously.

'Take it easy. It's going to be all right.'

'Belt up, bitch.'

Then she screamed. A long scream that paralysed everyone present. In a flash she had hopped down from the bed and, as if all her strength vanished when her feet touched the ground, slumped against the instrument table with its ligatures and sutures; a steel tray fell to the floor with a metallic crash, and wound retractors, needles and pincers flew everywhere. Miraculously the girl regained her balance, simultaneously tearing open a pocket in her black belt, and the next moment she was pointing a gun at them.

She swung it around wildly, pointed it first at Annika and then at the others on her way to the door.

'It's not good for you to get up just now. You have been bitten by a . . .'

'I know that. Shut up. And let me out. I've got everything under control again.'

With the capacity of a psychopathic patient in a fit of rage to make everyone around her freeze, the girl rushed from the room, leaving Annika, the anaesthetist and the nurse gawping. None of them could believe their own eyes.

'I can only repeat what I've said, Mr Kahn, that the whole thing happened so fast, we were so taken aback, that none of us managed to react.'

Annika was in the canteen looking out over the water. Darkness had fallen over the city. The searchlights that illuminated Sydney Tower had been switched on. Under the Harbour Bridge the propeller of one of the yellow water taxis from Taxis Afloat drew a white ruffle behind it. Closer in, one of the Kookaburra mahogany boats was on its way home with the day's last batch of tourists, and from the Circular Quay terminal small ferries and jetcats sped in all directions. Annika sipped her mug of coffee meditatively and swallowed the mouthfuls slowly.

Detective Superintendent Kahn was a thin dark man, without doubt younger than he looked with his pale grey downtown complexion from too much steel and tobacco smoke, and without doubt older than he let on by his behaviour. Annika didn't know what to make of him. There are people whose personas force others to make snap judgments about them. Those are the kind of people with whom one can foresee either a close and on principle lasting friendship or a lifelong enmity. She felt sure that in other situations his persona would certainly be useful, for instance when he needed to drive someone mad. In particular a small habit he had of pressing his tongue against his front teeth and producing a little sharp clicking sound, as if he was cleaning his teeth or on the whole disbelieved everything said to him, must surely rattle the most hardened criminal.

'Two porters sent in pursuit of a mortally sick girl couldn't catch up with her?'

Annika nodded.

'And then the cavalry arrived. And they couldn't find her either?'

Superintendent Kahn looked at her with narrowed eyes. Then he pressed his tongue to his teeth. Again that internal smacking sound.

'And the car,' he said, consulting his little notebook, 'a Toyota Troop Carrier, that should still be parked up there, should it? At Quarantine Head?'

'Unless someone has moved it.'

'This man? this' – he emphasised the word to express his disapproval of the hospital's negligence – ... *'bagsnatcher* ... how well did you see him?'

'Not specially well. Everything went so fast,' said Annika, trying to recall any conspicuous features in the man.

'Is it fair to assume that you suspect this man of taking the girl's bag to prevent us discovering who she is?'

'Otherwise it would be, in your terminology, a case of an extreme form of offence against property?'

Kahn shrugged his shoulders.

'We are in Sydney. Only a generation or two from the great penal colony.'

Kahn made a note on his pad. Then he looked at Annika.

'The man. Could he be her husband? Her boyfriend? Did no one at all speak to him?'

Annika shook her head.

'The Swedish couple said he drove in front of them. To show them the way to the hospital.'

'Can you describe him?'

Annika tried again to summon a clear picture of the man. She was not good at faces and even worse at names, a deficiency she had once been ashamed of until she had found out that many others shared it.

'It happened so quickly,' said Annika. 'You see, I took him for the couple's son or something like that. I thought he was with them.'

'Try. As hard as you can . . .'

'Tall, dark, about thirty, I should think. A scar. He had a scar on . . . his right cheek.'

'A scar?'

'A scar. From the corner of his mouth to just under his right eye.'

'The snake —' Kahn looked at his pad again — 'isn't it simply possible that it had crawled into the car? Doesn't that kind of thing happen?'

He answered his own question:

'Well, no, not if it was a . . . taipan. They don't live here. But are you sure it could have been a taipan?'

'I'm resting my evidence on the test,' said Annika. 'But we can't be quite certain until we get the results back from Melbourne. Why don't you just find the girl?'

'We are searching, Miss Niebuhr, we're searching. You look tired?'

'I *am* tired.'

'Were you also tired while you were seeing to the girl's treatment?'

'I can deal with a snakebite in my sleep. I mean . . . you know what I mean.'

'Tell me, what do you mean, precisely?'

'Kahn, the girl was dead. She was examined thoroughly. No pulse, no breathing, no brain function. Others saw it, not only I.'

'Suspended animation. You — if anyone — must know that concept.'

'Asphyxia. The other term has been abolished.'

'By a vote in the canteen?'

'Oxygen,' said Annika, sitting down with her coffee in the chair opposite him. 'There was hardly any oxygen left in her blood. The vital organs — brain, liver, heart — start to fail. The heart stops. Electric shock and vasoconstricting medication into the veins. Heart massage. For more than ten minutes. The brain can do without oxygen for a couple of minutes at most before catastrophe sets in. I was there. I saw it. She was dead.'

Annika took a deep breath. 'What I mean, Kahn, is that what happened is impossible.'

'Petrarch,' said Kahn.

'I beg your pardon?'

'Francesco Petrarca, Italian poet. After having been pronounced dead for twenty hours he sat up in bed and complained there was a draught from the window. Nicophanes Glycos, Greek Orthodox bishop, lay on his *lit de parade* for two days arrayed in his vestments, then sat up in the church at Mithymi.'

'That was long ago,' said Annika. 'No one can cheat technology today.'

'Plenty of breathing techniques can simulate a state resembling death. The globe fish, full of tetronotoxin, the fuga, you know, which only specially trained Japanese chefs may prepare. When things go wrong there, the dead person is put under observation for safety's sake. Some recover.'

'She died, Kahn,' said Annika tonelessly, fixing him with a gaze of determined disbelief.

'Did you examine her eyes?'

Annika, deep in thought, asked: 'What do you mean?'

'The pupils. Did you examine her pupils? The quickest possible indicator of brain death. Light on the pupils. The pupils expand when the brain dies, and after that do not react to light. Did you look for that?'

Annika felt a surge of irritation.

'Yes, Kahn. I examined her pupils.'

'Certain substances make the pupils expand. But when subjected to light they will contract. Slowly. Might you possibly have overlooked the contraction?'

Annika sighed and took another mouthful of coffee.

'I cannot explain what happened, Kahn. But I am sure that if we could find the girl and examine her we should get an explanation.'

For the first time Kahn smiled.

She looked at him enquiringly.

'There must always be a rational explanation. You remind me of your father, Miss Niebuhr. A fine man, your father. I'm smiling, because now I can see the likeness.'

'Did you know, Kahn, that when Einstein's great friend, Besso, lost his wife, Einstein wrote and told him not to despair, because "we physicists know, do we not, that time does not exist?" That, Kahn, is how my father would look at this case. You may smile. But what you are smiling at is in fact not the likeness between us, but the difference between us. And no matter how many questions you ask me, nothing will alter the fact that it is you, not me, who's faced with a problem. Someone tried to kill that girl. And it is your job, not mine, to prevent that happening.'

As usual there was heavy traffic on the four lanes of the Pacific Highway. The cars travelling north formed a long caravan of chromium, of light and enamel. A weary chorus of horns sounded at the lights and the numerous crossings of suburban roads out of town. Most people drove with their windows open in the intolerable heat. Arms hung down alongside doors, flopped on side mirrors. Now and then a youthful throbbing went past, but otherwise the rush-hour traffic merely let itself drag homewards.

Although Annika felt some anxiety about what had become of the girl, and even if the whole episode was both puzzling and sinister, she could still smile at the thought of what Simon Rees would get out of the story, and she already looked forward to telling him about it. Although in most cases he preserved professional secrecy with the discretion of a priest, now and then he had sketched out stories and events that Annika would have found hard to credit if they hadn't come from him. Simon's position at the Australian Security and Intelligence Organisation was not what you would expect when you heard that he had been enlisted from the SAS as an expert in data communication and electronic espionage. For almost ten years now Simon had been attached to the ASIO in the capacity of a psychologist, a qualification he had acquired on his own initiative concurrently with his military training. Although all the projects he worked on were by definition confidential, and even though in many situations this naturally set limits to how concrete he could be, in time Annika had built up a good idea of his work. She had read a number of reports, mostly perception psychology investigations, with passages of sensitive information blocked out, and several times he had asked for her comments. Likewise Annika knew that at present Simon's preferences were and had been for a long time centred on the paranormal, and what she and her colleagues had just witnessed was decidedly not something that could be dovetailed into the established medical picture.

In the twenty years during which Annika had studied snakes she had never had an experience to match this case of the young woman. Among the recorded cases she had read how in 1979 a taipan had killed a four-year-old boy in less than ten minutes. How a tobacco farmer from North Queensland who had been bitten only once in one foot, with medical help had taken three weeks to recover. From the *Medical Journal of Australia* she knew that Townsville General Hospital had obtained good results with repeated doses of serum, which routed the anticoagulating as well as the coagulating components in the venom, but also that these were treatments that continued for hours, and that a patient was hardly ever able to breathe by himself until at least twelve hours had passed.

Nature does not offer many biochemical weapons stronger than the taipan's venom, and why such powerful venoms have been developed by the taipan and other Australian snakes is still a partial mystery.

Annika's close friend, Harper Stone, a renowned biologist and palaeontologist, who occasionally published his well-informed illustrated articles in the *National Geographic*, once explained to her that heat is the simple and only cause. Because the stable climate of the tropics has traditionally offered ideal conditions for the evolution of the greatest variety of species in the world, he argued, they have become the breeding ground of the world's store of natural poisons. The enemies have themselves had many enemies, and in an equatorial belt stretching from Central and South America over West and Central Africa, on over South-East Asia, Indonesia to Australia, nature has assembled and distributed her depots of potential weapons of mass destruction, of which many are still unknown. It is also the case that *elapidae*, the family to which the taipan and the other dangerous Australian snakes belong, have deadly relatives in the tropical zones in other continents. African cobras and mambas, Asiatic cobras and kraits, and the American coral snake, are all members of the *elapidae*. Yet this does not explain the massive concentration of poisonous snakes in the Australian fauna. There are over one hundred venomous snakes in Australia, of which thirty – an extremely high proportion – pose a danger to human beings.

In 1894, when the French scientist Albert Leon Calmette, in the infancy of immunology, against the background of the discoveries of the American Henry Sewall some years earlier, marketed his snake antidote, *serum antivenimeux,* as a universal cure for snakebite, the reaction of researchers at Sydney University was tellingly enough a shrug of the shoulders: it doesn't work on ours. What from today's perspective might look like long-established myths about French arrogance versus Australian nonchalance turned out to underline a massive Australian problem.

Before 1955 a bite from a taipan was generally considered to be fatal, and it was not until Kevin Budden, who took a special interest in snakes, made his legendary contribution that the world was given an idea of this snake's venom. Budden was up in Cairns collecting snakes when he managed to catch a taipan almost two metres long in a heap of rubbish. As he stood beside his car, about to drop the snake into a sack, he lost his hold on it, and it struck repeatedly at his thumb. People rushed up and tried to kill the snake, but Budden prevented them. He was treated with tiger snake antidote at a nearby hospital, but he soon sank into unconsciousness, and next day, totally paralysed, slipped away. However, he had been able to emphasise the importance of getting the captured snake alive to the Commonwealth Serum Laboratories in Melbourne. Annika clearly remembered the graphic description that the naturalist David Fleay, who had been called in to milk Kevin Budden's taipan, gave of the snake's eyes in his book *Talking of Animals*. Everyone who has come close to this snake recalls the shining orange eyes with their clearly marked folds indicating permanent anger, the thirteen-millimetre-long venom teeth, short for a normal poisonous snake but long for an Australian one, sharp as injection needles, and the mouth that never opens until it is really in earnest and, when that happens, resembles a triumphant grin with the muscles of the venom pumps markedly visible on the head, which widens out above the otherwise slim and graceful neck region and which, very aptly, is reminiscent of an old-fashioned stick grenade.

The scientific term for a lethal dose is LD50, the number indicating how much venom expressed in mg/kg is needed to kill fifty per cent of a batch of laboratory mice. With a toxin count for the taipan of only 0.064 and an average dose of venom which in dry weight was four times greater than that of the common tiger snake, after Kevin Budden's death it was obvious in strict scientific terms why there was such a high mortality rate in connection with this snake.

When Annika's parents occasionally had visitors from Denmark or Sweden, she found it extremely difficult to convince the guests that they should forget any ideas they might have picked up from tourist brochures of leaving the asphalted areas of the country in order to experience Australia, and instead buy a book about how to survive Australia. They thought she was exaggerating, which of course she was, but when she thought about it she couldn't in fact recall a single Australian family who had not at least once in their life, even in Sydney, been obliged to remove a poisonous spider from their kitchen cupboard or call on professional help. In circles other than those she frequented, she had the impression that people did not have much knowledge of precisely how many things could go wrong at the seaside, what measures you could take to prevent something going wrong, and what you could do when or if something did go wrong. And finally, leaving aside biologists, herpetologists and doctors, it was rare to come across someone who could identify more than two or three of the venomous snakes that in high season were commonly to be found both in the parks and the suburbs of Sydney.

'Think of cyanide,' said Annika, when she noticed that her message wasn't getting through properly. She had learned from experience that when something seemed too strange to people, too abstract and too absurd, well-known quantities could help reality to penetrate.

'Cobra venom is about forty times stronger than cyanide. The most venomous Australian snakes are fifty times as poisonous as the cobra. So you can work it out for yourselves. Wear thick shoes and socks and take a compression bandage with you if you're going into the bush. So you've been warned.'

According to the Aboriginals one animal is mightier than all the others – the snake. In the aboriginal world picture, the sky is an enormous snake, which bears the rainbow on its sides, while young warriors carry the sun and the moon. When Kookillo Dhamarandji told Annika about the world picture of himself and his forefathers for the first time, she recalled how in childhood her mother told her stories about the Midgard serpent which wound itself all the way round the world in the World Sea, so that it bit itself in the tail. And about how Thor could not lift it when it assumed the shape of a cat, and how he went out with Hymer the giant and caught it with his fishing line and walloped it with his hammer.

No other creature has been the object of so much worship as the snake. In the era when the concept of time was still a matter of changing seasons, the Mayan priests and Greek astronomers prayed to the serpents of the night sky in the form of stars. They were worshipped in the Middle East, they were sacred in China, the Mediterranean, in Scandinavia; the Aztecs, the Adena Indians and the West Africans held them sacrosanct. The serpents were everywhere, they held everything together. But nowhere has mythology depicted the snakes' role in the creation story more clearly than in the Australian aboriginal tales and Annika fell head

27

over heels in love with their story when Kookillo Dhamarandji related it to her. Because even in all its glowing naïvety, at the same time it was so logical and clear. It claimed that before the Dreamtime, the land lay in the Rainbow Serpent's belly, and on its way through the landscape the serpent spat out rocks and hills. Seen through the eyes of today it is not hard to grasp that waterways and rivers resembled snakes, and that there were snakes in the sky, and that an important element was connected with these snakes – water. According to the Australian Aboriginals, one being created the land and time, and when the precious water poured down from the heavens, that being manifested itself – as a rainbow, the Rainbow Serpent, which Kookillo Dhamarandji, who came from the Yolngu tribe in north-east Arnhem Land, called the *dhuwa*.

Apart from her mother's readings and a few other random events, Annika's memories of Denmark were scanty, and they offered, as far as she could see, no plausible explanation whatever of why she had later on developed the interest in snakes which, with the passing of time, had become the real *raison d'être* of her life. Even if the great mathematician Henri Poincaré's ideas on principally non-integrable systems corresponded very well to large areas of Annika's emotional life, in which various elements often made it impossible to work out her whys and wherefores, she was in no doubt that her interest in snakes was closely linked to an important aspect of the Australian soul – its drama. She was still quite small when her family moved to Australia, and although later, during the obligatory trip to Europe, she paid a flying visit to Denmark to see her sister, who had deserted and gone back to the little country, she did not remember much of it, and what she did remember was a deep and all-embracing feeling of cosy security.

As far back as Annika could remember she had been fascinated by snakes. Like that of other Australian doctors who on encountering victims of venomous snakes in A & E departments are gripped by poikilothermal curiosity, Annika's interest was concentrated on elapids, but that had begun at a much earlier point in her life, and the intuition that snakes were to have a more than usual importance for her came after her first visit to John Farrow's reptile park up at Brisbane. Farrow was already then a living legend because he had survived a crocodile attack simply by giving the beast such a drubbing that it eventually released its hold on him. He was never shy of showing off his stomach scar, which in time became indistinct and covered by an expanding paunch, although not totally invisible. And even the attack, which Farrow, to the great delight of the Aussies, embroidered with more and more and increasingly dramatic details with the years, thrilled not only the media but also Annika. At that point, at fifteen years old, through her father and his home library with its blackboard and chalk lines, she had developed an intense relationship with the exact sciences and therefore, with a youthful appetite for life, thirsted for a more colourful and exciting access to it. This she found in John Farrow, who was already putting on a daily show for visitors, in which he demonstrated the lightning attack of crocodiles by leaping down into their watery cage and posing with gigantic net-pythons, and – all of it in the effective mixture of entertainment and education beloved by the Australians – described the local venomous snakes in a gripping and knowledgeable manner.

Later on Annika's mother greatly regretted having been the one who had taken her daughter to the reptile park, where she spent her time for the following five summers, officially on holiday but in reality acquiring and developing her passion for reptiles, and was soon assisting John Farrow and Kookillo Dhamarandji not only by cleaning paths, as was reported back to Sydney, but in repairing and installing air-conditioning for newly arrived and irritable boas.

She was filled not with fear but with pleasurable tension the first time she milked an eastern brown. The sensation in her hand when the venom fangs as if in spasm punctured the rubber membrane on the little glass tube, and the deadly lymphoid fluid slid down inside it. Or when she picked up a funnel-web spider for the first time, the weight of that lump, the bristling legs, the desperate cricking of the neck trying to direct the one-centimetre-long venom teeth towards what had seized it from behind. It was the thrill of standing so close to death, which could come through a little scratch one did not feel. The consciousness of death, which is the most exalted proof of our consciousness of life and unique to human beings. Some higher apes grieve over death like us, but they do not comprehend death as we do, in the incomprehensible form it sometimes assumes in our imaginings. It was that very fact. That death assumed a form, a little hairy body, or a long scaly flatness, or long tentacles that in the microworld of the jellyfish activated a whole battery of rockets which in a few minutes could kill a human being or cause permanent disfigurement.

Annika's mother, who came from Rättvik by Lake Siljan in the Swedish Dales, had the same unbending antipathy to change as Zorn, the painter from her homeland, so just as she insisted on transporting her Swedish country-style furniture in large containers, first from Rättvik to Bagsværd in Denmark and later to Sydney, she would have preferred Annika to have followed in her footsteps and aimed at the teaching profession she herself had given up so early in favour of the man who had sealed her fate at a midsummer celebration outside Tällberg.

Many children during their development exhibit in a particularly concentrated way a split evident throughout the whole history of western culture – the split between the rational and the irrational, between enlightenment and infatuation, between mother and father, and Annika followed this pattern.

During the sixties her father, Aage Niebuhr, was a promising young nuclear physicist at the Niels Bohr Institute in Copenhagen. Under the influence of Sheldon Glashow, who at that time was in contact with the Institute, he pursued – in contrast to many other physicists – Glashow's calculations, in an attempt to establish an association between low nuclear power and electromagnetism. But he could not find a solution to Glashow's problems with renormalisation and the unsatisfactory zero positioning of the power-carrying particle mass, and the renormalisation problems Abdus Salem and Steven Weinberg later encountered. In a weak moment he repressed the fact that the most epoch-making discoveries have been made by coincidence and mental potency alone, and adapted himself entirely to the belief that the only way in which one could verify Glashow's neutral Z-particle was in a sufficiently powerful accelerator. Therefore when at about the same time he received an invitation, as did a number of other scientists, to work on the five-kilometre-long accelerator to be built for the Sydney Space Centre, he did not hesitate for a moment. All home moorings were cast off, and the family departed. To Annika, for whom Jutland was the farthest place she could imagine, the sight of the red Martian desert beneath them, which continued hour after hour, seemed just the same as if they had quite simply – and without it actually surprising her – left the planet.

In Australia nothing was as her father had expected. The political winds in New South Wales changed, grants were withdrawn, the syndicate supporting the project as commercial sponsor went bankrupt – in other words there was no accelerator. Instead Annika's father found work at the Observatory in Eppig. Through the long night hours he stared out into space. He dutifully but unenthusiastically took part in a series of partial projects; he contributed to routine observations of red shifts, wrote reports on the Magellan clouds and also went around the circle of gratings on the exterior of the telescope dome with a certain cosmic fulfilment in his body, when the supernova exploded one night in April 1987 and the sun rose in the morning in an unusually clear and almost holy zodiacal light. But as a whole his life had been a disappointment.

Financially he and his family never suffered hardship. Annika's great-grandfather, Knud Gustav Niebuhr, the first in the family to become alive to the potential of the Australian continent, had consolidated the family fortune as early as the 1920s by lucrative investment in the small-boat industry, when Broome was still the centre of the world's pearl fisheries. He was a doctor like Annika, but had started out, after taking his student examination at Gammelholm School, by studying engineering. During the first year of the war he was with the Danish ambulance service in Le Tréport for a couple of months, and later volunteered for the *Hôp. militaire Buffon* in Paris.

31

He worked as private assistant to Dr Danysz at the Pasteur Institute before returning home and marrying Judy, an Australian he had met in Paris. He specialised in the diseases of women, became clinical registrar at Section A of the maternity department of the Danish National Hospital, registrar at the department of women's diseases at St Joseph's Hospital and microscopist at the Radium Station and the Cancer Committee, before his wife's homesickness manoeuvred his fate to Australia, where in a short time he created his fortune, lost his wife and returned to Denmark.

Despite a certain talent for squandering, among other things through a rash investment in connection with big sapphire finds in the Willows Gemfields, his son, Cai Gustav Niebuhr, who, without physically leaving Denmark, tried to emulate his father's adventures in Australia, managed to make no more than a symbolic inroad into the immense wealth now at the disposal of the family.

There was thus more than enough left for Annika's father to do more or less what he pleased with his life. But riches and material freedom from care can be as hard to disregard when one has them as when one does not. Aage Niebuhr dreamed dreams of scientific prowess. But the dream of particle impact at speeds close to that of light had faded from his inner sight after the unforeseen adversities he had met with in Australia. The vision of being able purely physically to measure the Lilliput world of nuclear fission, and thus be seconds from the beginning of all things, had vanished. There remained only an all too tangible and physically determined realisation that in the world of reality not everything goes according to one's deserts. Stubbornly, but also with a certain bitterness, he still spent his days on his calculations. Now gravity had to be united to the four familiar forces of nature, accelerator or no.

In comparison with this man, her father, Annika, where intellect was concerned, was, she knew, a midget on her knees. But when people pointed out the likenesses between them she could still, without renouncing their familial intellectual relationship, note with some relief that it was in a projection of the differences that she saw herself.

She had always felt there was an immense irony in the Church having for centuries been able to subjugate people by forcing them to believe in something so vast that it was beyond human comprehension both mentally and physically. And that there was a corresponding irony in the fact that science has had the good fortune to convince everyone that what is small, almost unmeasurable, which only few understand, and fewer can relate to, is the really essential thing. So even though Annika had chosen a scientific subject, medicine, her real passion was her interest in snakes. For her father, who would rather have seen her engaged in fundamental research, this was a development he didn't like, and for her mother, to whom the romantic Swedish painters and poets of the nineteenth century were sacrosanct, it was a development she couldn't grasp.

Annika turned off towards The Spit, which would take her home via Manly to Bilgola and Whale Beach. She bowled through the wealthy districts of Northshore, where she herself grew up and where her parents still lived. Just before the golf course at Balgowian she turned in to the filling station at Sheila Sue, tanked up and bought herself a supply of mineral water.

She balanced back from the shop across the forecourt enjoying the feeling of the ice-cold bottles against her body. There had hardly been a cloud in the sky for three weeks, and the humidity had steadily and calmly climbed to almost a hundred. Annika pushed open the car door and got in.

It all happened so quickly that she failed to react. She had just put the key into the ignition when she realised she was not alone in the car.

The hand that grabbed her round the mouth was small and bony, but it was strong. It pulled her back against the headrest, and at the same time she felt the unmistakable sensation of a pistol against her temple.

Annika said nothing, didn't even try, and the first thought that rushed through her throbbing head was that Simon Rees would scold her. How could you possibly leave the car unlocked? No matter where? It happened quite regularly that his protective, now and then almost fatherly feelings for her welled up in him, and Annika knew she would be lying to herself if she didn't admit she was flattered at eliciting this urge to protect. It was Simon who had provided her with the Browning she kept at the bottom of the Hepplewhite chest in her bedroom, it was Simon who had taken her out to the shooting ranges at Stowe's Corner and taught her how to handle it so it didn't only pose a threat to herself, and it was Simon who had encouraged her to take lessons in self-defence when she made the decision to live alone. She had once before found a use for the expertise that had been devoutly instilled in her at the training station down at South Inning. It happened one evening after she and her friends had been for a drive down to The Rocks. A man had assaulted her, and she had turned and kicked out in an arc, a circular kick, in one movement and without so much as stopping to think. She just managed to see the pole in the man and then kicked into him, into that column, past his face, as she had learned, with such force that one of his teeth was chipped, two others were loosened and, as far as Annika could judge by a superficial glance, he also received

34

a slight fracture to his nose. But the martial arts never became a natural bodily response for her. Two years of tae kwon do, two years with fists and feet, mostly feet, had been enough for Annika, although she still did her daily twenty arm bends, on her knuckles, still did the splits with a regularity that might give the uninitiated the impression that she found a sexual delight in it, and could still feel a childish pleasure in precision training by switching off lights in her house with her feet. But what repelled her, indeed filled her with revulsion, was the semi-religious fug in which the noble art of 'the empty hand' was wrapped. With a respect she had scarcely shown for the Danish, Australian or Swedish flags – and certainly not at all after devaluation – she bowed to the oriental symbols for two years with an earnestness amounting to the comical, and without ever knowing what the symbols meant. There was no giggling – that incurred punishment training – and this robotic discipline, which was a directly logical extension of the vacuous assumption of exotic rites and foreign flags, had such a repugnant effect on Annika that she stopped just before she was about to take yet another belt test.

Of all the defence systems in the world the only one that could have been of help to Annika in the present situation would probably have been eyes in the back of her head, and while a voice behind her explained in terse, unambiguous terms that the hand over her mouth was about to be removed providing this was not taken as an invitation to alert the whole filling station, she had enough to do collecting herself and regaining normal breathing after the shock.

The voice was a woman's, and after a glance in the rear-view mirror Annika swiftly realised it belonged to the girl from the hospital.

'Who's got my things?' she said, as she lowered the pistol so that it less visibly pointed at Annika's neck.

'There was a man . . .'

'Who?'

'We don't know . . . but we assume he took . . .'

'Assume?'

'It all happened so fast,' said Annika. 'He was carrying the bag at one point, so we think he took it . . .'

35

'Shit,' said the girl, and Annika could see in the mirror that she was leaning her forehead against the back of the headrest. She didn't look well – she was pale, and sweat ran down her face.

'What was in it? Money? Credit cards?'

'My purse. I had everything in my purse. The problem is, I can't remember what everything was.'

'I don't get it.'

'I can't remember everything that was in it. What did he look like?' she asked.

'Tall, dark-haired . . . are you sure you're all right?'

The girl nodded, and in the mirror Annika saw her smile.

'One question is whirling around in your head, isn't it, Doctor? How? How did she manage it?'

Annika met the girl's eyes in the mirror. She didn't reply.

The girl smiled again. She leaned forward towards Annika and whispered: 'Why don't you just feel happy that I'm alive and well?'

'I do. I just think you don't look well. Why won't you let us help you?'

'There's no one who can help me. Someone's after me.'

'Who?'

The girl grimaced, as if a sharp pain ran through her.

'You don't want to know about that . . .'

'Why don't you go to the police?' said Annika.

The girl made no reply. She leaned the pistol against her forehead, then moved it from cheek to cheek to cool herself down.

'Are you sure you can't remember anything particular about him? Special marks? You must be able to remember something? Did he limp? Did he lisp?'

'A scar,' said Annika. 'He had a scar.'

'Where?'

'On his face. On the cheek. The right one.'

'Kessler.'

'Who?'

The girl rubbed her hand wildly around her face and hair.

'This heat. It drives me crazy. Why is it so fucking hot? Can't you switch on the fan?'

'It won't help,' said Annika. 'Now, put down that pistol and let me help you. You really aren't well.'

'Was there anyone else besides him?'

'Kessler?'

'The man with the scar.'

'Didn't you say he was called Kessler?'

'Were there any others besides him?' The girl leaned back in the seat and rested her head after repeating her question.

Annika shook her head.

'No, he was alone.'

'I don't understand it,' said the girl. She turned her face, sat still for a moment and stared thoughtfully out of the window.

'I don't understand it.'

They sat for a while without speaking. The girl gazed blankly out of the window while Annika now and then glanced into the rear-view mirror. The girl sat with the pistol to her face, meditatively pushing her lips to the stock.

Finally she straightened up and laid her face on Annika's head-rest.

'Stay here for ten minutes. I have a car back down there. And I want to be well away before you get up to anything. If the police ask about me, I'd appreciate it if you didn't say anything to them about this.'

'I promise.'

The girl looked into Annika's eyes in the mirror. Then she opened the door and started to get out.

'What is it you don't understand?' asked Annika.

'There are people after me. People you wouldn't want to be after you. Believe me, you don't want to know anything.'

'But what if I do?'

The girl remained on the seat behind Annika with one leg out of the open back door.

'I don't really know what's going on just now. But if anyone comes to you asking about "Atlas X", you'll know they won't wish you any joy.'

'What is "Atlas X"?

'*That's* something you don't want to know about.'

As promised, Annika stayed on until the girl had disappeared. She noticed her hand shook slightly as she took out a cigarette, which she smoked before starting the car. She felt helpless. It was obvious the girl wasn't well, but there was nothing she could do about it. She had no idea what her name was or where she was going. All Annika could do was pray she could keep herself alive by some unlikely means. She stubbed out her cigarette. Then she drove out of the forecourt, trying to put the thought of the girl out of her head.

In the nature of things, no theory is perfect, for if it were it would not be a theory but a synthesis. One of the great weaknesses of neo-Darwinism is its lack of the ability to explain transitional forms. The great leap in evolution. There is still debate about *Archaeopteryx*, the feathered lizard, being the transitional phenomenon between lizard and bird, and the scientists who study human development are hampered by the fact that intermediate forms are rare in geological strata sequences. Nor are there any simple answers where snakes are concerned. Is *Pachyrhacis problematicus* the solution? Did snakes originate in the sea and not on land? The learned scholars disagree.

Among Annika's many commitments was her work as recorder on a large-scale project including scientists from Colombo University, Oxford University and the Liverpool School of Tropical Medicine to survey the life and activities of sea snakes in the Pacific area. She had been in contact earlier with the medical faculty at Colombo, as the Sri Lankan doctors had initiated several research programmes with the aim of developing more effective antidotes to the local snake venom, and she had agreed and looked forward to the new project, because it meant she would get a chance to do some diving.

She sat at the wheel giving only scant attention to her surroundings, trying to detach her thoughts. In three days she and Mike Lewis would head off for the Great Barrier Reef, and while she was happy at the prospect of the work she also enjoyed the idea of being part of a team whose investigations might provoke perspective-widening discussions among minds more capacious than her own about the possible missing link of the snakes, or at least produce a mass of new information on the life of the sea snakes, which had hitherto enjoyed so little study.

In an attempt to distance the events of the day, as she drove she went over her shopping list and mentally crossed off one or two items she had already bought, but the thought of the girl kept whirling around in her head.

It was not so much the pistol. She was moderately conversant with firearms from her training and from Simon. It was the fact that she knew her thoughts would go on churning around the girl without being able to find a convincing explanation for what was going on. She ran her gaze down Mike's shopping list again, but came to the conclusion that there were some things she couldn't get hold of now. She switched on the radio then turned it off again. Her thoughts returned to the mysterious scene at the hospital, but she could not make head or tail of it.

Of course, asphyxia was not a phenomenon solely relegated to the past. Annika had read numerous descriptions of cases, and had herself experienced some. But in almost all the cases she knew of, cold had been an essential factor. With the consumption of alcohol or medication. The pathogenic picture would often look convincing: no pulse, no heartbeat, no breathing, no movement. And even the body temperature would be abnormally low. In itself low body temperature is never a reliable parameter for death. Not so many years earlier many people who could have been saved, in particular fishermen, perished in cold waters. At that time there was still widespread ignorance of the fact that on principle if the surface of the body is heated up before its interior, a catastrophe ensues. The musculature of the fine capillaries will open up and the blood pressure vanishes. But if the body is heated from inside, centrally, with warm liquid in the large body veins, the body will normally raise its temperature by about half a degree a minute, and even a loss of temperature of over ten degrees can be restored. Not in spite of but because of the cold, the heart and brain and other vital organs will not be harmed. When Annika and Mike Lewis went to see James Cameron's film *The Deep* down at Hoyts, some people left the cinema when the young woman drowned at the bottom of the sea and was afterwards resuscitated. Reality is a rare guest in American films. And unwelcome when it appears because, paradoxically enough, it can create a lack of credence in relation to the fiction.

But when all these indicators occur collectively in an acute or an intensive care ward, with the organism connected to the electrocardiograph and machines registering pulse, blood pressure and the oxygen content of the arterial blood, it is pretty certain that if death should ensue it will not be as a result of some transient virus.

Annika could not describe what had happened in words, and she knew that in future she and the others who had been present would probably refer to the episode as a 'technical error' or some such term. Like diagnoses that began with words such as 'primary' or 'essential', which in reality often hid the fact that the doctors did not fully understand what they were talking about. They might mutually shake their heads over the apparatus, even perhaps physically shake it, and agree with each other that 'you can never rely on those computers', even though the greatest achievement of the computer is and always has been to show us that we can never completely rely on the human being.

It was this more than anything else that contributed to the discovery of chaos theory, which Annika, lacking a faith, made her own. Chaos theory emerged in the year she was born. In the winter of 1961, when the meteorologist Edward Lorenz was working at his Royal McBee computer, which contained a simple model of the weather, and about to print out a single sequence, he did not realise he was going to shoot yet another bullet hole into Newton's already well-perforated world picture.

Lorenz too first put the blame on a mechanical fault when a new transcript, which should have been identical with the previous one, instead of showing conjunction, exhibited an astonishingly great divergence. Instead of repeating the whole sequence from the start, Lorenz had chosen to type in the initial criteria himself, as he had them from the first transcript, in the middle of the sequence. The computer saved six decimals, while the transcript, in order to save space, only operated with three. And when Lorenz typed from the first transcript, he typed only three figures. That made all the difference. The number of decimals. One ten-thousandth part.

For Lorenz this was a lesson in the great effects of small influences, and for science yet another disproof of Newton's view of the world as a great orderly magnitude of inexpressible linear tediousness. Annika belonged to a generation that dutifully and with aching heads had solved differential equations and never set a question mark after either them or their quadratures. Merely because they form the foundation on which many centuries of Western technological triumph have rested. No one ever told them that those which, after much head-scratching and intellectual rigour, were finally resolved were not representative of differential equations. They were not even in the majority. They were among the small number of differential equations that *can* be solved at all.

Lorenz had no reason to doubt that the systems of arithmetical notation used by a man whose laws of movement and gravity had made it possible to predict the existence of the planet Neptune in 1846 at precisely the place indicated by the figures, and who had so dazzlingly impressed generations with his simplified, well-rounded world order, could be defective. That a thin layer of varnish concealed a veritable chaos. And Annika had no reason to believe otherwise than that the recalcitrant numerical system she dragged herself through with toil and trouble in her student days assumed an elevated universal status, that the figures were sparkling mathematical crown jewels, a magical, man-made interpretation of nature's numbers and not mere decimalistic freaks.

'We know more than people expect, and much, much less than

they think.' That was how Harper Stone expressed it, when he literally stood in the middle of the cloud of Cantor dust that was whirled up in the wake of the discovery of complex systems, deterministic non-periodic currents and the incomprehensible patterns of fractals. Harper Stone had gone up south-west of Borroloola to study spiders. He repeated the attempt of the American entomologist Terry Erwin in South America to let off a poison cannon under a single tree and then see what fell down. Terry Erwin's starting point was to collect beetles from a single tree. From a limited ecosystem. A tropical lime tree, *Luehea semanii*. Several beetles had specialised in living on that tree. The treetops of the impassable rainforests were practically new ground for scientists. No one had any idea what was hidden in the forests up under the roof of the jungle. At the foot of the tree they placed a row of large funnels in thin aluminium film attached to bottles containing seventy per cent alcohol for conserving the fallen insects. When the poison cannon sent its death-dealing cloud up through the crown of the tree it was not long before it sounded as if a local hailstorm was ravaging the jungle. Down from the tree, one single tree, fell not only beetles in vast numbers. Down came more different species of ant than there are ants in a medium-sized European country. Down plummeted whole groups of anaesthetised insects the world had never known. Down fell the generally accepted opinion that biology now only needed to find and describe a couple of million insects and spiders and place them in their respective taxonomic groups. Down dropped the idea that the work would most likely be concluded in a not too distant future. Down sank instead the realisation that they had only just started on a task that would never be completed. Something similar happened to Harper Stone up in Arnhem Land. When he delivered his slide lecture at Sydney University it was obvious that the close-packed audience were faced with a man who had gone out to create a comprehensive view – and had lost it.

'I would not even suggest that we multiply the number by fifty. For we simply do not know how great a number of species we don't know; but it is large,' a dizzy Harper Stone announced to the hall.

Simon Rees was an eager listener when Annika dished up stories about Harper Stone and his discoveries. And Simon Rees too could contribute accounts of chaos – chaos from the urban jungle.

'The problem isn't the information in itself. The problem is the quantity,' he said. 'Would you believe, Annika, that when the Cold War ended, the NSA had only analysed about twenty per cent of all the monitoring carried out.'

Annika was of the opinion that Simon's habit of frequently using examples from American Intelligence and not from the ASIO was probably due to the Americans not being his cup of tea. He often used the Gulf War as an example of how not only raw data in the form of reports from the field and digital satellite photographs, but also uncensored publicly available news coverage, was misinterpreted to a huge extent by CIA headquarters, by the Pentagon and by the White House. As a rule Simon was fond of showing up American bungling or ineptitude and incompetence by the CIA. He entertained Annika with stories of how during the Gulf War the American observation satellites registered at lightning speed the Iraqis' anti-aircraft radar so that the F-117s and self-guided Tomahawk missiles could take them out, but also how the military on the ground worked with fourteen different reception systems for intelligence information, of which only two were mutually compatible, and he revealed how at one point the fate of a whole world lay in the hands of an American president who was so much of an actor that he often demanded his intelligence briefs served up as a quick video show. But in her heart Annika realised that Simon ridiculed the Americans and their bunglings as a cover for at least two manifestations of impotence. Partly a long series of betrayals of the land he loved. Australia's convenient position in relation to the Far East, added to the fact that the country had one of the largest deposits of uranium, had, in Simon's view, reduced a country independent only in theory to function as the USA's stepping-stone to the Pacific. Just as Denmark, at least during the Cold War, had functioned in the Baltic region, and as Canada did in the north-west. The other kind of impotence lay in the intelligence service as such.

But at more serious moments he exhibited a third strain of impotence, almost identical with Harper Stone's.

'The satellites don't see as much as some people hope, or some fear.'

Annika had always felt there was an extremely optimistic strain in chaos theories. She had never regarded chaos as a postulate of impotence. Nor as defeatism, nor as despondency, nor as weary futility in the face of the insurmountable tasks perceived from the viewpoint of a firmament of shaky ignorance. Merely as a correction of a centuries-long misreading of the world.

Annika knew the deterministic chaos that absorbed Harper Stone, which Simon Rees could not avoid even if he wished to. She knew about it from her own profession. The cause of nine out of ten heart diseases was uncertain, many medications were prescribed without an exact knowledge of their effect, spontaneous recoveries were an inexplicable but welcome assistant in the course of an illness. But the episode with the girl was puzzling. No one, no one rises from the dead without an explanation, sensible or no.

Her father would see it differently. As if with a mental adze he split his way into the atom's nucleus. Large, unwieldy quantities like cell walls collapsed with a crash in the world of quanta, numbers flew to every side like knots and splinters to end up in an accumulation of heavy material, an equation that could not be stated more briefly. Just like the apparently happiest aphorisms of language, the equations were formulae of an incomprehensible, universal and above all compressed character. Like a sculptor, he chopped his way piece by piece, chip by chip, into the nucleus. With blind faith that with closer knowledge of the initial beginnings of a system, and with the use of the natural laws that apparently operated everywhere in the universe, he would be able to calculate his way to the system's behaviour with approximate validity. The episode of the girl was an aberration and therefore not worth taking into account. A disparity in an otherwise clear calculation. Something one could ignore. That was the difference between them. Annika knew that there was an explanation. And that there was every reason to believe it was nonsensical.

Her hand came to rest on the mobile, but she resisted the temptation to ring Simon. Out of consideration for June they had agreed to call each other in the daytime and as far as possible avoid phone calls that in June's unreasonable world of jealousy and unfounded suspicions might be interpreted as more than they actually were. Annika respected this agreement. But she could not ring Mike either. There were only three days until they set off. Tomorrow they were going out for a meal to run through the final details. Because of the confused course of their relationship, he might misunderstand an unexpected call. Men.

And so that evening when Annika drove home, it was to a state of solitude.

Annika lived in unnecessary luxury out at Whale Beach, where the most conspicuous reminders of Denmark were the pile of letters from her elder sister, J.P. Jacobsen's Danish translation of Darwin, the antiquarian fourteen-volume edition of the *Works* of Goethe with an introduction by P.A. Rosenberg, and the Bang & Olufsen hi-fi on its revolving turntable in a corner of the room.

Her father, who was lavish about everything except his emotions, had bought the house for her when she married the zoologist Jay Morgan, and he did not take out any kind of mortgage on the house when they separated the following year. Jay Morgan and Annika had met when Annika was in the middle of her term as house physician at Sydney Hospital. He happened to be in the A & E department getting treated for some infected scratches from a koala bear when Annika fell out with a consultant she felt was being irresponsible by treating a small girl, who had apparently been bitten by a vicious roughscaled snake, with repeated doses of serum. Her reactionary superior had brought the girl close to death because he refused to believe that a double dose of anti-serum could lead to anything other than a doubly great catastrophe. The dressing-down Annika gave the consultant earned her a rebuke, but probably saved the little girl's life, and Jay Morgan witnessed the scene from the waiting room. He convinced both himself and her – with the eloquence bestowed on him by a glance at her legs – that it was her courage that had smitten him.

Jay Morgan introduced Annika to a number of the scientists, among them Mike Lewis and Harper Stone, who had since become her friends. He also initiated her disgust with Australian men. The argumentativeness that had apparently attracted him at the hospital was not at all to his liking within the four walls of home, particularly if it took the form of a rebuff, when, quickly losing his past eloquence but still inspired by a glance at her legs, 'sudden passion' overcame him. The house at Whale Beach was too big even for two, it was too far from Sydney, and for that reason friends and acquaintances never just dropped in. These three reasons, which in the first flush of love had made the house ideal, in fact had lessened Annika's enthusiasm even before they moved in. But she had grown used to living there, and after a year had passed, the only thing she was tired of was her husband.

The divorce proceeded – outwardly at least – without any great drama, and she left her childless marriage with the knowledge that she would never again take a husband, at least not an Australian one, but also with the conviction that it was essential for her to pursue her interest in the elapids.

Sometimes, on her way home to the empty house, the quiet district and the big silent rooms, she would be seized with a slight melancholy. When that happened she sought compensation in loud music, television pictures without sound, talking to herself. But in time she learned to deal with these fluctuations of mood, and in quick succession she turned down the music, shut off the television with the remote control, put a stop to her vacuous monologue. The period following Jay Morgan and her wild early youth in Sydney taught her that solitude could become familiar in an astonishingly short time. And without making or wanting to make solitude a martyrdom, Annika discovered that she actually set great store on being alone.

Now and then when she reflected on her marriage, not on the loss of it but on how it had come about, she found it hard to point to a specific reason for having said yes to Jay Morgan. It is said of family relationships that a strong and domineering father will produce a daughter with evasive characteristics and a pronounced weakness in making choices, and even though Annika was always on guard against the psychological templates of popular science, like everyone else she felt they applied to her now and then. In the case of Jay Morgan, choice was not an issue. He was older than she was, he was intelligent, he had, like Simon Rees, some enchanting premature touches of grey in the hair above his ears and above all he was very commanding. She had repressed the memory of the scene in which he must have been down on his knees, but when she thought back on it, she found it hard to hear Jay formulate his appeal as anything other than an order.

Neither Simon nor his wife June, and particularly not June, understood why Annika did not just move in with Mike, whom Annika now and then mentioned to them. But it was not so simple. Isolation can subvert. It can destroy and erode. But it can also corrupt. And quite early on in her solitary life Annika was able to recall a number of situations in which it was not an unconditional advantage to be two. June always spoke with enthusiasm of the idea of being a twosome when other people were present, at a party, or when there were just the three of them, herself, Annika and Simon. But she did it in an unexceptionable manner which covered her perfectly against any possible counter-attack. Outwardly it sounded as if she was genuinely worried about Annika being alone, but if she had really been convinced of that she would not have avoided the subject so adroitly when the two of them happened to be on their own. She and Annika were not intimate. Not to that extent. There was too much between them. Simon. And much else. Simon was reserved and more careful about his opinions, but Annika could not decide whether this trait reflected her own relationship with Simon or that with his wife.

Annika was well aware that she had dragged Mike through the worst tortures a man can be dragged through. Something that had fallen like a pale, disabling melancholy on his soul at the moment they first met, she had, with the help of all her rejections, in time stretched out into a psychosis-like depression which occasionally seemed to threaten to break him completely. When she first realised this she started, in order to balance the account, to go to bed with him. That only worsened the situation, and afterwards she reproached herself fiercely for not realising it. She had imagined that by introducing a physical element into the ethereal status she felt she had acquired in his imagination, she could put their relationship into a more tolerable perspective. Tolerable for her. For she was in no doubt that he, leaving aside his momentary yet brief emotional dives, was in a state of daily euphoria from some human chemical or other. Worse than this was the fact that Mike clearly exhibited some symptoms that she herself, albeit to a more controlled extent, had sometimes felt in her relationship with Simon.

'I don't want to get married. I don't want children. I can't be satisfied with one lover. I'm just like every other woman. It's pure chemistry, Mike. You'll be one of the ten per cent of men who change the nappies of a kid who's not theirs. We'll make love, and I'll go straight into town and let someone else get me pregnant. Have multiple orgasms. I'm sorry, Mike. But that's how we are. Unfaithful and not to be relied on.'

But none of this had any effect. And Annika realised that Mike had reached an advanced stage of his crisis.

'I'm on my own, Mike. Can't you understand that? I like it.'

Annika was very fond of Mike. They went diving together, and they enjoyed a friendship she would be very loth to lose. He was one of the most insistently persevering men Annika had known, and she was convinced that a woman who had not learned to enjoy solitude like herself would have given way long ago. In quiet moments she pondered on how differently men made their approach to a woman. Jay, who merely came on like a steamroller, and then Mike with his long, dogged perseverance. It struck Annika that both of them took great risks, where a woman would have protected herself much more. It struck her also that she herself reacted in a very contradictory manner when Mike eventually withdrew a little and found his attraction cooling. She caught herself missing his fervent pleas and thinking that if only he had been slightly less impressed by her, perhaps ... She also caught herself considering whether she had kept him in the role of rejected suitor because he, like her, had feared their friendship would fade when the wooing, the tender glances, caresses and compliments were no longer part of their common language. But she also caught herself thinking that that was exactly how a woman would think, and she rejected her bad conscience again as the expression of a gender-conditioned reflex. She maintained her right to persist, locked up her solitary life in her mind as a well-defined axiom, fumbled in the air for solid objects that slipped between her fingers when she tried to find material form for the things that must not be changed, despaired when the substance in her life that must be defended against intruders, and that ought to be something which could be seized on to hit people over the head with when they came too close, was merely something that seemed to slide along her skin like turbulence or wind. The truth, she knew, was that what she attempted to grasp as a concrete dimension was her own searching, her own cross-country run in a world where each new position offered only a brief happiness and a pointer to yet another post. She searched by sunlight and lamplight, read line after line, ploughed through page after page, book after book, work after work, bookshelf after bookshelf.

In a creation myth from Dahomey in West Africa, the first human beings were blind until a python, a god of wisdom, opened their eyes to the knowledge of this world. To Annika this myth had always held a double meaning. The snakes had been a route to something greater. Her exemplars had always been universalists like Goethe, Darwin, Poincaré. Like Goethe she wanted to straddle the centuries, look down, look up, look to the side, get the overview that led to insight, gain a firm foundation in a world in which she knew there was no firm foundation, in which each great discovery can only be called great if it simultaneously perceives how small it is, in which continents drift apart, and in which even the galaxies are islands moving away from each other. In this world of infinite existential excursion, the snakes were her centre. The power centre in which she found her strength. The point from which she manoeuvred. In the hunt for answers. Large and small. New questions. Other answers. More questions. When at times her head threatened to short-circuit, she reminded herself that this was good for the brain. That each investigation, that all students of the mind – Mike Lewis included – supported the fact that the brain was improved by training.

When Annika reached her house, sited right out on the point on three split levels, she activated the garage door and drove in.

She almost fell over the diving gear and bags in the hall, forgetting she had put them out with the idea of finishing her packing in the morning. She pushed her way through T-shirts, socks, Allen keys and various awls and spanners. Next she went on a round of the house, switched on lights, picked up the remote control from the glass table in the living room, put on the stereo, turned it down straightaway, switched on the television and switched it off again at once, went on humming a snatch of song from the car radio, and then fell silent.

She went into the kitchen, took a Braeburn apple from the fruit basket and munched big bites of it. Tired and dazed with the heat, she rested her forehead against the fridge before opening it. She took a jug of diluted apple vinegar out of the fridge door, opened the small freezer underneath and found the ice tray, dropped some ice cubes into the jug. From the open fridge she got out a jar of acacia honey.

Simon always said he couldn't understand how she could get it down, but Annika had drunk it for as long as she could remember. It had been her mother's idea, and in time had become one of her own few but lasting idiosyncrasies. Vinegar with everything. Wine vinegar with food, apple vinegar morning and evening, but in contrast to her mother, who was a slave to Martlet's Honegar, Annika preferred to control the quantity of honey herself. Her mother, who found a kind of confirmation in the fact that it was vinegar that had been used to moisten Jesus's lips on the cross, maintained that apple vinegar came from an old Swedish household recipe, but Annika suspected she had read D.C. Jarvis. Wherever it originated, Annika could find no objections from a medical viewpoint. All things considered vinegar is a dilute of acetic acid in water. Acetic acid is an organic material, which like the amino acids is found everywhere in space. It is a weak acid, which on account of the carboxyl group gives vinegar its sharp taste. Moreover, Annika knew everything about the excellent properties of vinegar. She knew that vinegar, like no other medium, could neutralise in under half a minute the extremely violent pains suffered by people in the north when they had inadvertently become entangled in the highly dangerous tentacles of the sea wasp, and when she discovered that she could also use vinegar acid as a rust remover, she changed her whole arsenal of cleaning materials and replaced it with vinegar and acetic acid for lime-scaling, supplemented by only one universal cleaning fluid.

She picked up the *Herald* from the kitchen and placed it folded on the tray, but as life had taught her never to go to ascetic extremes she supplied herself on the way with a bag of cashew nuts lying on the table.

Annika put jug, glass and honey on the tray and walked back into the living room. She pushed open the French window with a creak of wood and went out on to the terrace. The pump was humming quietly in the pool, water gurgled in whispers, transparent little splashes dented the surface, there were clinking smacks at the corners of the pool and slopping along the edge. She took an ice cube from the jug and let it slide down her throat, opened the bag of nuts and, starting modestly, quickly went on to small handfuls.

As she opened the newspaper she fell into a reverie and her thoughts turned for the last time that evening to the girl.

The girl had remained sitting up straight for ten minutes. Why hadn't she left the car? If the snake had bitten her at that point, immediately after she had sat down, as was implied by the Swedish couple's explanation, why hadn't she hurried to get out?

Annika searched for logic, meaning, cogency in the sequence of events. But there was nothing. There was merely a strip of linked small mysteries within the greater mystery: what was she doing in the car, why was there a snake in the car, how could she come back from a clinical death that was evident and visible to all those present, and how could she get up so quickly? Annika played with various possibilities in the form of shock reactions, but they did not cohere. For however she manipulated the possibility of a hypersensitive reaction, of poison, of antidote, nothing could explain away the four bite wounds, which in any case meant that she had received a powerful toxic assault that no one, either with or without treatment, could just shake off.

This illustrated why such confusion about Australian snakes prevails among the public and why doctors, biologists and herpetologists have such difficulty explaining when they attempt to classify snakes in a kind of toxic order of rank. Just like physicists, medics often favour a simple summarising sentence encapsulating the whole matter, and Annika frequently disappointed people when they – especially the press – tried to extract a clear answer from her about which snake was the most dangerous. The disappointment turned into incredulity when she stated that it was hard to determine clearly which was the most poisonous, but that naturally she could refer them to various books that gave estimated and rounded evaluations.

Queensland Museum has developed criteria incorporating five different factors of significance in a snake's bite: the potency of the venom, how much of it is injected by the snake in each bite, how long the venom fangs are, the snake's temperament, and how often it strikes when it attacks. The venom of the fierce snake, *Oxyuranus microlepidotus*, also known as the small-scaled snake, the western taipan or the inland taipan, because not until the snake was rediscovered in 1967 was it realised that it was not only a variant of the taipan but an independent species, is almost doubly as potent as that of the taipan. It was this that led to headlines all over the world in various journals, when on the basis of the LD50 value it was possible to calculate that in one bite the snake could put paid to 250,000 mice. But the fierce snake's fangs are not as large as those of the taipan, so it does not inject so much venom, is far less aggressive than the taipan, and does not make a series of bites like the taipan. The common brown snake would also surpass the taipan if it were a matter of pure toxin, its own being considerably more potent than that of the taipan, but the taipan's discharge of venom in a single bite is sixty times as great and, measured in LD50, taking into account both the height of the toxic danger as well as the average portion in a bite, it is forty times as dangerous as the common brown snake.

But even with these adjustments and proximate parameters the picture remains vague. When Annika had once looked back through the annals at the tests on pigs made by the Commonwealth Serum Laboratories at the end of the 1930s on the Reevesby Island tiger snake, she discovered that its venom was two or three times more potent than that of the common tiger snake, while later results showed one to two times when the test was carried out on mice. At Whylla Annika had once milked a black tiger snake from Kangaroo Island which with an evident pleasure that looked like delighted obsession bit into the rubber lid and discharged a dose of venom almost six times the average quantity from a tiger snake. Chaos rules in the world of snakes, and there are no simple answers. It is a case of two systems meeting. A human one with an ingeniously coded defence mechanism meeting a system of venoms coded to circumvent that defence. The danger lies in a series of variables. Whether one is a child, or old, how much one weighs, how one's chemistry is composed, which snake it is, how much it injects, how many times it bites, where and how it bites, what treatment one receives, where and how one is treated. It is endless.

The Aborigines up in Arnhem Land are – with good reason – wary of white doctors and particularly uncommunicative about their methods for cures, evolved and refined through thousands and thousands of years. But once, Annika succeeded in worming out of Kookillo Dhamarandji how they treated snakebite. Out on the island of Elcho, where Kookillo Dhamarandji came from, he said they used to scrape the carapace of a particular black beetle the size of a cockroach with a red patch on its back. The substance obtained was rubbed on the bite. Together with the inhalation of special leaves the beetle's carapace had an anaesthetising effect. Before this happened the bite was cut open and as much venom as possible sucked out. The Aboriginals knew that keeping calm was important. Sometimes a child that had been bitten was placed under a tree, while the guilty snake was caught, tied up and hung in the tree with strict instructions that if the child did not survive, neither should the snake. Even though Annika would always recommend Dr Sutherland's method and would never encourage anyone either to cut or suck a snakebite, there was considerably more sense initially in the native practice than in that of the white population when it helplessly confronted these hydrogen bombs of nature. Right up until 1912 people were treated with strychnine, which caused the death of a small girl that same year; as late as 1903 doctors suggested in deadly earnest that the patient should swallow a venom fang from the same type of snake that had bitten them, and before then the treatment was alcohol and no rest whatsoever. People who had been bitten danced like mad things. Danced themselves to death.

'*Marngit*,' said Kookillo Dhamarandji with an ironic glint in his eye, when Annika described to him her predecessors' highly dubious wisdom. *Marngit*, wise man, medicine man.

Annika rose from the table and carried the tray with jug and glass and empty bag into the kitchen. Then she went out into the hall.

She stood for a while gazing at the mess of clothes and gear. She was tired, but decided nevertheless to get the heavy packing done with. She packed her mask, snorkel and flippers.

On all fours she sorted the piles of clothes. And when finally she sat there moving the heaps around to no purpose she stopped. A few piles of shorts and T-shirts remained. There were still three days before they set off. Domineering father or no, a woman must only be deprived of the right to postpone decisions to the last moment under strictly controlled conditions.

Annika stood up and went in to have a bath. Half an hour later, when, with a towel wound round her hair like a white terry turban and another around her body, she crept into bed, a comfortable fatigue simmered in her arms and legs and head.

She switched off the lamp behind her, laid her head on the pillow and pulled the sheet tightly round her. Solitary people do not live long. Solitary people commit suicide more than others. As early as the 1950s, scientists at McGill University in Canada demonstrated that isolation sends human beings mad. Luckily, thought Annika, scientists at Brighton and Loughborough in England have now shown that one sleeps best alone. Then she fell asleep.

The sunshine ran along the floor and clung to the lowest part of the wall in ripples of light. Annika had opened the door and wound the blind right up so that cool air could come in during the night. She lay swaddled only in a white cloud of mosquito netting for the same reason, and the first thing she did, muzzy in the head and dehydrated, was to reach under the net for her bottle of mineral water.

It is the heat that brings out Australian snakes. The worst time is when the temperature changes suddenly in early summer, which corresponds to early winter in the northern hemisphere. December is particularly bad. By far the majority of the total of five hundred people treated each year for snakebite in New South Wales are bitten in December.

Annika knew, as did the others at the Prince of Wales, the Westmead and the Orange hospitals, that the first heat wave gave rise to an infantile cycle that repeated itself year after year. It began with the snakes. In late summer after the first bites, the hectic activity in the Australian A & E departments, the reports in the media and the warnings of the experts, everything slowed down merely to be overtaken by a fresh cycle: the spiders went out on a hunt for mates that led them into the houses of Sydney, into people's piles of newspapers and into their beds. To Annika it seemed as if many people in Sydney tried to ignore the fact that the plum-sized spiders occasionally found indoors must of necessity have come from outside, and even she was surprised the first time Harper Stone – as they sat chatting one evening on her terrace – showed her with a torch exactly how many big webs had been spun between the trees in the darkness of the garden.

Heavy with sleep, and drinking from the bottle of water, Annika stumbled into the living room and switched on the television. The sun poured in through the windows and the pictures on the screen were diluted by the morning light as they emerged. The row of Sabatier knives beside the fruit bowl sparked off the light as Annika moved on into the hall with screwed-up eyes.

She picked up the newspaper and morning post, went into the kitchen again, put on some coffee, prepared a plate with slices of juicy yellow and spongy melon, green kiwi fruit slices, apple and banana. The ice clinked in the jug of apple vinegar, and fragrant grey steam rose from the coffee cup on the tray as she walked into the living room to slit open her post.

Sometimes Annika had the irrational feeling that you could delay the contents of an envelope that had arrived by leaving it unopened. She also knew from friends with dodgy finances who practised this principle that it worked. When she came to a thick brown manila envelope she felt an inexplicable reluctance to open it. At first she put it aside and turned to watch the ABC news which, bathed in sunlight, resembled the transmission of some kind of divine séance however she altered the position of the screen. She chewed at a furry kiwi rind, but then pulled herself together and slit open the envelope, which resembled those she sometimes received from Simon.

At first she was surprised that it bore no sender's name. And yet more surprised when she took out the contents. Three sheets of A4. Colour copies of three scans. Positron Emissions Tomographics. At the bottom of one of them the paper was covered with a small sequence of scans. Another had a small cross-section model of the human brain, beside which was sketched a three-dimensional model brain. No text. No letter. No report. No analysis, no data, no figures. Annika studied the three colour copies. The same brain. She turned them over, one by one. No text. No name. No explanations whatsoever. When she looked more closely she caught sight of a faint system of arrows above various shaded areas in the PET scans and on the three-dimensional drawings. With some difficulty Annika was able to localise two of the arrows to the ventricles. On the other she could also glimpse an arrow by the hippocampus. As far as she could judge the third copy represented activity in the sight and hearing centres. When she studied the copies even more closely she noticed a diminutive initial mark in the corner of all the copies. 'MJ.' Annika sat for a while puzzling over the sheets. It irritated her that at this moment she lacked Mike's expert eye, which would undoubtedly be able to see what she could not make out.

As she was about to put them back in the envelope she discovered something else in it she had overlooked: a drawing. She saw at once what it represented, but her attention was first caught by a quotation written on a slant at the top of the picture, a quote she seemed to recall as a slightly modified sentence from the description of the seven wonders of the world by the Greek archivist Philon. 'What the eye of the soul has seen cannot be destroyed.' It was clearly in Simon's hand, and she well knew how he delighted in the old Greek philosophers they had discussed so often, but she could not understand what the whole thing was about. She knew this much: Simon was not good at drawing, so she puzzled over who might have devoted both time and energy to making such a detailed one so effectively. Not least because of the fact that the drawing portrayed her – it was a sketch of Annika's face.

She gathered all the papers and replaced them in the envelope, went inside and put it in the drawer of her bedroom chest, where she kept her pistol. Still not quite awake, she noted that this day had begun just as the one before had ended. With a mystery.

Annika felt quite convinced that out of the two kilos of sunshine that strike the earth each second, at least one kilo hits Sydney.

These were the days when Annika regretted not having invested in a cabriolet rather than the little off-roader she was now driving. She closed her eyes and imagined the roof pushed back to allow the breeze to blow cool air over the car, and the whole way into Sydney she sat airing her hand on the open window. But it scarcely helped. The air was so hot and so damp she was almost suffocating.

There is nothing you can do in the humid Australian heat but drink water. Water, water, water. And that doesn't seem to help much anyway. Even before reaching Manly she had finished half a litre of mineral water, and when the traffic came to a halt just before Manly she took out yet another bottle. She tried to get hold of Simon on her mobile. But in vain. She put her head back and drank from the bottle. Half asleep, she let herself be drawn in towards the centre, past the green peninsulas, islets, bays and inlets, past the beaches and the scattered groups of houses with tiled roofs on the cliffs, with the sparkling white eye of the sun on the water everywhere.

Dazed, Annika sat nodding in the sluggish traffic as she approached Harbour Bridge. The water beneath was a white jumble of fluttering sails, a Ken Done sailing idyll, with the big Manly ferry on its way out from Circular Quay, the small boats around the Matilda catamaran heading for Taronga Zoo, and a pointed white cruiser from Captain Cook chalking a line of wake behind it on its way across the belt. Puddles of sunlight lay on the cars in front of her, the open space before the Opera House shone and the glare flashed off the curves, even the spotted carpet of tourists in front of the semicircles emitted reflections before the sudden rainforest-like darkness of the financial district's skyscrapers, sharply outlined and towering, fell around her, immediately after she had passed The Rocks.

Annika spent most of the morning shopping in the Queen Victoria Building down by Darling Harbour, and while her list sent her around the old rectangular floors of the hunchbacked building with all its freshened-up pastel colours, she made use of the time to reconstruct in her mind the previous day's events. She was struck with a sense of unease; perhaps they had made some mistake or other. Naturally she was relieved that the outcome had been a happy one, but worried over the girl having had a relapse at a point when she had received serum and was stable. She recalled a statistic claiming that almost half the antidotes stored at the regional hospitals were either old or antidotes for the wrong snakes in the area concerned. But when she checked the packs of antidote at the hospital later in the afternoon she found no fault with them. And none of the packs had been on the shelves for more than a year. She contacted Taronga Zoo, the Australian Reptile Park at Gosford North, the Australian Wildlife Park, but no one knew about or had lost a snake. And the hospitals, the Royal North Shore, St Vincent's, the Royal South Sydney Hospital. None of them had treated a girl corresponding to Annika's description of her. She rang Sydney Hospital and the Poisons Information office. No one had called about a snake.

Towards evening Annika was washing her hands in front of the mirror in one of the department toilets when she was bleeped from reception. They told her they had sent a man desperately in need of a smoke to the hospital canteen, where he was waiting for her.

'Kahn,' she said, repressing a little smile.

'This is totally informal,' said Detective Superintendent Kahn. 'I just need to ask a couple of questions about the treatment of the girl yesterday. As I understand it, you were in charge of her treatment?'

'I gave express orders for her to be given another dose of serum. Her papers show she received it. If it turns out that . . .'

'But you yourself were not present when she presumably had the second dose?'

'No, at that point she was stable.'

'Why give her more serum, then?'

'It is a purely routine procedure. I would have given her a third and a fourth . . .'

'As far as I've understood, not everyone agrees that repeated doses of antidote are harmless? This . . . cocktail?'

'It is entirely theoretical. Polyvalent serum kills no one. There has not been a death since the 1960s. *Contraria contrariis curantur.* Opposites cure opposites.'

'Not everyone agrees with you?'

'Not everyone knows as much about snakebites. Listen, Kahn, I can tell you have been talking to another doctor. Without doubt an older doctor. In earlier times allergic reactions did occur, particularly in people born before 1940. There is an explanation for that, Kahn. At that time many had become oversensitive to horse protein in childhood. There is an explanation, Kahn. Even in the Dark Ages there was an earlier Dark Age. And if you think we are too lavish with our doses today it's nothing compared with the overdosage given then. In order to protect the children. From diphtheria and lockjaw. It worked. Unfortunately it made them vulnerable to serum.'

'Why didn't you treat her with taipan serum?'

'Because we don't have any taipan serum.'

'Why not?'

'Because we don't have any use for it. Normally.'

'You could have requisitioned some. From Taronga Zoo?'

Annika looked at Kahn angrily.

'Kahn, have you found the girl?'

'We're still searching.'

'Since you're so clever I don't understand why it's so hard to find her.'

'It would have been easier if you had kept hold of her.'

'What are you trying to say?'

Kahn sighed.

'I just want to definitely exclude the possibility that there could have been an . . . abnormal reaction . . .'

'We do not keep taipan serum because we have no taipan in our area. We keep the antidotes for the groups of snakes we do have. And then we have the polyvalent serum. In the north they have taipan serum. Down in Victoria they don't need the polyvalent one. All their snakes can be neutralised with a mixture of tiger snake and brown snake serum. In Tasmania tiger snake serum is the only one they need. Tiger snake serum can neutralise the eastern small-eyed snake, Collett's snake, the spotted black snake, red-bellied black snake, the copperhead snake, the roughscaled snake, the eastern small-eyed snake and several Indian and American snakes. The polyvalent serum may not cover the total volume, but it covers every constitution. In theory I would not exclude someone dying in spite of all this, but I can assure you, Kahn, that it would never, never make someone leap up like a jack-in-the-box and start to behave in a manner best suited to an American thriller film.'

Kahn heard Annika's lecture out in silence. She had steadily worked herself up into a fury and finally stood before him in an almost threatening pose with a fist clenched close to his face. When she came to herself she was on the point of telling him about her confrontation with the girl in the car the day before, but the sight of the speculative look Kahn was giving her determined her to stay loyal to the girl and instead to be difficult, an urge she excused as stemming from the irritation he had the knack of making her feel. She let her arm drop and went back to the window.

'Miss Niebuhr, have you anything particular against immigrants?'

'No. But I have against silly questions. And the heat. Which serum,' said Annika with her back to Kahn, 'do you think we use against the king brown snake?'

'Brown snake serum.'

Annika turned round with a smile.

'Black snake serum. Do you think, then, Kahn, that the king brown is a brown snake?'

'Isn't it?'

Annika sighed.

'It has been repeated over and over in newspapers and on TV. Moreover, it has been given another name: the mulga snake. Why is it people don't listen?'

'We can't all know everything about snakes,' said Kahn.

'Have you any children, Kahn?'

The Detective Superintendent nodded.

'Two.'

'Then you should.'

Kahn got to his feet. And for a brief moment Annika regretted having torn him off a strip. She felt a sudden need to smooth things over, reinstate the detective.

'Those tiresome cases, Kahn, that have appeared in the press, were where too little serum was given. Either because it was thought too expensive, or because there was not enough. And they involved deaths . . .'

'Her glove compartment was open. It fits well with the Swedish couple's descriptions. Could there have been a snake in the glove compartment?'

'There are two possible explanations for what happened. One is that there isn't an explanation. The other, that she is partly immune. If she has been regularly exposed to taipoxin, in theory she could have developed immunity. It happens to some herpetologists. Snake-charmers use it. There are two possibilities in frequent bites. Either you become immune to the venom, or you drop dead at the mere thought of it. She may have developed immunity. But I don't think she has.'

'Illegal export of snakes is not exactly an unknown phenomenon here, Miss Niebuhr. What I mean is, she might have brought the snake herself?'

Annika shook her head. She had kept a trump card for last, and it was as if Kahn felt it. He looked at her.

'Why don't you think the girl is immune, Miss Niebuhr?'

'She didn't move for ten minutes, Kahn. For those ten minutes, which roughly correspond to the precise time she had to get out of the car, she sat there without moving. And do you know why, Kahn?'

'No, Miss Niebuhr. I don't know.'

'She couldn't.'

Kahn looked at her uncomprehendingly.

'Ophiophobia. Snake phobia. For ten minutes she was able only to raise her arm and push open the door. No poison can have paralysed the girl, as the couple described it. The person who placed the snake in the car may have known this about the girl. Known that she would not move at the sight of the snake. Known that she would not have been able to. They may have known how she would react. Or not react. The greatest miracle is that that alone did not kill her.'

The moment she had spoken it was as if Kahn was filled with a visible satisfaction, and Annika had an uncomfortable feeling that she had said something she ought not to have said.

'Simon Rees. Does that name mean anything to you?'

Annika looked at Kahn in surprise.

'Yes.'

'You know him?'

'He is a close friend. Why do you ask?'

Kahn stood up.

'The car was hired via England. Through a firm in Brockham, Surrey. By Simon Rees.'

Some psychological research supports the theory that women's voices have a more calming effect on both sexes than men's. This is why women's voices are used in many civil and all military automatic telephone systems. When, for the fifth or sixth time, Annika had listened to the same entirely or partly automatic women's voices on the line with no other message than that Simon was neither here nor there, she would have been grateful to have heard a man's voice.

Annika gave up trying to get hold of him. She had been struggling to get through ever since she had parted from Kahn. First at the number he had given her for the ASIO, then the one she only knew belonged to some barracks at an unspecified distance from Sydney. No one had any idea where Simon was.

Just before she entered the Imperial Harbourside close to The Rocks, she rang his mobile, but only got his answerphone. She left a message for him before switching off her own phone and snapping it shut.

Mike had arrived. He rose and came to meet her when he caught sight of her, and it struck her how separation can change your impression of others. She could barely remember when they had last seen each other, but it was a long time ago, and, thought Annika at the sight of him, far too long. He kissed her cheek and gave her a hug, then led her by the hand to the table he had reserved. He looked good. He was tanned, had just had a haircut; he was wearing a coal-grey blazer over a black T-shirt. And he smelt good.

On the drive there she had worried a little about how the evening and two weeks at sea together would pan out. But now she could hardly wait to set off.

Mike ordered for them while she took the opportunity to go and 'powder her nose'. As she walked through the restaurant, where couples and small groups sat by candlelight looking out on the Harbour Bridge with its pearly rows of lights over the black water, it struck her how hard it is to get away from the fact that you are a townie. No one who has lived in isolation for a good while can avoid wallowing in almost pathetic joy at seeing people socialising. Naturally, Annika had nothing in common with these people. At heart she knew that in conversation with any of these diners she would very soon get bored. As they would with her. There is nothing so provincial as a big city. The really important topics are trivialized, perhaps for the sake of clarity, and seemingly the importance of things grows in proportion to their elusiveness. Swiftly shifting moods of fashion, just as hard to predict as the weather, sweep in discreet whispers from customer to customer at the restaurants currently most sought after in the ever-changing big city picture of what's in and out.

People might try to explain to her that you couldn't live without the city. And would stare incredulously if she tried to explain to them that the only problem with solitude is that as a solitary you have no one with whom to share the joys of solitude. All the same, on this evening in the softly lit restaurant, she felt embraced by a warmth which, she felt, she had been missing for ages.

Annika laughed to herself. She realised how long it was since she had gone out and how much she valued it when she did. She realised too that the last time she had seen Mike was also the last time she had had sex. With astonishing, almost disturbing speed, the mysterious events of the previous day were reduced to marginal trivia.

Before the mirror in the ladies' loo she ran a pale pink lipstick over her lips, rubbed them together, straightened her hair and then returned to the restaurant in the same expectant mood as when she had left it.

Like Simon Rees, the still youthful Professor Mike Lewis was a student of the brain. Mike documented what was known about the human brain, Simon what one did not know was not known. Mike worked at St George's Hospital, and naturally he knew about Simon from Annika's mentions of him, but otherwise she had tried to keep the two apart. Not because Mike, in spite of his sworn fealty to the new neuroscience, was too rigorous and disinclined to talk about things he could not actually see on his scanners, but more on account of the emotional hassle Annika thought a meeting between the two men would probably cause.

On her way over to the table a tinge of anxiety assailed her. There was a proclamation, an announcement, in the air.

There *was* an announcement in the air, as it happened, but it was not the announcement Annika feared – it was worse.

'What's her name?' asked Annika, trying to look as unconcerned as possible, when Mike let slip the unexpected news.

'Kim. Kim Duncan. Duncan and Schwartz. The lawyers. It's her father. Duncan, that is.'

Even though Annika knew she ought to feel relieved and grateful, those were not exactly her feelings at that moment. She felt she had been escorted out of Mike's emotional life pretty tactlessly, roughly and completely without warning. She raised her glass of wine as calmly as she could to her mouth, and when Mike, with an incomprehensible and in her opinion far too big and hearty appetite concentrated on his plate, she swallowed the contents in one gulp.

Mike was clearly in need of telling all, so Annika decided, while trying to preserve a remnant of pride by simulating a friendly interest in the girl, to get as many of the formalities over as quickly as possible.

'Is she very young?' Annika asked.

'Actually, she's only twenty-four,' said Mike.

Far too young, thought Annika, far too young for Mike.

'That's not so important,' she said. 'But what does she say about you going out sailing with an—' she hesitated before completing the sentence – 'old sweetheart?'

'She knows we're just friends,' said Mike with a big smile, and Annika reached for the wine bottle herself, shaken but still under control. In her head a somewhat confused dialogue was going on, which chaotically on the one hand forbade her under any circumstances to say anything undignified, on the other to conceive any sympathy whatsoever for Mike's newfound love. At one blow she felt reduced to a share in the All Ordinaries index, which suddenly, without any good reason, had taken a nosedive, and as she felt the wine going to her head she comforted herself by thinking she had merely been taken unawares and just needed to get used to the idea. Over the years she had known Mike he had naturally, she knew, had other lovers, just as she herself had, but never any who had needed a special proclamation, and it was not easy in a few minutes to lose the status of fêted icon and occasional sex partner to become an intimate but quite indifferent conversation partner.

In the midst of it all Annika felt a strange, pleasurable enjoyment in working herself deeper and deeper into the martyrdom whose nadir she was steadily approaching with each question. She increased the self-torture by assuring herself by stolen glances that he had seldom if ever looked so good as this very evening.

'Does she think we'll sleep in separate cabins?' asked Annika, well aware, as she heard herself utter the words, that it was a question that was equally, even if inadvertently, directed at Mike. But he managed to slide away from the part of the question that referred to him.

'I don't think,' he said, dividing a small piece of fish on his plate, 'I really don't think she's given that a thought. She hasn't mentioned it, anyway.'

'But do you think she takes it seriously?'

With an irritatingly calm and self-satisfied expression, Mike thought she probably did. 'But she is a decided young lady. She knows what she wants. And I don't think she is thinking about competitors.'

Annika sat there a while, feeling as though she had actually been slapped in the face. She allowed herself, partly in a state of transport, partly on the verge of tears, to feel the full impact of total humiliation. For a brief moment she had a suspicion that the whole thing was a cheap trick, something Mike was trying out on her to provoke a reaction. To force her into the open. But it was no trick. She put the glass to her lips and swallowed mouthfuls as if the wine was the very fluid that kept her alive. She forced herself not to look at his hands busy with knife and fork or holding the stem of his wineglass. But like a man, she imagined, who fuels his desire by looking at a woman's foot, her gaze constantly returned to those long slim hands, and she could feel her breathing grow faster and her cheeks warmer.

After the fifth glass of wine a witch took up residence inside her, whom she drowned immediately with glass number six. And by glass number seven she had regained so much control over the situation that she could focus again on what, against all expectations, had become the major theme of the evening: how she was going to seduce him. Gone was any thought of the snake and the girl and the hospital, of Simon, Kahn and Mike and her coming expedition, wiped out was every decorous reticence or respect for this twenty-four-year-old girl, about whom, she registered from a great distance, Mike was still smilingly muttering plaudits.

Seven glasses of wine had lifted Annika up into a whirl, a glowing state in which the only thing she could think of was a bedroom softly lit by candles, and those hands striking little blue sparks all over her body. All her concentration centred on making use of the effects of seven glasses of wine, preventing him from consuming the same quantity so that he could excuse himself from driving her home because he had been *drinking* too much, and on the other hand ensuring he had sufficient to make a glance at her legs, which she discreetly took care increasingly to bare, lead him to forget any restrictions self-imposed as a result of his new sweetheart. Like all women, Annika knew that the limit to a man's declared fidelity or merely theoretical good intentions, over which he slips when he is filled with explosive and unscrupulous lust, is the most fluid limit in the world, and she was really not sure whether the alcohol had had any great effect on this, but inwardly she was sure Mike had passed that limit when they were in the car on the way to her home at Whale Beach.

To think that it was this slightly dry young professor who had once said of her that there was a slanting hint of wolf in her eyes. That she had such markedly Swedish eyes. No woman, no matter how erudite and how focused on her subject and her career, can live without such words; anyhow she could not, so it was of less importance to her that he had said it, like Jay, under the inspiration of quite a different area of her body. For Mike was fundamentally different. He was gentle, thoughtful and even poetic at times. And in any case, she had warmed to his words.

Also, she had him to thank, in a way, for still being in reasonably good physical shape. For while the mind is active the body is neglected, and Annika had to admit that without their diving trips her body would slowly but surely have deteriorated. She had never, except when very young, taken much trouble over herself. She had a pot or two of creams on her bedside table, a bottle with a faint scent of Bulgarian rose; for festive occasions she used a touch of mascara, and when necessary took more trouble over her usual monthly leg-shaving. But otherwise her house and life were empty of aids other than those aimed at making her more knowledgeable. And her training had not been undertaken in a conscious attempt to hold the normal deterioration of time at bay. It was an inherent objective, even before her flirtation with martial arts, as a necessary preparation for her dives with Mike. When they sometimes went down with oxygen bottles to a depth of five atmospheric pressures it was essential for her body to be in optimum condition.

The only troublesome factor about this physical rearmament was that it intensified a sexual urge that under other circumstances would perhaps have been an active and welcome aphrodisiac, but in the light of her solitary life had an occasionally disturbing effect, and led her mind in all kinds of fruitless directions. She could look back on her childhood without the least feeling of shame either then or now, remembering her hands buried in her crotch, the round wet handful of the vulva, and with the pragmatism of the Niebuhrs in her blood she had acquired her implement, a small, shiny, battery-driven vibrator. With its whirring point against her clitoris in little circling movements a couple of times a week she maintained her auto-erotic life, which, apart from the diving trips with Mike, one or two occasional one-night stands, her press-ups and Kegel exercises, was free of physical excess.

As she sat in the car gazing at him it was not in triumph. No mature educated woman with any respect for herself toasts a victory over a twenty-four-year-old girl. But in her weaker moments Annika had realised that her feelings for Mike penetrated more deeply than the purely erotic and purely comradely. In those weak moments she had now and then played with the idea of a more permanent arrangement, but each time she had even begun to approach the idea of submission, she had quickly hardened herself and rejected the daydreams. Experience had taught her that submission smacked too much of capitulation in a negative sense, and all the years she had spent creating a life that suited her well and did not cause any emotional harm to others ought not, could not be thrown away and labelled as 'no good'. As she sat looking at him she thought that perhaps she was not so well insured against the slow grind of the years on the mind as she had believed. She did not know whether it was the prospect of the companionship she and Mike had enjoyed being threatened in earnest, or whether it was just her intoxicated state. She concluded her inner discussion by opting for the latter. When one is alone, one either breaks down because of the loneliness or fills the empty space with worthwhile interests, and with each new thing that takes up space in one's life, something else must give way. There was nothing in her life to be thrown away. She had changed the gasket on her siphon trap herself after the garden hose went on strike, she had emerged victorious from the battle with a blocked lavatory, and even in deeply sentimental moments she had coped. She decided to concentrate on the moment, which, given her tipsy state, was a task in itself.

She checked whether anyone had tried to ring her. Even though she was not on call they might have phoned from the hospital. They had not. Neither was there a message from Simon. But Detective Superintendent Kahn had tried to get hold of her. He had left a message for her to call him back and asked if she had seen the news. She looked at her watch, about to ring him, when she happened to look at Mike and thought better of it. She snapped the phone shut and put it back in her pocket.

Whether it was the drive, the heat, the air or the wine she could not tell, but everything seemed to hit her at once and went whirling around as they got out of the car.

They kissed the whole way up to the house.

'This isn't my style,' said Mike as they reached the door.

'Nor mine either,' said Annika, giggling. 'I'm not the one who has found someone else.'

She got out her keys with some fumbling, opened the door and switched on lights. Mike stayed in the doorway. She went over and kissed him, and he returned her kiss, and Annika pulled him in through the door backwards, but then he stopped kissing her; and that was annoying, she thought – he kissed so beautifully. She pulled his jacket down his arms, kissing his neck.

'This is wrong, Annika.'

'Hmm. That's what makes it absolutely right,' she said, slipping her leg between his.

'But what shall I say to Kim?'

Annika kicked the door shut behind him.

'To Kim Duncan? Lie. Say it was nothing special.'

Nothing, thought Annika, nothing can stop us now. And with her dress hauled up over her hips and her pants hanging just under her left knee, and with a hard bulge between her legs, she crawled up over Mike, at the same time pulling at his belt, and with her free hand took hold of the remote control, activated it and at once turned down the sound. She put it down and turned back to Mike, and now with both hands she unbuckled and slowly unzipped his trousers. As in a surrealistic dream the television images silently began to float out into the room. Channel 9 had had a news helicopter above the water just off Manly Wharf. She immediately recognised the *Langevin* in the pictures, taken that afternoon. She saw the police cars on the road and the body floating on the water. And there was a close-up of the dead man as life-savers and divers lifted out the body. She stayed where she was, sitting astride Mike, but every function in her body stopped short. She reached for the remote control and turned up the sound. But even before she heard the voice she knew that Simon Rees was dead.

In 1907 Dr Duncan MacDougall gave an answer to the question of the soul's weight. Dogs have no soul, and a human soul weighs between eight and thirty-two grams.

Annika looked at the steel scales fixed to a stand behind the perforated steel table, and simultaneously battled with a mental distaste against the physical wellbeing that had filled her in the refrigerated room when they fetched Simon.

MacDougall's calculation and conclusion, published in the journal of the American Society for Psychic Research, was based on the statable drop in human body weight occurring at the moment of death. Even though MacDougall's discovery does not, in the scientific sense, rank above the naïve patchwork division of the brain by phrenology, it is worth noting, thought Annika, as if to shield herself in an oddly mechanical manner, that the assertion has never been disproved. No one has proved that the soul does *not* weigh somewhere between eight and thirty-two grams. But that was small comfort.

Simon lay on the stainless steel trolley. Pale and unmoving. Annika had seen too many dead people to allow herself to be overcome by the situation itself, but the sight of Simon dead, lying there right in front of her, was overwhelming and unreal. It takes time for some things to filter through and settle so that they can be comprehended. Like great discoveries. Great emotions. Like Einstein's lambda. Like quantum mechanics. Like chaos theory. Like death. Like body fluids that depart a corpse through a perforated autopsy table, or fluids from the organs shortly to be placed on the small steel dissection table with its pierced surface, placed on top of the table with as little apparent use as a bed tray.

'Doesn't it seem strange to shoot yourself on a boat?' asked Annika.

It was the meaninglessness she was challenging rather than the abnormality of the death. The symbolism, the philosophical more than the physical facts, and Annika took this as an indication that grief was about to unleash itself within her, but that when it seized hold of her it would be so overwhelming that she would be obliged to approach it indirectly.

Simon loved his boat. It was actually the most fitting place for him to end his days, if it had to happen. She still remembered the date: 26 January 1988. The two-hundredth anniversary of the British invasion of the country. The three of them together on *Langevin* in the harbour among thousands of masts. Herself, Simon and June. June in a state of constant nausea, which could have been due as much to Annika's presence as to the fact that June was not a good sailor and therefore only ventured on board on really spectacular occasions, or when she felt her proprietary marital rights threatened. Annika and Simon were as festive, well oiled and fatuous as the rest of Sydney. Fireworks and the endless rows of white masts. Sydney bathed in foaming light. Like a painting, a watercolour, by Turner.

'Death is always a mystery,' said Conrad Hawke kindly. He pushed his narrow steel-rimmed spectacles into place, while a photographer took pictures of Simon on the table from every possible angle. A young pathologist followed all Conrad Hawke's movements intently. Silently, and with the respectful demeanour only death and a leading authority can evoke, he handed Conrad Hawke a Dictaphone. And Conrad Hawke smiled over the top of his glasses.

'Right, then, we're ready now.'

Simon lay on the table, stiff, white and pale with a hole in his chest.

Mike had been magnificent. He had offered to stay with her for the night, yet when she had recovered from her initial apathy she had asked him to leave. She had felt a deep need to be alone. The rest of the night was hazy. She had drunk the half-bottle of pastis she had in store, which finally rendered her unconscious but now was taking its revenge physically and mentally. She was sweating, her head throbbed, and she had to concentrate the whole time on not throwing up. She scarcely remembered some phone calls. To her father. And to the hospital, where she reported sick.

As Conrad Hawke was obviously wanting to begin his task, Annika tried to pull herself together as well as her seriously handicapped brain would allow, because she knew this would be the last time she would see Simon and because she was sure that Simon would never, never consider taking his own life.

Annika went over to the table and Conrad Hawke obligingly made room for her. She leaned down over Simon's face and studied the bullet hole in his chest. The skin around it and pieces of skin had been drawn inwards and downwards into the hole. She carefully lifted his head and shoulder and ran her hand down his back, searching for an exit on that side.

Conrad Hawke's comments sounded like an echo of her own thoughts.

'Calibre .22. I should think. Not strong enough to penetrate either the cranium or the body twice. Not even at close range. The bullet is inside. In the mess it has made.'

'Which makes it popular for liquidations, doesn't it?'

'For many purposes, Miss Niebuhr.'

'Have they found the weapon?'

'There are divers in the harbour. They should find it soon. Did Simon have a .22?'

Annika nodded.

'Well, then . . .'

Conrad Hawke looked enquiringly at the young pathologist. Then he bent down over Simon's body and made a Y-shaped cut.

As Annika walked towards the door she could feel Simon's head and his body in her hands. He was cold. The second main proposition of thermodynamics is simple. And correct. Heat never flows from a cold body to a warm one. Simon's final lodging was an unheated hostel. A warehouse for the dead. An object stored in a shelving system of stiffened souls. She recalled the dissections of her student days at the Glebe mortuary in north-west Sydney. The encounter with the unavoidable termination of the life process which you had quickly to harden yourself against when faced with it. In the long corridors and the unceasing fug of formalin.

Here, in the mortuary in A Department, the light was off and the temperature was kept down to two or three degrees. The processes of putrefaction are halted by such a low temperature. Snakes cannot survive at such low temperatures.

'Prepare for a surprise, Dr Hawke.'

Conrad Hawke turned his face to Annika. He smiled kindly at her over his spectacles.

'If life has taught me anything, it is that the one thing you cannot prepare yourself for is a surprise.'

Annika pushed the door shut behind her. She stood still for a few moments, gasping for breath with closed eyes. She had been paying off a debt to Simon Rees, and she felt she was far from finished with her instalments. Now it was too late. She hated herself for it, but she had a clear feeling that if she didn't take a couple of aspirin in a very few minutes and wasn't immersed in a bath full of big ice cubes, she would die herself. Then she opened her eyes to hear a voice she knew just beside her.

'You have some influential friends, Miss Niebuhr.'

Detective Superintendent Kahn stepped coughing out of a cloud of grey smoke.

Annika closed her eyes.

'I suppose we all have our contacts?'

'With the dead?'

Annika turned to Kahn.

He nodded, looking down at his shoes, which rocked up and down, almost as if they expected some formal approval from above.

'I knew Simon.'

'I realise that,' said Kahn. 'Strictly speaking, you should be at work today, shouldn't you?'

'I needed to see him.'

'You do not rely on the police carrying out a thorough job themselves?'

She looked at him.

'As far as I can see from my daily *Herald*, the Sydney police are not exactly spotless. If only half of what has been claimed by the press is correct, it's probably only organised crime that is more organised.'

'There are black sheep in all flocks, Miss Niebuhr. Even in your ranks.'

'I needed to see him. For private reasons.'

'Why didn't you ring and ask his wife for permission?'

'On several occasions my father has turned out to be more effective.'

'I could have stopped you.'

'Why didn't you, then?'

Kahn muttered something impossible to hear. He concentrated on the Camel cigarette in his hand, which was smoked right down to the printed brand name above the filter. He looked around desperately for an ashtray, but there was none to be seen. Finally he dropped the stub and trod it out with one shoe. Then he rubbed either an irritating remnant of smoke or years' weariness from one eye and looked at her.

'After the incident of the girl at the hospital you must admit your turning up at Simon Rees's post-mortem seems strange?'

Annika nodded.

'I told you, we were friends.'

'Friends?'

'Friends.'

'It has come to my notice that you sometimes travelled with Simon Rees?'

Annika nodded.

'Once or twice.'

'But he was married?'

'Simon worried about his health. I examined him a couple of times. I went with him on a couple of his . . . journeys. But at most it had a therapeutic effect. At times he got neurotic about his heart. Oversystolic, double beat, you know. But there was nothing wrong with his heart. Apart from the weaknesses we all suffer from now and then.'

He smiled, satisfied.

'Aha, the heart. That heart. Did Simon Rees's wife know that you accompanied him on his trips sometimes?'

'I think you should ask her about that.'

Kahn looked at her sullenly. Then he dug some papers out of an inner pocket. He checked through the contents and then passed a photograph to her.

'Here. Take this. Look at it.'

Annika reluctantly took the picture and looked at it. She recognised the girl. From the hospital. From the car. She studied Kahn, who looked at her with satisfaction, and gave it back to him.

'Is it her?' he asked.

'Where did you get it from?'

'I take it you knew Simon Rees worked for the intelligence service?'

Annika nodded.

'You're always a tad suspicious when that sort of person either drowns or shoots themselves, aren't you?'

'Gaia Jessup. Apparently she was among his clientèle. They say she did not turn up as arranged. Either yesterday or the day before.'

'What project was she working on?'

'That,' said Kahn, '"they" don't want to go into.'

'Have you found her?'

Kahn shook his head.

'Miss Niebuhr, was there anything between you and Simon Rees?'

'Am I under suspicion, Kahn?'

'By his wife?'

'You know what I mean.'

Kahn felt in his pocket for his cigarettes. He lit yet another.

'The body of Simon Rees was found shortly after I visited you at the hospital yesterday. At present everything points to suicide. We have no precise time, but we know he can't have been in the water very long, and in any case you have an alibi for the whole day. No, you are not under suspicion for anything at all.'

'Who informed the police?'

'A young couple. Saw him from the promenade floating on the surface.'

'Why are you so sure it's a case of suicide?'

'Well, who would want to murder Simon Rees?'

Annika fought rising nausea. Her head was throbbing violently and she was about to suffocate with the heat.

'It was only a question of a couple of trips. We arranged it so we could be seen. As friends. I looked after my work. Simon saw to *his* things. You can have the dates and years. Simon loved his work.'

'One thing doesn't exclude the other?'

'Simon also loved his family.'

He smiled and gazed at her intently.

'There's nothing like an answer that sheds light on a question that has not yet been asked.'

'Any girl would be attracted to Simon. What are you after, Kahn?'

'The girl. Unhappy love. Perhaps she is carrying his child. Perhaps in a moment of . . . libidinous excitement he made promises he was unable to keep.'

'Simon did not give way to . . . what did you call it? A moment's excitement.'

'How do you know?'

Annika made no reply. And Kahn went on with his theory.

'Simon Rees sees no other way out. He knows her. He knows her fear of snakes. "The tickets are in the glove compartment, darling." It goes wrong. Simon can see no other way out than to take his life.'

Annika began to walk down the corridor.

'Was your relationship with Simon Rees only friendly?'

'I read some reports for him now and again. Made a comment. Gave an opinion.'

'What did the work consist of?'

Annika turned to answer him, still making her way backwards towards the exit.

'Even now after Simon's death I consider that to be classified information. But "they" will no doubt put you in the picture if you ask them.'

Kahn came towards her.

'After the lecture you gave me yesterday on snakes I have read a little about them. I understand there is one snake that differs from others: the death adder. From the available literature on the subject I understand that it strikes with a speed of one two-hundred-and-fiftieth of a second, and that not only in theory but also in practice means that one can be struck two or three, maybe four times without noticing it at all. I also understand that it is the only Australian snake that does not flee when approached. That you can stand right beside it without anything happening. But the moment you tread on it . . .'

'I'm not quite sure what you're getting at.'

Annika opened the door and quickly went outside. Kahn gaped at her open-mouthed.

'Where are *you* going?'

Detective Superintendent Kahn gallantly passed her a handkerchief. Annika half blindly accepted it, while hauling the upper part of her body up out of the rubbish bin beside the benches and the bristling yellow and white displays of flowers in front of the building.

'Why don't you tell me about your relationship with Simon Rees?' asked Kahn.

'It was,' said Annika, fishing in her pocket for a lozenge, 'just after my divorce. I wasn't myself. I don't really know what it was

Michael Larsen

about. I am not good with emotions. It was something to do with drugs. I was leading quite a wild life. Simon helped me. Set me on an even keel again. I'd rather not talk about it, if you don't mind.'

'But the relationship was absolutely platonic?'

Annika nodded. She sat there with Kahn's handkerchief folded up in her hand.

'And nothing you know of can explain this dramatic action?'

'Kahn, Simon was the last person on earth who would consider taking his own life.'

'Nevertheless . . .'

'He would have shot himself in the head, Kahn. There is no lesion in the head?'

'We often see it the other way round, believe me . . .'

Annika gave Kahn such an unfathomable glance that he started to twitch. She passed him his handkerchief, somewhat hesitantly. He took a quick look at it, clicked his tongue and shook his head deprecatingly. Annika dropped it into the rubbish bin.

'What were you going to say to me in there?' she asked, sitting up.

'That regardless of your good connections, Miss Niebuhr, they do not set you above the law. If you know of anything I ought to know, I should be grateful if you would tell me.'

Annika looked at him thoughtfully.

'*Situs inversus*. Conrad Hawke will give you the information when he has obtained it. I should guess, but of course it is only my humble opinion, that it will exclude suicide.'

Kahn rose and stood for a moment without speaking. Then he smiled uncertainly.

'Now is the moment you are going to tell me that in reality Simon Rees was left-handed.'

Annika looked at him for a moment, then turned on her heel and started to walk off. When she reached the corner of the building she turned towards him and called out:

'Close, Kahn. Close.'

*   *   *

Annika's heart bled to see June in this state. There had always been a mutual bond linking them. Simon. He had also stood in their way.

When June appeared, Annika had a foolish feeling of being unwanted, and almost regretted coming to see her. June stood in the doorway, her face blank, saying nothing, and for a second Annika was afraid she would be turned away. Then she realised that June's central nervous system had been so heavily sedated that everything she saw around her had to be dipped in a mental developing fluid and kept there for a while before anything revealed itself clearly. Annika went up to her with the flowers she had bought hanging by her side.

'He isn't here,' said June, her gaze stiff, speaking slowly in a voice that sounded as if it felt surprised at what it enunciated.

Annika put her arm around June.

'I know. I know.'

'I went in there with the children. I think it was the right thing. Now they know where their father is sleeping.'

Annika bit her lip. She visualised the two small ones. Simon's two daughters. Naturally they had, like two seismographs, caught on to what was not said in so many words, which they would not have understood any better if it had been.

And poor June. She imagined June had not slept much, if at all, her eyes were dull and swollen. She had wept until a pill had cut her off from the grief and pain. Like all women with classical features, June's looks were balanced on a fine line between beauty and asthenia. Without foundation, rouge and the emphasis of mascara she seemed quite pale and anonymous. With her war paint on she could knock everyone flat.

Annika drew away and the two women went inside together. Annika looked around her.

'Where are they? The children?'

'They are with my mother,' said June. 'Would you like anything?'

Annika smiled gently and shook her head. She followed June

into the living room, which was overflowing with flowers. Many of them looked as if June had just thrown them down, overwhelmed by sudden meaninglessness or lack of enough vases. She stopped Annika, who had bent down and begun to pick the bouquets up off the floor.

'Just leave them. I don't know what to do with flowers. Not now.'

Annika ignored her, filled her arms with bunches and went into the kitchen to look for vases in the cupboard.

'Are you quite alone? Is it wise to stay here alone?'

'The police have been here. There's been someone here the whole time.'

Annika arranged the last bouquets and turned off the tap. She went back into the living room.

'Would you like me to stay?'

June hesitated for a moment. Then she shook her head.

'Someone is coming later.'

'Oh, June.'

Annika went over and embraced her. Never before had Annika felt an absence as such a strong presence of something lost. It filled her body like a slow slide and erosion that would become an avalanche if she stopped moving for a moment. Occupied herself with something. Said something or other. She feared each moment that June would break down and weep, for then Annika would lose her grip on the situation. But she realised her fear was unfounded. Lifelessly, June allowed herself to be held. She would give in so far. Up to there and not a centimetre more. Quietened by barbiturates. Otherwise the embrace would have been almost unthinkable. Annika had nothing to regret. She had not come for forgiveness. She pulled slightly away from June and looked at her. Behind the fogginess there was a point that did not yield. Something she could not reach. A small, tight and hard knot that could not be split into pieces. Even if they had bound her fast and bled her with the all-embracing love that resides in the extension of a drop of morphine.

June looked at Annika vacantly.

'They say he had someone else. That it was because of her that he . . . that he . . .'

At that moment the telephone rang, and for a brief moment June recovered herself and went to answer it. From the conversation Annika could hear it would take some time.

She went over and opened the door on to the garden. A fine veil of fluffy cloud had spread over the sky above the town and laid a protective filter beneath the sun. Annika walked towards the open door that led down on the other side of the pool to Simon's study.

Inside the room the first thing she ascertained was that the plug for the computer had been pulled out. Behind it she noticed that one of the screws was loose, and guessed that they had quite simply removed the hard disk.

Simon's desk was usually tidy. But its orderliness bore witness to the fact that work was going on. Usually papers were lying on it. Letters. Now there was almost nothing. There was a Rolodex card index, a numbering machine, a stamp, a ballpoint pen and an empty notepad, an empty tray and letter scales. That was all.

Annika shot a sidelong glance at the door. She didn't feel too good about the situation but decided she might as well get it over with, and sat down at his desk. One by one she pulled out the drawers just to find out that what was left in them showed above all that something else had been removed. She looked at his Rolodex and started to leaf through the cards. She recognised several of the names of friends of Simon and June, and came to the conclusion that if there had been cards with important numbers or cryptic notes, they were not there now.

Instead she ran her eyes over the metal bookcase and pushed herself towards it on the office chair. In front of it there was a filing system on wheels. She separated off the hanging files, glanced down them, pulled up one or two documents, but there was nothing but private papers. She got up and started to pull out the few subject files and ring binders left in the cabinet. Nothing.

85

Michael Larsen

Her gaze fell on the books at the end of the bookcase. She ran a finger over them, reading the titles sideways. There was a four-volume encyclopedia, a couple of legal textbooks, dictionaries. J.B. Rhine's book *The Faculties of the Soul*. She pulled it out, shook it and put it back in place. *Deuteroskopie* by Horst. An old book with its spine worn and crooked. She cautiously opened the pages, but there was nothing. Gurney, Myers and Podmore's *Phantasms of the Living* and *Proceedings of the Society for Psychical Research*, Volume 10, London, 1894. There were several volumes in this series. Nos 1, 2, 6, 8, 11 and 12. Annika ran her finger on farther. There were books by Grof, Jung, Moody's two books on *Life after Life*, *The Tibetan Book of the Dead* in two volumes, and even a French edition of Herrlin's *The Unconscious World of the Life of the Mind*. When she came to Richet's *Experimentelle Studien auf dem Gebiete der Gedankenübertragung* she noticed that something had been pushed down among the pages. She picked up the book quickly and opened it.

Inside were two black-and-white photographs printed by the Anglo-Australian Observatory, together with transcripts of notes and columns of pairs of numbers, and she managed to see a row of calculations before she heard June walking towards her out by the pool. Hastily she gathered up the papers, folded them, pushed them down inside her trousers and sat down on the office chair.

'Have you found anything? Anything compromising?'

Annika looked up. June stood in the doorway.

'I was looking for something to write on. I wanted to give you some numbers.'

June's gaze wandered from the pen to the notepad open on a blank page, and then enquiringly to Annika.

Annika reached for the pad and pen.

'He was behaving so strangely. For the last two weeks he was quite beside himself.'

Annika looked down at the pad as she replied:

'How do you mean, strangely?'

'Strangely in the way a woman notices, Annika.'

'I haven't seen him for the last two weeks.'

'Well, you weren't married to him.'

Annika looked at June, lowered her head again. She put down the pen, folded the paper a couple of times, rose and gave it to June, who took it hesitantly.

'I have a few things to see to,' she said.

'One thing before I go,' said Annika. 'Simon's chief. Do you have a name?'

'Is this the right moment, do you think, Annika?'

'I think it is the worst one. I would never ask, unless it was . . .'

'Nothing, nothing is as important, Annika.'

June stared at her and looked as if she was struggling with all her might to keep back her rage.

Annika nodded and walked towards the door silently. She went through the house with June behind her, and in the hall edged past the mirror and a large glass vase of flowers to reach the front door. June, behind her, stopped and picked something up from the wall shelf underneath the mirror. As if moved by a sudden impulse.

She stopped Annika in the doorway.

'Here,' she said, handing her an invitation to a private view. 'We shan't need this. Now. He will be there. Osborne.'

Annika looked at June. She wanted to say something, but didn't know what. Perhaps it was to justify a desire to let something out, but Annika imagined she saw a question take form in June's eyes. Something that perhaps could be let out. It was June who had lost her husband, yet it was she who looked as if she had a question that would be unseemly on a day such as this, and which self-respect prevented her from asking. Annika wanted to help. If it was really so simple.

'June, you know I thought a lot of Simon. But we were never . . . we have never . . . they are not thinking of me when they say he had someone else. And what they say doesn't fit.'

She saw that June was battling to formulate something that would not pass her lips. How she could hardly bring herself to say it. But then it came.

'Wasn't there ever anything between you?'

'Yes, there was,' said Annika, grasping the door handle. She leaned towards June and gave her a quick hug. 'You.'

Annika thought she could see a smile behind June's otherwise sorrowful and tortured face. Without knowing if she had the right, she sent back a crooked little smile of her own.

On the way down the steps, Annika turned round.

'How shall I know who he is?'

'John Osborne. He's hard to miss.'

Annika sat on the bench beside the south-eastern tower of Harbour Bridge, smoking a cigarette. Her gaze ran along the bars, the wires and the pipes up under the bridge's heavy steel construction. The massive lattice-work rose up from The Rocks and on the other side of the water ended its arc at Milson's Point.

She took a last pull at the cigarette, dropped it and stubbed it out with her shoe. Then she stood up and started to walk alongside the harbour towards Campbell's Cove, past the Geological and Mining Museum, in towards the terminals at Circular Quay. Up on the bridge the traffic flowed slowly like an uneven belt, but even through the honking of the horns she could hear low snatches of jazz carried over the water from Sydney Opera House and the Forecourt Restaurant, coming in waves among boats and ferries leaving the terminals with people on their way home from work.

Annika passed the newly restored warehouses and harbour restaurants of The Rocks. On the space in front of the buses little clumps of gentlemen in evening dress and women in ball-gowns were on their way out along the little peninsula of the Opera House, its small plateau here and there illuminated by the last rays of light shining through the gaps in the skyscrapers behind her. In shadow beside the terminals at Circular Quay other tourists hurried towards the long queues at the ticket booths, in shorts and short skirts. Here and there gays and lesbians in costume were giving out fliers for their forthcoming Mardi Gras parade.

Annika made her way by side streets to the little Italian restaurant

La Grotta, where she sat down outside and ordered a mineral water and a cup of coffee.

She hesitated a little before taking out the papers. In principle there is no difference between picking up an old book in a dusty second-hand bookshop and finding a banknote between the pages, and carrying a large sum in cash to the bank. Or having just removed some papers from the home of a deceased acquaintance. The feeling is completely irrational, and it envelops even the waiter who takes your order, blameless passers-by and the windows of nearby houses. You think they know about it. You think the whole world is watching you.

Not until Annika's order was in front of her and she had lit a cigarette did she relax, get out the papers and put them on the table in front of her.

She saw that the two black-and-white photographs really did come from the Anglo-Australian Observatory. The pictures were of the kind she had often seen in her father's study: a small section of the firmament that could be anything at all taken in any direction; it could be from our own galaxy or an observation of a far-distant galaxy, it was impossible to determine. Annika placed the two pictures side by side on the table. They seemed to her to be completely alike.

Three pages of calculations were stapled together. Annika thought the first page held correlated numbers, co-ordinates of some kind. Some resembled geographical co-ordinates, but it all looked strangely incomplete. A few pairs of numbers had been ticked off, as if they had received some sort of endorsement, others were furnished with a minus. Next came a row of columns which continued on page two and looked like the commencement of a specification of something or other, but the whole thing was bereft of accompanying explanations. In the middle of the mass of columns the specification changed into a row of digits that were quite obviously calculations, accounts, and Annika quickly ran her eyes down to the bottom of the third sheet in the hope of finding a kind of total that could elucidate what the whole thing was about. But there was no concluding explanation.

Annika knew people who could not stand the sight of too many numbers. It was not quite so bad for her. But digits – and like these in total confusion, large quantities and apparently most reluctant to communicate their potential message – had never been to her taste. Not at school, not when she was a student and certainly not when, seized by the urge to comprehend quantum mechanics on more than a purely superficial level, she spent several years of her life penetrating Heisenberg's matrix algebra, a moderately successful venture. She knew there were physicists who seriously thought matrices and logarithms were simple, that mathematics itself was plain sailing, but she had more sympathy with those who had succumbed in the battle with abstractions.

Annika looked down at the table and made a brisk decision. She could sit staring at the papers for hours without ever getting to the bottom of them and discovering what significance they were hiding. She didn't need to do that.

Annika was never one to go running for help. She worked out her own budget, she filled in her own tax return, and her meticulousness about her petrol consumption and systematic checking of the fuel indicator in her car had once led her to demand that a service charge be cancelled. At first she had noticed that the car had not been doing what it should to the litre, then she had examined the wheels and discovered that one front wheel was burning hot when she had been out driving. Finally she had confronted her garage with the problem, and although at first the mechanics had protested their innocence, it turned out that one brake drum had in fact been fitted too tightly.

Annika rolled up the pictures and papers and put them in her pocket. She left money on the table, rose and left. She had decided to do what other mature women do when they are really in need of help: ask Father.

Three flambeaux were burning outside the Kim Keyser Gallery. One was attached to the brickwork above the door, the other two were on either side of the steps.

Annika walked up the steps and handed in her invitation. On the small landing from which another flight of steps led up to the actual gallery, two ceremonially painted Aboriginals were playing. A didgeridoo droned out its ominous centrifugal sounds, while the other man beat time with a stick.

Annika walked past them smiling. At the end of the staircase the Kim Keyser Gallery opened out into two high-ceilinged rooms, with exposed black-painted beams and whitewashed walls.

On the second landing catalogues were being distributed by, Annika guessed, representatives of the Cultural Aboriginal Society. She took one and glanced at the items on show. The exhibition was called *Adjusting Dreamtime*, and included watercolours, works in oil and acrylic, and small sculptures.

As Annika began an inspection of the hung paintings and free-standing pieces, she tried discreetly, in the crowded hall, to catch sight of a man whose bulk would single him out. She saw him at the end of one room on his way towards an open door that led up to an isolated terrace. She glimpsed a waiter and an outdoor bar encircled by flickering torchlight, and headed for the door herself.

'Do you like it?'

A tall, dark-haired man was in front of her. He gave her a friendly smile, and standing there straight and tall in his dinner jacket he seemed, Annika thought, to have stepped out of *Gatsby*. The man, whom Annika didn't know, flung out his arms to emphasise his question.

'Who are you?'

'Frank Kiesworik. From the American consulate in Brisbane.'

He gave Annika his hand; she took it hesitantly.

'Annika . . .'

'Niebuhr. I know. I know your father.'

'Everyone knows my father. How do you know who I am?'

'A consulate must keep informed.' He smiled a disclaimer. 'June called me.'

Annika looked around at the walls. Did she like it? It seemed as if the only manner with which Western culture had failed to behave when confronting other cultures was dignity. As if it had only been able to express extreme patterns of reaction. People had either annihilated or given way to exaggerated veneration when they had encountered the unknown and unfamiliar. Right up into this century Aboriginals had been shot, as had been the Indians of North and South America. And in Australia now, as in America, it seemed there were no limits to how admirable people considered the native inhabitants were, even though, as Kookillo Dhamarandji himself admitted, it had been the original culture that had wiped out many of the continent's great mammals.

There were so many of these exhibitions in Australia. Some were good, others were rubbish, but there seemed to be no discernment these days.

She thought of how she had drunk the soft fresh water straight from the rivers flowing into the sea from Fraser Island. Water that nature's unsurpassed powers had filtered through layer after layer of sand for two hundred years and so was some of the cleanest water in the world. How she and Mike had seen humpbacked whales playing in the waves of Platypus Bay on the way to the Great Barrier Reef, of how she had swum with dolphins, of how art, not always but often, takes and will always take second place to that which it seeks to imitate. And she thought how arbitrarily we evaluate everything, and how dependent these arbitrary judgments are on completely personal preferences. And of deep-rooted, inward and grotesque systems of penitential acts that are supposed to redeem the past.

'Taste is so individual,' said Annika. 'I once attended a conference in New York, when a woman in all earnestness praised the city water supply. There was so much chlorine in it that I would not even have used it in my swimming pool.'

He smiled.

'Did you know Simon?'

'Did you?'

'Simon was in the Gulf. I was in the Gulf. At that time our work touched on the same things. We met there. We got to be mates.'

'Simon never mentioned you.'

He smiled.

'Simon never mentioned *you*.'

They strolled on towards the door.

'Simon didn't like Americans.'

Frank Kiesworik's face creased into a big grin.

'Who does?'

They went on a few steps without speaking. Kiesworik walked with his eyes on the floor. Then he said:

'I wonder what made him do it.'

Annika looked at him.

'Do you want to know what I think, Mr Kiesworik?'

'Frank.'

'Frank. According to a strictly logical deduction the Americans caused Simon to take his life.'

'I beg your pardon?'

'Do you remember when American scientists scared the life out of everyone with their investigations into cholesterol a few years ago? Simon was worried about his heart. Unnecessarily, as it happens. He watched over his cholesterol like a hawk. But it was not too high. It was, rather, too low. A low cholesterol content in the blood is reputed to cause a lack of serotonin. Serotonin is a signalling material between the nerve cells, and if it is lacking the brain will be under-stimulated, and this can lead to depression and possibly to suicide.'

Frank Kiesworik smiled uncertainly.

'That was an analysis with a number of uncertain factors, I think. Moreover I gather you do not think it was suicide?'

Annika stopped short, but tried to keep hold of her self-possession.

'Why on earth do you gather that?'

They had reached the door on to the terrace. Frank Kiesworik looked at his watch and excused himself with an uncomfortable air. He feigned a smile. A broad one. To smooth things over. Annika saw he realised he had said too much, which reinforced her feeling that when men are really pushed into a corner they almost always respond with affront camouflaged as polite withdrawal.

'Who dares guess why a woman thinks the way she does? I know you are meeting Mr Osborne. I won't hold you up.'

'You're very clearly in the picture.'

'The job.'

He shrugged his shoulders. He placed his hand on her shoulder blade and slid it up her back in a singularly affectionate gliding movement. Then he took himself off to a group of other Americans.

On one other occasion in her life Annika had had a rush of panic like the one that now nailed her to the floor. She was in a flat in King Street, surrounded by people she did not know and had never seen since. It was just after her separation from Jay. They were like whales that for some mysterious reason make for a coast and together perish. Afterwards she could not tell why she had ended up there; she was sitting among people who were lying down and whom she did not really know, and not until she sneezed by mistake over a snow-covered mirror and sent a little cloud of powder into the air did she feel something was very wrong. She recalled getting up and walking across a floor, and how she had wondered why people stayed there prone. And then it seemed she fell and could not get up again. As if someone had grabbed hold of her. Pulled her back. She had no specific reason for being there.

She remembered a sudden paranoid feeling that she was wasting her life away, and she realised that she had a life, and that she was about to lose that life. She fled as from a black hole from which no flight is possible; there were the vacant staring faces and this hollow desperate feeling that she must get out. Then the flat was stormed. They surged in through the doors. That was how she met Simon Rees. He gathered her up. Shook her. In combat gear and carrying an automatic.

'Do you want to die? Are you tired of life? Or are you tired of the life you are leading?'

And that, she thought, sounded so moralising and evangelical that she spat in his face.

'I know your father.'

'Give him my love, then.'

She had put the room, those people, this penury, behind her. Supported by Simon Rees and Harper Stone, she had worked her way away from it all. But one thing never left her, and that was the memory of that massive attack of fear. It stayed with her for a long time, but gradually she learned to force herself to look at it as a parenthetic overreaction. She knew that it was not. She knew in her heart she had been dangerously close to a degraded and loathsome side of humanity. It was this loathsomeness that coursed through her there in the art gallery, and she felt an overpowering urge to turn round.

Only Kahn knew of her suspicion. She had confided nothing of it to June, and Annika was convinced that Conrad Hawke would not think of looking into and reformulating her vague intimations as a concrete suspicion of possible crime.

She had come to meet John Osborne. In the hope that by talking to him with watchful artlessness she would be able to inveigle enough out of him to enable her to isolate the meaning of the mysterious PET scans she had been sent. Their possible connection with Simon's death. In an attempt to discover more about Simon's link with Gaia Jessup. In the hope of getting at the real identity of a man called 'Kessler'.

Now she was not sure she should have come. And now she was no longer sure about what she wanted and would dare say.

John Osborne stood over by the railing of the terrace. Dark, powerful, large. For a moment it seemed to Annika that he was the equal in intellectual power of her own father.

He smiled contentedly. Demonstrating that body's strength by gently rolling a brandy around in a large balloon. Even that goblet of a glass seemed frail and small in his great hand. While with an appraising air he sent the amber liquid up the sides of the glass, where it left a transparent film, he laid one hand on the metal. Then with the other he lifted the glass to his nose and sniffed, discontentedly, the aromatic scent, after which he turned his face to Annika.

He shook his head in resignation.

'We seem to get everything wrong in this country. In France they recommend narrow tulip glasses for brandy. It was never the right idea to drink from these goblets. We reverently serve brandy with coffee, even though everyone knows that that mixture is quite as revolting as the combination of coffee and juice. Now and then, you know, I understand the arrogance of the French. Where that is concerned we're pretty comical.'

His tone of voice calmed Annika, and she forced herself to laugh. But inside her head the questions churned around. She thought if she could just get through this conversation she might get some peace to think everything through clearly again.

'In Sweden they say coffee without brandy must be a revolting blend.' Osborne smiled in amusement. 'What do you suggest we do about it?'

He went up to the waiter behind the bar and ordered another brandy in a smaller glass. It was almost hidden in his hand as he brought it over to Annika.

'Here. Try it. Courvoisier. Cordon Argent. Hand-warmed. Smell.'

Annika took the glass and breathed in a whiff of fruity scent sneaking up from the little glass.

Then Osborne passed her the big glass, and Annika took in the strong, sharp cloud of spirit that rose up towards her.

'It's the same Cognac,' said Osborne.

Annika recalled France. The high point of the obligatory tour of Europe. She remembered the scent that hung over Limousin, which gave body to the oak casks in which the brandy was matured. She remembered Paris and Provence, which reminded her of the Hunter Valley, she recalled the rosé wines, the goat cheeses and black olives from Nyon. She remembered the ancient sunshine blazing down over endless fields of lavender, the medieval village idyll that clings to stones and tiles, cobwebs in wind-furrowed gables, spun so decoratively that it seemed as if the very spiders had been instructed to carry out their craft with pride. She remembered bakers sweating to produce the best bread, vintners who appeared to feel a spiritual rather than a commercial pain at putting up with a harvest of second-class grapes, the old-fashioned small farmers who cared so much for their beloved animals that you might think they had chosen the wrong business. She remembered a country where chaos ruled without leaving behind anything but the most excellent order. She remembered respect and pride. And love. And she found it hard to imagine how that same country could harbour a felonious Marseilles and lay everything waste with atomic clouds beneath distant atolls.

Annika looked at Osborne in amazement. Maybe she read something of all this in him, and maybe not, for although it was obvious that his heavy figure hid a gourmand, it wasn't possible to see whether the shabby dinner jacket hid a hedonist.

'Just a few days. And we should have been French. Strange to think of, isn't it? Just a few days. But you weren't born here, were you, Miss Niebuhr?'

Osborne put down his glass. With slight difficulty and heavy breathing he withdrew a cigar from his inside pocket.

'How do you know that?'

'I know your father. From television. And the papers. Denmark. Small country, that Denmark.'

'Have you been there?'

Osborne struck a match, and with long silent pulls he brought a glow down through the cigar leaves. A puff of smoke and the odour of sulphur buffeted Annika in the face. Osborne blew a great cloud of smoke into the twilight, and then Annika hit on the characteristic trait she had been searching for. People with power resort to brutal changes in a conversation. It is a way of ensuring that they only talk about things that really interest themselves the whole time. Quite simply he did not reply to her question but instead asked one that *en passant* he furnished with further sub-questions which he answered himself.

'Have you heard about the inscriptions up at Jinmium, Miss Niebuhr? I don't understand,' he said, pointing at the gallery behind them, 'the art in there. I can't see what it's meant to represent. But the archaeologists' work up there. Fantastic. There we beat the French by several lengths. What are their cave paintings? The Lascaux cave? Twenty thousand years old? Thirty thousand? And ours? Almost two hundred thousand years old?'

'Of course, no one knows yet what those signs mean,' said Annika.

'What if,' said Osborne, ignoring Annika's objection, 'we had to rewrite the whole history of evolution? What if that Out-of-Africa theory is wrong?'

'Maybe it is the most probable one.'

'You know about the disagreement over the pyramids?'

'Which one?'

'The dating. According to these new theories, which are, you must admit, alluring, the pyramids are eight thousand years older than has been assumed. The Egyptologists shake their heads. But why shouldn't there have been other fantastic cultures before ours? Their knowledge of pi? Sprung from nothing? Their undervalued knowledge of the stars? We have a desperate lack of faith in the capabilities of our forefathers. The Babylonians discovered asphalt – two thousand years before we did. What if everything started here? In Australia? Or the Egyptians had been here? They had boomerangs too. And we have pyramids here too.'

'The scholars don't have any artefacts to confirm those theories.'

Osborne mumbled reluctantly. An assent that was served up as a rumbling protest.

'Until recently it was thought that agriculture began ten thousand years ago. Near the Euphrates and the Tigris in Mesopotamia. The finds at Buka indicate that agriculture started there as early as twenty-eight thousand years ago. Taro root with stone tools. Hard to get around that. There's the Wollemi pine. Unknown a few years ago. Now it's the botanical sensation of the century. A hundred and fifty million years old. Everyone thought it no longer existed. It was right in our back garden. We have a magical country. And now these stone signs up at Jinmium.'

Annika cleared her throat.

'No one can be sure what they indicate.' Her tone was admonitory.

'Human beings before homo sapiens. Thinking people. Creative people. Before Out-of-Africa? Makes the view that the first Australians immigrated here fifty thousand years ago from New Guinea look a bit shaky, eh?'

Annika looked around restlessly. And in spite of the pleasure he took in airing his own philosophy, Osborne seemed to pick up the signal for a change of subject.

'There's too much for us to explain. That was why I always supported Simon in his projects. I don't believe in ghosts, Miss Niebuhr. I'm far too rational. But I can't see any explanation for many of the phenomena Simon and his people have described. Video films of the measuring apparatus with their electromagnetic interference. Both the first and the second time the sceptics talked about faults in the measuring equipment, and of course we believed them. But when the same faults went on occurring?'

'Can you remember the excitement when Parkes Observatory received those mysterious signals from space, and they believed they had made contact with intelligent life? Radio signals with a frequency of 2.3–2.4 gigahertz? Always at the same time of day. It looked promising right up until someone wondered why they always came at mealtimes. My father told me it turned out to be their own microwave oven that was sending the signals.'

Osborne gave a roar of laughter. Its course was like a roll of thunder. First the big crack, then a few half-suffocated coughs considerably assisted by the cigar in his hand, then a few more rumbles until it finally died out.

'The Niebuhr scepticism. The famous Niebuhr scepticism. Now I understand why Simon chose you as a critical adviser in his investigations.'

Annika looked at him.

'How did you hear about that?'

He smiled.

'It's my job to know, Miss Niebuhr. I have to know about that sort of thing.'

'I've been living with the illusion that I was anonymous.'

'Simon did too. And so you were and are in a way. But I'm the one with the responsibility. Obviously I know about it.'

Osborne looked up at the night sky with narrowed eyes. His tongue was busy getting hold of a tobacco leaf which he manoeuvred right out to the tip, from where he picked it up with two fingers and flicked it out into the darkness.

'Is it possible that Simon was having an affair with another woman?'

'Out of the question,' said Annika.

Osborne turned his back to her and looked out over the garden and the sea. The weather was breaking up. Even in the dark it was clear that the stars were vanishing behind thicker and thicker layers of cirro-cumulus drifting in from the southeast.

'I can't understand this business with Simon. Why should he take his own life? Have you ever met Gaia Jessup, Miss Niebuhr? She took part in some of his investigations.'

'I never met any of the people involved. I assisted with scientific explanations. Where I could. But I never participated actively.'

'I seem to remember some tests in which you yourself took part.'

'That was as a passive participant. I never saw the results, and I cannot claim to have experienced anything myself that could corroborate the hypotheses relating to the project.'

'Simon used several independent supervisors.'

'I have never had uninicited visions. In short, I don't have much faith in the phenomenon, so I really doubt whether you can have found my contribution of much use.'

'Simon achieved impressive results in some Ganzfeld experiments. That will be further researched.'

'Both Edinburgh and Stockholm have had dramatic results with their Ganzfeld tests. But it seems no one really understands them.'

Osborne drank up his brandy. He took another gentle pull at his cigar, inhaling deeply.

Annika looked around her. Inside and now outside as well, the dinner-jacketed guests, who all unmistakably resembled embassy staff, took up most of the space.

'There are a lot of Americans here this evening. I didn't realise that Americans took such an interest in aboriginal art?'

'The ambassador from Canberra is here. The local consulate has turned out in force. I think their interest in native art is genuine enough. They have just about annihilated their own now, of course.'

He turned and gazed at Annika intensely.

'Simon was working on a project. "Atlas X." Did he ever mention that to you?'

Annika shook her head. And inwardly trembled. She repeated the words in her head. It was 'Atlas X' that Gaia Jessup had mentioned to her in the car. Annika tried to appear unaffected as she replied.

'No,' she said. 'I've never heard of it.'

Osborne studied her. Then he mumbled something. Apparently satisfied with the reply.

'I don't like the thought of there having been something between Simon and this Gaia Jessup. There was something very wrong about that girl.'

'What do you imagine? That she was blackmailing him?'

'Something like that. Perhaps she knows something she shouldn't know.'

'But what could that be?'

The feeling started that night. From the moment she left the gallery until she was in the taxi she was convinced that every step she took had been watched.

More clouds were drifting over the town from the south-east, drawing a dark sky behind them. The wind was getting up. Annika felt the first drops on her cheek and got into the taxi she had hailed in Goulburn Street. She asked the driver to take her to the hospital, where her car was parked.

At no point in her life could the word 'jungle' applied to the big city have held more significance for her. All the way home she noticed people's rapid movements, the quick exchange of glances. In the rear-view mirror she saw cars following her. There are people who find something pathological in paranoia. In the natural world it is a tool for survival. And it is not directed at the fellow species but at presumed enemies. In human beings it is directed at our own species. That is what defines it as pathological. But the really sick thing is that it is well founded.

Over the sea the sky lit up as flashes of lightning drew their forked branches down to the water. The inner depths of black clouds were visible for brief moments like illuminated faces. Then a rumbling began that slowly moved away from Sydney.

Annika switched on her TV. A supposedly serious American news channel was showing an ad for the station itself. One of the station broadcasters announced that if an event, such as when Jesus rose from the dead, or when Moses divided the waters, should occur again, that channel would have the first reporters on the spot to cover it. In a voice-over, it was emphasised that this reporter was just one of the station's many renowned employees. Annika sighed in despair. This was the channel that Simon had once used as an example when he wanted to show how absurd it is to talk of man's 'free will'. He was amazed that the world could pay so little heed to the fact that yet another religious movement had committed mass suicide in sectarian fanaticism, when everyone who is otherwise willing to search their heart will realise that all existence implies some degree of brainwashing. But millions still followed the world on a television screen, where ostensibly reliable hosts enthusiastically reiterated their own names.

Annika switched off.

She went out on to the terrace and sat down on her wet sun-lounger with a glass in her hand. At first, under the parasol and on the part of the seat where the teak was worn and grey and dry. Then she moved slightly to the side. And then sat right out in the rain. Rain at last.

Not even half the American population believes in Darwin's teaching on the origin of species. You can drag them through a museum of prehistoric saurians and yet seventy-five per cent of them are ignorant of the fact that dinosaurs existed before man. You can pelt them with carbon-14 investigations, ice-nucleus borings, dendrochronological results, lithostratigraphic or biostratigraphic analyses, potassium/argon dating, uranium dating and fluorine adapted tests, and still, with a neurotic's precision, they will go on their knees every night and pray to a white-bearded man reminiscent of a cross between Father Christmas and a benevolent uncle. Such behaviour would lead to sectioning if it didn't occur within a Western mindset. Every four years and during great crises, the American President also reinforces this religious fealty to a man with a white beard.

There are no figures for how many nations throughout history have regarded themselves as specially chosen. Out of them all the Jews with their biblical story have been the most successful. Like all good fiction-makers they stole a little here, a little there, from the Sumerians, the Babylonians and the Egyptians, and stirred it all together, and not even the horrors of the World War in which another nation was seized by the same disastrous belief in their own exclusivity has made them think better of it.

The Aboriginals have not been above doing the same thing. Kookillo Dhamarandji had often regaled listeners with stories of the numerous tribes who considered themselves to be God's chosen people.

It was an American, an embassy man and thus by definition an agent, who was aware of her suspicion that something did not make sense about Simon's death. That something did not add up. That something was completely wrong. The ASIO *is* the CIA. So Simon said. But how did Frank Kieoswork know about her suspicions? It had to be Kahn. Only to Kahn had she voiced them.

The telephone started ringing, but Annika took no notice.

It was Simon who had once explained the whole political background to her. She needed him now.

The Australian Security and Intelligence Organisation had been created at the end of the 1940s, and according to Simon it had been this that led to the relinquishing of the remnants of what had been a dubious independence. With the conservative Sir Robert Gordon Menzies at the helm during the 1950s and 1960s, and with the UK–USA Co-operative Intelligence Agreement, whose precise brief only a very few know even now, but which also included Canada and New Zealand, the Americans to all intents and purposes took over the government of the country. The agreement meant that the British and American intelligence services could freely and without hindrance operate in Australia.

Simon, who hated politics, knew all about politics. Annika, who thought it was important to know what was going on, was politically naïve. If she had been in any doubt about that Simon had put her straight, and though she was miffed she had to admit he was right. She wasn't interested in politics. Not in the sense that she studied its shifts or kept herself au fait with which decisions were politically motivated and not merely good, sensible rulings. Simon knew that everything that happened was political. That was what he hated.

He told her about CIA operations in the name of ASIO. He told her about Vietnam, about how Australia, which had never had any quarrel with the Vietnamese, was drawn into the war by Menzies, and had to supply troops, had to sacrifice thousands of young people's lives – merely to carry out American foreign policy. He told her how ASIS, the Australian secret service that only operates abroad, on several occasions had acted in direct opposition to Australian interests – merely to realise American foreign policy. How ASIS agents had worked for the Americans and the CIA in Chile, and of how Whitlam had been put in his place when he discovered this. He told her about the secret American military installations, North-West Cape, Pine Gap and Nurrungar, and how the Americans, when they carpet-bombed Cambodia, launched their B-52 planes from secret bases in an unknown Australia.

In Simon's world there was no distinction between East and West,

North and South. Intelligence services were intelligence services, politics was politics.

'You can manipulate people into believing they are free, and into believing they are not free. In Australia it has been demonstrated,' he claimed, 'that the only thing democracy has over a totalitarian state is the right freely to elect a dictator.'

Science doesn't willingly acknowledge ghosts, and when it does they must only be its own. Scientists talked of neutrinos long before laboratories and nuclear reactors were able to confirm their existence. This was the kind of whirling ghost Simon had set rotating from his grave. An invisible, unremarkable and by and large colossal particle. The astronomers knew that an invisible dust cloud of neutrinos would hit the earth simultaneously with the explosion of a supernova. The result was ready before the figures had nicely arranged themselves in rows. A collecting tank in Kamioka in Japan surrounded by sensitive photon counters, filled with water and placed where Simon was soon to lie, underground, was ready to receive the fall-out from a dying star. A detector in a salt mine in Ohio was collecting the same information from the dead star. In the world of physics nineteen protons do not commit collective suicide. A far more likely explanation was that the protons had been destroyed by a massive attack from the neutrinos. That a supernova had exploded somewhere in the universe. Simon was Annika's dying star. She could still picture him as he lay in the mortuary. If pushed into a corner, would he have been able to take his own life? No. The declaration of suicide concealed another one. A much more probable explanation. Simon Rees had been trained by the SAS. He was an élite soldier, a major in the combat force. It takes an élite soldier to kill an élite soldier. Not merely a casual criminal.

Unless they found toxicological traces in his blood, it was unlikely that he would have allowed himself to have been taken by surprise like that. He would have fended off a gun pointing at him. He would have defended himself.

Solid Simon. Faithful Simon. Simon, who loved June and his two daughters. Never. Annika could call to mind people who were capable of taking their own lives. The Australian suicide statistics for young people were among the highest in the world, and at Sydney University they actually studied suicide. But Simon. No. What Simon had passed on was a message. Information. Perhaps he had known the people who killed him. Perhaps, perhaps he had asked them not to shoot him in the head. To pass on a message. Or in a final desperate attempt to survive. His own people. Perhaps they had not known that.

The telephone started to ring again. This time Annika rose, went in and picked it up.

It was Kahn.

'You should have told me about it, Miss Niebuhr.'

'I did not want to meddle in the investigation.'

'I just didn't realise one could live so long. With the heart on the wrong side, I mean.'

'It happens in one case out of ten thousand. Only half of these survive, the rest die from heart complications. Those who do survive live just like the rest of us. Some with related problems, others without them. Simon was one of those who feel no side effects. Simon's *situs inversus* was only partial. And on the whole he suffered no resulting illnesses. Kahn . . . no one knew about it.'

'You did?'

'Well, I was close to him. And checked him over now and then.'

'But no one else can have known?'

'Kahn, there are two kinds of human beings. Those who find it amusing that other people should think their hearts have stopped, and then those who try to hide their abnormality. Simon belonged to the latter group. He felt insecure about it. And he hated the thought of anyone knowing. It was mentioned nowhere in his papers. It was a malfunction. Something he wanted to forget.'

'It doesn't change anything.'

'What do you mean?'

'We have found the pistol. A PPK calibre .22. It was a little way away from the boat. It is Simon's. And the ballistic investigation confirms that it is the weapon that killed him. He most probably dropped it when he fell overboard.'

Annika took a deep breath.

'How many people have you told that I don't believe Simon took his own life?'

'None.'

'Then if I were you I would examine your car, garage, telephone, ballpoint pen, cigarette packet, lighter and the wall covering in the corridors of the morgue. Because somebody knows.'

II

A flock of seagulls rose in a fluttering cascade above the low wall that divided the promenade in Manly from the wide sandy beach. A breeze from the sea worried at the frayed pines all the way along the wall, and out in the surf youngsters lay on their stomachs on their surfboards, waiting for the wave that would carry them in, sitting or standing.

Annika sat lost to the world, buried in a pile of newspapers, at a table outside the Manly Ruben with a view of the Steyne Hotel, as Mike crossed the Corso and came towards her. The *Telegraph Mirror*, the *Age* and the *Australian* lay beside the *Sydney Morning Herald*, which she was slowly skimming through. Only that and the *Mirror* had a notice about Simon, which left her none the wiser.

When she caught sight of Mike she put her sunglasses on the table and stood up. They met in a long and close embrace, and as she made to draw away he held her fast for a few moments more. Annika felt herself relax.

'How are you?'

She merely nodded. And then they slipped apart and sat down on either side of the table. Mike hailed the waiter, who came up with the menus.

Mike perfectly understood when she said they would have to postpone the sailing trip for a day or two. He told her he had a few problems with the motor, and began to describe them in detail, but Annika did not listen, and she quickly got the impression that the thoroughness of his description was a way of helping him visualise a solution to the problem.

'But this is all trivia,' he said with an ironic glint in his eye.

One of his hands moved over and laid itself on hers. 'It'll do you good to get away from here.'

As he spoke she realised that though she had felt a great desire to get away she had an equally great one not to leave Sydney before she had cleared up the mystery of what had happened.

Her smile was pale and automatic, and Mike seemed to feel he should tone down his happy mood; he immersed himself in the menu in concentrated silence. Annika studied hers as well, but she did not read it, and when the waiter came she ordered only a mixed salad and a mineral water. Mike chose a salad too and also ordered a glass of Pinot Noir. The waiter took the menus and removed the used ashtray from the table.

'In the morning,' said Annika, 'it was yesterday, the same day as Simon . . . something came from him in the mail. I'd like you to take a look at it, if you would?'

Mike spread his arms in a willing gesture, but Annika shook her head.

'It's at home. PET scans. Copies. They may well not mean anything, but I'll bring them down to the boat. I'd like your opinion.'

'Was that the reason?'

'Reason for what?'

'That he took his life? Was he ill?'

Annika lit a cigarette. That idea had not occurred to her. All things considered, the scans could have been of anyone. It was not possible to tell. At first she had assumed that the microscopic 'MJ' was a kind of identification mark, but that was not necessarily the case. But when she thought about it she rejected the idea. If Simon had been ill he would have confided it to her. She was one of the few people he had told about his *situs inversus*, and those who confide in only a few often confide many things to those few. She could not see why he should have been selective about this.

'I don't believe,' said Annika, 'that Simon committed suicide. I believe he was murdered.'

She inhaled, and then thoughtlessly blew out a cloud of smoke that floated over towards Mike, who leaned back in his chair and tried to wave it away. For a moment she had quite forgotten his asthma.

'Why . . .'

He tried to complete the sentence but couldn't, and instead stretched out in his chair, trying to get his inhaler out of the pocket of his tight jeans. He put it to his mouth and took a suck or two.

'I'm sorry, Mike. I don't know what I . . .'

Annika stubbed her cigarette out in the ashtray.

He brushed off her apology with his hand as he sat quietly until he felt better, and then the waiter appeared with the food and drinks.

When he had served them and gone, Mike was himself again.

'It's not only the smoke,' he said. 'It's just as much the weather. It's been foul lately.'

'Is it a good idea to go diving?'

'It'll be all right. The air is better out there. What did you say about Simon? I thought the police said it was suicide.'

Annika took a piece of bread, broke it and spread butter on it. Then she began to tell him.

She weighed her words carefully as she put him in the picture. She explained that she thought there was a chance of her seeing a preliminary post-mortem report, and that it would mean a lot to her to see Dr Hawke's conclusions. She mentioned the drawing that had accompanied the scans, but in order not to cause him unnecessary worry she omitted to say what it represented. And she didn't touch on Osborne or Kiesworik at all. She did not mention Gaia Jessup and her link with Simon, nor what she had found in Simon's study.

'Those scans,' said Mike, starting on his salad, 'if they are not of Simon, who are they of?'

Annika shook her head, chewing. She took a mouthful of water and poured out some more.

'I don't know. But the drawing was furnished with a quotation. Simon had written it. "That which the eye of the soul has seen cannot be destroyed."'

'What did he mean by that?'

'That's what I'll try to find out. And I have the feeling there's an error in the quote.'

Mike held his wineglass at an angle and stared down at it thoughtfully. Then he put it down without drinking. He laid his hand on hers and looked at her.

'Are you sure you wouldn't rather stay in Sydney until the funeral is over?' he said.

Annika put down her knife and picked up her glass of water. She knew the answer he didn't want to hear, and she didn't want to give it to him.

'I'm not much good at funerals,' she said. 'Simon would understand.'

Mike got out his inhaler again and took a couple of deep sucks.

Annika drank the last of her water and was getting out her money when Mike stopped her.

'I'll pay,' he said.

Annika looked at her watch and stood up.

'Ring me when the boat is ready,' she said.

He smiled, stuffed the inhaler back in his trouser pocket and gave her outstretched hand a squeeze.

'Remember he worked for Intelligence, Annika,' he said.

She smiled and nodded.

'That's going to kill you one day,' she said.

Then she left.

Libraries can make you painfully aware of your lack of knowledge. Annika often wondered if that was the reason for the half-empty rooms that greeted her when, as she often did, she frequented the great library of Sydney University.

In these halls with their ranks of green bankers' lamps over the small cubicles, with their worn old tables and chairs, the endless rows of bookshelves and rolls of microfilm, she had spent many hours of her life.

She sat reading in one of the cubicles with a stack of books beside her. It was quiet in the dimly lit room. Besides herself, only one student and the librarian were present, and now and then someone would go past along the corridor outside. Fresh air came in from the high windows but there was hardly any sun in the room, which was as dark as a chapel.

The original text, or rather a copy of the ancient text, was brought from the Orient to Europe a thousand years ago. For a century or two the book suffered an unknown fate before turning up at the university library in Heidelberg, where today it rests locked inside a box. Some historians doubt the authenticity of Philon's list, in which the descriptions of the world's wonders are in a single piece of poetry among a number of other texts of the same era.

The book she was looking through was Simone Levy's *Seven Wonders – Wonder Why*, in which Antinatros of Sidon, not Philon, is still held to be the man who – in 100 BC – set down the account of the ancient buildings for the first time. This was the book in which Annika could remember having first come across the story of the old wonders of the world. Other, later books which the librarian had helped her find contained reproductions of Philon's text, and notwithstanding what the various sources stated, there could be no doubt about the source of Simon's quotation. But there *was* an error in his version.

'What is seen in the mind's eye can never be destroyed.' She had remembered correctly. 'Never' had become 'not' in his version. Her memory had not been playing tricks, but, she thought, she did not know what she dare assume from that, for she could not rule out the possibility that that was precisely what had happened to Simon.

Annika gazed vacantly in front of her, tapping her cheek with a pen.

The very room she was in was full of that kind of faulty quotation. Some were due to an exaggerated but undoubtedly sincere faith in a memory that had failed. Others to slovenliness or laziness or pure cheating. Scholars who through the ages had miswritten and misrepresented fact in order to make hypotheses work. Bulky tomes by respected authors, published by distinguished publishing houses, had never been guarantee of the pure and honest truth, something

Annika had found to her cost many times over the years. And this arsenal of information, these endless quantities of compressed knowledge that at the beginning could seem intimidating – even to her – turned into a slightly more manageable amount as she gradually read her way into the discrepancies that appeared, as in her accumulating thirst for knowledge she searched far and wide. At first they created confusion, a confusion that was later sharpened into scepticism and finally became a merciless criticism of sources.

She recalled how she had once lost a case of Wynn's Cabernet Sauvignon 1971 from Coonawarra to Mike in a bet. Annika seemed to remember a book on semiotics which, in order to emphasise some points on repetition as a stylistic device, had used the example of Ingrid Bergman's 'Play it again, Sam' from *Casablanca*, and the book did the same thing. But Mike, who loved *Casablanca* and had seen it innumerable times, maintained, correctly, that that precise phrase is never uttered in the film. We make connections, we ourselves create the images and carry the misunderstandings further. Like the experiment made after the Dutch air catastrophe in 1993 when a hundred people were asked, a year after the accident, to describe what they remembered from the television pictures of the plane that crashed into a block of flats in a suburb of Amsterdam. Over sixty per cent could remember the pictures, and many gave extremely accurate and vivid descriptions of the catastrophe, but they were all pictures in their heads, for no television pictures of the moment of the accident existed. Or like the picture of the background radiation taken of the COBE satellite in 1992. It resembles our idea of an expanding universe to such a degree that many, including textbooks on astronomy, believe that the picture shows the universe, while it is merely a picture of a small section of the sky.

Within her own proper field as well, Annika could find serious errors and misunderstandings. Respected British zoologists could still take it into their heads to publish books in which they recommended the tourniquet for funnel-web-bite, even though it had been known for years in Australia that Sutherland's method works as well on funnel-web-bite as on snakebite; and Annika found it particularly comical that examples of theories thought out behind a desk in the northern hemisphere were applied to conditions in the southern one. A few years ago a Swedish psychologist propounded the thesis that many of our phobias are innate, and explained the fear of creeping things as inherited from our forefathers. Experiments with rats had shown that a rat never forgets where it received an electric shock. The experience of pain, ran the argument, causes some glands above the kidneys to produce hormones that affect amygdala in the brain, and from there the impulses travel on to other regions in the brain, which ensure that the unpleasant experience is never forgotten. The psychologist considered that it was the same recollection of pain which nervous forefathers had kept in their genes. In Annika's opinion this smacked rather too much of Lamarck and adapted giraffe necks, and the psychologist in question was obviously unaware of the Brisbane experiments, which to the horror of all Australian parents proved that the widespread human loathing for snakes is acquired and not instinctive, which was made clear when they found several children playing with and stroking some of the most dangerous snakes in this world.

After having spent half the day in the library finding references and reading, Annika closed the books. She had got no further. She rubbed her tired eyes and sat on for a while with the books in front of her, lost in thought.

She knew there was a hidden message in that text. She just did not know what it was yet. The renowned correspondence between Victor Hugo and his publisher after the publication of *Les Misérables* came to mind. Hugo had gone away, but regretted it and wanted to hear news of his book's reception. '?' he wrote to his publisher. '!' the publisher replied. Information does not need to take up much room. What is or rather is not there is what endows meaning.

Annika rose and packed up her things. The student did the same, a young man with untidy hair, skimpy steel-rimmed spectacles, wearing a T-shirt, worn jeans and trainers that squeaked on the floor. While Annika went around putting books back on the shelves, the young man went up to the counter with some order slips.

There are about three thousand recognised medical journals in the world. In order to keep up to date, one must read at least fifteen to twenty of them regularly. At the beginning of the nineteenth century there were in all one hundred scientific journals. Today there are several hundred thousand. The whole thing is a slavish adherence to the exponential law of development of the scientific historian Derek de Solla Price. Annika found it fascinating that at any given point in time the world knew more than it thought it knew, and less than it imagined. That a link between some of the contents of these books could almost be guaranteed to provide a cure for a terrible disease or a signpost to a hidden treasure. That as a whole we do not know the sea, that we know the sea far less than we know space, which we do not know especially well. But Annika understood how difficult that might be to accommodate in a world where the television media constantly tried to postulate and perhaps even believed in their own conclusions. A mechanism that could only function if the world around them were laced into a tight corset, and 'buts' and 'ifs' were sorted out in the cutting room. Where a raindrop the size of northern New South Wales served as a precise evaluation of the next day's weather. Perhaps people did not know they could go into the university library. Or perhaps they just visited the State Library of NSW. Or maybe the whole thing was just too overwhelming. Perhaps that was why people didn't just come tumbling in from the street, and maybe that was why Annika always sat here surrounded only by students who felt obliged to turn up.

And perhaps that was why it was more likely for Annika to notice that the only person besides herself should choose exactly the same time to sit down and to leave. And from the moment when she walked out into the street, and the young student followed her at a distance, she was no longer in any doubt that he was certainly no student.

In the evening, when Annika left the district around Darling Harbour and Chinatown after polishing off a tandoori chicken and oceans of mineral water in Azads India, she made her way towards her parents' house.

She swung out on to Dixon Street, crossed Goulburn and Liverpool Street and was driving alongside the park when she noticed in the rear-view mirror an aubergine-coloured Mazda 828 sedan; because of its attractive colour she could remember it having been parked a little way from the restaurant. It stayed behind her the whole way past St Andrew's Cathedral, where the last of the sunlight flowed like a veil of orange silk high up around the tessellated spires, over Market and King Street and on towards Harbour Bridge. When Annika stopped at a red light she lit a cigarette and glanced in the mirror – the Mazda was still there.

Annika used the waiting time to check her mobile. There was a message from Mike saying he had now definitely localised the problem, and would have the boat ready to sail in half a day at the outside. In the middle of the message Annika heard the alarm signalling that the battery was low, and as the message from Mike was the only one, she put the phone back in its holder just over the air vent and plugged it into the cigarette lighter to recharge.

When the traffic moved on and they were approaching the bridge, she decided to turn off and drive underneath the Cahill Expressway down to Bennelong Point and the Opera House. After she had passed the ferry terminals and come right out to the curve of Sydney Cove, the Mazda was still behind her, and Annika realised it was following the same absurd route as she was – the route that would take them back in precisely the same direction they had come from. Annika consulted the petrol gauge and saw the tank was almost full, then made up her mind to go on driving round and round until the car behind got the message that it had been noticed.

Darkness fell slowly over the city, and when for the second time she reached the area of Woolloomooloo with its old warehouses and the whores in the streets around King's Cross, the neon lights shone out like entwined red and blue pulsing veins on the façades of the buildings. She drove on through Darlinghurst with all its bars, bistros and Cambodian, Mexican and Vietnamese restaurants, and here discovered that the Mazda had disappeared.

Despite the disagreements that arose now and then between Annika and her father, she knew that if anyone on whom she totally relied could decipher the mysterious papers and pictures from Simon's office, it was he. She also knew that a man like Simon, who had emphasised time after time that eighty per cent of all intelligence activity was based on information from publicly accessible sources, wouldn't keep anything in a book unless it was important. And she knew in her heart that although she found it easy enough to get worked up by and about her father over many things, she would never forgive herself if anything happened to him on account of her. Therefore she rarely let the prospect from her rear-view mirror out of sight until she had once more rounded the southern end of the town.

When you cross Harbour Bridge you do not only cross a social divide. You also cut straight through the illusion that the old British imperialism ever succeeded in becoming more than a thin phalanx in this country. A strip of old sandstone houses and sporadic outbreaks of Victorian monumentalism along the coast. Of disused whaling stations beside the sea and deserted windswept mining towns inland. The northern part of Sydney with its immense wealth, with the parklike gardens of Kirribilli, straggles out into pure wilderness and untamed nature. A single hour's drive divides one of the world's metropolises from the eternal blue mist of the eucalypt forests in the long humps of the Blue Mountains. Behind them is a world of marsh flies, mulga scrub and mesa mountains, and far into the continent at Ayers Rock, where some of the Aboriginals think the Rainbow Serpent lives, the eye is met by apparently endless desert. In only an hour you have left behind the dizzying pleasure yachts in Sydney harbour basin and the precipitous financial centre behind Utzon's shining shells to find yourself in clouds of dust, bumping over rough red stone roads behind a farmer's dented four-wheel-drive pick-up with his surly barking sheepdogs in the back.

Annika's parents lived in northern Sydney just past Kirribilli with its well-tended gardens, tall cypresses and endless evening hum of sprinklers, and Annika found it quite appropriate that her father, with his view of natural science, could walk around on lawns where the shrubs were kept trim and above all sparse.

If simplicity is an expression of beauty, then Newton's equations are beautiful. What he described in his elegant laws of motion was the clearest expression of simple logic whereby the universe was held together that one could imagine. They were classical laws for the courses in which stars and planets revolve around each other. Not only did he make the spatial discoveries of Copernicus and Kepler correspond with the theories of movement of Galileo and Descartes, not only did he make the much-sought-after connection between heaven and earth, he also elevated human intellect to almost divine proportions – if only it had not been for one snag: the equations don't fit.

What Newton found was not rules for the universe, but exceptions. His absurd ideas of absolute time were crushed by Einstein. His macroscopic scaffolding broke up like a shaky matchstick model when it met the quantum world, and when it met chaos his idealised notion of a simple, static universe was split into the atoms that were unknown in his own time, and this turned out to be the beginning of the end of the universe in which everything was predetermined. What Newton's geometry enabled him to see was not an elephant. It was at most a section of a groove on the arse of an elephant.

It seemed to Annika as if those who reached out for God's knowledge were always sent back, not with deeper insight into this universe, but with a sharper sense of our incomprehensibly limited knowledge.

Annika lived beneath a vault of knowledge when she was a child. She learned fairytales from her mother. By Andersen, Grimm, Lindgren. From her father, on certain conditions and much, much later, science. For a long time, she recalled, she went around in the mistaken belief that fairytales, with their close-ups of smiling moons and talking stars, provided the really reliable representations, while the books that she consulted more and more often in her father's library contained only a very limited knowledge of life as it was played out in space. The illusion vanished when she learned to read. Annika's mother's teaching did not extend to a more thorough introduction to the azimuth and precession, because, despite her marriage to a physicist, she preferred the fairytale image of happy heavenly bodies. Annika's father's pedagogic abilities were more or less non-existent. To him objects that seemed small were really large, and this grandiosity in the smallest parts of existence forced him to use a vocabulary that in itself was hard to penetrate. And if he was reticent about his feelings, he was downright uncommunicative about his scientific pursuits, so that on the whole Annika listened and read and by herself acquired her knowledge of the meridian and the equatorial system of co-ordinates, of zenith and nadir, and it was greatly to her credit that with a child's ability to extract necessary information she orientated herself almost as correctly on the night sky as on the streets of Sydney at a relatively young age.

The firmament is known as the poor man's accelerator. This was what her father, with other astrophysicists and astronomers, had been advised to study when Sydney gave up its dreams of putting the world of particles into gear. When Annika had reached the age when she no longer posed the most elementary questions, her father grew more favourably disposed to her taking part in a proper dialogue, and she and this reductionist professor emeritus quite frequently spent a night in the library together during an eclipse of the moon. With a mutually silent agenda that excluded certain topics.

Behind her, obliquely, she could glimpse the Southern Cross over the lights of the city. Today one can take bearings to the south by looking at people's parabolas, but at one time it was the vertical in the Southern Cross that navigated people due south with unerring exactitude. In the northern evening sky the stars were more distinct. Annika reflected that at the sight her father would agree that this evening, too, these clouds of gas and dust obeyed the laws of Kepler and Newton. Reflected on how they, father and daughter, in their own awkward fashion, were bound together. On how children, no matter now seemingly improbable at times, are inextricably linked to their parents for good and ill. On how the lover of poetry and the unraveller of mathematical knots ran side by side in her veins, and on how long it might take merely to get *them* to agree. On how many attacks she had launched against him, attacks that in reality had begun as a discussion in her own mind, and how the vitalist in her had merely projected her opponent into the physical world.

As she was driving up to Harbour Bridge the telephone rang, and Annika hadn't a second's doubt about who it was.

'Mike?' she said as she picked it up.

There was silence at the other end.

'I don't know who Mike is, but I should be obliged if you didn't replace your receiver, Miss Niebuhr.'

Annika wrinkled her brow. She listened to the buzzing on the line. And pondered on the voice, which had a deep and markedly metallic tone. Almost as if the speaker had a tin bucket over his head.

'Who is this?'

'I sent you some papers by post recently. Copies of some scans.'

Again she was silent. And again she listened to a faint noise that filled the receiver, and strengthened when the voice came, but in a strange manner that did not disrupt the speech. She guessed that the person was using a voice distorter, and that this somehow interfered with the telephone.

'Why?'

'Simon asked me to.'

'Simon is dead.'

The voice hesitated.

'Yes, unfortunately. Have you had time to look at the pictures, Miss Niebuhr?'

'Yes. Why are you distorting your voice?'

'Just a security measure. What can you see?'

'A brain.'

'Do you see a normal brain, Miss Niebuhr?'

'I see a brain.'

'Try to study it a little more closely, Miss Niebuhr. I am sure you will find it extremely interesting.'

'Wait, wait. Something is written on it. I . . .'

'I cannot talk any more about it now. I have been obliged to make some changes of plan. You will be contacted when necessary.'

'What plans?'

Then the connection was broken at the other end. Annika sat holding the phone for a moment in bewilderment, then put it in place again. A cold shiver ran down her back and she felt a quivering around one eye. She lit a cigarette and went on across the bridge. When what was necessary?

Annika stopped in a neighbouring road for almost ten minutes with her eyes fixed on the rear-view mirror before starting up again, and as she drove the last stretch with extinguished lights and turned in through the gate in the wrought-iron fence that surrounded the large property, she assured herself by glancing in the mirror that no one was following her. Then she drove up the drive and parked in front of the porch. Straight away her mother came out to meet her.

When Annika looked at her mother she sometimes tried to imagine how she herself would have behaved as a mother, and whether she would have met her children with the look her mother mastered – a look that combined reproach and anxiety in such a precisely measured blend that in one second you were reduced to the child that has no defence against its vague accusation.

'You look ill. Are you getting enough to eat? Are you drinking your . . . ?'

Annika went up the steps. She gave her mother a hug.

'Every day, Mum.'

Her mother read a series of details as if they were written on various parts of Annika's face. Then she ran a hand through her daughter's hair. Annika thought of the way Frank Kiesworik had slid his hand up her back.

'Terrible about Simon. Was it the right thing to have gone down to see him?'

Annika kissed her mother's cheek.

'I think so.'

Annika went on through the open door into the hall and, looking around her, asked for her father.

'Where is he?'

'Where do you think?'

She found him in the library, bent over the massive desk in the light of the small, squat table lamp, as so often before wreathed in cigar smoke and a blizzard of calculations. Behind him the blackboard with half-erased equations and arcane chalked numbers. Oculars and colour filters in red, blue and yellow were cluttered around him, and in the doorway on to the terrace a catadioptric telescope, a Schmidt-Cassegrain, stood on a tripod.

He did not notice her as she entered the room, and she did not speak and interrupt his calculations.

As a child you learn at least two ways of connecting with an adult. The direct and the indirect. The direct way is the soliciting, enquiring, insisting, begging and finally almost shrill commanding. The indirect consists of breaking something or other. Annika made her way straight towards the motorised equatorial mounting with gaff suspension, which ensured that in an hour the axis of the telescope traversed fifteen degrees parallel with the rotational axis of the earth.

'Don't touch.'

He didn't even look up from his papers. But that was unnecessary. Now Annika knew, which with him you could not always be sure of, that her presence had been registered. Then she went over to the desk. On it she placed the sheets of calculations and columns and the two photographs from the Anglo-Australia Observatory.

'I wanted to ask you to look at these.'

'Not now.'

'I didn't say it had to be now.'

He looked up.

'Conrad Hawke rang. He said that your definition of surprises agreed very nicely with his own.'

Annika nodded. She went across to the terrace door and pushed it open. Behind her she felt him pulling the papers towards him. Cigar smoke oozed like gas-blue clouds, an astral interior fog, drawn by the draught from the door.

'But we may not interpret it in the same way,' said Annika.

She dropped into one of the two chesterfields with a little coffee table between them, which stood in front of the bookcases of leather-bound books. She leaned her head back and gazed up at the chandelier, her thoughts returning to the mysterious telephone call. Plans? What plans? She threw a glance at her father, who put down his pencil and took a pull on his cigar.

In principle there can be no greater gulf than that between particle physicists and theosophists. Centuries of conflict between the Church and science are not a patch on the gap that exists between the holists' intuitive feeling for meaning and correlation and the hide-bound, morose scientists' explosions of material in kilometre-long accelerators. In reality they are completely identical. Both camps pursue one single all-explanatory formulation, whether it appears as a formula or a revelation. But where the holist, when it all grows too complicated, prefers crude and convenient generalisations, one can at least be sure that in the end the reductionist works to find a solution, and when Annika observed her father she noted with a satisfied smile that he was already busily occupied in studying the photographs.

'What's this, then?' he said with the papers spread out on the table before him.

'I don't know, and I have to ask you to be a little discreet. I'm not sure what it's about, but I am sure they are not meant for public consumption.'

'What does that mean?'

'I'm not saying it's anything illegal. Just that you shouldn't tell anyone you have them.'

'Hm,' he said, looked down at the papers and then put them together again. 'I'll take a look at them.'

There is a difference between how we intellectually and existentially apprehend and understand concepts. Naturally, Annika realised at an early age that medical science was born in the image of natural science, but it was not until later, when she became existentially adult, that the symbolic irony in the fact that rather than breaking with a pattern in reality she reinforced it was revealed to her in earnest.

When Annika finally chose to study medicine instead of biology or zoology, which would have been the most obvious subject, she explained it to herself in her weaker moments as a deduction – a logical consequence of these firmly established patterns. In stronger moments she saw it as a triumph, as she emphasised – in discussions with her father as well – the completely concrete, daily results of her calling as opposed to the theoretical indifference of physics and biology. In Annika's mind there had always been an element of revolt in her choice. In contrast to her father, who had been lost for years to the outside world in his inveterate hunt for a union of compartmentalised theories, Annika fulfilled a role that was beneficial to the patients with whom she was in daily contact. She did her best with the chances she had to educate people. To share her knowledge. Report after report, the latest a comprehensive investigation in the *Medical Journal of Australia*, showed that children in almost a third of the registered cases of snakebite received no, or only ineffectual first-aid treatment. When she was able, Annika gave lectures in schools and appeared on the media if requested.

In her life and through her ordinary contact with scientists, Annika had met two types: those, and they were in the great majority, who developed the humility of an ant towards the forces revealed to them, and those among whom she was ashamed to have to include her father, who without respect and intuitive understanding subverted nature and incorporated a dynamic in their ego that was otherwise confined to the universe – expansion. As if by an unwritten collective law, the first type almost all developed a disarming self-irony. The other type developed into misanthropic, reductionist and totally humourless characters. This flaw in Annika's father's personality derived from a bitterness that had culminated in the CERN accelerator's verification of the Z particle, and because Annika was thus able to locate the time and place of the misery she could also occasionally look on this man, who was her father, with a certain tenderness. But she looked with scorn on the fact that it was precisely his humourless cocksureness and his dated mechanistic view of the universe which had made him so popular on the weekly TV programme *Scientific Week*.

Annika stubbed out the cigarette she had just lit in his silver and mahogany ashtray, a fiftieth birthday present from her mother. She went over and laid a hesitant hand on his shoulder. She knew he loved his daughter. But over the years their relationship had grown into an exchange of achievements. She knew that was where she would find his love. Over the years she had learned to be careful about making demands, that love must be expressed in a way other than is natural to it. That it is limited. By generations. And generations before them.

Even before she had closed the door behind her, she heard a pencil being drawn along the edge of a ruler. In mummified concentration her father was drawing parabolas and curves for the laws of the universe as his daughter left the room. She herself walked down the steps lost in speculation about the mysterious phone call in her car.

Her mother followed her out.

'Won't it give the wrong impression to go out sailing now?'

'What d'you mean?'

'Shouldn't you be at the funeral?'

'I *have* said goodbye to Simon.'

Her mother looked worried.

'Have you?'

Nobody can pinpoint an ache like a mother. Take the right bearings on something that had never been resolved. Activate a sore point. If a father hits the mark it is by mistake. Men are different. They are used to hiding their feelings and so do not see it. The important thing. Love. Out of sight is out of mind. Men are not familiar with love. Therefore women are obliged to be. In many ways Annika was like her father. Especially when confronted by her mother.

Annika knew well enough that she had never revealed a word to her mother about what she had once felt for Simon. But she did remember talking about him several times. It had been unavoidable. Sailing trips in the *Langevin*, a meeting in India, journeys in the East, barbecue evenings at Simon and June's house. She knew that at best her father had listened, but her mother had understood.

As Annika walked up the garden path to her house she could glimpse a bit of the Serpent's Head out in the north-east firmament. The Serpent is the only constellation divided into two, the head and the tail. It is often portrayed in old aboriginal bark paintings, and it was an important constellation for the ancient astronomers. Then it was all in one piece. To the ancient Hebrews, Arabs, Greeks and Romans the Serpent and the Serpent-Holder were one constellation. But later it changed. Stars have displaced themselves in relation to one another. The star that once oriented the Egyptians to the north is now in the Dragon constellation. Mathematical fictions exist for us. We have invented them because we cannot do without them. If we did not make use of imaginary notions about what the universe looks like we could not orientate outselves at all. The error occurs when we believe that we are decoding what we read into the system. Newton was totally human in his physics. He needed something to hold on to. But there isn't anything to hold on to. The universe does what suits it. And we don't know what that is.

Her father would be sure to take a few days to decode the pictures and sheets from Simon's office, and she knew in her heart she would have to ring Mike and call off the trip, and try to explain to him that she couldn't go anywhere at the moment. No matter how much she wanted to, she couldn't leave Sydney now. She knew she would have no peace of mind before she heard the result of the autopsy, and she knew she had to find out what the strange phone call meant. That she had to know what Simon had meant by that quotation.

She switched on the light and looked at her watch. She thought for a while and had already picked up the telephone when she discovered the light on the answering machine was winking. She wound the tape back and listened to the message. It was from Kahn and it was brief.

'Meet me at four o'clock tomorrow at Le Kiosk. I have something for you.'

Annika opened the autopsy report – Simon's medical record. She leafed through the papers. Identification papers, copies of fingerprints, photographs, analyses of the stomach contents, toxicological tests, a complete autopsy report with conclusion, the police report, copies of receipts for personal possessions and copies of newspaper articles. Elements in the *corpus delicti*. She searched for a certain line and found it: 'Presumed suicide'.

Annika pulled her sunglasses down her nose a little and looked over them at Kahn disbelievingly. He shrugged.

'The shot was fatal. Immediately. More or less. Hit the main artery. He might have known it. He had a good doctor.'

Annika directed her gaze away from the sea in across the park at the end of Shelly Beach. A small flock of galah cockatoos sailed along in a pink cloud above the treetops in the direction of St Patrick's College. She looked down at her empty cup and started to scrape at the hard crust the frothy milk from the cappuccino had left on the inside.

'All suicides shoot themselves either in the head or the heart. It is completely unpredictable how a calibre .22 will behave when it penetrates a human body. Simon was not the sort of man who would take his own life. And he was above all not a man who left anything to chance.'

Kahn put his arms on the table and clicked his tongue. He took out one of his Camels and lit it. The next words he uttered came out rounded by the smoke rings that left his mouth in small puffs.

'I admit the shot looks strange. But we have no technical data that would indicate a crime of any kind. And we have no witnesses.'

'And you have no suicide note?'

'We don't need one.'

'A man like Simon. Trains as an SAS soldier. Discovers the depths of life. Trains as a psychologist. On a quest for answers. To the mysteries of life and human beings. Who lived for formulating and describing problems. Don't you think he would at least try to sketch out the motives behind such a momentous decision?'

'Perhaps. I have come across dyslexics who left half the draft of a novel. Politicians who vanish without so much as a syllable. Lawyers who forget to make provision for their family. People in Simon Rees's situation do not act rationally.'

'I'm not talking about exceptions. I'm talking about probabilities.'

'I never talk about probabilities. I talk about concrete examples.'

Annika leafed through the report. She pulled out a piece of paper.

'They found traces of blood on the deck. Simon's blood. I thought you said he died instantly.'

'Almost instantly.'

'After which he staggered up from the cabin, took two or three steps and threw himself into the water?'

'Fell, Miss Niebuhr. Did you see the film of Kennedy's murder? I think that what people felt was totally crazy was the interpretation of the "magic bullet". The one that had apparently gone in and out of Kennedy's body five or six times. The selfsame bullet. But it was a manipulated representation. I remember we were once chasing a drug addict along King Street. Finally a young officer saw nothing for it but to shoot the man, who was about to break through a fence. The autopsy showed that the man had been hit in five or six places. But the officer had fired only one shot. We saw a "magic bullet" then. Reality can look absurdly unreal. But as a rule there is a rational explanation. Even if it appears to be really irrational.'

'I don't think you presented your theories on asphyxia like that.'

'I am a policeman, Miss Niebuhr. If I just humoured everyone I'd never get to know anything.'

Influenced by Kahn, who stubbed out his cigarette in the ashtray at that moment, Annika took one out herself. Kahn stretched across the table and gallantly lit it for her.

'What about the girl?'

'We know the snake was in the glove compartment. The forensic people have found traces of scales and mites. I had no idea snakes carried mites.'

'It's very common. In captivity. How did she get into the car? Wasn't it locked?'

'The key was in it when we found it.'

'Is there still no trace of the girl?'

'We're still searching.'

'I'm surprised she isn't considered a possible suspect.'

'What do you mean?'

'I met John Osborne at the private view. He has a theory that the girl had something or other on Simon.'

'She may well have had.'

'But then why does it not occur to anyone that she may have shot Simon? Simon hired the car. The girl gets into it, opens the glove compartment and ... whoops, a snake. Simon dies the following day. They may have had an appointment. Which Simon broke. She may have decided to take revenge. To kill him.'

'Miss Niebuhr, we are not regarding Simon Rees's death as murder. Not at all, at the moment. Read his wife's statement. Simon Rees was not well, his state of mind was low, he was not himself. Depressed. Dispirited.'

'I don't understand it.'

'What don't you understand?'

'It's as if murder is not to be mentioned at any price. As if they're intent on sticking to suicide. You'd think this affair with the girl would be received with open arms.'

Kahn glanced around swiftly in all directions, and also out of the corner of his eye at the tables behind them, where the conversation from the guests was merely a faint mumble broken by the sound of cutlery against plates.

'Now you seem to be assuming some kind of conspiracy. I cannot go along with that. Shall we stretch our legs?'

He put his hands on the arms of his chair and looked at her encouragingly. Annika stubbed out her cigarette and rose.

He stretched out his hand.

'I'd better take charge of the report.'

Annika picked up the report and passed it to Kahn, who insisted on settling the bill, though making light of it.

'Oh, I only have big notes. Have you any change?'

Annika stared unbelievingly at what he had put on the table. It was not money. It was something that looked like a folded photocopy of a newspaper cutting. She picked it up quickly and put it in her pocket, took out a note for a small sum and laid it on the table. She passed Kahn a couple of coins. He smiled as if nothing unusual had occurred.

There was not a cloud in the sky and hardly any wind. They walked along the esplanade until they came to some steps that led down to the beach. The ocean was flat and stretched out like a smooth, almost jade-coloured cloth. The waves broke on the beach with a regular foam of spray, but not until a good way out did the breakers rise at long intervals in a weary dark green line from point to point, before collapsing with a hollow boom.

'Why do you think someone knows about your suspicion?'

'Frank Kiesworik. The consul at Brisbane. The American. He was at the private view. He gave himself away. Do you know him?'

Kahn shook his head.

'Who cleared up at Simon's home?'

'Who do you think?'

'The ASIO?'

'After all, he was employed by them.'

Kahn stopped and took out a cigarette. He sheltered the lighter flame unnecessarily when he lit up, and sweetish blue tobacco smoke spread around him. They strolled down to the water through the sand and the spaces among people's towels.

Annika kept her hand on the newspaper cutting she had in her pocket and waited for Kahn to enlarge on it.

He looked around him before he began.

'A month ago a whole family died in a car crash a little south of Brisbane. The Johnson family. It had been raining. Their car skidded after aquaplaning, slid over into the opposite lane where it was struck by an articulated lorry. The passenger vehicle burst into flames. Three people perished. A family, the Johnson family, were smashed and burned past recognition. Those are the bare facts you will read in the article from the *Courier-Mail*.'

'How is this connected with Simon?'

'Mark Johnson had a peripheral contact with the ASIO. The article does not mention that.'

'Mark Johnson?' said Annika. She remembered the little 'MJ' mark on the scans, but when Kahn asked in surprise whether she knew him she chose to conceal her knowledge of the scans.

Kahn pulled at his cigarette.

'All notes in electronic form have disappeared without trace from Simon Rees's private computer. We have tried to reconstruct the files. Without success. Regardless of whether Simon Rees or others deleted the information, it was done with unheard-of perfection. There isn't a scrap to get at.'

Annika looked at him enquiringly.

'But?'

Kahn smiled.

'The ASIO had been there before us. But I knew there were two mobile telephones. Simon Rees had one and his wife, June, another. Simon Rees's mobile was at the office. So we thought. For God knows what reason he happened to take his wife's phone to work that day. Therefore the ASIO didn't touch the phone at their home. They thought it was hers. But it wasn't. It was Simon Rees's.'

'So you heard the message I left for him?'

Kahn nodded.

'That wasn't very nice of you. At that point he was regarded as a suspect.'

'Where is it now?'

'Naturally I passed it on to the ASIO people. Oh, yes, that's something I haven't told you, Miss Niebhuhr. The ASIO have now taken over the investigation themselves.'

'What about that phone?'

'One of the hundred numbers in the memory cannot in any circumstances be explained away. It is on a par with a fingerprint. The papillary lines of numbers, if you like. The number has been disconnected now. But it *was* the number of the Johnson family. Simon Rees knew the Johnsons.'

'I still find it hard to see the connection.'

'Do you? You, who see a conspiracy in two people merely talking to each other?'

'But the accident was an accident. Or wasn't it?'

'Do you know the medical officer of health in Brisbane?'

Annika shook her head.

'Kate Carpenter. She carried out the inspection of the bodies. Kate Carpenter is a working scandal. She's pretty much an alcoholic; it's said she has never done an autopsy without a cigarette in her hand, and she makes a beeline for all the young interns up there. But she's a fiendishly clever pathologist. And even when she's more than half cut, there's something in her that sees everything clearly. The bodies, or the remains of them, were taken to Brisbane. She let slip an interesting comment one night to one of my colleagues up there. It was a day or two after the accident. She felt she could allow herself to have a small one, because she hadn't been seeing double. She thought the journalists had, though.'

'And what did she mean by that?'

'All the newspapers based their story on a telegram from the Australian Associated Press. Those that carried it. The Associated Press got their information from the police. There were no journalists at the accident. One is tempted to say because it was raining. It was a busy evening with many other important events on. The photograph printed of the car had been taken by a freelance photographer. It was in a couple of papers. That photographer works occasionally for the police.'

'So what did she think about that?'

'She thought the papers had exaggerated. She thought she had performed a post-mortem and identified two bodies. She thought the papers had written about a person who had not been found. That one passenger was missing. She never saw the third body.'

Kahn stood looking out over the water. Thirty metres out it rose in a green wave that lay like a straight line almost from one end of the beach to the other. Halfway along, the wave broke in the middle, and the two parts fell slightly out of line. Annika needed no explanation for why he always spoke when the waves broke, and when they were close to groups of children.

'What shall we do now?' she asked.

'We?'

'I should be glad to help . . .'

He smiled.

'Oh, no, Miss Niebuhr, you misunderstand. I don't know what you will do, but I have not considered doing any more.'

'Married with two children. Is that what you mean?'

'It's not that banal. Even if I wanted to or could proceed with the case, I couldn't justify it. I have no technical evidence that so much as hints that Simon Rees did not take his own life.'

'What do you think happened?'

'I don't know. Perhaps he really did take his own life. Perhaps he was implicated in the accident up there. Perhaps that was why. Or perhaps you are right. Perhaps he did ask not to be shot in the head. In the hope of surviving the first shot. Or to tell us something. I don't know what you are going to do about it, but I *cannot* do more.'

'Why are you telling me this?'

He leaned towards her. Whispered.

'I know something about the way the ASIO works. The fact that an intelligence service is not subject to parliamentary control is of course no guarantee for its ensuring that it can always justify its actions?'

'I don't follow.'

'I have driven the route the Swedish couple say they took with the girl. If they had gone the direct way, along Sydney Road, it would have been impossible for them to overlook the sign for Manly Hospital. But they did not take the direct route. They took a zigzag course through Manly. Only after Manly did it become the direct way. Over Spit Bridge to Mosman. Our friend, the handbag snatcher, drove in front and set the direction. Despite the risk that the girl might die, he thought it was important for her to get to the Prince of Wales hospital. Why?'

Annika looked at him, bewildered.

'Since you, Miss Niebuhr, are the only person at that hospital with a direct link with Simon Rees, I can come to no other conclusion than that he or someone thought that for some reason it was essential for Gaia Jessup to get to you. For you to see her.'

'But in what way should I be involved?'

'I hoped you would know that yourself.'

In this age's desperate search for the self, lying has become the indicator that distinguishes us most clearly from other species. When we are looking for the quality that makes certain animals seem equal in consciousness, characteristically enough we select a bad trait. Using the uncertainty factors that allow them to distinguish between acquired and spontaneous, consciously misleading actions, primatologists have discovered that only great apes and, most of all, chimpanzees possess those qualities.

To Annika's way of thinking lying was a rare, occasionally necessary, but above all unwelcome device. And she was not at all happy about lying to Mike. Her whole life and being were geared to precision and candour, so that lying, or tactical deceit, as the primatologists choose to call it, was always unexpected when she encountered it, and in its isolated form alarming. Especially when she met it in herself.

The meeting with Kahn had solved one problem and created another, but Annika's dilemma was the same – she would have to lie to Mike.

She was weighed down by four bulging bags as she crossed the wide pavement of George Street that evening with her last purchases. The streetlights were on, and from inside the sepia-coloured buildings that housed the Museum of Contemporary Art light came flooding out of the great picture window facing the street. Annika used the pedestrian crossing and made for her car, which was parked beneath the awning just outside the Ken Done shop.

Annika had never managed to fabricate the lie that was to have bolstered her wish to cancel their trip or postpone it indefinitely. Now she would *have* to work it out. With another one. Because the route would have to be altered. She neither could nor would make herself let Mike in on all the facts of the case. Partly because he would never allow her to get mixed up in something that involved the intelligence service, partly because she knew it would wound him deeply to know that she and thus he were suddenly uncertain about why she was really going on this cruise. Was it on account of Simon? On account of Mike? Or on account of her work? He would fully accept the latter reason – the first would finish him.

Besides, she wanted, at least that was what she told herself, to protect him. If he knew nothing, less could go wrong. For that reason she had considered and just as quickly rejected the idea of taking a flight to Brisbane. She could fly there and be back again in Sydney in half a day. But if the ASIO were really dogging her every movement they would know about it. They would know where she was going and who she intended to see.

On the other hand, a visit to Brisbane under cover of their expedition was almost perfect. If they had tapped her phone or listened in on her conversations with Mike they would know the tour had been long in the planning, and that there had been no secret about their destination. It would be more difficult to follow her at sea. And above all the whole thing would seem perfectly natural. It would look as if she had given up trying to find out more about the case. There remained only one problem, and that was the planned route.

Mike had suggested they should make the voyage out in two stages. They would call at Port Macquarie and tank up, stay the night, then potter on to Coffs Harbour and thence to Brisbane for another fuel stop. From there they would go up to the reef, and when Annika had finished her work, and if they had time, they could go into Brisbane and spend a few hours there on the way home. That was what Annika wanted to change. Although she could rein in her impatience enough not to take a plane to Brisbane immediately, she didn't want to wait for almost two weeks to speak to Miss Carpenter.

She knew they would have to go into Port Macquarie to tank up, but also that from there they could get to Brisbane on one tankful. Instead of arriving at Brisbane in the evening they would be able to cover the last stretch in the morning and in that way could have most of the day in the town. They must get to Brisbane. As quickly as possible. The conjunction of the initials 'MJ' and Mark Johnson, ASIO and Simon could not possibly be a coincidence. A well-oiled pathologist in Brisbane held the answers. Maybe not all of them. But perhaps some. Annika just had to speak to her.

Annika unlocked her car and manoeuvred the bags on to the passenger seat. She picked up her phone and rang Mike on the boat. Mike knew that when Annika was in the area she would on no account miss the chance of seeing John Farrow and Kookillo Dhamarandji; she had already prepared him for that. That could be her white lie. That her only chance of meeting both of them would be during the next couple of days, as Dhamarandji was going home to see his family for several weeks.

Mike warned her it would be a tough trip, and she would have to take the wheel part of the way.

'Don't you trust me?'

'About boats?' he said, laughing. But he didn't protest further. He felt it was up to her, as she was the only one who could foresee how much time she would need for her research.

'Where are you now?' he asked.

'I'm on the way home to finish packing,' said Annika.

'I should be finished with the boat about midnight,' he said. 'If we're to keep to plan we must get up early, so ring me if you make any changes.'

'I'm not going to change anything.'

Feeling slightly uncomfortable about the method but well satisfied with the result, Annika set the phone down on the front panel. She was about to start up when she glanced in the rear-view mirror and saw the aubergine-coloured Mazda a little behind her on the other side of the street.

*　　*　　*

141

In his description of the seven wonders of the world Philon wrote of wonders spoken of by all but which no one had seen. You could describe the coffee at Il Paradiso Trattoria in the same way. For three generations the Macri and Romeo families, who owned the place, had kept the details of their blend of coffee secret, which of course hadn't frightened the customers away. All the way up to the restaurant, which is in the Food Hall arcade midway between Cremorne and Neutral Bay, the Mazda had stuck behind her, but when somehow she seemed to have shaken off her pursuers, and as Annika and Mike as a rule lived on powdered coffee while they were at sea, she decided to go in for a taste of something a bit more exotic. The mere thought of having them following her the whole way out to Whale Beach made her shudder, and she felt her palms sticking to the leather-covered steering wheel as she parked the car. Not until she reached her house would she have anything at all to defend herself with, and she thought how easy it would be for them to force her over the cliffs out on the peninsula.

An uncomfortably fast heartbeat accompanied the rhythm of her stride, which grew faster and faster all the way through the arcade, and not until she sat smoking a cigarette with her coffee did she feel any better. It calmed her to see all the people, and she gazed around from table to table, where couples and families sat talking, separated by tall green palms and ferns. But then she realised she had only bought herself a temporary respite. If they were still there when she left the restaurant she would be in the same plight. The moment she walked out of here, the moment she stepped out of the arcade, she would be on her own again. And immediately the feeling of calm while surrounded by customers in the restaurant turned into a horrible suspicion. When a young couple sat down at a table close by it struck her that she had no picture of her pursuers. It might be a solitary man who came, it might be two women together, it might be a couple, and although she kept telling herself she was overdramatising everything, an unpleasant and, she thought, hopefully ungrounded fear had already got the better of her.

She rose resolutely and put some money on the table, then went in and asked where the pay-phone was. The waiter showed her, and Annika swiftly inserted money and called her parents.

She exchanged a couple of casual remarks with her mother and asked to speak to her father.

She could hear him leafing through his papers as he picked up the phone in the library.

'I thought you had left,' he said.

'We're going early tomorrow,' said Annika. 'I just want to emphasise the need for discretion. It wouldn't be a good thing for you to mention the papers I gave you to anyone at all.'

'I understood that,' he said.

'I just wanted to make sure,' she said. 'If anyone asks whether you have them you must say no.'

'Which papers?'

She paused. Then she smiled and laughed to herself. With relief, but also because she suddenly felt silly at having reacted so strongly. No one had seen her drive up to the house. No one could know anything. She was worrying unnecessarily.

She shook her head over the foolish panic that had seized her, which she could easily manage to turn into curiosity.

'Have you found out anything?'

'I have a suspicion of what it may be, but I haven't got around to looking at it properly yet. Ring me when you get back from the trip.'

'In a word?'

'You'll have to wait.'

'Just two words?'

He hesitated and she could hear him rummaging around in the piles of paper.

'Interesting. It looks interesting and maybe a bit alarming.'

'Alarming?'

'I'm not saying any more. I may be wrong. Ring when you get back.'

The Mazda was on the other side of the street when Annika walked out of the arcade. She couldn't see who was in it behind the shaded windows. Nor how many. She lit a cigarette and looked around her. The traffic was dense and there were people in the street. The streetlights were on and the shop windows were lit. Here she was secure. She made a swift decision, threw down her cigarette and trod it out. Then she walked quickly past her own car and started to run across the street towards the Mazda. But the moment she reached the middle of the street, among the passing vehicles hooting at her, the Mazda's lights came on, and with a screech of tyres the driver turned out into the road. For a brief moment Annika thought it was making straight for her. A car behind the Mazda braked so violently that it skidded before the driver could straighten up, so that it just missed Annika, standing as if thunderstruck on the central pavement. The aubergine Mazda vanished with a roar of acceleration in front of her. Down the street. Away.

Annika stood looking around her in some confusion. She hadn't planned what she would say to the driver. Let alone what she would do. Perhaps she had merely wanted to demonstrate she was not blind. Even though she was glad the car had gone, still it had taken her by surprise. There had been no need to do that. They could merely have chosen to ignore her. They could have rolled down the window and shaken their heads. They could have made fun of her. It was absolutely clear that they had recognised her. If there had been only a theoretical possibility that the pursuit through Sydney had some absurd explanation, now it was quite certain that someone was following her. What was new was the fact that for the first time Annika realised she might know the people in the car.

The creationists think the idea of evolution conflicts with the second law of thermodynamics. They maintain that since life has apparently moved from simple to complex, and that the second law of thermodynamics says that the universe moves from order to steadily greater disorder, a clash must exist between biology and physics. Thus in this way God, with his magic wand, could be reinstated. But the creationists forget that entropy, the huge amount of disorder, only grows in closed systems, something every woman who has lived in a permanent relationship with a man can vouch for. The amount of mess increases. The piles of clothes get larger. Disorder mounts up. And in the same way that the earth is an open system that takes its energy from the sun, a woman is obliged to get help from a cleaner if she isn't to despair or drown in chaos.

Annika smiled at the sight of the open cupboard doors in the bedroom and the jumble of clothes on the bed, and she laughed over her attempts to put right the muddle that surrounded her, whose only redeeming feature was that at least she had created it herself. It was only when she came to the scans, and with two fingers gripped the end of the revolver's trigger guard, that she realised she was not responsible for all the mess. In the layers of briefs and T-shirts there was no particular hierarchy, but there was one principle she never departed from, which was that no matter what else was put in the drawer, the revolver was always at the bottom. That served two purposes: partly so that even an unlikely accident would not happen if she rummaged in the drawer, and partly so that she would never have to waste time searching for it should it ever be needed in a hurry. Now she saw that it lay on top of the scans.

It was then Annika heard the garden door slam against the frame. She stood up, frowning, with the revolver in her hand. She knocked out the magazine to make sure it was full. She put it back in the stock and the magazine slid into place with a hard clack. At that very moment all the lights in the house went out.

She went through the loading motions and stood perfectly still with both arms stretched out before her and her left hand over the right one holding the stock. She could see nothing. A thief could strike her head off before she had time to react. When she occasionally darkened the whole house and lay out on the terrace to look at the stars, she always waited for a quarter of an hour for her eyes to get used to the dark. She did the same thing now.

She listened and waited, and as no sound was to be heard, and she slowly started to make out the contours of the room and the furniture, she began to walk down the passage.

She slowly advanced, carefully opening the doors of the small storerooms along the corridor.

It was warm and damp, but as so often there was a light breeze from the point, and at intervals she could hear the banging of the garden door.

Over the years Annika had grown used to living alone. But once or twice during those years she had come close to experiencing intense fear. It had happened when she woke abruptly in the middle of her REM sleep, when she clearly felt that state of total paralysis she knew the organism slid into in that phase of sleep. It had taken her by surprise and almost frightened the life out of her, because the extremely sharp feeling of anxiety, which occurred in full consciousness, had been accompanied each time by a conviction that was greater and stronger, that someone or something she had to escape from was in the room with her. Nightmare in a state of complete consciousness. Encapsulated in fear, with a sure knowledge of what was happening, incapable of action. This was the feeling that accompanied her down the passage and which left her only slowly.

The electricity meters were right at the other end of the house, and she tried to comfort herself with the thought that it might just be a simple fuse.

When she came to the end of the passage and was in the open kitchen, it became easier to see her way. The large windows let in the moonlight, and the marbled reflection from the pool outside glimmered on the ceiling.

She took the three steps down into the living room, which lay in darkness, and over to the stairs and on to the last small area containing utility room, lumber room, guest room and bathroom.

She pushed open the door of the utility room, which was in total darkness, and fumbled her way to the meter.

At the same instant the garden door slammed to behind her, and at that instant she turned round and her hand struck the edge of the door hard. The revolver flew out of her grasp and the pain in her hand was so sharp that for a moment she could pay no attention to anything else and so did not sense where it had landed. She had lost her bearings and merely concentrated on not screaming out loud.

Then she stiffened. There in the dark. Stock still.

Marine biologists talk of a phenomenon they call 'hot' water. It occurs when a large concentration of poisonous jellyfish has been removed from a pool. Broken-off tentacles remaining in the pool will still be active, even though they are disconnected from their host animal. The water will be 'hot.' The minute capsules of the threads, the nematocysts, still fire off poison at everything that comes into contact with them. If you put your hand in you will be stung by the microscopic capsules of poison lying in wait in the water.

Now Annika felt she was standing in a pool of 'hot' water. That the slightest movement would kill her. That the presence of death was around her.

She felt her heart beating hard, and the pulse in her neck worked as if it would burst the skin. She did not dare look round. Could not move.

In her head she heard Simon. 'Tai kwon do, because in reality you haven't a chance in hand-to-hand combat with a man.' She had been trained to use her legs. And to react like lightning to an attack. To concentrate her strength into an explosion at the end of her foot or the end of her outstretched arms and firmly clenched fists. But in situations where she had been able to see her opponent, and her knees hadn't turned to jelly. The darkness had surprised her, and she stood there struggling to control her situation. To transform the fear into an explosion of aggression. She tried to calm down by talking silently to herself. It was the garden door she had heard, it was the utility-room door she had struck. There was no one but herself in the house. She knew that if anyone really was there, she hadn't a chance if she did not get the better of her fear. But she also knew she was fighting with an evolutionary injustice. She would have to find her way to the point in her brain that contained both fear and rage. Into the R-complex. The reptile brain. The centre that dealt out blows. That centre which is always in readiness in a man.

'Surprise, aggression and speed.' Simon on the lawn in his garden.

A mentor testing the abilities of his pupil. But no matter how quickly Annika spun herself round to kick, he warded off her feet. To June's pique he grinned, and with his arm around Annika went up to the house and the other guests. June's excuse was that she loved Simon, but Annika couldn't understand that she didn't see you should only fear what is hidden. 'Three factors,' said Simon. 'Mutually dependent on each other. If one factor fails the others suffer.' That is how élite soldiers attack. The SAS, the SEALS, the Danish hunting soldiers. That's how snakes attack.

Of course it was not the place, and of course Annika was clowning – she could not take it as seriously as Simon. To her the physical training was above all a means of restoring mental balance, but she also learned from it that she would never be able to foster this killer attitude that, when it came to the point, was effective because it was committed to the question of survival even before it was posed.

She felt that someone was standing in the doorway. And that she was weak and afraid. But then it seemed as if something went away. The feeling of the presence of a person vanished, and shortly afterwards she heard the front door close.

She stood in the dark for a little while. She was breathing fast. She did not move.

The telephone began to ring, but she did not answer, and she was recovering her composure only slowly. She felt strange. Relieved. And humbled.

Annika found her way to the relay and switched on. No fuse had blown.

On her way to the telephone she heard a car accelerating along the road, but although she ran to the front door and opened it a crack, she failed to see it.

She went back and picked up the phone.

It was Mike.

'I just wanted to know if you're about ready.'

'Yes,' said Annika. 'Now I'm ready.'

She went down and found the revolver on the floor of the utility room. Then returned to the bedroom and packed it and an extra magazine at the bottom of one of the bags, with the scans. She put the last T-shirts in and a stiff Driza-bone oilskin jacket on top. Fetched the briefcase containing the taxonomic schedules and papers from Colombo University and packed that too. Then she made a round of the house, put out all the lights and made sure all doors were locked.

Lugging the bags, she went into the kitchen and over to the rack of kitchen knives.

She noticed one knife was out of place, and with a thoughtful expression pushed it straight.

Then she left the house.

Sydney's numerous small islands and peninsulas make it look as if the land masses are floating like lush green pontoons in a world of water. Since the sea has eaten its way far into Sydney to the north at Manly and a long way in westward to Parramatta, where Harbour Bridge and the Opera House lie in the middle of the harbour entrance, and where white boats, fluttering sails and smooth shining tiled roofs sweat in the sun, the town has a fashionable air. But the real luxury is found around northern Sydney's Beauty Point.

The marina lies just on the other side of Spit Bridge near Pearl Bay, as you drive towards Sydney, and even in the dark Annika could identify the big cruisers and pleasure yachts anchored up along the pontoons. In this company, where the largest private motor cruisers were like small ferries, Mike's boat, an Endeavour 2000, was only one among many, but because Annika knew where the cruiser was she caught a glimpse of Mike from the bridge.

Apart from her short-lived marriage to Jay Morgan, Annika had been pretty lucky with her male friends, and even though some Australian men could drive her mad now and then, when she thought about it she had always felt happiest in the company of men. Mike, Harper Stone, Simon, Kookillo Dhamarandji, John Farrow.

All of them were reticent introverts but also shrewd and self-assured. Men to whom you could confide your feelings without fearing that they listened and then later turned those feelings against you. In her early youth, with its female friends and relationships, Annika had had one or two shattering frights, which showed her that you shouldn't let your women friends censor private matters.

She soon learned that confidences needed an element of undignified sensation in order to build a solid friendship between two women, which made Annika slowly but surely weed out a number of those friendships. She did not find in men these conditions of mutual hostage-taking in which what seemed to Annika horrific trivialities and trifles appeared to fulfil all demands for real substance. With men you could safely speak out; all the rubbish that Annika, like all other women and men, sometimes had to get rid of was forgotten. And you were never later confronted with what in Annika's relationships with her women friends often seemed to her to be beating about the bush, distortions or direct untruths, although she did not for a second doubt that they were painfully correct rehearsals of deeply hurtful outbursts of feelings, that one only wished to forget. So Annika was careful not to engage in any dodgy dealing with the men she knew, but instead tried to keep to essentials. It was easier for her than she would have believed, and once that was clear she realised that when it came to the art of managing a tight emotional economy, she had inherited more from her father than was immediately comprehensible and perhaps desirable. In time she learned to accept that this emotional exclusivity, which other women regarded as eccentricity, was a part of her personality, and that you cannot run away from the person you are. Even in a country like Australia, which will not go down in history as one that brought in an unconditional law to allow for ambitious women, Annika had always felt at ease in company with 'her' men. She was accepted on equal terms and they had the same attitude – that there was an exterior world which, after the tumultuous youthful years they had all been through, was at least as thrilling as the interior one.

Only in her relationships with Simon and in particular with Mike had the constants been shifted slightly. If she were to search her heart about her feelings for Simon, she would not be able to deny a certain emotional engagement that went further than the purely professional and friendly, an engagement that had increased in intensity over the years, although she was also certain that she had never made a direct pass at him. But Mike was more of a problem.

151

Michael Larsen

Annika got out of the car and lit a cigarette. Laughter and noisy chatter could be heard from the fish restaurants farther out along the quay square; otherwise all was quiet among the parked cars. She did not think anyone had followed her, but stood there waiting for a while. Finally she took the smoke from two quick drags deep into her lungs before dropping the cigarette. She pulled her two bags from the seat and shut the car doors. She knew they had been in her house. In her drawers. That they must have seen the scans and the drawing. She wondered why they had left them there. But her head was buzzing with fatigue, and there was nothing she could do about it. If they had got anything out of them they were wiser than she was. She walked along the bridge, lugging the bags.

Mike was kneeling on the afterdeck with the hatch of the motor-well open. Annika stepped carefully past and put her bags down on the thwarts in the pantry. She went out on the bathing platform and leaned against the rubber dinghy lashed to the rail with snap hooks. She stood in the shadow of the big glass-fibre hood mounted on bars farthest aft and joined to the big flybridge, which served as a roof for the whole bathing platform.

There was plenty of room on board. Underneath the deckhouse ceiling, on which the large white flybridge rested like an advanced American spaceship, were three cabins, two of them aft and out in the stern, *en suite* with toilet and shower. A couple of steps midships led downward to the galley, which included all modern comforts: oven, microwave, hob, ice machine, hot and cold water, stereo and television.

'I thought she was ready,' said Annika, teasing.

Mike made black prints on the oilbag beside him. Then he turned to her and dried sweat and hair from his face with his wrists. He stood up, stretching his body awkwardly from the cramped position he had been in. Then he pulled a cloth from his pocket and wiped his hands on it. He looked at her and smiled.

'She *is* ready.'

Annika followed him in to the sink, where he rubbed oily jelly on his hands before turning on the tap and washing them. Then he dried his hands, took a bottle of mineral water from the fridge and drank until there was none left.

He sat down in the galley. Annika turned round and flopped down on the bench on the other side of the small table.

'I'm so tired,' she said, leaning over on to the table.

'Go and lie down, then.'

'I must unpack the car.'

'Where are the keys?'

Annika turned her hand over and opened it.

Mike took them.

Annika lay there blinking. Then she fell asleep.

She woke to find him almost carrying her down the steps from the saloon to the cabin right forward under the foredeck.

Dazed and shattered with exhaustion, Annika threw herself on to the double bed.

'Don't undress me. And don't try anything.'

Mike began to undress her.

'You won't feel a thing.'

She smiled.

'That's what I mean.'

She lay listening to Mike rummaging around. She felt really conscience-stricken at not doing anything when there was so much to organise, but she was quite simply unable to move a muscle. Her body and arms felt like cement, and her eyelids, which she was fighting to keep open, sank down again and again like heavy covers. She lay for a while listening to the creaking of the boat's fenders against the quay. She looked out of the small rectangular porthole. She thought of Simon. Of what the whole thing could mean. Gaia Jessup, a girl Simon had known. Who was she? Simon's cryptic message? The scans, yes, the scans, she must show them to Mike, but not now, not yet, not yet.

When Mike got into bed beside her, she knew she had been asleep.

Gone. But she had no idea for how long. He lay there a while without saying anything. She felt his hand caressing her back and she mumbled some throaty sounds to tell him that wasn't a bad thing to do. She kept her eyes squeezed shut because she was assailed by her bad conscience over not explaining the situation to him. She didn't like going on a voyage with a hidden agenda, perhaps the real agenda. When Brisbane was done with, when she had been to see Kate Carpenter, what then? What if that visit did not make her any the wiser? What if it did?

For someone driven by dual motivation in everything she or he undertakes, it can be hard to separate the main from the connected reasons. Instead she turned her attention to Mike's caresses on her back, and slowly dropped off.

He lay behind her on one elbow, supporting his head on his hand. All was quiet in the marina, and now and then she could feel him turning his face, as if he expected to direct it at something that had a form. But there was nothing. There was the water around them, the creaking of ropes, otherwise nothing.

'Annika?'

'Mmm.'

'Don't you ever feel lonely?'

Annika replied sleepily with closed eyes.

'You've asked me that before.'

'But then you lied.'

'Not exactly.'

Annika pushed her bottom backwards, and she felt Mike's arm slide in under her face, while the other came to rest beside her stomach.

'Sometimes,' said Annika, 'sometimes I feel it's hard to live alone. In fact I feel it gets harder and harder the older I get.'

'What's holding you back, then?'

'I also think it gets harder and harder to live with someone.'

Behind her he fell silent. And slowly her eyes closed again. She smiled at the thought of his half-erect penis which she could feel through the blanket. Then she fell asleep.

*   *   *

Late in the night Annika opened her eyes. Cautiously she sat up in bed, and almost imperceptibly shook Mike awake.

'There's something in here,' she said.

'What is it?' said Mike. His voice was low and sleepy.

'A snake. Why are you whispering?' she asked.

He didn't reply. Then he suddenly opened his eyes.

'The only absolutely safe thing you can do at this moment is talk. Snakes can't hear voices. They're on a different frequency. You can even scream if you want to. If you can do it without moving.'

'Why,' he said, raising his voice slightly, 'do you think it's a snake?'

'Because,' she said, peering round in the darkness, 'it's just crawled up on to the bed.'

They lay for a while unmoving. Annika tried to localise the snake, but even though her eyes had accustomed themselves to the dark, only the bedside table, the bed and a bag just beneath the porthole could be made out clearly. She tried to imagine how the snake saw them at this second. As flickering infrared heat rays, as computer simulations, splotches of heat, images like hospital thermography scans. The probability was that it had slid down to the deck and was moving along the glass-fibre edge.

'Are you sure it was a snake you saw?'

'Put it this way, the only thing I'm not sure of is whether it's left the bed or crawled down under the blanket.'

'Is it dangerous?'

'Mike, here in Australia everything that's bigger than a little fingernail is dangerous.'

* * *

When confronted with a taboo, a vice, a flaw, Annika had always been on guard as a girl, when she occasionally abandoned herself to a reductionist admiration similar to her father's. But in more sober moments she realised that every passion taken seriously in the Western understanding of the term science necessitates a commitment to things as they appear in their molecular form, and she had also learned early on that in the world of the electron microscope there can be an almost perverse satisfaction in seeing the great toxin molecules at work. When Harper Stone was preparing his great encyclopedia on Australian spiders, *Spiders' Web Rebuild*, Annika had assisted him in the laboratory of Sydney's Macquarie University as he pursued his theory that necrosis, caused by *Lampona cylindrata*, might be due to an infection of microbacteria in the spider's mouth parts and not – as assumed – a particularly villainous toxic potpourri. They found themselves in historical surroundings. It was at Macquarie that Merline Howden and Dr David Sheummack led the first research team in the history of the country to be able to chart the complete structure of an animal toxin.

In order to isolate the critical components they began with samples of *Atrax robustus*, greatly feared in and around Sydney. In the chromatographs they separated the various components, measured the contents of the small samples by ultraviolet scanning, and in order to identify the isolated toxin protein's molecular structure they placed the individual toxins in the sequencer. Here, to their astonishment, they made the discovery that the venom from a *Missulena occatoria* was apparently stronger than the venom in *Atrax robustus*, an assumption that has since been verified. During the whole course of the work Annika spent her time amid rubber tubing, leads and centrifuges with a restrained but steadily increasing admiration for the elapids. For their venom. For their purity. The venom from *Lampona cylindrata* and many of the other Australian spiders will unrestrainedly start to destroy the skin around a bite – a wound that may or may not heal. If one survives. The American rattlesnake first removes all the layers of skin around a bite, then the venom gets going on the flesh beneath and in the worst cases lays bare parts of the bones. The same monstrous parameter of destruction is followed by the six-eyed crab spider, *Sicarius hannii*, in South Africa. But almost all the Australian snakes, through millions of years of evolution, have concentrated the toxins in different chains of swift-working nerve poisons, the toxins' Grand Cru, which in a sophisticated ensemble, almost symphonically, go on the attack, but in the case of most of them remarkably cleanly, like the vowel sounds of language, and on the whole without engendering local pain. With death in mind, it's true, but not with all-encompassing destruction as the aim.

The Australian snakes' venom operates on several different levels, but first and foremost acts on the central nervous system. It has complex mixtures of proteins and enzymes, all with different aims. They are so complicated that no one has as yet been able to produce the venoms artificially. Most of the venoms contain at least two neurotoxins, which act respectively on the pre- and post-synaptic side of the nerve cell opening. With pre-programmed cunning the various toxins work with and for each other in a manner reminiscent of intelligence on the molecular level. It was previously thought that the destruction of the red blood cells carried out by certain snake venoms was due to a specific toxin. Now we know that it is due to certain neurotoxins able to destroy muscle fibres in the body, but apart from these massacres there are very few toxins that deliberately attack the muscles. On the whole a mechanism that is attacked can be compared to a machine that on principle is fully functional – it merely lacks a starter. And for the same reason it is often seen that a snakebite in itself does not cause significant pain.

Harper Stone, who had been bitten by cobras on several occasions in India and Thailand, described his experiences to Annika as almost mystical.

'If I were a poet and not a scientist I would say that human consciousness arose when some remote ancestor was bitten by a snake,' said Harper Stone.

The moment Annika leaned over the side of the bed she saw its head coming into view at the foot. Even in that faint light she was in no doubt: it was a taipan.

'Lie still, Mike. It's on its way over to you.'

The snake glided slowly over the blanket near Annika's legs. When it reached the wall it turned round and rolled itself up in the hollow between Mike's legs. Annika guessed it to be slightly more than one and a half metres long. She followed its movements carefully with her eyes, and out of the corners of them glimpsed Mike, staring stiffly in front of him. It was obvious that her assurances to him about speaking had lost their effect. Each movement that Annika made now would immediately be registered by the snake. Beneath the blanket she could feel that Mike was sticky with sweat and paralysed with fright.

'No matter what happens, Mike, lie still. Imagine you have no legs. That this isn't happening. That you're not here in this cabin. Just lie still.'

Annika tried to orientate herself in the cabin space. She looked around for something she could put the snake in. Slowly she drew her feet towards her and cautiously moved her legs out over the edge of the bed. Then she quietly rose and walked over to switch on the light.

'It's moving,' said Mike.

'Lie still. It's got mites. It's irritable.'

They are on their way across the flat desert in the Jeep. They're in South Queensland. Beneath them the earth is a broken mosaic of red sand and clay. Soft ribbed sand dunes and scattered mulga spinneys are visible as far as the eye can see. Annika and Kookillo Dhamarandji. Alone out in the outback. To catch fierce snakes. They are searching for the systems of tunnels where they live for most of their lives. Annika is driving, and Kookillo Dhamarandji stands on the platform, from where he can spot the snakes. They are out early. About nine o'clock in the morning. At this time the snakes are replete after a night spent hunting rats in the passages, they are cold and therefore lethargic. They have come up to absorb warmth, but only for a short while. Then the heat becomes too intense, and they vanish into the tunnels again. With their narrow heads that are blue-black and glistening like inkcap toadstools. This is where Annika learns to catch snakes with her bare hands. She is seventeen.

Kookillo Dhamarandji jumps down from the vehicle and runs over the desert floor when he catches sight of the first one. Annika stops the Jeep and runs after him. The snake tries to get away, but when Annika reaches him Kookillo Dhamarandji has already caught hold of its tail. He holds it up over the ground at an angle of thirty degrees while the snake tries to wriggle free. Annika holds the sack ready, a sack rounded like a fishing landing net. She knows how to twist it when Kookillo Dhamarandji thinks he has the snake under control. Venomous snakes are helpless when they are held by the tail. But because Australian snakes are so big they can still cause problems. The smaller young ones, which are quite as venomous as the adults, are too quick. The mature ones are too big.

'Ready?' says Kookillo Dhamarandji.

And Annika has the sack ready.

He lifts the snake up away from himself, and for a brief moment it hangs loosely in the air, then Kookillo Dhamarandji lowers it carefully into the sack, which Annika fastens by twisting.

'It isn't difficult,' says Kookillo Dhamarandji, when they have caught a couple. 'You just have to be calm, resolute and focused. When you've got hold of it you mustn't take your eyes off it for a second. One mistake, and you're finished. Let it run away from you. If it turns towards you, step aside and pull its tail so it runs forward again. You must see that it runs away from you the whole time. And keep calm. If you upset it, it will attack.'

And so it is that Annika catches her first fierce snake. It had not been sanctioned by anyone. Not by John Farrow, and certainly not by her father and mother, who believed that all Annika did at the reptile park was sweep floors and feed the animals. But she had begged Kookillo Dhamarandji to teach her how to catch snakes. And he had indulged her.

Since then she had caught and milked dozens of snakes.

*   *   *

Annika found the sack, which had been thrown down or placed on the afterdeck by the narrow ladder gangway. From there the snake had made its way down to the cabin.

She opened her bag and got out her mobile telephone. She woke up Harper Stone and explained that she had decided to catch the snake on her own. He promised to come as fast as he could. Next she got out a compress bandage in case something should go wrong. Annika always had a compress bandage with her. And like the other doctors in Sydney who followed her example, she was laughed at by colleagues who thought she overreacted. But the truth was that by using Sutherland's simple method of tightly binding a compress, one could buy twenty-four hours in which the venom would not spread through the organism. This worked for all snakes, and for the funnel web spider, and Annika had often witnessed, when she and colleagues came to remove a correctly positioned compress, that only then did the venom explode into the body.

She thought for a few moments about how to get the snake away. They were not far from the hospital, but Mike's asthma was a problem. If either of them were to be bitten, it would be best if she were the one. Mike knew what he would have to do. The worst thing was that in the confined space they both risked being bitten.

Other snakes, even cobras, are civilised compared with Australian snakes. The cobra only strikes forward. The taipan strikes in all directions. Reluctantly only. But when a certain mark has been overstepped – with rabid fury. The cobra's strike radius is limited to the length of body it has raised above ground. Australian snakes are not limited by anything whatsoever. Once their anger is aroused, they hurl themselves through the air with their whole body, which makes it almost impossible to avoid being bitten.

In theory venomous snakes, unlike constrictors, cannot hoist themselves by their own bodies. But the Australian snakes do not adhere to any formal theory. As a rule they are large. Several metres long. They flog themselves into the air. And lifting them up by the tail does not guarantee anything whatsoever.

They were dealing with the worst possible conditions. The narrow cabin offered no place to which the snake could make an orderly retreat, as it would normally prefer. And if it flew into a rage the cabin certainly did not offer any room for a retreat for Mike and Annika. The problem was that as long as it lay between Mike's legs it was as hard to kill as to catch.

Annika lifted up the blanket cautiously. Immediately the snake rose with a hiss. But it made no attempt to strike out at her. From a suitable distance she cut down on all her movements so that they were very slow, and she did this for long enough to ensure that the snake felt she posed no threat, and that it had an impression of how big she was and that there would be no point whatsoever in striking. When it had understood this, what she was hoping for happened. It moved off to the right, away from Mike, over the edge of the bed and away along the floor.

Annika saw it disappear through the narrow door of the cupboard, an extension of the cabin. She fetched the boathook and a torch and shone it in through the crack. It lay curled up, and was clearly frightened. When she had assured herself that it was not so scared that it might suddenly decide to shoot out of its refuge, she ordered Mike to get out of bed.

'Jesus fucking Christ. What's going on here, Annika?'

'Take the sack. I don't know, Mike. I don't know.'

'Why don't we wait for Harper Stone?'

'Because we don't know how long it will stay where it is.'

Mike grabbed the sack and took his place beside Annika, who kneeled down and cautiously pushed the boathook in towards the snake. It did not strike but rolled aside, still in its defensive position in the shelter of the cupboard door. When she and Kookillo Dhamarandji caught snakes up near Brisbane, they gradually stopped using aids of any kind and only caught those they could seize by the tail. Snakes are fragile. Even the improved types of forked sticks with rubber nooses often inflicted unnecessary damage. But in this case Annika would gladly have hurled an anvil at the snake if she had had one handy.

She gave it another jab in the side but it still did not come out. But the third time it did. Like a missile, and only because of the cupboard door, which its body burst open as it threw itself forward, did it mistake its aim. Annika had misread it, and in a split second she was certain she had been bitten or was about to be. But then it made yet another unexpected move. Instead of attacking again it retreated to the steps up to the pantry, and when Annika saw this she was on to it like a flash. She quickly threw herself down and grabbed its tail, lifted its body off the floor and slowly began to pull the snake towards her. At once it turned to attack, and at precisely that moment Annika stepped aside, simultaneously drawing the snake back farther. The sequence was repeated, and the third time it occurred Annika was sure that if the snake hit her it would no longer be as a warning. It would inject at least half of its enormous reserve of venom.

'Now,' said Annika, and Mike stretched out the sack towards her. She pulled, let go, and seized the snake farther away from its tail while lifting it up in one movement.

'Lower down!' she shouted to Mike, who at once put the sack down at floor level.

By stretching her arms up high Annika could get enough of the snake free of the floor to lower it into the sack and still keep as much weight down near the snake's head so that it would not be able to pull itself up of its own accord. Calmly she directed the snake's head down into the sack.

'Now, lift up the sack and close it as soon as it's right down.'

And Mike closed the neck of the sack like lightning, when the last of the taipan had vanished into the darkness.

He looked at her.

'Annika, what's going on?'

Annika secured the top of the sack with a short length of rope.

'I don't know. Honestly, I just don't know.'

They were sitting in silence on the foredeck with the sack beside them, drinking a beer, when Harper Stone came on to the boat.

Michael Larsen

Annika rose and gave him a hug when he had manoeuvred his large body across the flimsy narrow gangway.

'Beer?' said Mike, already on his way to the fridge. Annika let go of Harper Stone, who nodded at Mike and then dropped down among Annika's bags on the pantry thwarts.

Sitting there, tanned, almost scorched-looking, muscular and with his thick chest hair bristling through his T-shirt, he could easily be taken for an inveterate beach bum from Bondi Beach.

Harper Stone was like a landscape. An eroded cliff that anyone living in his vicinity would never see any change in throughout his life. As far back as Annika could remember he had gone around in his sleeveless T-shirts with his long hair combed back behind his ears, stiff, unruly and slightly shiny, as if he washed it only in seawater, and striped as if bleached by the Sydney sun. Other people Annika had known, fellow students and childhood friends, and those she met later, changed to the point of unrecognisability. She knew she must have passed by schoolmates who had seemed complete strangers to her. Harper Stone was always the same.

'Ugly customer to find in your bed, eh?'

Annika smiled.

'Which of them?'

Mike pretended to give her a slap. He handed Harper Stone a Fosters. The three of them drank a toast. Mike emptied half his beer in one gulp.

'Annika can't explain it,' said Mike. 'But even here in Australia surely it would be rare to find a taipan with a predilection for the sea?'

Harpet Stone observed Annika, who said nothing, and almost as if he glimpsed a wordless message in her eyes, he put down his bottle and said:

'Sure, a jealous young girl. They can hit on anything, Mike.'

Mike stood up grinning and flung out an arm, as if in surrender, and then went below.

Harper Stone laid his dry hand on Annika's hair and affectionately let it caress her cheek.

164

'I read about Simon. How are you, love?'

They talked a bit about Simon, a bit about the coming trip, then a yawning Harper Stone pulled himself together, finished his beer and rose.

'Give my regards to everyone at Taronga,' said Annika as he picked up the sack.

'Give mine to the folks in Brisbane. Tell Farrow I'll look in on them up there soon.'

'Will do,' said Annika.

She held on to the stanchion supporting the cockpit cover as Harper Stone rocked down the gangway.

Of all the men Annika had known, Harper Stone was the only one who seemed to live by an actual mating season. Each year in early spring, not only various parts of his anatomy became erect but his whole nature, and he scrupulously skittled everything he found to aim at. Then suddenly this instinct fell into a kind of torpor and he spent the rest of the year absorbed in his research, more or less uninterested in sex. Late in summer his eyes lost their sparkle, he became harmless and uninteresting, lovable, comradely and erotically detached to the point of being irritating. To Annika, Harper Stone had always been a man one could easily fall in love with, but to no earthly use. As a friend he was second to none.

'It was sweet of you to come,' Annika said to him, as he flopped down on to the quay.

He smiled and waved to her.

Annika went back across the bathing platform. She got out her mobile and sat down on a white plastic chair. She dialled Kahn's number.

'I hope I'm not disturbing you?'

'I was asleep, Miss Niebuhr.'

'A friend of mine, Harper Stone, is on his way up to Taronga Zoo with a taipan. I think it's the one that was meant to kill Gaia Jessup.'

Mike knew his boat. He loved his boat. Which wasn't his at all, but his father's. To begin with, the maintenance of the boat was carried out by hired help, for Mike's father did not want to be more involved with it than he was with his female acquaintances. Wisely enough, he abdicated from the bridge and left maintenance and the right to command to 'the Lad' without making any change in the ownership. In return Mike was expected to invite his father and the successive lady friends on easy-going cruises in and around Sydney on selected bank holidays.

A boat's state can be assessed at a glance. Even if it is a thirty-foot-long yacht of almost eight tons. And Mike had made himself familiar with every detail of the *Endeavour* and treated it like porcelain. He and Annika took turns in keeping the logbook and in time, expertly and patiently guided by Mike, she picked up many of the boat routines, but it was Mike who had the broad unifying overview. He kept long lists, as if in a car repair shop. There were routine checks for short trips, and special long schedules for use on longer excursions with cross-sections for everything from daily housekeeping for emergency provisions, towropes and radar reflectors to oil checks, reserve filters, spark plugs and impellers. He had systemised everything once and for all with the small adjustments experience had told him were necessary to effect preparations in the best possible way. He went about them in an orderly way, working quickly, well organised as he slavishly followed his lists and the routine he had worked out over the years. He had acquired a wide knowledge of chart signs, cloud formations and deviation curves, and in this way he himself became the final decisive part of the comprehensive machinery which, trailing a small bubbling wash, passed silently out through the bights of Sydney.

It was early morning. Annika sat with her hands on the stern rail and let the wind blow in under her shades and through her hair. A sharp salty scent rose from the water they moved through with a light hissing sound, accompanied only by the quiet hum of the motor.

The *Endeavour* was built for high speed and Mike increased speed when they were out on the open water. The planing hull, with its deep soft curve, lands softly on the waves at speed, but the lack of a proper keel prevents it from counteracting drift when motoring slowly.

It is extremely ironic that each generation, and in particular this one, which has so eagerly taken up the idea of evolution, sees itself as the high point of development in the strangely implied sense of a terminal point, no small contradiction in terms.

In the teaching of physics Annika received at Sydney High, Rutherford's model of electrons in circuit around the nucleus was used. This was in the mid-seventies. She remembered the discussion about the positively charged particle, the proton, and that a particle that had no electrical charge, the neutron, was also linked with the atomic nucleus. These were the smallest constituents of life, indivisible elementary particles. At that point physicists had known for years that this was incorrect.

Outside her own narrow circle Annika often met with the view that on the whole the world was clearly understood – which seemed to her to confuse information and knowledge – and that people's greatest source of irritation was that doctors could never agree to what extent a new miracle cure was sound or was burdened with side effects, and were mildly astonished that the big television stations, which generally broadcast reports of accidents in seconds, when things really came to a head, such as after a plane had crashed into the sea, could not produce continuous, accurate coverage with a steadily increasing line of development and a satisfactory climax.

Michael Larsen

People could sit for hours, noses to the screen, being stuffed with vapid nothings, and for their part the media struggled to live up to their own fiction of reality, never able to deliver the goods, helplessly subject to the rage of the elements.

The history of humanity resembles that of the individual. Every human being reckons on an existential refuge. Newton's understanding of the world was dependent on a constant, an imaginary grid stretched out over the whole universe, from which everything could be measured. This grew into the fixed star system, which was founded merely on distant stars that were not so unmoving as Newton had wished. For the ordinary person it may be education, a lover, a wife, a husband, a child, a career that makes up the bearings along the route. With an underlying dream that then things will fall into place and everything come to rest. And sometimes the aim can seem so liberatingly close, within reach, but just as the outlines of a fixed structure are glimpsed, the unity is atomised, and the person sees laboriously collected components and doggedly amassed nuts and bolts turn into a belt of bolts and screws in a sirocco that never slackens.

It has never been otherwise. The trail of inadequate systems and defective interpretive models in the history of man is endless. When the atom theory had been generally accepted by the physicists, which occurred at the turn of the century, the same physicists were of the opinion that on the whole everything was now understood. But everything moves. Everything that was not, like Simon, dead, moves. The earth, which once in other parameters of understanding lay at the centre of everything, rushes along at about thirty kilometres a second, rotating obliquely around its own axis, in its elliptic course around the sun, which itself rushes along around the centre of the Milky Way at about 250 kilometres a second, and the Milky Way, which itself moves with its whole shining belt at an unknown speed in the local supermultitude, which again moves in relation to the average distribution of matter in the universe.

She turned and looked up at Mike. The skipper. Enthroned up there on his flybridge. It might well be that it is quantum mechanics which makes the whole thing possible, from the radio receiver to the engine in the bowels of the boat, but Annika enjoyed seeing him in operation. It pleased her to watch people doing what they were good at. Seeing their capabilities unfold. Watching people practising their craft. Reductionism can be beautiful if it does not also attempt to make the whole into a single part. Or the individual parts into a whole. Mike did not stand outside, observing this system. He was a part of it. He handled this boat as he dealt with a patient in the operating theatre. He practised his craft. Diligently prepared and with respect. And if anyone should ever be inspired to unscrew her lid she would demand that only Mike should be allowed to rummage about inside her. Mike did not approach the open sea in arrogance. He did not pretend to know every choppy wave in this ocean. He did not confuse bearings with axiomatic truths. Nor half-truths with truths.

She stood behind him on the bridge with her arms around his middle and her face against his back. The Manly ferry crossed in front of them, the first sailing boats met the wind, and as they passed Grotto Point they saw de Fortier's beautiful gaff-rig putting out from the point at Dobroyd.

They had not mentioned the night's drama.

The first colour to disappear is red. After five metres. Farther down, at a depth of fifteen metres, orange goes, another three metres and yellow no longer exists, sixty metres down there are no more greens, and at seventy-five metres depth, which Annika had never been down to, blue vanishes. Newton thought the speed of light was unchanged under water. It is not. Nothing is unchanged under water. A dive is like a stepped unreeling of reality.

It was Mike who had taught Annika to dive. While he was studying he worked at Mike Ball Dive Expeditions, and when he finally persuaded Annika to go out with him she received meticulous instruction, and not in Australia. In spite of living in a country with a two-thousand-kilometre-long reef he suggested to Annika that they should take a holiday together in the Maldives. At that time they had known each other for only a year, and Annika was filled with reservations at the idea because she felt it smacked overmuch of sweet music and solitary sunsets, and moreover she baulked at the thought of travelling so far to reach something they had on their doorstep. 'Believe me. You won't regret it. There's nothing like an atoll reef,' said Mike. That was true, and he was right. His tactics worked, in the way a nervous child can be introduced to the sea for the first time; you can be happy splashing about in a sheltered little pool near the sea. The atoll was like that. They needed only to go into the water a few metres before the reef enclosed them with only a few openings into small labyrinthine paths out, which you could follow as your courage increased. For almost two weeks they lay there, wearing masks, snorkels, flippers and white T-shirts to shield them from the sun that they completely forgot in their entrancement at the explosion of colour beneath them. Emperor fish with quivering striped bodies and black Zorro masks, zebra-striped picasso fish with prominent jaws and swelling yellow lips and yellow doctor fish splashing in the tidal currents around the tall staghorn corals raising their antlers from the sandy bed to the surface. When they returned to the surface now and then to exchange experiences, and Mike convincingly put names to the shoals of fish, they saw flying fish playing ducks-and-drakes on the surface of the lagoon. Then they dived again, down to a rain of red sea goldies over sea-fans like clumps of elder, shoals of white-breasted doctor fish with blue bodies and yellow manes drifting over the flat plate corals of the seabed, and parrot fish and morays shooting up from the sand like exclamation marks.

On the Maldives too they continued the erotic relationship they had begun a short time earlier, for even if the long sun-drenched days underwater competed hard with the attraction they felt for each other, in the evenings and night after night they were, after all, two people sharing temporary quarters in a cabin on more or less a desert island. Everything came together on the island, and even if Annika might have felt a momentary doubt about the sudden intensity that had entered the relationship, she had nothing but gratitude for Mike, because he had opened her eyes to a world she had really known only from books and films. As she had foreseen, their intimacy was normalised to a more moderate degree when they were back home, and apart from one or two slight disagreements they had succeeded on the whole in maintaining a hard-won equilibrium between friendship and love. The only thing that did not undergo a marked change was Annika's relationship with the sea, and it was not long before she enrolled with Moby Dive, from where she obtained her final diving certificate later in the year.

They lay at anchor thirty nautical miles from Brisbane. It was late afternoon, Port Macquarie was behind them, they had filled up and shopped, and then at last had caught up with some sleep. After a night on the boat they would be able to make Brisbane to the north in a couple of hours.

They were on deck going through the usual checks. Seeing that the buoyancy compensating jackets and bottles were in place, that the suits were in working order, the lead-shot belts in the right position, that the air passages functioned, the hoses were not entangled, that there was plenty of air for the dive.

Mike was the one who insisted on going into the water. He wanted to test the equipment so that they could make adjustments in Brisbane should it be necessary.

The very proximity of Brisbane had filled Annika with an unpleasant sense of uneasiness, and she did not feel much like diving. She looked at Mike, and her bad conscience over exposing him to danger returned. Over not telling him what she was really about to do in Brisbane. She tried to explain to herself that it would merely make the situation more dangerous if he were aware of it, and stubbornly attempted to convince herself that Brisbane had nothing to do with the problem but rather was concerned with the solution. She would tell him all about it later. When she herself knew more of what was going on.

When they jumped from the platform at the stern Annika's thoughts were still somewhere else, but when she struck the surface and received a blow from the bottle on her neck because she had forgotten to hold down the BC jacket, things went better as she realised how long it was since she had been diving, and how good it can be for the soul to have everything else shut out.

Earlier, before she had come to know Mike, the sea had always been a means of cooling down when you lay basking in the sun at Bondi or Manly or down at Whale Beach. And if she was cautious about acquiring a more physical knowledge of the sea and the deep, it was because she was all too knowledgeable clinically about the things that could go wrong, and the dangers posed by the sea.

People in Sydney lived in happy ignorance of the powerful toxins of Australian sea creatures, which can kill a human being in a few moments.

Along the city beaches they had grown used to false security from the helicopter patrols ceaselessly on the watch for sharks, and although there was a great deal more to worry about than sharks, there were still many people who didn't bother to keep inside the areas of patrolled bathing beaches. Once, when Annika worked at Sydney Hospital as a house physician, a young man was brought in who had been harpooned by a sting-ray during a snorkel trip off Coogee Beach; another time a ten-year-old boy who had been collecting old cans on the beach unfortunately thought that the insignificant little octopus lying in a rusty tin was cute. Only four minutes passed from the time it pierced his hand with its parrot-like beak until he was completely paralysed, and he survived only thanks to an alert lifeguard on his way home from work who saw him floundering about at the edge of the beach. Most octopus bites, in any case rare, may well be painful but are not dangerous. Only the Australian blue-ringed octopus, *Hapalochlaena maculosa*, has developed the TTX poison which potentially makes it one of the worst things you can touch in the sea. It is of course mostly of academic interest whether a victim dies of suffocation or drowns because all the muscles in the body cease to function in a few minutes, but although the first death to be registered took place in 1954 Annika, like most zoologists and biologists, did not doubt that this fatality must have had precedents. Tetrodotoxin, which is closely studied by neurologists, is a cunning poison which nullifies the electrical impulses along the nerve paths in a few moments; after a day or two the venom vanishes, leaving no trace that can be discovered in a post-mortem. But in contrast to the globe-fish, whose venom is in its tissue and other places, it is only a bite, often not noticed, from the octopus which releases venom. Annika and Mike often saw it when they were diving off the cliffs at Camp Cove just at the entrance to Sydney Harbour. At rest it is almost as hard to distinguish from its surroundings as the stonefish, but if you approach it too closely it displays its iridescent alarm system of blue siphons and rings, which shine brightly on its body and arms. It is the equivalent to the snake's hiss of warning and the rebuff of a woman.

Of all Australian sea creatures one is feared above all the rest. It floats through the water like a ghost with its transparent cloak around it. It has no brain, no heart, no vascular system, it consists almost entirely of the element it floats through, water, and yet it stores up one of the most powerful poisons in this world. *Gaywarr*, as Kookillo Dhamarandji called it – the box jellyfish. *Chironex fleckeri*.

Several people die every year in appalling agony on the northern coasts when they are tangled up in its several-metre-long threads, equipped with thousands of millions of small torpedoes. If you try to remove the threads, more poison is fired off. In Australia more people have died from box jellyfish poisoning in this century than from the sum total of shark and crocodile attacks. Simon had once told her that no white person had given much thought to this creature until Japan was involved in World War Two, and the Australians started to train their soldiers in counter-attack up in the Northern Territory and northern Queensland. Some died, and several hundred were knocked out of the running when something or other they did not recognise attacked them underwater and in a few minutes paralysed and disfigured them and inflicted terrible pain.

Annika and other doctors and various museum directors had from time to time pleaded for more detailed information on the dangers posed by many Australian creatures to be made available to tourists, who unsuspectingly threw themselves into the waves or out into the bush. It is not difficult to sell a country like Australia. The climate and kilometres of beaches make large parts of it a tropical dream. Which it is. But it is also a continent that gives houseroom to the world's most venomous creatures, and there is no reason to conceal the fact. Harper Stone and his colleagues at the Northern Territory Museum often quoted the example of the young American photographer's model who was eaten by a crocodile in a river in Western Australia in the mid-eighties. This didn't drive the tourists away, as had been feared, although the episode attracted a good deal of attention. On the contrary, there was a marked boom in visits by American tourists, who obviously couldn't get enough spectacular experience. But it was hard to get the argument through to the authorities. Just before the Easter holiday the Environment Ministry sent out a notice to the citizens of Sydney warning that forty different species of poisonous snakes were about to prepare for the coming winter by hoarding food, so the greatest caution should be practised not only in the bush but also in suburban gardens. The string of alarm calls from worried citizens to the National Parks and Wildlife was fairly constant, so the experts had to go and remove diamond pythons from people's trees in the north and south and black and brown snakes in the western districts of Sydney, but no co-ordinated official warnings were issued to tourists about snakes, spiders or jellyfish. Annika's sister kept her informed about the tourist catalogues and inadequate guides that unfortunately did not pass on the simple guidelines for travel around the country and how to cope in the bush, or how to deal with stings and bites if attacked.

Annika felt better under water. In the sea. As so often before she assumed this was because all the senses except sight were put out of action one by one the moment you turned round on the surface and dived.

With the aid of sonar, whales can communicate through the water for over seven hundred kilometres. In principle there is nothing mysterious about this, as water is about eight hundred times denser than air. But to people who calculate the locality of a sound source by reckoning the time lapse taken by the sound to travel from one ear to the other, it actually means that it is impossible to determine from where underwater sound waves emanate.

Mike was a responsible diver, with more experience than Annika had. But because of his asthma she was the one who kept a watchful eye on him. Today the roles were reversed. Although the anchor chain showed that the current was strong, they were not using a partner line, so Annika kept close to Mike while he marked out the route. As if he sensed all was not well with her, he did not go more than fifteen metres down, and turned round frequently to signal that if she wanted to go up, they would. She signalled back that everything was fine.

They went up after half an hour.

On the way to the surface they made the usual safety stop at five metres depth. For three minutes they stayed face to face, keeping an eye on each other's eyes; they checked the depth recorder and watched the time. Then they went up.

They lay on the surface for a while before swimming over to the boat. Mike looked at her enquiringly.

'You seemed a bit far away.'

'There's something I want to show you.'

Annika wore only a white towelling robe when she opened the zips of her bag and took out the scans. She picked out the drawing and put it in the bottom of the bag with the revolver. She straightened the T-shirts, then zipped up the bag and closed the cupboard door.

Mike spread the scans out in front of him on the small table in the pantry. He put on his reading glasses and looked from one to the other. Picked each of them up, looked at them close to and put them on the table again.

'We don't know anything?'

'Nothing.'

'Man, woman, young, old?'

'Nothing.'

'"MJ",' he said, studying one of the sheets closely. 'Is it a name?'

'Probably. I don't know,' said Annika.

He shrugged his shoulders resignedly, then took a ballpoint pen out of his pocket and started to point.

'I can only say what I feel it resembles. And it resembles schizophrenia. Look at the references to the ventricles. For the hippocampus. The limbic system has shrunk, the ventricles grown larger. Typical of schizophrenia. A small hippocampus. Often seen in schizophrenics.'

'But' – Annika took one of the A4 sheets and turned it round – 'in principle it could well be a completely normal brain we're looking at?'

'But why would anyone scan a completely normal person? You know what a PET scan costs. Besides, if you look closer, there are arrows pointing to both the frontal lobe and the basal ganglia.'

He turned the papers, so she could see them correctly. He put one hand on the paper, pointed with his pen.

'We know that in schizophrenics there is reduced activity in the foremost part of the frontal lobe. The dopamine is the central thing. Signalling material. Schizophrenics get an explosion of messages. A hundred television channels working simultaneously. A thousand. With the indicators we have here my guess would be that we are looking at a schizophrenic person.'

'And we can't get any closer?'

'I can give you at least ten theories on what triggers off schizophrenia, but it wouldn't make either of us much wiser. Some are very imaginative, not to say rambling. Some claim to have proved that life in a big city can trigger schizophrenia. You've got no idea at all of the context of this?'

Annika looked at him. But she decided to say as little as possible. If she mentioned the drawing and went on to enlarge on the initials, if they were initials, it wouldn't be long before she was talking about Simon's contact with a man called Mark Johnson, who lived in Brisbane and had once worked for ASIO, and unfortunately met his end when he and his family were squashed under an articulated lorry.

'There was the drawing. And Simon's quote. But I can't find out what he meant by that.'

'What is the drawing of?'

'It's just . . . a line drawing. But it's the quotation I'm thinking of.'

'I'm not with you.'

'I can't see whether he means something I have seen, or something this person has seen.'

'What might you have seen?'

'You know I sometimes read reports for him. Looking for errors. Evaluating neuropsychological test results. Banal things. Checking measurements. Sight, hearing and so on. But I can't exclude the possibility that I may have seen some more sensitive information and just didn't realise it.'

She saw that Mike was looking uncomfortable. She laid her hand on his arm, but he rose and went over to the small fridge.

'That explains the snake,' he said, crossing his arms and his legs and leaning against the fridge. 'Are we running away? From the intelligence service?'

Annika smiled. She stood up and went over to him. She took hold of him, squeezed herself under his arms and kissed his throat.

'That's why you're so distant? You're thinking about it all the time, aren't you? Who killed Simon. But what if he did take his own life, as the police say?'

'Hmm. Do you really want to know what I'm thinking about?' said Annika, pressing herself against him. She lifted off his glasses, put them on the table and kissed him. She felt his hands creep down her back, and how he carefully lifted up her wrap and put his hands on her buttocks. When he gripped them and she could feel a hard bulge between her legs, she pulled away and looked at him.

'I'm just going to have a shower.'

'Annika, we . . .'

She turned and hushed him.

'We won't talk about it any more. I'm sorry I brought it up. Not another word about Simon.'

If Annika felt bad as she took her shower she felt even worse when she left the cabin again.

Just two candles were alight on the small table in the galley and one beside the stove, where Mike was prodding at the frying pan where a little blue lake of flames from the Cognac was sizzling. He had laid the table with napkins and crystal glasses, and a bottle of wine stood in a bucket of ice.

Annika sat down at the table in her bathrobe, but at the sight of the table and the bowl of fresh fruit quite forgot to rub her hair dry.

She picked up the wine bottle and read the label. A white Sauvignon from Brown Brothers of Milawa. She came up behind Mike and stretched to look over his shoulder.

'What are we having?'

'Tasmanian lobsters. Flambéd with brandy and stuffed with apples.' He stirred the small saucepan on the other burner, in which was a little of the lobster eggs with chopped garlic, basil, tomato and cream. 'But we can put something in the micro if you'd rather . . .'

She slapped him affectionately and went over to the table again.

'I'm speechless. I hadn't realised I should have brought an evening dress.'

'There are no rules about dress in my establishment,' said Mike with a smile.

'Good,' said Annika, as she unfastened her robe and let it slide off. It fell around her feet and she stepped out of it and sat down at the table.

When he turned and glanced at her, she crossed her legs and leaned in over the table.

'What are you up to, Mike?'

'I just thought you needed a bit of spoiling. Do help yourself to wine, won't you?'

Annika poured herself a glass.

'What about you?'

'Yes, please,' he said.

She poured him a glass and went to sit near him. She leaned her head against his back.

'What'll Kim Duncan have to say about this?'

He turned with his glass in his hand and smiled.

'Who?'

Loners, who either go out to eat or hastily swallow a dull sandwich, are suckers when someone suddenly displays great culinary art and serves up a feast in the grand style. If you also have a guilty conscience about the happy host, you're in a very tight corner. And if you are open to romance, you're defenceless.

When Annika looked back on the loves of her life she could not recall one of them that had not been unhappy. In a way it was actually that which defined being in love for her, at one and the same time an unreasonably insupportable and wonderful condition of pain, which, when you were young and had the strength for it, was extended and kept artificially alive far beyond its proper survival date, and which, the older you became, needed to be harpooned at an early date to prevent the worst miseries.

As Annika gradually matured she realised that the obsession that drew her into new relationships was not a special case but a fundamental aspect of her personality, which unfolded with precisely the same force each time she threw herself head over heels into a new unhappy and binding love affair which, regardless of whether she wanted it or not, occurred about every other year. She tried to shield herself as well as she could. She tried to direct, plan and control as much as possible, for it was a hopeless prospect. Annika found the idea of twosomeness, of love, infinitely wonderful, but not, at least in her own case, durable. The only permanent love affair she knew was a passion for the very idea of love.

Annika knew in her heart that she had to go and see Kate Carpenter, but as she sat there opposite Mike she was confused all the same about the emotions she felt swirling around inside her. In her life she had grown so accustomed to pursuing trails and questions that it had become completely natural to the way she operated never to doubt the rightness of the impulses and inclinations that drove her. Only when they sat there eating and chatting did it strike her that no one was demanding of her that she should do anything at all in connection with Simon's death. No one had ordered her to visit specific persons or ask questions of anyone. She could cut out Brisbane, go to the reef with Mike, write up her report and send it to Colombo, and not a soul would object. But that was not her way. She knew that. And after Kahn's hint and the phone call to her car it had become clear to her that she herself was involved in a way she did not understand. She could not just leave it now. She had to know.

She sat studying Mike in the light of the candles. Perhaps it was the closeness of Brisbane which had triggered these strange reservations and considerations. Brisbane was like a crossroads. A place that could draw them together or in opposite directions.

Annika lifted her glass.

'Tell me about Kim Duncan,' she said. 'What *is* going on between you?'

Mike sat regarding her. As if to read the answer she wanted to hear. Or the answer she could stand. Then he bent his head and smiled.

'Kim Duncan . . . Kim Duncan wants children.'

Annika kept a mouthful of wine in her mouth before swallowing. 'I see,' she said.

She pushed herself away from him a little and picked up her robe, put it on and patted the pocket for her cigarettes. When she had lit one she took care not to blow smoke over Mike.

'And what does Mike Lewis want?'

'Mike Lewis,' he said, picking up the bottle and pouring them both wine, 'Mike Lewis wants children too . . .'

'Well, then, everybody's happy.'

'With you.'

Annika picked up her glass, drained it and held it out to Mike, who poured again. She felt sure she was not herself. Definitely not herself. Normally with this kind of conversation she shuddered, as you do when someone draws a piece of chalk down a blackboard. Now instead she felt a special warmth spread through her.

Annika was fond of children. But for all the wrong reasons. She could not comprehend the panic that had seized the friends in her circle. Reluctant sweethearts were cast off posthaste, and moments later stomachs grew big and happiness was apparently unlimited. Dubious donors were summoned to the most desperate, others set up relationships that from the start were doomed to end in divorce and fatherless infants.

Annika had been present at a family gathering when her nephew, Tobias, took his first faltering steps. They all clapped until he grabbed at a table and with a big smile plumped down on his nappy-padded behind. It was a lasting memory for the family. But to Annika it turned into a whole story. An internal vision of an ancient history, and Tobias became an object. Something that could be studied. Brought out and turned around again and again. She had looked at her father, but had had no idea what he was thinking. Whether he had merely felt a tug of pride in his grandfatherly role, or if he too had been engaged in exploding little Tobias in an internal accelerator. Annika consoled herself with the thought that she was not crazy. It was just that her head functioned differently. Neither worse nor better. Just differently.

To Annika, Tobias's first bipedal steps became an illustration of the greatest anatomical feat in developmental history. Millions of years of evolutionary history gathered into one moment of overwhelming suddenness. The human model, created only a million years ago, perhaps, the total reconfiguration with forward-transposed *foramen magnum*, with the S-shape of the back, short pelvis, strong *gluteus maximus*, long legs instead of short, short arms instead of long, and precision grip. Created from the first hominid tribes, long before *Homo erectus*, long before the expansion of the brain.

To Annika the unsteady steps were also symbolic. The child's first steps are the most beautiful, when the stride has become more than a mere stagger and less than a distance between two places to sit down. When children walk because they can, there is nothing they dislike more than being helped with this skill. For adults life becomes a lasting hunt for something to hold on to, support themselves by, cling to. A faith, a partner or a stimulus.

Annika wanted to live in her solitude until she was not merely obeying a convention by sharing her life with someone else; she wanted to go through this world alone, if that was how it turned out. She wanted to understand the world. To falter, walk, stand and fall, stumble, totter, sway, stand and fall. But move along the whole time. Forward. Even if it was with a child's stagger.

She looked at Mike. Mike would be a good father. She looked at the table, his setting. The dishes, the candles, the napkins he had brought with him specially for this meal.

She had considered it once. It was with Simon. And it had happened some years earlier. She had had the feeling in her body. The desire. But something held her back. A reservation due to a reservation in Simon. It was obvious that even though he might decide to begin a relationship with her or someone else, he would never leave June and their little family. Annika saw no future in it. Perhaps she had never felt it strongly enough, or else in reality Simon had been useful to her in that he did not stand between her and the world, but quite simply shielded her from the world and its conventions. He existed. As a theoretical possibility. A distant dream.

Annika liked Simon's firmness. And it had never occurred to her to challenge it in earnest. Now she looked at Mike across the table. And she could almost fall in love with the resolution that was an extension of Mike's visions for them both. For Mike there was one. And she was that one. It was romance, and Annika understood it. He did not need to say anything; his table, his arrangement, had said it all. But, as she knew, it was a romance that was impossible to live with. Mostly because you knew that at some point you would have to live without it.

'You know how I am, Mike.'

'I also know how it would be for you.'

Annika felt herself reddening and instinctively shook herself inside her robe.

'Are you cold?' he asked.

She shook her head, but inwardly felt herself suddenly relegated to puberty and the first nervous trysts, and as she stretched out her hand for her glass to have something to hold on to, she felt it shake like a stupid girl's.

'More wine?' said Mike, reaching for the bottle. But Annika placed her hand over the glass.

'You don't know me well enough.'

'For how many years do I have to know you to know you well enough?'

'I don't know you.'

'I don't know our child.'

'You're splitting hairs.'

'I only mean . . .'

'I promised not to talk about Simon any more. Now we won't talk any more about children.'

Annika couldn't make out what was happening to her. Mike was an old friend, and if there was one thing she could agree on with her women colleagues it was that old sweethearts don't suddenly sweep your feet from under you. If there had been anything, it had been there the whole time, and what has been but is no longer there will never come again.

Perhaps it was because Mike, in spite of everything, including Kim Duncan, was an ally in solitude. An institution that Annika would always and forever fight for, but which she had grown tired of defending against all those who had known it only as a temporary crisis in their lives.

No one like the solitary has to both explain and defend their deviant behaviour while at the same time, and in a strange way, having to sanction the blessings of coupledom. Serve up hair-raising descriptions of the dizzy abysses of solitude, as if only a singularly indefinable fear in certain situations can assure the rushing couples that it is better to stay put than hurl yourself out into the unknown.

When Mike came to her she was thinking that the most beautiful things in this world are black snakes who mate in a riverbed. These mortally dangerous creatures, winding and twining themselves as gracefully and gently as the double spiral of DNA. Like pennants. Or the soft flight of streamers through the air.

In her mind Annika turned a page in an old book on human anatomy. She placed her hands on his buttocks. Circled a finger around the anus. Massaged the entrance. She remembered her intern time, when shocked friends had consulted her because they were afraid their sweethearts were bisexual. She did not always immediately share her knowledge with them. Now and then she put her hands to her face just for fun and told them she herself had had a suspicion for a long time.

The area between the anus and the scrotum is particularly sensitive. Pressure here midway between scrotum and anus will often produce a quicker erection, and stimulus here often produces as much pleasure as it has on the sexual organ itself. It is presumably due to the effect of deep-sited nerve ends, since the mucous membranes in the anus are not specially sensitive.

When Annika heard Mike approaching his climax she inserted the top of her finger into him, but when he came she hardly felt it. Nothing but a sinking movement of the ring of muscles around her finger.

The Australian humpback whales, which you can encounter around Brisbane at the right time of year if you are lucky, are more numerous than biologists had feared for years. They had counted pods of them on their way from cold Antarctica to the tropical ocean of the Great Barrier Reef. They had no alternative. But it was the wrong method, for it has been shown that many of the sexually immature females remain in the Antarctic so as not to run unnecessary risks. Many biologists were also sceptical about the idea of there being white humpbacks, although according to Mike the fishermen of Hervey Bay had long known they were there. Earlier biologists had also believed that the deep sea, which is almost uninvestigated, was lifeless and deserted, right up until Robert D. Ballard found the metre-long tube worms and off Mexico the underwater vents that emit sulphur-rich water with temperatures of up to 350 degrees, and are thereby an authentic indication of the origin of all life on earth. Annika was always surprised at how most journalists managed to slip a negative role even into articles where they were otherwise clearly attempting to convey the joys of visiting a piece of unspoilt nature. They always used phrases like 'the last untouched piece of nature', 'nature's last unspoilt bastion', or 'the last unexplored spot'. Harper Stone thought it was because these people probably spent their whole lives in a city and so did not imagine there was more than a couple of hectares of rainforest left. And precisely the hectares they happened to have seen. That when they wrote about overpopulation they apparently did not allow themselves to be distracted by the fact that by far the greater part of the globe is unpopulated. In such a world, he thought, it is easy to be unaware that species we have long believed to be extinct still exist, that large new mammals are still being discovered, that great trackless rainforests still stand where no human foot has trod, and that you do not need to go very deep in the ocean to find a universe of strange fish, jellyfish and gigantic octopus that are hardly known to man.

But it was neither whales nor self-illuminating deep-sea fish which had accompanied the boat through the confusion of small islands off Brisbane River, but dolphins. They had swum beside the boat from Peel Island and only left it when Mike turned in towards King Island.

Annika put the kettle on for coffee, and while it boiled listened to the shipping forecast and wrote up the logbook sitting at the pantry table. She noted the hPc values on the barometer and added signs and numbers in the columns for wind, weather and sea conditions, and when she reached the small column for the voyage, bit the end of her ballpoint pen before drawing a little heart.

She closed the logbook and placed it on the coastal chart of Brisbane that Mike had been using. She went to get the sunblock out of the medicine chest and, as she had it open, checked it. As far as she could see, nothing was lacking. There were plasters, sterile gauze, cotton wool and elastic bandages. There were Sepan tablets, and she made sure they were within the date limit, because neither of them was prone to seasickness. There were painkillers, vinegar and hydrocortisone, immodium and chlorohexidin for disinfection. Everything that should be there was in place, and at the back of her mind Annika was well aware that she was merely hoping to find something missing so that she could buy a kind of indulgence by using her little excursion in Brisbane to get hold of something useful for both of them.

She poured the boiling water over the coffee powder in two mugs. While the steam was settling she sat down and covered herself all over with sunblock. Then she carried the mugs up the hatchway and joined Mike, who was sitting on the bridge at the helm.

Along the coast towards Wynnum the harbour area could be

187

made out with cold stores and terminals, gantries and dry docks. A big container ship right in front of them was crossing the wake of the Cat o' Nine Tails catamaran making for St Helena Island laden with tourists.

When you have grown up knowing that it gets colder when you travel north, it is hard to get used to Australia, where you meet steadily higher temperatures and humidity the further north you get. But although the sunshine in Brisbane was if possible even fiercer than in Sydney, the south-east trade winds blow harder in Brisbane and thus equalise the temperature difference a little. It is this dry trade wind, which blows most of the summer, that makes the beaches at all bearable to stay on, and it is the same trade wind that meets the powerful thermal low pressure of the interior of Australia and forces the temperature up to over forty-five degrees.

When they had motored upriver for a good half-hour after entering the mouth, Brisbane began to rise in a rainforest of civilisation. Low buildings and smaller tower blocks rose like reflected prints in the skyscrapers, shining in their glass coverings on the sunny side, and the impressive bridges threw big shadows over them when they passed underneath. When the Edward Street ferry and the Botanical Gardens came into sight, Annika went below.

She sat for a while picking at the little ankle chain of raw places her new R.M. Williams boots had left on both legs. It was really self-torture, and actually far too hot to wear them, but their advantage was that the laminated stiffening of the toes and the internal steel screws and stitching in brass thread would have a greater effect than a pair of sandals should she have occasion to kick anyone. Carefully she put her feet into them and pulled the leather straps. She found the article from the *Brisbane Courier-Mail* and put it in her pocket. She left the scans where they were. Then she glanced up to the pantry before getting out the revolver, knocked out the magazine and put it in place again. She put on a loose-fitting T-shirt, fixed the revolver firmly in the lining of her trousers, then put on a thin canvas jacket and fastened the belt.

* * *

Annika kissed Mike goodbye on the esplanade and said she would be back some time in the evening. Then she hailed a taxi and rode a few hundred metres before asking the driver to stop at the roadside, and paying him.

She left the taxi and walked along the streets of Paddington until she reached a telephone kiosk near Kate Carpenter's apartment. When Kate Carpenter answered, Annika apologised – without introducing herself – and said she had called the wrong number.

Outside the kiosk she smoked a cigarette, while from behind her sunglasses she kept an eye on the stairway. When she had waited for fifteen minutes she went up and rang the bell.

'Niebuhr? Are you the snake lady?'

Annika smiled at the intercom with a certain satisfaction.

'For a moment I was afraid you would say you knew my father.'

'In a way, love, that was what I meant. There was an article on him in *Women's Weekly*. He talked of you. What can I do for you?'

'Talk to me. About Simon Rees.'

There was a short pause, then Kate Carpenter replied.

'Just come up.'

She let Annika in, and Annika walked up the three floors to where Kate Carpenter waited for her in the open doorway with a friendly smile.

Every time Annika saw a woman smoker who was older than herself she remembered she should never have started, although she did not smoke a great deal. Cigarettes are sexist. Women get more wrinkles than men from smoking. And even if they stop they will always, in comparison with women of their own age, look considerably older than men who quit tobacco.

Kate Carpenter looked to be about sixty. But she could also be in her early fifties. It was hard to tell. She was a head shorter than Annika, and, although the rest of her stature was quite slim, her face had those slightly pendulous, grey and furrowed cheeks that made you think of elephant skin. As she stood in the doorway with moist lips, a glass of white wine in one hand and a little stump of a filterless Gauloise in the other, Annika had the impression that not only did she look older than she was but she also passed herself off as more sober than she was. Engaged as she was with glass and cigarette, she merely stepped aside with a welcoming smile so Annika could go in.

She closed the door behind them.

'I should love to talk to you. But probably about anything except what you have come to talk about.'

Annika smiled at her.

'Which means?'

'Just call it intuition, love. But we can also say that I read about Simon Rees's death in the papers. I've been expecting someone to turn up some time.'

'Why?'

With screwed-up eyes, as if it required great concentration, she sucked the last nicotine out of the short stub that glowed between her fingers, then with a thick underlip sent a quick cloud of smoke up past her face and stubbed the cigarette out in an ashtray on a table in the hall.

'That's what I don't want to talk about.'

Then she took Annika into the apartment.

'Come inside, love.'

She had a clear, sharp and penetrating voice, slightly hoarse, but she cleared it at regular intervals with a brief bout of coughing. It was of the very unfeminine kind that women who constantly smoke acquire, which did not seem to worry her in the least. When she drew breath deeply it sounded as if someone inside her was whistling.

There are occasional smokers, there are smokers, there are chain-smokers, and then there are passive smokers. Judging from the smoke-filled rooms, Kate Carpenter belonged to all four categories. And the whole flat was permeated, despite open windows and a fan in the ceiling, with a vague odour of wet woollen socks. Ambulance paramedics know the phenomenon from being called out to apartments where corpses have putrefied. A smell of dead bodies hangs over everything and is extremely difficult to eliminate. It is the same with tobacco smoke. No matter how much airing is done, or how often ashtrays are emptied, some stays. But it didn't worry Annika, who followed Kate Carpenter into the living room and sat where Kate indicated on a chair beside a desk in a work corner looking on to a back yard. For she smoked herself and was used to people around her smoking, and in hospital some doctors considered someone exceptionally high-principled if nicotine was the only stimulant they surrendered to.

'Why don't you want to talk about it?'

Kate smiled at her.

'Simon Rees asked that question too, love. Now he is dead. Would you like a glass of wine?'

'Did Simon call you?'

Kate did not reply. She rose, took out a glass from a display cabinet and put it in front of Annika.

Annika didn't feel like wine but decided it would be a good investment. While drug addicts at an early phase of their habit become paranoid about guarding their stuff, alcoholics seem to the last to think that others somehow sanction their misuse by sharing in it.

'I never understood that call from Simon Rees. I mean: why ask me when he knew himself?'

'What did he know, Miss Carpenter?'

She sent Annika an enquiring glance but still did not reply to her question. Without, it seemed, so much as thinking about it. Perhaps without having caught the question at all. She was concentrating on her own thoughts. And they concerned Annika.

'I have respect for women who can handle snakes. But I wonder what makes a young woman like you interested in snakes. Doesn't it scare the men away? I wonder, is it on account of your father?'

'In spite of my father, Miss Carpenter.'

'That's how you like to look at it.'

'That's how I see it.'

191

Michael Larsen

'Snakes are mentioned thirty-five times in the Bible. Did you know that? In St Mark's Gospel. After the Resurrection. Jesus says that those who believe in him will be able to "take up serpents".'

Annika smiled and shook her head.

'I'm not a believer.'

'That's because you are young.'

In the seventeenth century, James Ussher, Archbishop of Armagh in Northern Ireland, after a close study of the Bible, calculated that the world was created about 23 October, 4004 BC. Annika had learned from her father that in any discussion of possible life on other planets in or outside our solar system, American scientists still had to assure worried orthodox politicians that this discussion did not conflict with the fact that the universe is not older than six thousand years. Harper Stone had told her that one out of eight Australian biology students believes implicitly in the creation version of the Bible when they begin their studies.

Half of humanity is ignorant of the fact that the earth takes 365 days to revolve once around the sun. We live in a bizarre mixture of high-technological mechanical culture and highly developed medievalism, not only in the world as a whole but even in the educated world's own circles.

Ussher could believe in his calculation because he was unaware of the concept of 'deep time'. We first caught a glimpse of deep time at the end of the last century with the discovery of fossilised lizards. To a child and the uneducated, a hundred years ago feels like the remote past. To the educated it feels like a millimetre. When Harper Stone and other palaeontologists rest their eyes on a lump of amber that has encapsulated an insect, a leaf or a fungus, which despite existing for millions of years still resembles those we can find today, what they see is deep time. And if it were not for the fact that millions of years are nothing compared to the vast scale of deep time, which is reckoned in billions of years, the acceptance of a biblical character's involvement in the creation of species would give them the shivers. Simon was in agreement with Harper Stone that it is the concept of deep time that is the cause of well-informed theories of the universe existing happily alongside a far greater weight of intellectual illiteracy. Deep time is new to the human being. And, as with all new discoveries, it takes a long time for this picture of the world to settle, to penetrate all the layers of consciousness that make up a world populated by human beings. The Big Bang was not a huge explosion, since an explosion presupposes surroundings to explode in, the stars are not massive, as in the simplicity of her childhood Annika had believed, but clouds of gas and dust, and the clouds in the sky are not firm and soft, as she had felt they were as a little child in the Blue Mountains when her father asserted that they were standing in them even though they couldn't be seen.

It appears that there are two characteristics that can develop in the life of a human being. Either delight in or fear of what is seemingly futile. Annika had never had any use for the professed miracles of religion, for the world as it was in itself had taken shape ever more miraculously as her knowledge of it increased. Lack of knowledge is for the lazy, and in Annika's opinion there was something directly suspect in a book that makes itself out to be other and more than a mere springboard for others.

When she occasionally met an old schoolfriend who had gone in for a conventional life with a career and the appropriate reproduction after finishing her education, she did not sink into melancholy at the possibility of never becoming a mother, but instead rejoiced that her horizon did not end at some mental fog-bank about the turn of the century, that everything after that did not darken and turn into an uneasy fumbling for dates and the people and events attached to them, and that the whole thing did not halt at a reasonably correct date and a deeply impaled man from Nazareth. She enjoyed seeing figures like Jesus and Buddha and Mohammed slide into place in her consciousness as the comparatively modest personages they actually were in the far greater history of the earth and its development. She relished the fact that the endless immaterial lists of names of the British kings and queens in her head made way for more interesting characters such as Lucy, Peking man, Turkana boy,

Cro-Magnon man, *Australopithecus*, *Homo habilis*, *erectus*, *archaic sapiens*, *neanderthalensis* and *Homo sapiens*.

To Annika religious belief was on a par with capitulation. And she had always thought it must be pretty feeble to resign yourself to a few frayed fragments of parchments whose descriptions of the Flood were useless rubbish from the scientific point of view, but which, combined with archaeological finds, ice-core drilling, geophysical investigations and molecular biology, added up to a far more wide-ranging story, a story of the development of everything – evolution, in which man's role was constantly diminished concurrently with the appearance of further knowledge, and whereby a demythologised form of the Flood provided the interpretation of the catastrophes, climatic changes, which time after time have challenged the species.

Annika's development fell into two stages. When she was still very young and at school, she lived in a limited segment, a distillate of the world. Human beings cannot assimilate everything at once. You live in an extract. A form of grading. In a simplified image. The world that surrounded Annika was the world that formed her. She was big city, Sydney, beaches, cars, hospitals and snakebite.

It was when she met Harper Stone and he introduced her to deep time that her internal continental plates grated against each other once again, caused one world to founder so another could rise. Deep time grows within you. Like a child. It does not come into being as if by magic. The nature of deep time is, precisely, deep. It takes time for consciousness to absorb merely a feeling of millions of millions of years. Her father's world picture did not fall like a regime. It was taken over. Gradually. Little by little. At first she felt split in two. Because, enthusiastically spurred on by Harper Stone, she began to read in all directions. In a state of confusion which she recognised in the time and in her patients. Annika did not understand that in her search for knowledge she met, not a circumscription, but an expansion. In the belief that more knowledge would in the end assume an almost physical form, she did not understand that things did not fall into place but away from each other. At one blow she understood the frustration with which patients met doctors. Understood that people had lost the sense that civilisation and nature belonged strictly together, and that in a whirlwind of television broadcasts and newspaper headlines they had developed the idea that man had severed himself from nature once and for all, and that doctors were a kind of modern alchemist who, out of nothing and on the basis of almost miraculous medications, helped them to survive. That the same people who loathed snakes like the plague quite simply did not comprehend that among other things it was only on the basis of the components of snake venom, coagulants and anti-coagulants, that heart medicine and blood-thinning preparations could be produced. That the substance kistrin from the Malayan snake, *Agkistrodon rhodostomas*, counteracts the formation of blood clots. That secretions from the Australian green frog, *Litoria caerulea*, act against such different things as schizophrenia and bacterial infections. That epibatidin, a substance that affects hitherto unknown receptors in the human brain, from the triple-striped arrow poison frog, *Epipedobates tricolor*, is a painkiller two hundred times more effective than morphine.

Plate tectonic events and global climate changes can hit the psyche as they have hit the earth. There is an indisputable conjunction in the segregation of the hominids from the line that led to the African human apes about five million years ago and the expansion of the Antarctic icecaps. There is an odd coincidence between the formation of the Arctic two and a half million years ago and the explosion of species formation among hominids in East Africa. And there is a comic irony in the fact that Darwin, who tried in *The Origin of Species* to explain the inadequate finds of intermediate stages in the geological strata as a generally low incidence of fossils, did not live to see that his own book, in some extrapolated sense, became an example of precisely that punctualistic view we take of evolution today. That his own book became a kick-start to awareness of the same dimensions as evolution now and then gives a single species, after it has rested and developed largely without change for long, long periods.

Michael Larsen

If Kate Carpenter had asked Annika about her attitude to God ten years earlier she would probably have replied that she did believe in something or other. At that time she still possessed the authoritarian urge for strict, logical chains of causation, which concentrated everything in some kind of diffuse starting point, which probably had a human form in some inhuman sense. She still kept the historians' traditional and inbuilt assumption that history book titles also embraced all the details and that the concepts could not be reversed, their convoluted and mendacious version of human development seen as something stringently progressive. That selected extracts of the world were also themselves the story of the world.

But the history of man is a great mess, and the road we have travelled is, seen in the rear-view mirror, uneven and potholed and filled with just as many happy mistakes as clear-sighted prophecies. There are no clear parameters. There is not a linear course with its starting point in a historical retrospect that can legitimise an interpretation of this moment as a culmination, much less a temporary culmination.

Simon once told her that Aristotle, as early as 300 BC, realised that the earth was round. From Athens he could not see the star Canopus in the southern sky, but he could see it when he travelled farther south to Alexandria in Egypt. He also knew that the deep bow-shaped shadow thrown by the earth on the moon during lunar eclipses was a visible proof of his assumption. But many peoples have explained lunar eclipses as a cosmic serpent eating the moon. As late as 1972, two were killed and eighty-five wounded when Cambodian soldiers opened fire on the serpent.

As long as 2,200 years ago the Greek librarian Eratosthenes could calculate the circumference of the earth with astonishing precision, but on the other hand that was in a culture which had not the slightest idea of the proportional distances between the planets of the solar system and the vast extent of the universe.

Over two hundred years BC, the Greek Aristarch worked with

the idea that our heavens were heliocentric, with a globe revolving around the sun and not vice versa. But with his specious mathematical fiction, which grew into a more and more precise description of the planetary orbits while steadily becoming more erroneously based, Ptolemy managed to set man's universe and his placing within it completely awry, before Kepler became the first seriously to assess the real state of things.

Thoughts do not fossilise. And as Osborne had touched on at the gallery, Annika too had found it interesting to think that highly developed cultures might have existed before those already known, which have not left artefacts behind them but only vague hints in ancient writings. Or merely imaginative successors? Whatever, there is no doubt that the human mind can read the myth of an ancient forgotten knowledge into the past. That is what the story of Ptolemy tells us. Only when the pile of examples, the list of apparent proofs, are big enough, when the lie is big enough, can we be convinced of everything. That his epicycle theory in the *Almagest* was vital for the prediction of planetary positions and solar and lunar eclipses, even though it was all wrong.

Human consciousness had often seemed to Annika to resemble closely the development of life on earth. A hectic development of a large number of basic constructs, of which only a few successful ones survive and decimate the total number of creatures capable of persisting.

Although, after her flirtation with chemical stimulants, Annika had learned to stay clear of the strongest ones, still her brief experience of them had taught her an important lesson. That a byword is to let go. Of everything one believes and imagines about the world. That is what those substances force us to do, and what people with the benefit of that experience teach us. Free-fall gives insight and experience.

Simon always chuckled at those intellectuals who, as he said, 'looked to Buddhism when they were too wise to be Christians and afraid of just being themselves'. He considered that Buddhism's great illusion is its belief that it can surmount all conflicts. That it is a

197

balanced religion. Like the Newtonian world picture. On that point scientific insights agreed with him. In our world, nothing balances. Not at least in the sense of equilibrium. That is what chaos has taught us. The heart functions at its optimum in imbalance, the brain works at its worst when in balance.

The world is like our idea of it. Simple. The world is like our brain's picture of it. As our consciousness pictures it. Simple. We know from computer science what huge amounts of information our brain receives and processes each second, but also that only an infinitely small amount of this information reaches our consciousness. It is into this chink that God slipped.

Annika looked at Kate Carpenter, who had lit yet another cigarette. None of the forensic experts with a scrap of experience, she knew, had preserved any belief that hidden in the folds of the brain there should be a dwelling place for either God or soul. Maybe doctors in the old days of trepanation were able to keep a remnant of superstition in the peephole they bored through the cranium to the brain. But there are few doctors today who leave an autopsy without the feeling of having met the inanimate, the demystified.

'Why do you want me to believe that you believe in God?'

'Maybe I think it suits an old aunt like me,' said Kate Carpenter. 'Maybe I worry. Too much. About youngsters growing up. They don't give the impression of believing in anything at all. Maybe I'm just talking nonsense. But you must have something to believe in, Annika. How can you exist without believing in something?'

'But I do believe. I believe in all of it.'

Kate Carpenter grabbed the bottle and pulled it towards her.

'You shouldn't do that.'

She said this as if she was about to divulge something, but then stopped. The wine gurgled as she filled up her glass, but Annika put a hand over hers. She was already drowsy, and didn't want to get muzzy, but she couldn't suppress a certain admiration for Kate Carpenter, a woman capable of managing her work and doing it so well, into the bargain, that people respected her.

To change the subject Annika pointed to a picture on the table.

'Your husband?'

That loosened Kate Carpenter's tongue, and she talked about her husband, who had died ten years earlier, that her misuse of tobacco had begun long before that, but had found its real justification after his death, about his life of knocking about for Placer Pacific and their many mines, and the gold dust that had settled in his lungs and was finally the death of him. About her step-daughter who taught agriculture at Hawkesbury University in Sydney and visited her only seldom, which Kate Carpenter, as she emphasised with a wave of her glass, couldn't blame her for, and about her own life, which despite its meaninglessness had seemed full of meaning to her. Her memory was surprisingly clear, but as the conversation went on the words became more and more indistinct.

At last she yawned and stretched. Her eyes had grown small and red. She tried to rise but gave up.

'Make us some coffee, would you, love?'

'That will only make it worse.'

Kate Carpenter smiled.

'Yes, if you drink it neat.'

Annika smiled. She rose and went to the door on to the corridor that led to the kitchen at the other end of the apartment. But stopped when she heard Kate Carpenter mumbling behind her.

'It was . . . not so much the morphine. And the fact that none of them had soot in their lungs.'

Annika went back to the table and tried to look as unaffected as possible by the topic Kate Carpenter had introduced. She was afraid that if she showed too intense an interest Kate might regret her indiscretion. She walked past the table and over to the window, from where she looked down on to the yard.

'Are you talking about the accident?'

Kate Carpenter looked straight at her.

'I'm not talking about any accident, love.'

The sun hung low, quivering over the flat roof of the neighbouring block. A thin, crumpled line of violet-blue clouds lay out over the sea on the far horizon. In a gap between the buildings deep shadows crept over Brisbane River, mumbling in over the trees of the harbour promenade and the moored boats.

Kate Carpenter's fate was like so many others. If you live long enough you will know that in dealings with other people you invariably come to make concessions, which at the time they were made did not seem to have had a significant impact on your own opinions or beliefs. Now and then some of these collusions stand out like an accusation or a compromising of one's whole personality. When Annika and Simon once discussed politics, she found herself listening to a disillusioned man. Simon's world was made up of clean lines. High ideals and simple rules. And an absolute insistence on moral values. She never got out of him precisely what had given him his contempt for politicians, but he vowed that he would never place his trust in people who went into politics, which, as Annika pointed out, put him completely outside any influence. He admitted this, but as he said: 'There can only be one human monster on the way to the summit of power that's worse than the one who sells out his ideals, and that is the one who is able to get to the top but doesn't do it.'

In Kate Carpenter's case the complicated rules of the game did not get lost in obscurity. It was perfectly clear what was involved. For years Kate Carpenter had had a serious drinking problem, known about in certain circles. Those circles had made allowances for it, because she was particularly good in her field and carried out her work irreproachably. Certain persons in those circles who had displayed this magnanimity were now demanding the discharge of old debts.

But this time they had gone too far. Kate Carpenter had one thing left in her life no one could touch: her professional expertise. That was what they had offended against. And that was the reason why, helped along by her fuzzy state, she was talking now.

'I was obliged to obey orders. The forensic odontologist's confirmation came back. No doubt about the identity of two of the bodies. There were dentist's records for them both. The tooth roots confirmed their ages. Her wisdom teeth were fully developed, and there were obvious marks of wear on his. Aged about thirty-five to forty. One had several false teeth, the other a bridge. Both carried out by the same dentist. Bad work. The implants must have caused them discomfort. There were traces of gum inflammation in both of them. In a layman's eyes there were signs of insignificant inaccuracies. For a dentist two millimetres on the wrong side or a crooked screw thread is disastrous. The Swedes are clever with teeth. Branemark. Titanium screws. Solid suspension. I think that is the system they use in Denmark. Teeth are important. Teeth can drive people mad. Can make them see conspiracies around them. There was none of that. Not to begin with, at least. Only a bad dentist.'

'Isn't it very premature for two relatively young people to have had such comprehensive dental work?'

Kate Carpenter looked at her appreciatively. She nodded, as if pleased with a clever pupil's discerning question.

'There was another accident ten years ago. Also a car accident. They survived that one. Mark Johnson was no Niki Lauda. There was a court case. Obviously it inspired someone else to repeat the exercise. There's nothing so convincing as repetition.'

'What about the bodies?'

'It was said that the family wanted cremation. Sherylene Johnson's parents were both dead. Mark Johnson's mother is still alive, but she's ill and lives in the USA. She was touched that someone was looking after everything, and merely wanted the urns sent on to her.'

While Annika was listening with wrinkled brow she had fished out the article from the *Brisbane Courier-Mail*. She unfolded it and put it on the table in front of Kate.

'The paper mentions three bodies. I gather Mark Johnson had contacts with the ASIO. But as I understand you, it was Mark and Sherylene Johnson's bodies you did a post-mortem on?'

'You're quite right, my dear. There was obviously a third passenger in the car. The daughter. It was her body I did not examine.'

Annika sat thinking hard.

'What did they want to hide by removing the girl's body?'

Annika heard the office chair turning round behind her.

'What makes you think,' said Kate Carpenter, 'that the girl is dead?'

Annika turned to her.

'But Mark Johnson's mother has already had the urns sent?'

Kate nodded. And at that moment Annika realised what was preying on her mind. In an urn in America was a little heap of ashes. Maybe a couple of kilos. But they were not the ashes of a fourteen-year-old girl. Kate Carpenter had not merely had to pay off an old debt. Now she was paying off interest that would go on for ever. One telephone call and Kate Carpenter would be lumped with a problem – how to explain. The ashes would remain for the rest of her life. As a permanent threat. No one would ever dream of examining them. Unless there was a telephone call from Australia. Something in those ashes would reveal that they were not those of a fourteen-year-old girl.

'Cremation is carried out at no less than 1,800 degrees Fahrenheit. The furnace bricks can resist up to 3,500 degrees. For an hour. Normally. Most is pulverised. But not everything. There are always small pieces of bone left. Those are collected and crushed to the same size as granulated sugar. So you would think all traces would be eliminated. But they are not. Carbon is present in the carbon dioxide of the atmosphere and in all living plants and animals. There are three isotopes. Carbon-12, carbon-13 and the very sparse, radioactive carbon-14. The old type of carbon-14 dating needs large quantities of substance to be precise. The new methods do not demand this. Put remains of this granulate in an atom accelerator. That is sufficient. There are currently twenty to thirty laboratories in the world working with this technique. Now let us say that the remains of a dead rhesus ape that has been used in experiments have been put in that urn.'

'But surely a test will disclose that the atoms come from an ape and not from a girl?'

Kate Carpenter smiled. She slowly shook her head.

'But it would be able to tell something about the age of those atoms. The exactitude goes down to thirty years. Now imagine that an ape that has been preserved for many, many years has been used. I think people would find it very hard to understand how an otherwise capable forensic medic had been able to confuse a little girl with a laboratory ape. Exit Carpenter. We know she tended to like more than just a drop.'

Annika had listened, silent and amazed. Now she leaned forward in her chair.

'What is the girl's name?'

'Maria. Maria Johnson.'

'Maria Johnson,' Annika repeated. 'That's her. She's the one it's all about. It's not the father at all. It's the girl.'

Kate Carpenter smiled conspiratorially, as if she knew everything that had brought Annika to see her.

'Why did Simon Rees call you?'

'Just put the coffee on, then I'll tell you what Simon Rees told me.'

If you were God, a neighbour or a sniper on the roof of the house opposite, you would have been able to see Annika rise from her chair and stand as a half-figure in the top section of the picture. Walk away from the table and vanish out of the picture. A few moments later you would have seen the light come on in the kitchen. If you were listening in on the apartment, you would have heard the older lady humming. Otherwise it would be pictures without sound. You would see Annika take the glass globe of the coffee machine, see her filling it with water and then turning to put it back on the unit. From an apartment opposite you would be able to see two pictures simultaneously. Like a split screen. If you looked into the kitchen you would see Annika put a filter in the funnel; if you looked into the living room you would catch sight of the old lady taking out a cigarette and lighting it. If you could pick up the sound you would still hear her humming.

Michael Larsen

If you wanted to break into this chain of events, the perfect timing would be the moment when Annika in the kitchen opened the cupboard door to get out sugar bowl and cups. If you did that you would see two things that seemed to be mutually related. You would see the older lady's head jerk violently forward. In the kitchen you would see Annika stiffen in front of the open cupboard door. Seen from outside it would resemble a causality. It would look as if Annika's decision to open the door had had a directly physical and lethal effect on the person in the other room. If you then watched the sequence in slow motion, you would see in a nanosecond, before the older lady was hit from behind, the hole in the pane and the glass splintering, you would see her strike the table, red fractals squirting over it at the same moment, as if a technical pen had exploded in front of her. You would see the office chair slide on its plastic base because of the displaced weight, and you would see the older lady fall over on to the table.

You would see Annika turn away from the cupboard and, at first with hesitant steps, then at a run, disappear from the top edge of the picture, and next slowly come into view in the living room.

'Miss Carpenter?'

Annika stared at the pool of blood on the table.

In the 1960s at Lark Quarry there was found the only physically documented drama we have from the world of the dinosaurs. Annika's blood froze when she visited the spot with Harper Stone. Huge, deep prints of carnivorous dinosaurs, and a confused dotting of several hundred lizards that had been no larger than hens, lie before one in the desert protected by a roof and in the shelter of a big steel construction. A man like Kahn would love the place. Even a hundred million years later the crime is obvious, and it is easy to reconstruct the drama. There are traces of both victims and perpetrators. Side by side in something that was once clay or mud, and which later stiffened during a lengthy drought and was then covered by sediment during inundations, and finally preserved by large rocks and stones. The small lizards had been surprised when they were at the water hole to drink or graze and in chaotic panic had tried to escape in all directions when the dinosaurs set about them.

Annika gazed at Kate Carpenter lying lifeless on the table with blood underneath her. She pondered on how this would seem to someone who looked at things or wanted to see things differently from herself. She felt her legs shaking and yet stood there paralysed.

Isn't it true, Miss Niebuhr, that you were not in the apartment at all? Isn't it true that Simon Rees instructed you in the use of firearms? Isn't it true that technically you worked for the ASIO?

Annika stood gazing at Kate Carpenter. A few moments ago a human being full of life. A human being with a past. A merry widow, a mother, an alcoholic. But a living person. Annika looked at the window. The floor with slivers of glass. The silence. She contemplated the fate that had been intended for her. Whether the doctor in her or the human being should react. If that had been thought about. If that had been intended. Should she force herself over to the table and end her days in a hail of shot? Or should she stay glued to the floor and mechanically allow herself to be led away by head-shaking policemen? Or should she take to her heels?

If the room was bugged they would be aware by now that she knew too much. The sound of sirens came all too quickly. She considered what this looked like. What it had been intended to look like.

Annika got out her Browning and walked backwards cautiously to the front door. Her hands shook and she fumbled with the safety catch before priming the revolver. Gently she manoeuvred the door ajar. There was no one on the landing. Annika went out. She closed the door carefully and went to look down the stairwell. Right at the bottom she caught sight of two men on their way up, and quickly drew back so they could not see her.

She stood for a few moments to catch her breath. Then she went resolutely into the apartment again. Keeping an eye on the window opposite, she went straight to Kate Carpenter and the table swimming in blood. With a swift movement she laid her hand in the pool and smeared it over with blood. She picked up her feet one at a time and wiped the blood on her hands over the soles. Then she went back to the door, checking that her boots had left a trail of blood. When she was out on the landing she could hear the two men on their way up the stairs. She walked down the three top steps close to the wall. On the last step she stopped and pulled off first one and then the other boot. Then on bare feet she crept cautiously back upstairs and past the entrance to Kate Carpenter's apartment. Once up on the next floor she lay down flat on the floor with her Browning in front of her.

She heard the two men approaching below, and felt her heart beating against the floor. She had an unpleasant feeling that they might be able to hear it.

When the two men were on the way up the last flight before Kate Carpenter's apartment, she could hear them stop and whisper.

'She's got out.'

'Impossible. We would have seen her.'

There was a short pause in which Annika tried to picture what they were doing.

'She's still in there,' whispered one. 'She came out, heard us and went back again.'

'There's no sign. No trace of steps going back.'

'No more blood.'

Annika thought her heart would stop beating, as they were standing just below her in front of the door of Kate Carpenter's apartment.

'What about farther up? She might be there.'

'Check it, then.'

In an attempt to make no sound, Annika stretched herself absolutely flat on the floor, although she felt like confronting them and shooting and shooting to get it over with.

Intolerable seconds while she wondered if they had discovered her or not. Silence. If they came right up she was finished. They only needed to go up three or four steps and she would be seen. She lay with her head at floor level. A face might come into sight at any time. At the end of her field of vision lay the cock of the Browning she was trying to keep still.

'Nothing,' she heard one of them say. 'She must be in there.'

'That's what I said, wasn't it? Cover me. I'm going in.'

Annika lay perfectly still until she was sure both men had gone into the apartment. Then she stood up and crept down the stairs, past the door that was ajar and on down the stairway. Near the bottom she decided to go half a floor farther and vanish into the back yard.

She opened the door. She glanced nervously up at the roof of the neighbouring property and concentrated so hard on not being shot from above that she completely failed to register that in two quick movements she first lost her Browning, then stood locked fast in the vice of a pair of arms that held her hands so tightly behind her back that she might as well have been in handcuffs.

'Stand still.'

She knew the voice. She recognised his shaving lotion. It was Frank Kiesworik from the American consulate in Brisbane.

The order was superfluous. Annika was chained fast in his grip. He pointed over to the opposite side of the yard where she could glimpse a lifeless form lying face down on the stone flags.

'We must get you away from here. I don't know how many of them there are.'

'There are two up there,' said Annika.

He pulled her carefully backwards out to the street on the other side of the building. Just before he relaxed his grip on her she felt a damp, warm sensation on her back. She felt her T-shirt sticking to her and at once, when he released her, she turned round and saw that his shirt was covered in blood.

'My God . . . are you all right?'

With the hand holding the gun pressed to his stomach he pulled a handkerchief from his jacket pocket with the free one. He shook the ironed folds out of it, and Annika had the strangely detached thought that either it was newly purchased, or he was married. Frank Kiesworik held it to his stomach.

'I am a bit out of sorts,' he admitted, playing it down, with little trickles of blood running down over his hands.

Annika tried to take his hand away but he grimaced and pressed it still more firmly to his midriff. The blood oozed from between his fingers.

'Out of sorts?'

She got an arm round him and helped hold the handkerchief to his stomach. He took a deep breath, squeezed his eyes shut, but didn't utter a word.

'You can scream if you like,' said Annika.

He smiled again. With difficulty.

'Scream? Do you think I'm enjoying this? Anyway they always work several to a team.'

'Who are "they"?'

'Who do you think?'

Annika looked around them.

'Where's your car?' she asked.

He looked around himself, as if there were small holes in his memory. As if he only now recalled where they were.

'Over there,' he said, looking around watchfully. 'We must get away from here.'

He started to cross the street at a run and she tried to match her gait to his as he seized her hand and led her in the direction of the car. The car howled and flashed when he activated the electronic lock, and Annika ran round to the right side.

He came up to her by the door.

'Certainly not. Do you know what it cost?'

At that moment a car started up farther down the street, and with spinning wheels and furious speed a big black Mercedes ploughed towards them.

'In, in, in.'

He pushed Annika quickly into the car. Then brutally over into the passenger seat. Then he got in himself and started up.

He looked at her as he revved the engine.

'We must get you back on the boat.'

Then he let in the clutch and stood on the accelerator and they hurtled forward so fast that Annika felt as if something was pulling her backwards.

They rounded Charlotte Street at high speed, went on along Eagle Street, turned out on to Turbot Street towards the airport, and continued in that direction for a while. The black Mercedes was still visible behind them but it had been caught in a row of cars farther back.

Frank Kiesworik overtook wildly to get more space between them, and even though Annika held on tight she was thrown from side to side in her seat.

Behind them their pursuer was now out of sight, and when they drove back along the Boundary on the way down to Brisbane River, he had definitely disappeared. Kiesworik slackened speed as they rounded the Central Railway Station, but he was still driving so fast that several motorists hooted at them.

She sat looking at Frank Kiesworik. Apart from the blood there was something almost homosexually well groomed about him. From the scent of his shaving lotion to his newly polished English Lloyd shoes. From his glossy hair to his shirt, his black suit and the matching black opal in the ring on his finger.

As he sat pressing the handkerchief to his bloody shirt, Annika studied his hands. No sweat. She looked at his face again. Looked into it. She had seen brains like his on the PET scanner's computer images at the hospital. Lesions in the cerebral cortex in the middle of the brain. Fair game for limbic berserk rage. The neurologists' EEG curves with their complete disclosure of the lack of contact between emotion and reason. No emotion, no fear.

As they went through a red light at the last crossroads, Annika pushed her feet hard against the floor and put one hand on the front panel.

He looked across at her, still keeping up his speed.

'In theory you live longer the quicker you move. Unless, of course,' he said, grinning and looked across at her, 'it kills you.'

'You're a psychopath, you know,' she said.

He looked across at her with a smile.

'Does it make me more normal if I say I'm afraid of that too?'

'I didn't know intelligence people knew so much about physics and relativity theories.'

He turned to her again and then looked in the rear-view mirror.

'During the Gulf War we controlled many weapons from navigation satellites. The satellites contain hysterically precise atomic clocks. But space time and earth time are not alike. We used Einstein's theorems to adjust the clocks. Not everything you learn at university is useless.'

When they were down by the river he slowed down appreciably because his foot quite simply had become so weak it could no longer keep the acclerator pedal depressed. He slumped down over the wheel, his face fallen into a creased jumble.

Then he collapsed. Annika seized the wheel just before the car struck the wall. When the pressure of his foot left the pedal the car went dead. They glided on almost soundlessly, until the friction almost made the engine stall. Annika stretched her foot over the gear lever and down on to the brake pedal, and the car stopped. She got out and walked round it. She managed to get enough life in him to drag him over into the passenger seat. Then she sat behind the wheel and started up.

'We must get you to a hospital,' she said.

He looked up at her and shook his head.

'Someone will come and fetch me. A car will come and stop behind us soon. When I give the sign, you must just leave the car. Leave Brisbane immediately. And forget all about this business. Not a word to the ASIO. Not a word to the police. Not a word to anyone.'

'How did you know I was here?'

'I'm almost tempted to ask you what you were *doing* here.'

'Surely it's not unusual for a doctor from Sydney to visit a pathologist in Brisbane?'

Frank Kiesworik shrugged his shoulders. He straightened up as if the pain had subsided.

'Did you get the information you needed?'

Annika did not answer his question. She looked enquiringly at him.

'I hate to sound ungrateful, but if you've been following me all the time why didn't you stop them getting at Kate Carpenter?'

Kiesworik raised his eyes.

'How is it that everyone thinks the Americans can save the whole world? We didn't know they would go and kill someone.'

'Who killed Simon?'

He only shook his head vehemently and clenched his teeth. He pressed the limp blood-soaked handkerchief to his midriff and took another look in the rear-view mirror.

'What did Kate Carpenter tell you, Miss Niebuhr?'

'Why do you want to know that?'

'Just tell me what she said to you.'

'How did you know I didn't believe the theory that Simon took his own life?'

'If you did, why should you be so keen to meet Osborne?'

'What is your role in all this, Kiesworik?'

'I am a diplomat, Miss Niebuhr. A diplomat in the finest meaning of the word. I am the one who intervenes and smooths things out when American marines or permanent staff at the bases run amok in a bar and beat up Aboriginals. I am the one who tries to straighten out misunderstandings among the various services when they arise. If, and I emphasise if, the ASIO really have staged a murder of one of their own, we should very much like to know why.'

'Why?'

'I think I told you I knew Simon Rees.'

'Is that the only reason?'

He shook his head, puzzled.

'Can you think of others?'

'Do you think they would have killed me?'

Michael Larsen

'That probably depends on what Kate Carpenter told you.'

Annika thought back. She thought of the break-in at her house, she thought of the snake in the boat.

'I can't get rid of the idea that if anyone had wanted to kill me they could have done so long ago.'

Kiesworik looked at her with an arch grin.

'Maybe you've got a guardian angel.'

Annika looked at him. There was something in the way he said it that made her puzzle over whether he was merely chatting, insinuating something or encouraging her to supply him with information.

'Who?'

Kiesworik shook his head ironically.

'How should I know that?'

In the mirror he caught sight of the car Annika could hear rolling up behind them.

Again he put his hand on her back. From the shoulder blades he gently ran it up to the vertebra on her neck as she opened the car door on her way out.

'Go home now, Miss Niebuhr.'

Annika turned towards him.

'How do you feel about snakes, Kiesworik?'

'I hate snakes.'

Annika smiled thinly.

'I had a feeling you'd say that.'

'Go now,' he said.

Annika had kissed a cobra in India.

It was at the end of July a few years earlier. It was dangerous, childish and unnecessary. But when she found herself in the situation she could not resist the temptation.

She and Simon Rees travelled together. Their ways separated in Thailand. Annika was to meet Harper Stone in Bombay and travel with him south to Shirala for the annual Naag Panchmi festival – the festival of snakes.

Every Australian herpetologist must go to India or Thailand. To get to know the cobra, the mother of all the elapids.

Every year thousands of people lose their lives in Asia because of the cobra. The problem is the rice-fields and the fact that serum is costly and scarce. And also that the cobra, like the death adder, does not withdraw but stays where it is and if necessary strikes. Nevertheless they idolise the cobra in a blend of mythology and pragmatism. Just as the biologists in Queensland with their laborious fieldwork have come to the conclusion that without the elapids and the water pythons the area would be an explosion of rats, the Indians know that their crops are protected by snakes, which remove the worst pests.

Especially in southern India, in the little constitutional state of Kerala, the landscape is a veritable profusion of temples dedicated solely to snake worship. In most places the annual festival day in honour of snakes is a continuation of a millennium-long Hindu tradition, and the Indian pilgrims flock to the beautiful large temple statues of snakes to sacrifice and pray. In Shirala they dance with living, lethal cobras, and when Annika and Harper Stone arrived during the week of the great procession, the locals were in full swing catching cobras in the rice-fields.

In the Amba temple the snakes were set free in the courtyard, then gathered and carried in before the goddess of good fortune, the men holding the swaying cobras firmly by their tails. Out in the streets barefoot young girls in thick sarongs and flowered cotton dresses sprinkled colourful petals, camphor and sacred violet powders over the snakes' heads, and those girls who wanted to get pregnant, but who would not normally dream of approaching a cobra, kneeled down before the snakes and pushed their faces close up to their venom fangs. 'No one is afraid today. And no one will be bitten,' said one of the locals to Annika and Harper Stone.

And right enough, no one came to grief in that living belt of mortally dangerous snakes, which were rolled along on ox carts like majestic legendary figures, like gods. The centre of attention in a cacophony of drums and horns, of loud music from the grating

213

loudspeakers, of human noise from the overfilled streets, of shouts and screams from the mango and banana stalls, of roaring buses and cars, of the rattle from clay vessels and pots full of gravel, which were unceasingly rolled in front of and alongside them to distract them.

But Annika noticed something else as well. These people had generations of experience in handling snakes and a knowledge of when and how near they could go to them at given moments.

Mostly they handled the snakes in the same way as she and others did the Australian ones, by picking them up by the tail. But she also saw some who had a technique she had otherwise only seen at snake shows in Thailand and Malaysia.

It was this image, which had become almost physical, that she had recalled both times Frank Kiesworik had placed his hand on her back.

You can take hold of the cobra from behind. Place your hand gingerly on its distended neck and simply lay it down. Or you can grasp it tightly round the neck and slide your hand up towards the bulge. The moment the cobra feels the hand approaching the bulge it tries to escape from your grasp and slide down into the hand, so you have it by the neck. Completely defenceless.

Annika heard the car behind her start and drive off. She folded up her jacket, having turned it inside out, and slung it over her shoulder.

She ran along the esplanade under the trees. She dodged in and out among the pedestrians in the smog of car exhaust, the reek from fish and chip shops and the smoke from the outdoor BBQ restaurants.

Mike stood on the little swimming bridge as she ran up, gasping for breath.

'What's happened?' he asked.

Annika ran her eyes down herself. Even if she had wanted to she couldn't explain it away. Kiesworik's blood had stained both her T-shirt and her trousers.

'We must get away from here,' she said, walking past him. 'We must just get away.'

'When d'you want to leave?' he asked.

'Now,' said Annika, crossing the landing plank, throwing her jacket on to the steps to the flybridge and straight away starting to release the mooring lines.

Darkness began to fall over Brisbane. In layers of bright, almost transparent strips in the west, the sun hung in an open crack close to the horizon. The last rays made the houses along the northern side of the river stand out clearly. It was a calm evening. Only a light breeze stirred the river, and it felt as hot as the heated air from a car fan.

Annika went below as Mike reversed the boat into mid-river and started to manoeuvre it round.

She pulled the blood-stained T-shirt over her head and drew out the revolver before stepping out of her trousers. She put the gun in the middle of the bundle of clothes and stowed it all on a shelf in the cupboard.

As she soaped herself under the shower, she rested a hand on her neck. Again she felt Kiesworik's hand on her back, between the shoulder blades. Kiesworik. She repeated his name to herself.

Questions whirled around in her mind. Helter-skelter. And there was neither head nor tail to be made of any of it. She pictured Kate Carpenter at the moment she was hit from behind. She screwed up her eyes to shut out the image, felt how her hands shook, almost as if she were freezing.

Not until she heard a faint, growing rumble through the boat and knew they were on their way out of Brisbane did she begin to calm down.

A fourteen-year-old girl. Maria Johnson. Her father had had connections with the ASIO. Gaia Jessup. The snake. Someone or other, someone, had put a snake in a car. Gaia Jessup had let herself into the car. Why? What was she doing with a big canvas bag if all she had in it was her purse? Was she going to fetch something? Simon had hired the car. Simon knew Gaia Jessup. She was his protégée. His lover. Or his enemy. Simon knew the Johnson family.

215

Annika stood thoughtfully gazing out into the dusk on the other side of the porthole. The lights of Brisbane were coming on. And the great South Bank Parklands lay like a long dark oasis in the middle of the town with palms, shrubs and trees along the bend of the river, only faintly lit by park lamps and the torchlight of the clowns on the paths. Brisbane is known as 'the town of snakes'. It is said that when you get out in the suburbs, away from the centre of town, from the epicentre of concrete and glass, out to the villas, the apartment blocks and terraced houses, there is not a single house without its snake. Annika listened to the sirens rising and falling through the streets, among the buildings and out over the river, although it was impossible to pinpoint their direction. Some people find comfort in telephone bells, traffic noise and the song of ambulances in side streets. And others take pills to counteract noise. So the phone lines can hum, the traffic thunder and the emergency services rush along the streets. Everything is bound up in a big city. Into one great organism.

That is the great mystery. The universe. So vast, so far-reaching, so full of phenomena and laws we do not yet know. Within this mystery are other enormous universes of mysteries. Within them still more mysteries.

A murder is a mystery. It involves a victim, a murderer and a motive. This evening an ambulance would reach the apartment where Kate Carpenter lay. A daughter in Sydney would receive the tragic message. But before that all trace of the real criminals would have been removed. Someone or other would have the crime pinned on them, or reports would state that there was no apparent perpetrator of the horrific crime, nor any trace of one.

All human cognition suffers the risk of being led astray. By inexact information, by apparently unshakable empirical knowledge, by obscurely motivated manipulations.

Not only a philosophical system but now a scientific one too has verified the Socratic view. The only thing that increases is the extent of ignorance. It may seem as if our knowledge sometimes takes enormous strides, but beside these apparent fits and starts, ignorance grows exponentially the whole time. When man progresses by a centimetre, the universe extends by a galaxy. One murder becomes several. It began with the murder of Simon. Or with Kahn and his information about Kate Carpenter.

Newton's gift to humanity was not his demonstration of gravity. His gift was not the *Philosophiae Naturalis Principia Mathematica* with its parabolas and hyperbolas. which isolated and delimited; the gift was that it extended and created holes. His gift was not his precision, but his inexactitude, not his apparently faultless description of the universe, but its defectiveness, not his classical cogency but his inconsistency, all the inbuilt self-contradictions of his system. Newton drew on the old Greek ideology that contains as much nonsense as truth. The world was misled for 1,500 years by Ptolemy's ingenious circular system, which showed how wrong it can be to smother the universe in mutually dependent mathematical abstractions. To Newton beauty was on a par with simplicity. But the truth is not simple. The only simple thing is our true need for simplicity.

Annika searched her mind for a clear causal chain. Something that could be falsified. Something that could be attacked by doubt, a weak point where you start to question. But there was only a jumble of events. A muddy course in which it was impossible to point to anyone and say: he was the one who did it. Kiesworik, Osborne. Who had shadowed her in Sydney? Who had been in her house? Who liquidated Kate Carpenter? Who killed Simon?

When she came out of the shower she heard Mike calling. She got dressed, found her cigarettes and went up to the flybridge, where he sat at the wheel with a torch on the chart before him.

The high office blocks were fading into the distance in the twilight. They could follow them for a long time, watching them diminish, as they passed the numerous bends in the river. Up to the north over Queensland the monsoon clouds were thick enough to create an artificial horizon reminiscent of an unbroken chain of mountains. They met mostly fishing boats and ferries crossing on their way downriver, but when they reached the mouth and the ocean Mike had to make a sharp turn to starboard to avoid a yawl in which a young couple were struggling with the stern sail on the mizzen-mast.

He looked at her and rummaged in the pile of charts.

'What's this?'

He held up the drawing of Annika. She looked at him and knocked a cigarette from the pack. She crouched down and bent her knees slightly to shelter her hand while she lit it. A strong wind blew from the sea.

At first she was hurt that he had searched her things. Then she felt guilty and ashamed that she had not told him everything about the whole business from the start.

She took the drawing and studied it.

'I don't know.'

'What does it mean?' he said, slapping the paper. 'Why haven't you told me you are involved . . . ?'

'Because I don't know.'

'Know what?'

'How I'm involved.'

'And this,' he said, and held up the copy of the *Brisbane Courier-Mail* article. 'It was in your jacket. Everything is covered in blood. I wouldn't be wrong to assume this has something to do with Simon's death, would I?'

Annika shook her head.

'You didn't go to Brisbane to see your old friends.'

Annika shook her head again.

'But it was for your sake I didn't say anything.'

She took a step towards him and laid her hand against his cheek, but he turned his face away. He crumpled up the article and flung it from him.

'Bloody crap,' he said.

'I don't think it was very nice of you to go through my things,' said Annika.

Mike glowered at her.

'I don't think it was very nice of you to lie. And I only went through your things because I thought I'd overlooked something. Which I had. Obviously.'

'I would have told you about it,' she said.

Mike clenched his hands on the wheel, and a little white crown appeared on his suntanned knuckles.

'I can't understand why you didn't just tell me what it was. This makes it seem so suspicious.'

'I'm not sure you want to hear what's happened.'

'Tell me, Annika. Sit down and tell me.'

Annika sat down beside him in the little plexiglass wind scoop. She hesitated for a moment before starting to speak, considering whether she should lie again. Avoid involving him, forget everything, go back to Sydney. Perhaps it wasn't too late. Perhaps they would leave her alone. If she went home and forgot all about it. An unwritten mutual agreement that if she did not undertake anything, if she didn't talk to anyone, if she did not reveal what she knew, then they would not go any farther. A silent agreement? But she swiftly saw that the only person she was negotiating with was herself. Of course they would not let her be. She had witnessed a murder. Before her very eyes a human being had been alive one moment, dead the next. Murdered. She had been there in the apartment. At the moment it happened. She had seen it. Been there. She speculated over the lie they would fabricate. How the story would sound. Did she appear in it? Or did they believe they were so secure that they would do nothing, were they really so secure that they would simply wait until some over-zealous Detective Superintendent in Brisbane, if one existed, asked a series of unanswered questions, and then just put a stop to the matter, as they had put a stop to Kahn in Sydney? Of course they would not leave her alone. They would come after her. One day she would be shot, have a car accident or be hit by an oncoming truck out of control.

Annika began to speak. She told Mike everything. If anything happened to her, he would still be there. A fact that both calmed and frightened her.

She observed him as she spoke. When she had finished it was clear that she did not need to expand her story. He sat slumped in his seat, silent. It was as if he were trying to find further uncertainty in the tale she had unfolded for him. But the only question he arrived at was the same one she was grappling with: why?

After three hours they were out on the open sea. *Endeavour* shot over the waves at high speed, clouds of spray at her sides but with her bow raised completely free of the water.

They sailed through the darkness at almost thirty knots. Just south of North Stradbroke Island, Mike set the automatic pilot with information on the controls, position and the desired course, and connected the alarm. He gathered his charts, stood up, and together they went below.

Mike put the kettle on for coffee and then went over to the little table where Annika had sat down with the scans in front of her.

'I don't understand the drawing. But these,' she said, laying the three A4 sheets on the table, 'they are scans of a fourteen-year-old girl.'

Mike sat down opposite her.

'Impossible,' he said.

'What d'you mean?'

'That it's unlikely.'

'Why?'

'Because we would never be able to see positive signs of schizophrenia in a fourteen-year-old girl.'

'Surely you can't completely exclude that?'

'Clear symptoms first appear typically at twenty to twenty-five. In women most often later. And they are never ever visible at the age of fourteen.'

Annika bit her lip. She stood up and went to open the small fridge. She took out a bottle of mineral water and unscrewed the top with a squirt. Then she threw her head back and drank.

She passed the bottle to Mike and sat down again.

'Those words Simon wrote about something the eye of the soul has seen. A vision of something that cannot be destroyed, cannot be forgotten. It isn't me he means. He means the girl. It is she who has seen something. "MJ", Maria Johnson. It can only be that.'

'The parents' death? The people who killed her parents?'

'But why all those efforts to spread lies that she's dead?'

'Same reason. To get her out of the way. That might actually be an explanation.' He turned over the sheet illustrating a brain. 'The small hippocampus could be due to shock. Post-traumatic stress disorder. A violently upsetting experience.'

'But why undertake costly scans on a girl when you'd want her to forget what she has seen?'

Mike shrugged his shoulders.

Annika put her hand on the papers.

'It's something to do with her brain. Something or other they can make use of. What about this? I don't understand it,' said Annika, pushing over the A4 copy with the PET scan on top and the copies of scan sequences underneath.

'Hard to say. This one,' he said, pointing to one of the diagrams, 'could be some kind of trance condition. Hypnosis, meditation perhaps. A series of new methods has been evolved to extract various layers of consciousness from the scans. The sequence might resemble an attempt to cleanse the consciousness. There are examples of cases where someone in a meditative state has been asked to clean out brain activity. After that they are scanned. And again in a normal waking state. It's a bit of hocus-pocus, but in this way one can cleanse vibration from the deeper layers of consciousness and obtain an approximate picture of normal consciousness as it would look without disturbances. But I give up on these sequences. I've quite simply never seen so much activity in so many centres at the same time.'

'Simon was working on a project. A remarkable project. A secret project. Atlas X. What if this girl has certain . . . powers? Have you ever taken a scan of an . . . abnormal person?'

Mike bent over the sheets. As if he hadn't heard what she said. He spread them out in a fan before him.

221

'It's scary, actually, isn't it? A person hears a voice. A message from God maybe. The frightening thing is not that the voices are there. What's frightening is that now we can see it.'

'A . . . medium?' said Annika.

Mike looked up.

'A medium?'

Annika reached for the pen. She doodled on one of the sheets, thinking. She wrote the girl's name. Her age. She wrote Simon's name. Then she wrote: Simon's child? She crossed that out.

'I can't get rid of the idea that there was a reason for his citing Philon. Simon loved brief maxims holding various messages. He refers to the girl by using Philon. That she is a wonder. The wonders everyone speaks of but no one has seen. Simon undertook a lot of research on telepathy. What does telepathy look like in a scanner?'

'Now we're moving into a sphere where I must admit my knowledge is . . . inadequate. Thinking. Who knows what that actually is? Electrical interplay between billions of nerve cells? We've got enough to do to keep up with the connections that exist purely factually.'

Mike rose and went out on to the swimming platform. He stood there for a while before going up the steps to check the compass.

Annika sat there deep in her own thoughts. They were on the way home. South. *Endeavour* almost hovered over the waves. Far in, the lights along the coast glimmered. The Gold Coast with all its tourist hotels could be glimpsed like an elongated chain of light. Out here they were alone. Their stern wave foamed behind them. A few metres back and every trace of them vanished.

She went up on the bridge and stood behind Mike. He was studying the fluxgate compass. They shot along at over thirty knots, on an even keel; there was no list, and no disturbing choppiness. Underneath them lay a delicate mechanical device of small sensor terminals in cardanac suspension. No rotating compass card, only the control panel and digital compass figures. Governed by the underlying, wonderful world of quantum mechanics.

Annika knew she ought to feel at ease. Yet an indefinable sensation of unease rose up in her. She looked around into the darkness. But there was nothing to be seen. Neither behind them nor on either side.

'They know I know about the girl. They know I know the truth about what happened to her parents. They know I was there when Kate Carpenter was murdered.'

'What do you want to do about it?'

'They know I know,' she repeated to herself.

'What are you trying to say?'

'That no matter how you look at it, that knowledge is deadly.'

Annika paced around. She suddenly had the ominous sensation that something was very wrong. The darkness flowed around them. No trawlers or other cruisers in sight. They flew over blue-black waves. In the sky above them the shining ribbon of the Milky Way shone out like an exposure.

'Mike, could anyone have had access to the boat when we were in Brisbane?'

'I went ashore to shop.'

'We'll have to search the boat.'

'What d'you mean?'

'Mike, these people are killers.'

Millions of years before Edison invented the incandescent lamp, jellyfish, octopus, bristle worms, starfish and a wealth of deep-sea fish had evolved lighting systems supplying over ninety per cent of energy as light against the paltry five per cent of man-made electric bulbs.

Luciferin is a substance that combines with the enzyme luciferase, and if oxygen and energy are added to it, light is produced. It was one of Annika's great dreams to go sufficiently deep down into the sea to be able to see these natural lighting methods. But it was and remained a dream, for no one in this world could get her to even contemplate the idea of diving at night in Australia.

Sharks are everywhere around the Australian coasts. And in every harbour. Some of the world's largest white sharks are caught in Australia, and she remembered how a few years ago Melbourne had been plagued by a shark that cruised off the coast for weeks and laid waste to the beaches. Mike knew of her fear of diving at night, and it was he who on an earlier occasion had entertained her with stories of numerous attacks on fishermen and surfers along these very beaches of Stradbroke Island.

Total silence fell when Mike stopped the engine. After the high speed at which they had been travelling it felt like a landing when the motor died. Then there was stillness. Only the sound of waves breaking on the bow and the whisper of the wind over the crests.

Mike stood almost naked, getting his wet suit out of the locker. Annika passed him his mask.

'Do you want oxygen?'

He shook his head.

'No, give me a snorkel. And a torch.'

Annika watched him disappear into the water. She stayed by the ladder, looking into the darkness, following the cone of light under the water until he vanished under the boat. Then she started a thorough search on board.

She began in the bow with the bedroom cabin, the beds, the seat, cupboards, then the toilet, shower, cupboard by the stairs, seats and cupboards in the saloon. She found nothing. No trace. She lay down with the torch, and studied every weld and riveted edge at close quarters. Found nothing. Not a trace. She ended in the pantry, where she went through all the cupboards, checked the electricity, the cooker, the microwave, sink, fridge. Annika did not know what she was searching for looked like. She knew nothing about explosives. But she knew what the boat ought to look like. She would notice a lack, catch sight of something superfluous.

Now and then she went out on deck and leaned over the side to make sure all was well with Mike. She caught sight of the light of his torch beneath the boat, then went in to continue her search. But found nothing. Finally she crawled along the outside deck, along the side and up to the foredeck. She returned, searched the lanterns and stumped out on the foredeck again. She lay out over the bow and caught sight of Mike's blue cone of light in the water. He came up to the surface.

The water around the boat was steel-grey from the light; a couple of metres away it was black. He spat once he was clear of the surface, then stood in the dark, treading water.

'Nothing,' he said.

'Shine the light on the bow,' said Annika.

Mike swam from one side of the boat round to the other with the light directed on to it. Up and down, from side to side.

'Right, then.'

He let himself slide along the freeboard, lighting up the side of the boat, and Annika staggered back, holding tight to the handrail as she helped him up.

Mike crawled up the aft ladder and sat down on the edge. Annika sat beside him.

'What about the engine well?'

'If they had opened it to let out petrol vapour we'd have gone up in the air the moment I switched on in Brisbane,' said Mike.

'I don't understand it,' she said. 'There's nothing on the radar, no ships near by. We are alone out here, Mike. If they intended to kill us this would be the perfect place. But if they don't have a boat in the water, and if they haven't mined the ship . . .' Her eyes met Mike's, and as if they had had exactly the same thought at exactly the same time, they both looked up at the sky. And far, far away they heard the plane.

'Shouldn't we just wait and see?' said Mike, but Annika was already on her way below. She ran to her clothes, got out her revolver, knocked out the magazine, made sure it was full, and shut it again. She released the safety catch and picked up her mobile phone from beside the double bed. She heard Mike start up and set the boat in motion. She ran up to him and shouted.

'Get the rubber dinghy launched!'

She threw open the lid of the locker and pulled out her own wet suit. She searched among ropes and hooks, parachute rockets and smoke bombs for the hand flares, and extra batteries for the torch. Mike stood looking out into the darkness, not doing anything. He seemed to be thinking she was overreacting. The sound of the plane was still a good way off. But far away its lights were now visible. Mike hesitated, and it was as if the thought that they might be lying in the water in a few seconds hadn't struck him at all.

He looked at her as if she had gone crazy.

'What are you planning to do? Shoot it?'

'Yes. And then tell it we will surrender unconditionally. Now get that boat into the water.'

Whether it was the devastating prospect of deserting a boat worth over a million and a half, which was not even his own, Annika didn't know, but as he made for the wheel to take over from the autopilot, she seized hold of him and screamed:

'Stop the engine and launch that boat!'

At that moment a powerful searchlight hit them from the air, and the first machinegun salvo beat down like a hailstorm in the water on the starboard side as the plane flew past.

'Mike, we haven't got a chance here. Put the boat in the water.'

But Mike seemed paralysed. He stood apathetically gasping for breath. He looked after the plane, or rather the sound of it, as if he quite simply did not understand what was going on. Panic-stricken, Annika ran over to the rail and started to release the snap hooks for the rubber dinghy, but discovered it was also fastened with ropes in front. At last Mike seemed to come to life. He leaped up and turned off the engine, switched off all lights and ran over to the locker to find a diving knife. Back at Annika's side he cut the ropes she had been trying to untie.

Out on the horizon, straight ahead of their keel, the plane was clearly banking. It was on its way back, and soon the lights were visible. It was flying low and making directly for them. They were too late.

Annika stiffened for a fraction of a second. Then suddenly an idea, which she should have thought of at the start, struck her.

'Distress signal. Send a distress signal.'

Mike ran up to the control panel again and turned the key. But the engine didn't start. Above him she saw the plane coming straight at them. Annika aimed her gun at it. Mike turned and turned the key. But nothing happened.

The plane dived. The lights grew bigger, and the dark fuselage grew first fuzzy then clearer as it came out of the darkness. She saw a plume of flame as the plane passed over them and turned, just before it reached the boat, so the figure that was shooting could take aim at its target. Annika shot and shot and shot, and at the same time she heard the hail of bullets from above perforating all the way along the glass-fibre roof.

Almost without realising it she noted, with strange dispassion, that they were both still alive as the drone of the plane died out again. She stared up at the overhang, where a dotted line led at a slant from edge to edge.

Mike began to cough violently, still doggedly trying to get life into the boat.

Annika ran to the dinghy and released it. She threw it over the side, made the line fast to *Endeavour*'s rail and hurried over to Mike. He tried once more. 'This fucking ... boat ... won't ... start.'

'Forget it,' said Annika. 'Come on.'

At that second he got a spark of life out of it. Tired and coughing, as if it were slurping oil, it started.

Behind the boat Annika could hear the plane making another turn. Mike ran over to her, the engine still running.

'Did you send it?' asked Annika, one foot already in the dinghy. She stood swaying, trying to keep her balance.

He was unable to talk. Nodded hard. She seized his wrist but he pulled away.

'Inha ... my inhaler ... I'll die ... without ... it.'

'No, Mike.'

But he was gone.

Annika looked straight at the plane, approaching again from the stern. If they were not hit themselves, this time it would undoubtedly hit the engine well. She called to Mike. But he didn't come up. She called again.

With her hand on the rail and balancing against *Endeavour*'s side, Annika again took aim. She managed to think that in theory one could calculate the ballistic course of the bullets she was firing, but she also managed to think how immaterial that was, given the way she was rocking up and down. After that nothing was clear to her. She merely shot. She dropped the gun inside the rail as a wave pulled her and the dinghy down. Managed to see a big flash of light come from the plane. Then felt the hull of the *Endeavour* against her feet and just pushed off. She felt herself falling and then the water closing over her.

Hours might have passed. Or seconds. It might have been a dream. It seemed distant and unaffected by time.

Parts of the plane, pieces of wreckage from the boat were still burning and smouldering on their way down through the water. She rose to the surface.

Only the end part of the plane's tail was left afloat, as if it had pierced *Endeavour*, illuminated by the flames from the boat, and stinking, poisonous PVC smoke floated grey and black around the wreckage. She tried to get away, get free of the wind direction. Apart from the flames beating in the wind, all was perfectly quiet. Here and there the fire had ignited small bonfires of petrol, as if the sea were ablaze. Annika felt a violent pain in her head. She snatched a breath and dived again.

Again she rose up.

'Mike. Mike.'

Then everything went black.

III

When Annika opened her eyes she found herself alone in a large white room. From a diminutive window behind the bed-head moonlight streamed in, throwing a bluish light on the walls.

Slowly she tried to orientate herself in the room and in her mind. Within it was a severe but curiously distanced pain, and slowly she passed her hand up her cheek. She stopped when she felt plaster and gauze stretching from her cheek up to her ear.

'Do you ever think the future is something we are approaching – or something that pulls us along behind it?'

The voice came from somewhere beside her. It was calm, deep and slightly melancholy, almost resigned.

Annika slowly turned her face, and at first only his knees, his hands and the lower part of his chin were visible in the moonlight coming through the window. He sat astride a chair he had turned round and pushed between his legs. His powerful arms rested on the chair-back. Even before his face came into view she knew it was Osborne.

'Where am I?'

'You are in Sydney.'

'How long have I been here?'

'You came in yesterday. You have injured your head. It's better for you to stay calm . . . oh, well, you know that yourself . . .'

'What happened?'

'There was an accident.'

'An accident?'

'A boating accident. A helicopter from RACQ Careflight found you. You were rescued by the coastguard. Our people on the spot flew you here. What actually happened?'

Annika struggled to clear her head. A boating accident? Had he called it a boating accident? Slowly she remembered. Remembered Kiesworik and his help in escaping the ASIO. His warning about the ASIO. Now she was lying here. In the headquarters of the ASIO.

'I'm thinking of the fire. There must have been a fire immediately before the explosion, since you managed to send a distress signal.'

'I don't know . . . it's all hazy.'

Everything was black. But then suddenly it flashed back. The final seconds before the plane hit the boat. Mike. Had he jumped before the plane struck? She couldn't make him appear in the glimpses she saw. She saw the rail, the spurt of flame, the explosion, the pressure, the water, and the ascent to the surface, the poisonous smoke, her grip on the dinghy's painter, and then everything went black. Had she crawled up into it by herself? And where was Mike?

She tried to get the rest of the room into focus but failed, and as if Osborne, with something resembling sympathy, had read her thoughts, he rose and sent a cloud of blue tobacco smoke towards her.

'We haven't yet found his body, Miss Niebuhr, but I think you'll have to prepare yourself to face the fact that Mike Lewis did not survive.'

'Wasn't he in the dinghy?'

'You were alone.'

'But the boat was ripped to pieces when it blew up. If he is dead, his body would have come up, wouldn't it?'

'I hate to sound macabre,' said Osborne, 'but as you say yourself, the boat . . . was blown to bits, so perhaps . . . he was as well. Perhaps he is still caught in a piece of wreckage the divers overlooked. And then . . . then there are the sharks.'

'Oh God . . .'

'I am sorry, Miss Niebuhr. I'll leave you alone for a while. Maybe you should try to go back to sleep. We . . . we are checking you on a monitor, there are doctors here, so if you feel ill you can' – he stretched over her to a button on the wall just above the bed – 'just press here.'

Then he straightened up and walked to the door. He opened it and stood fiddling with the lock.

'If you leave the room just remember to leave the door unlocked, or it will slam after you. I am the only one with a key. There are clean clothes and toilet things on the chair.

'There is a toilet and bathroom down there to the left,' he said, pointing down a small staircase. 'You cannot get out of the front door down there. You have to have a card to go the other way. Just along to the left is our well-stocked canteen.'

'I'm not hungry.'

'I just thought I'd mention it. Try to sleep for a while now. I'll be back in the morning.'

'What is this place?' asked Annika.

Osborne turned to face her.

'You are safe here.'

Annika did not wake up until late in the morning. She knew that if she did not get up out of the narrow, uncomfortably hard bed at once she would fall asleep again.

She sat up and rubbed her eyes. Her head throbbed at each movement she made. She felt the bandage carefully, and looked around for a mirror. But there wasn't one. She moved her arms cautiously to get her shoulders loosened up; they felt bruised and tender, and she saw she had blue and yellow blotches all down her arms.

The room was almost square. Beside her was a wheeled table with television and video, not switched on, a bedside table with a small lamp, and a telephone attached to the wall. The big panorama window gave on to an asphalted space. She went over and looked out.

In the adjoining building she could make out behind a large glass façade some activity in a high-ceilinged canteen. On her right an old coffee-maker stood on the windowsill, beside it a pile of plastic cups with spoons, sugar and cream in small packages. Further to the right in the corner was a small alcove with a washbasin and towels.

Along the wall adjoining the corridor was a galvanised metal cupboard close to the door. There were two strip lights on the ceiling. She went over to the door and pressed the switch. The strip lights clicked and flickered wildly. She switched off again and went to sit on the bed.

Thoughts of the boat and Mike came back to her, and she hid her face in her hands.

She stayed in that position until she heard a key in the lock.

'You were seen in Brisbane, Miss Niebuhr. What were you actually going to do there?'

Annika looked at Osborne, calmly drawing at his cigar as he sat opposite her on the chair. She wasn't sure about what and how much she dared tell him, and why he was bothering to ask at all.

'Is this an official interrogation?' she asked.

Osborne looked at her in astonishment and shook his head.

'I am asking because a murder has been committed up there, and we are helping with the enquiries. Kate Carpenter.'

'I visited her . . .'

'We know.'

'Yes . . .'

Annika looked at Osborne irresolutely. She couldn't make out why he was playing games with her, and wondered what medication they were giving her. Surely they knew what they knew?

'According to the witness statements we have, you must be one of the last people to have seen Kate Carpenter alive. So naturally we are interested to know what happened.'

Witness statements? Annika stared in disbelief at Osborne, who confused her even more by nodding encouragingly.

He took a pull at his cigar and leaned towards her.

'What exactly did Kate Carpenter tell you?'

Annika hesitantly told her story. But she left out Kahn, she left out Kiesworik, she left out the whole story of the murder she had seen; she restricted herself to the content and edited out all circumstances as she spoke and lied about the conclusion to her visit to Kate Carpenter. And as she listened to the story while telling it she realised how crazy it sounded in its censored edition.

Osborne smiled at her.

'What do you think of that story yourself?'

'What do you think?'

'That it sounds like the story of a paranoid alcoholic. The story of a disturbed female.'

'Why should she make up such a story?'

Osborne shrugged his shoulders.

'Brisbane. Maybe not exactly the most amusing place on earth for a widow who likes her tipple rather too much and has seen too many corpses in her life?'

Annika smiled.

'Almost Kate Carpenter's own words when she tried to imagine the objections that would be made to her story by the people she was afraid of.'

Osborne looked intently at her. As if he were searching for small changes in her face that might give her away, tell him something, say something about how much she had told him of what she knew, or whether she was keeping quiet about anything.

'Did Kate Carpenter say who was supposed to be behind this presumed great conspiracy?'

For a brief moment Annika was uncertain. She ransacked her memory for a name, an organisation, a designation, but it became clear to her that she and Kate Carpenter had not discussed precisely whom they were talking about. It had been implicit in the conversation that it concerned the ASIO. But had she actually ever mentioned the ASIO?

'"They" and "them" are pretty flimsy terms, aren't they? I wonder: was she talking about the local police who were investigating the case? You must understand, Miss Niebuhr: I do not claim not to know about Mark Johnson and his tragic fate, but I can assure you the ASIO was not mixed up in that accident.'

If Osborne's guileless expression concealed anything but sheer ignorance, he was an unusually clever actor. A characteristic one can expect to find in certain people, but which Annika found hard to link with Osborne.

Annika remembered the scans she had been sent. They must have come from inside. From a person or persons inside Osborne's own organisation. From people Simon relied on. The thought struck Annika that perhaps someone quite different was behind Osborne. A grey eminence neither she nor Osborne knew. Someone who ran an intelligence service inside the intelligence service and sent out murder squads when necessary.

Annika looked at Osborne but hesitated before replying. She remembered talking light-heartedly to Simon once about the working methods of the ASIO – a chat that sprang from a perfectly serious discussion on the importance of double-blind tests. How so many of the investigations of recent years into inexplicable phenomena had produced dramatic results which had prompted intensive research into the subjects, but which soon turned out to be practically useless because the influence on the research of the supervisor, the independent assessor, had been severely underestimated. She recalled how they had turned the famous example of Einstein's prediction of the deflection of light upside down. A group of British scientists confirmed Einstein's epoch-making prediction with photographic evidence from an eclipse of the sun in 1919, but it later appeared that the errors in measurement were quite as big as the effect the scientists had sought to prove, and that it was presumably owing to their foreknowledge of the desired result that the measurement succeeded. The whole thing ended in drunken babble in which a pair of Simon's male friends, who had stuck it out, enthusiastically contributed half-sick anecdotes of how they had seduced young women in the bars of Sydney. They did this according to quite simple principles, which consisted of putting endless questions to the female victim they had picked so in the end she thought that the monologue she had in reality carried on was part of an extremely pleasant and affable conversation. Even though it was late at night, and they – the men – had drunk a great deal, when the coarse jokes went too far Annika felt obliged to stand up for her sex, and she exchanged glances with Simon across the table and grew even more angry because she knew his silence was not grounded in simple sexism but that under no circumstances did he intend to come to her rescue because he considered them in principle to be right. To him it wasn't a question of chatting up or rather listening the pants off a woman, but of human behaviour, of psychology, and on that point he was, thought Annika, now and then hopelessly honest. That was one of the few occasions when they hit a core of cynicism in his personality that was hard for her to accept, for even though she knew she ought to love the fact that a human being is able to function normally despite having observed the simple and impoverished mechanism with which human intercourse is often carried out, she still wished he would take her part. What she wished for, and perhaps it was unreasonable, wishful thinking, was a gentle softness at the heart of his character, but it didn't exist, he was uncompromising through and through. When they were alone he lifted the veil of the interrogation methods they used, and how remorselessly they had learned to apply manipulation. He told her about the inhuman interrogations they were put through both in the military and in the ASIO in preparation for active service.

'Everyone talks under interrogation. At some point or other. But you can delay it. By sticking to just a few statements. And by trying never, never to answer the actual questions.'

This it was, those words, which flew through Annika's mind. But she was walking a difficult tightrope. As well as having to forget truthful aspects of her own history, she needed to remember the omissions and lies she had chosen, and simultaneously she must try to work out Osborne's strategy, his tactics, find out what it was he wanted from her, why and when he was bluffing. She was not trained for this kind of thing. He had done nothing else most of his life.

It was the way he inspired confidence she must fear, watch out for. In other words she should be careful of his whole character. This large body of Osborne's that seemed both good-humoured and jovial, and which to a certain extent Annika avoided being hypnotised by purely because for a brief moment in the gallery she had seen another side of him through a crack.

'Kate Carpenter was not specific. She did not say precisely who had—'

'Kate Carpenter was not specific. There was 'someone' there, and 'they' were 'those' who . . . Miss Niebuhr, you really are far too intelligent to fall for—'

'I am also too intelligent to believe that Simon committed suicide. Simon did not take his own life. Simon was murdered.'

Osborne nodded, eyes closed.

'But still . . .' Annika stopped short and looked at him. 'Why are you nodding?'

'Because you are right.'

'About what? Right about what?'

'About Simon being murdered.'

Annika didn't know what to say. She tried to concentrate, silenced by the unexpected admission, as if she was not sure whether Osborne was serious.

'Then why are you trying to make everyone think he killed himself?'

'Discretion, Miss Niebuhr, discretion. The case of Simon is a bit . . . embarrassing. We are trying to solve it, but it is a case that demands a certain tact, certain care. Indeed, Simon was murdered. Are you satisfied, then? And yes, we have people working on the case. Satisfied?'

'Not until you catch the people who killed him.'

'Was that why you went to Brisbane, Miss Niebuhr?'

'Yes.'

'To find Simon's killers?'

'Yes.'

'Why in heaven's name did you end up at Kate Carpenter's?'

Annika did not reply. She had prepared herself for a trap – and had walked straight into it. Now she owed him an explanation. Her reason for going to see Kate Carpenter. He had lured her. Surprised her with an unexpected announcement. Given her an admission. And thus had lured her into an explanation that only gave rise to new questions. Impossible now to make a retreat and withdraw her statement in any credible fashion.

'Just find the people who killed him,' said Annika.

'We shall,' said Osborne, raising his voice, 'when we know who it is. When we are quite certain of who it is.'

'Whose toes are you afraid of treading on, Osborne?'

He looked at her. Then he said sharply:

'It's not courteous to ask a woman's age. But it is downright rude to refer to a man's weight.'

'I only meant . . .'

'I know what you mean, Miss Niebuhr. We merely don't want to draw any hasty conclusions. That's all.'

Osborne stood up. He went slowly towards the door.

'Have you told me everything that might be of interest about your rendezvous with Kate Carpenter?'

'I don't know what you mean by interest.'

Osborne sucked at his cigar. Stared patiently at the ash. But there was no glow.

'Somehow I think you do, Miss Niebuhr. What first gave you the idea of seeking out Kate Carpenter? It's quite simply beyond my understanding.'

'Somehow I don't think it is . . .'

Osborne put his hand out to the door. He smiled at her.

'Does anybody know where I am?' asked Annika.

Osborne shook his head and pointed to the telephone on the wall.

'But if you are thinking of your family, you're welcome to ring them.'

'What about the girl? Is the girl here?'

'Now you should rest for a while.'

Annika rose and went over to the window looking on to the courtyard. A few cars were parked down at the end. Both civil and military.

'Am I being held here? Am I forced to stay here?'

'You can leave the moment you wish to,' said Osborne.

'It's a strange place . . .'

Osborne opened the door.

'I actually thought you might like it. This was where Simon worked.'

Annika stood lost in thought at the window, staring blankly ahead of her. The first glimmering of dawn lay on the adjoining building, the dull grey barrack-like wing that, apart from the glass façade of the canteen reflecting images of cars and trees, extended its uniform length along the courtyard. She was in a building, a complex, a construction like a school somewhere north-west of Sydney.

A mathematics lesson at Sydney High, she recalled, had preoccupied her. Although at an interval of many years it did not seem to have been an epoch-making event, she realised, on looking back, that that one lesson had played a central part in her eagerness to learn and had thus contributed to marking out the course of her life since.

Goethe hated logic. And mathematics. To Annika mathematics had always been a necessary evil. There was no doubt about its usefulness. Nor about her young, rebellious spirit at that time, then otherwise occupied by unhappy and irrational love affairs. Her objections to it stemmed from its desire, its urge to be unique, her attitude undoubtedly the result of growing up in a home in which mathematics was just a tool – a tool for physics.

Many years later she could still remember the lesson on infinity. The lesson in which they learned about the quantity of quantities. The lesson in which they had to reconcile themselves to the incomprehensible paradox that one lived in a universe that apparently had no limits. The lesson in which they learned about Russell's paradox, that the majority of quantities are apparently not members of themselves, but that some are, and that others again, paradoxically,

Michael Larsen

are both. The lesson in which it became really clear, as it had become clear to generations before her, that there was something they were never told, that there was something that could not be told. The lesson in which the perception of the concept of reality began to slide. The lesson in which mathematics for the first and, as far as she remembered, the only time became philosophical and thereby interesting.

Since that lesson her life had been one long search for explanations. An explanation of why elapids are so widespread in Australia, when every herpetologist knows that venomous snakes are the last of the snakes to originate, and that in the nature of things it is impossible for descendants to colonise a part of the world before their ancestors in the species. Of what a placebo is in reality. Of what it is, which all statistics substantiate, that enables thought to control and affect the course of a disease.

The funny thing was that during her hunt for explanations, she naturally ended up at what had been the starting point of it all – the question of the quantity of quantities, and the explanation that there was no simple explanation, no definitive proof, no definitive, unshakable and indisputable conclusion.

What the great mathematician Bertrand Russell, with Alfred North Whitehead, tried to prove was the possibility of creating a system that contained no self-contradictions or paradoxes. Worried first by the discovery of non-Euclidean geometry, which questioned whether mathematics dealt with reality at all, next by all the quantity-theoretical problems that Cantor's teaching on quantities had given rise to in the previous century, mathematicians and philosophers sweated over the fact that the paradoxes would probably not disappear, and that they needed a work that could once and for all put things, and specifically mathematics, in place as a consistent system, a system without self-contradictions. Carried along by a monumental conception of the limitless abilities of mathematics, the result was the voluminous work, *Principia Mathematica*, published between 1910 and 1913.

Like so many other young people, at that age Annika was

absorbed in the loops and metamorphoses of the painter Escher, Mandelbrot's fractals, the paradoxes of Zenon and Epimenides, and spurred on by the opening in the armament of authority and the apparent certainty that attended teachers during her schooldays, she read herself straight into the proof delivered by Kurt Gödel in 1931, that not only was the *Principia Mathematica* only good for throwing out with the bathwater, but that all systems which claim to be able to prove everything are doomed to failure, precisely as Newton's differential calculation is unfitted to handle things that are irregular and thus can only be used on linear systems in which cause and effect are linked by proportionality.

When she left school it was with a mental image of the ideas of Rutherford and Bohr on the atoms. Like so many others of her generation she ran around with Bohr's working model of the behaviour of atoms as demonstration of the real picture of the world of atoms. As a system of peaceful planets and suns revolving around each other in serene, fixed courses. Bohr's idea was like Newton's when he was working on Kepler's picture of the planets and Galileo's pendulums and falling bodies. When Annika became aware that she was going around with a picture of the smallest parts of physics that was basically wrong from top to tail, which had never been intended as teaching material either in schools or universities, and which Bohr had only made use of in order to advance the work of formulating a serviceable atom model, she determined to read her own way into the heart of the new physics – quantum physics and Heisenberg's principle of uncertainty.

It was a decision she had never regretted. And it became the happy dementia of a teenager's diffuse and semi-romantic ideas of trying to preserve herself intact and untouched by an exterior world that was apparently only bent on extinguishing light after light in the very years when the world seemed so fantastic and so unreasonably and unrealistically wonderful. So many things fell into place, and if she had been high on joints and wired from her reckless use of various synthetic powders in the unstable periods of her life, it was nothing compared to the way in which the apparently unruly dance of innocent electrons had been enough to make her high. The reproaches turned on adolescence, turned on an educational system that insisted on making you think in boxes and straight lines and strict causal chains, which welled up in her during the years when quantum reality unfolded before her eyes, were soon turned to gratitude, for it seems to be a fundamental rule in this world that young generations will always turn against their progenitors and their picture of the world and thus always discover precisely the world that is otherwise withheld from them.

It was also clear that even for the great physicists there were limits to how much an established picture of the world could be dismantled, before they too had to capitulate and turn against what they themselves had brought about. Like Einstein and the unhappy war he waged against himself and the quantum theory he helped to produce, but which he never really cared for because he was still imbued with remnants of Newton's thinking.

She also perceived that Young's renowned double-column experiment was doomed to be ignored even though it showed clearly that light consisted not only of particles, as Newton had asserted, but also waves, not merely because it was sacrilege to launch an attack on a man like Newton only a hundred years after his death, and on top of that by a countryman, but also because there are quite simply limits to how much and especially how quickly the world can move in the interpretation of itself.

Finally it became clear to her why so many young physicists of this century, after the discovery of quantum mechanics and chaos, had dug up Goethe again and patiently read their way through his thorough scientific examination of colours and reflected afresh on his ideas of a more open science.

Thus suitably armed, she launched the attack on her father and classical mechanics. She didn't know why he held on to mechanics as an unbroken quantity and a dominant characteristic of this world, when he knew it was not, but she guessed that it had a similarly reassuring effect on him and the numerous viewers as *Scientific Week* had.

When Galileo the space probe turned back to earth for the second time to gather acceleration for its journey to Jupiter, it happened within seconds and metres of previous calculations. Such an unheard-of precision must by definition attract an almost superhuman faith in human prophecies and in the solar system as a system that works with clockwork precision. And her father was happy to pass it on. But when Annika saw the programme, she knew that these excellent preliminary calculations were carried out for a space with planets and moons that do not at all live up to our theoretical expectations of them. That astronomers at MIT in Boston had demonstrated on one of the most powerful computers in the world that the solar system behaves in as chaotic a way as does life on earth. That metaphorically speaking the planets gambol around among each other. That chaos reigns even in space.

Up to this moment Annika had never regretted the course of her life. A life in books in search of still more knowledge had made her own existence meaningful. Had filled her with a respect and love for this world, this universe, whose all-dominant characteristic made it an inexhaustible source of potential interpretation.

But it was also this curiosity that had driven her on to the moment in which she now found herself. She thought of Mike, of the boat, of the explosion, and that it was she who had brought them both into that situation.

She sat gazing blankly out into space. And for the first time in her life she knew the full significance of feeling alone.

Osborne let himself in about midday in the company of two men. One of them a young man in a suit and tie like Osborne, the other middle-aged in a white coat.

Osborne introduced the two men to Annika.

'Dr Lucas Henry, Miss Niebuhr. Henry worked in the same section as Simon. He just wants to have a look at you.'

Annika gave him her hand and smiled.

'How are you today, Miss Niebuhr?'

Annika still felt weak, sore and pretty knocked about, but she smiled at him and nodded.

'And special agent Kevin Cooper,' said Osborne, and indicated the young man, who put a tray on the table with a friendly smile. On the tray was a bowl of salad and an unopened bottle of mineral water, and beside them a sandwich wrapped in foil.

'We gather you are not eating anything,' said Osborne, again looking to Agent Cooper. 'Cooper will see you safely home when you are ready. But first' – he smiled at the young man – 'he will make us all a cup of coffee.'

Cooper went over to the coffee machine, picked up the globe and poured water into it from the tap in the small basin.

Lucas Henry sat down in front of her and pulled carefully at the plaster, which brought tears to her eyes, and then pulled more and more from her cheek.

'I think some air will be good for it now.'

'What does it look like?'

'A bad graze. It will heal up well.'

Osborne cleared his throat.

'We need to know who gave you the idea that Kate Carpenter might have had some special knowledge relating to Simon's death.'

'Why don't you tell me instead what really happened in the accident up near Brisbane?'

Osborne looked at her, then down at the floor, looked at Cooper, who had taken up a position with his back to the big window, looked at Lucas Henry.

'As you described it. As it was described in the press notice you mentioned. There was no mystery about that accident. I don't know where Kate Carpenter got that idea from.'

'All that fuss . . . about a girl who died in a car accident a month ago? Why don't I believe you?'

Osborne studied her for a moment and hesitated slightly before answering.

'The only thing,' he said, getting up and going towards Cooper, 'the only thing that is not correct in the telegram is that three people died. The girl . . . the girl is not dead. When the accident took place the girl was here.'

'So I should believe some of Kate Carpenter's story, but not all of it?'

Osborne nodded.

'And Kate Carpenter's sudden death has nothing to do with the case?'

He looked at her.

'I didn't say that.'

'Is it normal for the intelligence service to go around like this, falsifying death certificates?'

'It's highly abnormal.' Osborne looked at Cooper, whose gaze faltered. 'It's abnormal, anyway.'

'Why did you do what you did?'

'To protect her.'

'Protect her against what? "Herself and others"?'

'Something like that.'

'So the ASIO took . . . possession of her? Declared their right of possession to the child? Is that legal? Were there no relatives who could . . .'

Osborne interrupted her.

'Miss Niebuhr, the girl is sick. Medically and legally the arrangement was fully responsible. We are not, perhaps in contrast to what you think, on the lookout for laws to break. And regardless of anything else, it would be completely irresponsible, that . . . this girl is . . .' He looked at Lucas Henry. 'Help me, Doctor.'

Lucas Henry sat down in the chair opposite Annika.

'Maria Johnson is not . . . quite normal.'

'I have realised that.'

'She is in fact somewhat . . . unique. She has certain abilities that . . .'

'Are you helping her? Or is she helping you?'

Lucas Henry threw a glance at Osborne, who was standing by the window looking down into the courtyard. He turned and for a brief moment his eyes met Henry's. Osborne nodded. A detailed explanation had been granted.

'It was Mark Johnson who originally contacted Simon, because his daughter had something wrong with her. For quite some time she had suffered from certain inexplicable attacks. Resembling epilepsy. Blackouts. Mark Johnson had heard very good reports of Simon and asked him to see the girl. I assisted Simon with some of the investigations. When he hypnotised her he discovered she was troubled by a series of frightening visions that kept recurring.'

'What did she see?'

'It wasn't altogether clear. At the beginning, Simon and his colleagues took her through a whole series of tests. She was better for a time, but then things went wrong again. She had severe anxiety attacks, and for periods we were quite unable to communicate with her. Simon spent oceans of time on her. You know how he was with children. It was decided that she should stay for a longish period at this . . . place, so we could get to the bottom of her problems. Mark Johnson agreed, and after we had gone through a mass of formalities it was arranged for her to receive a certain kind of teaching here. She was well looked after.

'As she improved and had remained stable for a long period, Simon started to involve her in some of the projects he was working on.'

'What projects?'

Again Lucas Henry glanced at Osborne, who made no objection.

'You will recall the exposure of the CIA's parapsychological programme? Center Lane, Sun Streak, Stargate. A favourite child has many names. We had a similar programme, which Simon was in charge of. "Atlas X." Gaia Jessup, whom I gather you have met, was also involved in that project. To start with Maria Johnson was Simon's patient, but she ended up as part of the clientèle. There was a link between her unstable mind and the abilities she turned out to have.'

'Are you trying to tell me the girl is telepathic?'

'No,' he said, looking at Osborne again. Annika noticed that his forehead was starting to sweat. He turned to Annika again. 'I am trying to tell you that Maria Johnson is quite exceptionally telepathic.'

The coffee machine emitted a series of resigned sighs, and when it eventually died in a long-drawn-out snore, Cooper went over, poured coffee into four plastic mugs and distributed them.

Lucas Henry dug a pack of cigarettes out of his lab coat's breast pocket. He put down his papers and lit up. Annika asked for a cigarette.

'I can't really recommmend that.'

'You can't really recommend smoking at all, can you, Dr Henry?'

Lucas Henry smiled and gallantly knocked a cigarette out of his pack. He lit it for Annika.

'As far as I understand,' said Annika, inhaling deeply, 'not a single scientifically substantiated experiment exists confirming the reality of telepathy.'

He looked at Annika with an uncomprehending frown.

'That is quite simply not so, Miss Niebuhr. There are plenty of investigations that support the idea.'

'But also others that do not?'

'Have you heard about the Russian rabbits? Pretty macabre. But convincing. A mother rabbit was fitted with electrodes in her brain; the electrodes were attached to immensely sensitive measuring equipment. Then the mother was taken down in a submarine to a depth of several kilometres, while on land her babies were killed one by one. Each time this happened the Russian scientists registered violent electrical activity in the mother rabbit's brainwaves.'

'Has that been tried on human beings?'

An expression of distaste crossed Lucas Henry's face.

'I don't fully understand your scepticism. The Russians, the Americans, the English – they are all working on these things. Did you not yourself take part in Simon's experiments?'

'I read through some reports. The results I saw were not impressive.'

Lucas Henry rose to his feet. He went over to Osborne. They whispered together, then Lucas Henry turned to Agent Cooper, who first looked at Annika then left the room.

Lucas Henry went back to his chair and sat facing Annika again.

'You do know about the phenomenon of "remote viewing", do you not, Miss Niebuhr?'

'By hearsay. I have never seen it in action.'

'Physicists from the Stanford Research Institute in California introduced the term, and surely Stanford can pass muster even for a highly trained woman like you?'

'I think it is problematic that it is not possible to verify these phenomena in controlled experiments.'

'How do you think Newton and his contemporaries got on with gravity? Before Einstein's space curvatures and Maxwell's local fields of electrical and magnetic forces? What do you think they did with the idea of the earth pulling at the moon? With the idea of invisible forces working in vast empty space? But which apparently had no effect on two people standing precisely opposite each other?'

'Are you talking of quantum mechanics and non-locality?'

He shook his head.

'Of Jung's acausal relations? Synchronicity? Superluminal connections?'

'We don't have a word for it, Miss Niebuhr, for we quite simply do not understand the mechanisms that make it possible. But allow me to remind you that there is nothing in Einstein's general theory of relativity or in quantum mechanics that prohibits wormholes and time travel, so you can decide for yourself which you find most strange.'

'What are you trying to say?'

'Miss Niebuhr, you never saw the results. Simon was working on strictly classified material. He didn't show you the results. Not all of them.'

'I don't get it . . .'

'Do you or do you not have a revolver in the third drawer of your chest of drawers in the bedroom? A Browning?'

At that moment Cooper came into the room again. In his hand he held a clear plastic bag with a small label attached to it.

Lucas Henry reached back and took hold of the bag. He held it out towards Annika.

'And is this the Browning in question?'

'How can you find a weapon but overlook a human being?'

Annika looked at him. She threw a glance at Osborne by the window, who looked at her expectantly without otherwise batting an eyelid. It was Cooper who replied.

'It was in the dinghy. Beside you.'

Annika tried to remember the final seconds on the boat. Before the plane hit them. She remembered shooting like a madwoman at the aircraft above them, but she also remembered losing her balance, falling backwards and dropping the gun. On to the boat.

'I didn't have it. Not at the end . . .'

Osborne cleared his throat.

251

'The revolver was found beside you in the boat. As was your mobile telephone. Both are intact and you will get them back when you leave here. Now try to concentrate on this.'

'Simon knew I had it. He got it for me.'

'Is it true that you have a dilapidated book with a red spine on your bookshelf, which . . . moves you when you turn to page sixteen? To a sentence that includes the word "*mislykkede*"?'

'The Danish edition of Goethe's collected works. Volume One. P.A. Rosenberg's foreword on his "*mislykkede farvelaere*", his ineffective theory of chromatology.'

'Why does it move you?'

Lucas Henry looked at her with sincere surprise. It was clear that this was a point which had disorientated him, something Annika could not blame him for.

'It's probably a kind of wistfulness. Goethe's clash with Newton's *Optics*. Goethe worked with his chromatology ideas for more than forty years of his life, and he himself regarded it as his most important contribution to world literature. He was misunderstood and wrongly understimated and misjudged for two hundred years. Today we know he was right. That there were grave errors and limitations in Newton's view of light. That Newton's wavelengths in the spectrum don't tell us a brass farthing about the nature of colour.'

'You are very fond of Goethe?'

'I greatly admire his feeling for complexity. His sense of the coalescence of things.'

'How do you account for the fact that Maria Johnson was aware of it?'

'Simon could have told her.'

'She wrote the word "*mislykkede*". In Danish.'

'I taught Simon a few words of Danish. I don't remember whether "*mislykkede*" was among them.'

'"*Rødgrød med fløde*", "*æbleflæsk*", "*ærlighed*" and "*kærlighed*". Forgive my pronunciation. But those are the words and phrases Simon thought he had learned from you. Red jelly and cream, pork with applesauce, honesty and love.'

'What exactly are you trying to tell me?'

'I am trying to illustrate some of Maria Johnson's abilities.'

He picked up his mug and took a mouthful of coffee.

'I can assure you I have never been in telepathic contact with that girl.'

'I am not saying you have,' he said, putting down the mug. 'What I am saying is that she has been in contact with you.'

Without a word he pulled an A4 sheet out of his briefcase. He placed it in front of Annika and turned it around slowly until it was straight.

'Considering she has never seen you it is a very good likeness, isn't it?'

Annika put her hands on the paper. As if to feel her way to the secret that must be hidden in the lines of the drawing. The drawing that had been sent to her. The picture of her face. She looked enquiringly at Lucas Henry.

'This is a copy,' he said. 'We can't find the original. But there is no doubt that the drawing represents you, is there?'

At one time Annika had three assumptions about the world. That she had a fair understanding of relativity theories; that this was a good thing as she expected them to come to play some role in her life; and that quantum mechanics, as technical and inaccessible as it seemed, was something she did not need to acquire a deep understanding of, since it could only have a limited meaning for her everyday life.

All three assumptions were wrong. The relativity theories had no influence on her life, and her father steered her swiftly away from the delusion that the theories had any connection whatsoever with philosophical relativism and the phrase 'everything is relative', and that they – wholly against her expectations – focused on the precise aspects of physical reality that are not relative. And quantum mechanics was the revelation which – she found – enveloped her and everyone else from the time they got up until they went to bed. It was the foundation of all modern natural science. Without it hospitals would know nothing of microsurgery, molecular biologists would not have an analysis apparatus to interpret X-ray diffraction data, and we would not have space probes to search the remote areas of space with their electronic brains. There would be no mobile telephones, no lasers to read the magnetic strips on everyone's credit cards, no digital clock radio would stand on the bedside table, there would be no stereo systems, no portable television sets and no computers.

Heisenberg's uncertainty principle, which in essence consists of two central equations, killed off the dream physicists had of fundamentally understanding reality.

The spidery little equation $\Delta x \Delta p > h$ doesn't immediately look much, but when it emerged in the 1920s it shook science.

In the equation, h represents Planck's constant, and the Greek letter delta, Δ, is used to indicate small increases in the variable. Provided one knows precisely where an electron is, so that Δx is equal to nought, then Δp in principle will become infinitely great, and one will not have the remotest idea of where the electron will travel in the universe, because in order to know where it is one must hit it with light, and this will disturb it and influence its speed in a completely unpredictable manner. This is the Heisenberg equation which says that the more precisely one attempts to determine an electron's position, the more imprecise will be one's knowledge of its speed. And vice versa. The other equation $\Delta E \Delta t > h$ tells the same story of the relation between two other physical variables – energy and time.

It was actually the term objectivity which died with these equations. Until then classical physics had believed that fundamentally there was no lower limit for how precise measurements could be. There was.

What Goethe was querying, and what has always been the declared working method of science, was that one observed and searched for clues, from which one created one's theories. But very often the reality has been different. Scientists created their theories and then undertook their observations and searched for the clues that could support the theoretical basis. Physicists, who for centuries had grown accustomed to thinking of the universe as something that functions with clockwork precision, and according to theories that could be verified by experiments, suddenly had to get used to the idea that the dream classical physicists held of nature as an easily understood, clarified and measured entity was not necessarily shared by nature itself.

Today it is not hard to understand how physicists, who at the turn of the century were busy digesting Einstein's dramatic rewriting of the laws of nature and his impressive prophecies, which emerged as the most excellent in classical physics, shortly afterwards found it hard to accept that they would have to make adjustments to the parameters of our ideas of reality. That there is a reality that snaps its fingers at our ideas about interaction, forces, push and pull, heave and let go, a world in which the order of factors is not trivial, that the set of rules according to which the world works on its most fundamental level is imbued with indeterminism and probabilities.

Annika's way in to quantum mechanics was an article in *Reviews of Modern Physics* which she found on her father's desk. It discussed a repetition of a series of the classical experiments undertaken by Tony Klein and his colleagues at Melbourne University, and in its conclusion established that not only electrons but also neutrons and protons, indeed all particles and waves, are neither particles nor waves, but both. That not only is there no picture in the atomic world that represents a clearly observable solar system of planets circling each other, but that there quite simply is no useful picture at all of what goes on. That no analogies from classical physics can be utilised in the atomic world. That apparently electrons can be in two places at the same time, that we can only obtain a limited knowledge of them when we are observing them and have no idea whatsoever of where they are and what they do when we are not.

When Annika was very young she would have sworn she would never become interested in the diffuse peek-a-boo of the electrons. But after studying details of the Aspect experiment of Paris, which produced an experimental proof that the quantum world, despite its strangeness, patently is our world, when she looked back to the 1960s' formulation of Bell's theorem, which in principle settled the lengthy disagreement between Einstein and Niels Bohr in favour of Bohr, she realised that it satisfied something far more fundamental in her, as no doubt in most people, namely the feeling of duality. That everything can be dissected and yet not, that everything is made up of detached parts and yet combined, that one can feel, sense and abstract, but also think, analyse and discard, and that everything, when all is said and done, ends up in knots and Greek paradoxes. That we and the electrons are inextricably bound up in an uncertain process which no one understands.

By using Schrödinger's wave equations one can force a determinism into quantum mechanics which makes all forms of electronic apparatus possible. All the way from atom bombs to hospital equipment. But it does not alter the fact that it is part of the human condition not to know anything with certainty. That in a way reality only takes form when we look at it. That we ourselves take part in creating it. That only at the moment when we send a gentle gamma shower down into the dark do we know whether the electron is there. That even with a little low-waved gamma ray we shall influence the reality we see, so that, when we look at the very smallest component the picture is jolted. That it is owing to us and our efforts to obtain a clear picture of the world. And that this disintegration of the picture is the sharpest picture of the world we can get.

Annika put down the drawing. Nothing travels faster than light. And the drawing only had meaning if something had moved at more than the speed of light. Annika looked at it again.

She had no explanation.

The moonlight shone in through the little window in the wall when Annika woke up late that evening. Osborne was in the chair beside her.

Annika sat up. Swung her legs down from the bed, bent over and tried to clear her head.

'How are you feeling, Miss Niebuhr?'

She smiled at him, stood up and walked stiffly on unsteady legs across the floor to the window on to the courtyard. She pressed her forehead to the pane.

'Is there any news?' she said.

Osborne did not reply. She heard him get up and come and stand behind her.

'You mean of Mike Lewis?'

With her back to him, Annika nodded.

'I'm afraid you will have to accept the fact that we shan't find him.'

She turned towards him. Looked up at his big face.

'He might have been picked up. By a ship.'

Osborne said nothing.

Annika felt it coming from right inside her. As something she could not possibly control. Like an undercurrent, a landslide, a crack-up. She put her face against Osborne's chest and flung her arms around him.

He put his arms around her hesitantly. In her mind's eye Annika saw a strip of images from a nature film that had once touched her deeply, when a young antelope on the African savannah ran up to and tried to find safety beneath the stomach of a cheetah, thinking it was its mother. Executioner and victim equally confused. The cheetah had no idea what to do. Tried to hit out at the antelope to make it go away. The young antelope, which still did not understand its mistake in its efforts to find a safe place, and the cheetah, which needed a creature in flight to activate its natural instincts. A collective short circuit in nature's system.

The side of Annika's face rested against Osborne's chest. She could not go on. She was exhausted. Dispirited. Helpless. She no longer had the strength to leave or to find out how everything connected.

Osborne stroked her hair.

'Why don't you just get it over with?' she said. 'Why don't you just kill me?'

Osborne pulled her away from him.

'But why should we do that?'

Annika let her face fall back on his chest.

'There was a plane. It exploded when it torpedoed the boat. The divers must have found the wreckage. Of the plane. And bodies.'

Osborne did not reply. He stood holding her for a few moments. Then he pulled her over to the bed and put her down on it. He tugged the cord of the little lamp on the bedside table, sat on the chair by the bed, and took her hands in his.

'You should have said that, Miss Niebuhr. You should have told us that at the start.'

Annika looked at him, biting her lip.

'You're lying to me, Osborne. Or is there someone who lies to you?'

'Or are you lying to me? You still haven't told me what took you to Brisbane. What made you seek out Kate Carpenter?'

Frank Kiesworik had fished for the same information. But with the decisive difference that he had saved her life.

'Have you talked to Frank Kiesworik, Miss Niebuhr?'

'Why do you ask that?'

'Ah, well, I just have a feeling you have been talking to the Americans. Kiesworik? Kleff? Holden?'

'Didn't we once sign an agreement with the Americans that ensured they did not engage in espionage in this country?'

'When has a written guarantee from the Americans ensured anyone against anything at all? You'd better wake up, Miss Niebuhr. Have you been talking to the Americans? What have they told you?'

'Doesn't it amount to one and the same thing? What you know, they know?'

'Just because you invite a friend in, it doesn't mean he also has admission to the marital bed. What have they told you?'

Annika made no reply. Then he grasped her wrist and raised his voice: 'What have they put across on you?'

She did not answer, just stared at him.

'The CIA spent over a hundred million dollars on Star Gate,' he said. 'The Red Brigade's kidnapping of General James Dozier in 1981. Their mediums failed the test. The American air attack on Libya in 1986. The mediums were to find Gaddafi. They did not deliver. They had more luck with their pictures of North Korean building works in Korea's demilitarised zone and the drawings of secret Russian U-boats. But the judgment of the American Institute in 1995 was that the results were too poor. Why? Because the Americans are fucked up.

'Maria Johnson is fourteen; she has never been abducted by little men with big black eyes. Over seventy-five per cent of the American population is convinced that the American government is hiding important information on UFOs from them. It is the same with ESP. They have made experiments themselves that reveal that the Americans are inclined to believe in ESP, which throws doubt on all their results. It is a vicious circle. The researchers working on ESP are also very positive about it. It affects the results. Which again will be better than they really are.

'Miss Niebuhr, the Americans are after Maria Johnson. No alien beings have carried out experiments on our Maria Johnson, no one has sent probes into her, no one has behaved indecently towards her. In other words, she would be perfectly normal if she were not so abnormal.'

'Where could she have got those abilities from?'

'On the whole all known cases of psychic powers which cannot be explained turn out to be linked with very violent events. Grievously painful experiences, experiences of death at a very early age. We know from all the tests that the younger a person is the better. Where children are concerned it is almost perfect.'

'But Maria Johnson . . . she was not involved in that car accident, or whatever it was.'

'No, but she was involved in another accident.'

'I don't understand . . .'

'I thought Kate Carpenter had told you. Maria Johnson and her parents survived the first car crash. But her sister did not. She and her sister were wedged fast on the back seat of the car. For over an hour Maria Johnson, at the age of four, was held there helplessly watching her sister slowly die.'

Annika closed her eyes.

'You see? The perfect impregnation, if you'll excuse the expression.'

'You frighten me, Osborne.'

'You know what I mean. Now tell me why you sought out Kate Carpenter.'

'You know quite well why I went there.'

'Describe now what really happened in Brisbane.'

'What really happened?'

'With the Americans, Miss Niebuhr. Try to find the logic of our wanting to do away with you. Why do we allow you to go on living now?'

'Because you want something from me?'

'Then why should we try to kill you at the start? It doesn't make sense, does it? You can see that for yourself, can't you? Now try to apply the same critical view to the Americans. What did they want from you?'

'They helped me . . .' said Annika.

'Tell me what happened, Miss Niebuhr.'

Hesitantly Annika started her story. She still kept quiet about Kahn in the hope that Osborne would forget the reason for her going up there at all, and then supplied him with all the details of her visit to Kate Carpenter that she had omitted in her first description. Next she told him how she had escaped from the apartment, about the men on the staircase, about Kiesworik in the back yard, about their flight in the car.

When she was done, Osborne sat looking speculatively in front of him. Then he smiled.

'I can certainly understand why you were confused.'

'What do you mean?'

'Did you see the men on the stairs?'

'I heard them . . .'

'And they spoke with an unmistakable Australian accent?'

'I think so . . .'

'And Kiesworik's bullet wound. Did you see it? Did you examine it? It would have been natural for a doctor to look after him.'

'What are you trying to say?'

'Afterwards in the car. Hard to be on guard against a man who has just saved your life, eh?'

'What do you mean?'

'First establish trust and then go to work.'

'Reminds me of what you've been trying on.'

'He pumped you, didn't he?'

Osborne stood up and shouted into her face: 'They tricked the arse off you, Miss Niebuhr. They set up a whole performance. Masses of special effects. And you never discovered it. And then when you had been softened up, Frank Kiesworik could put the questions he wanted an answer to, couldn't he?'

'I . . .'

'Filled you with lies. And then bang . . .'

'Didn't see it . . .'

'Bang . . . bang . . . bang.'

Annika shouted.

'I didn't say anything. Because I didn't know anything. And as you have the girl, I don't understand all this. What is it you want?'

She looked at Osborne and sat down. Silently. Only then did it dawn on her. Only then did she see daylight.

'You haven't got her. You haven't got the girl, have you? Simon got her away. You don't know where she is.'

Osborne looked at her inscrutably. He pulled out a cigar, felt the covering leaves, softly knocked one end against his index finger, turned it around between his fingers.

'That's why I became interesting. I knew Simon. How much did I know? You thought I was in on it? Knew where she was?'

Osborne sat down heavily. He rubbed his eyes and mumbled.

'We still don't know how he got her out of here. We know Gaia Jessup was involved. But we can't find her.'

'What about the snake? The snake in the car?'

'I merely give my orders. How things develop I leave to others. But we were obliged to give her and Simon a fright that could not be misunderstood.'

'You could have killed her.'

'Miss Niebuhr, I have seen Gaia Jessup "die" so many times that I honestly doubt if there is anything at all that can kill her. We have had her subjected to electrocardiographs when it looked as if she made use of them like a game of Ping-Pong. That girl can screw her pulse and heartbeat up and down as it suits her.'

'How does she do it?'

'She doesn't even know that herself. She says she concentrates. On not concentrating. I don't know if that makes you any the wiser.'

'Why didn't you just grab Gaia Jessup if you knew she would get into that car?'

'Because we didn't know where she had the girl. There was money for Gaia Jessup in the glove compartment. We know Simon had planned to get the girl out of the country. We confiscated the money. But we were obliged to let her go.'

'And Simon?'

'We had our people with him down on the boat. But only to talk to him. It was not until later that day that he was found dead. I don't know what happened. But we'll find out. We'll get hold of whoever killed him, all right.'

Annika remembered Gaia Jessup's warning. She kept quiet about the meeting she had had with her in her car. There were jarring notes in all the stories she had heard. Frank Kiesworik might be full of lies. Osborne might be. Gaia Jessup might be.

'There's something I don't understand, Osborne. If everything was going so smoothly, why should Simon be so set on getting Maria Johnson away from here?'

'It was Simon who experimented on her, Miss Niebuhr.'

'That wasn't an answer.'

'Simon was responsible for her.'

'But you were his chief?'

Osborne looked down. He put his cigar on the table, folded his hands and circled his thumbs around each other.

'Simon pushed her too hard. He ... I don't know, he pushed both himself and the girl too hard. We had some internal disagreements.'

'Simon would never let a child come to any harm.'

'Miss Niebuhr, I think you will have to revise your opinion of Simon. Maria Johnson's condition ... her condition has not been stable the whole time.'

Annika rose and walked around Osborne.

'Her father wanted to take her out of the project, didn't he? Mark Johnson regretted the decision. Her family wanted her back.'

Osborne looked at her intently.

'We had nothing to do with their death. But ... the accident happened a short time later. Simon misunderstood the whole thing.'

'I suppose objectively one cannot blame him for it.'

'Miss Niebuhr, we know there was a leak. We know the Americans tried to influence Simon.'

Annika shook her head firmly.

'Do you know what Simon thought of the Americans?'

'He knew Frank Kiesworik. We don't know whether Simon told him anything. But we know that Kiesworik knew about the girl's powers. Somehow or other he knew about Maria Johnson.'

'So the accident was no accident?'

Osborne looked at her speculatively.

'You have talked to Kate Carpenter yourself. There were strong indications in the investigation that it was not, but we do not know.'

'What would the Americans get out of killing the Johnson family? That in itself would not get them the girl.'

'But it put the ASIO in a bad light. In Simon's eyes. And so we chose opportunism. We made sure we had the girl.'

'Which strengthened Simon's belief that the ASIO were behind it?'

Osborne looked down.

'That . . . is a possibility.'

'It undeniably resembles a coincidence.'

'I like the way you put it, Miss Niebuhr. It resembles. It also looked as if the Americans were protecting you from us, did it not?'

'How can this girl mean so much to them?'

'Believe me, she does.'

'She's only a child.'

'You still don't understand, do you?'

Osborne went over to the wall telephone. He gave a couple of orders. Annika heard him telling Lucas Henry to come in. At once.

Annika looked at him enquiringly.

'I want to show you something,' he said.

Lucas Henry put a pile of videotapes on the small table. He had a folder in his hand. A report, sketched graphs, diagrams, which Annika could not read from where she sat, a stack of pictures.

He sat down and looked at her.

'We know from autistic patients that the brain can release quite enormous powers of calculation. We can't explain it. From neurologists we know that people whose numeral centre is damaged can still calculate in probabilities, approximate figures. Ask them what two and two make and they give the wrong answer, but ask them what it makes approximately and they have the feeling that it's close to four. Why? Suppose the brain holds quite other potentialities? Potentialities we know nothing about? Or that we have known, but forgotten?'

Osborne wound the video on.

'I'll show you one or two sequences from our observations of Maria Johnson in the sleep laboratory. If you have an explanation of what is going on we'll be glad to hear it.'

He activated the start button. Nothing happened. Osborne pressed the fast forward button, and something began to show.

Annika stared at the screen. So that was what she looked like.

Maria Johnson. A pleasant, almost beautiful girl of fourteen. Shy, with a slightly awkward manner. She was in a bed, enveloped in electronics. There were electrodes on her arms, her legs, her chest and her face. A comprehensive set-up. There was a counting meter at the bottom of the screen, and at the side, information on pulse-rate and brain and heart activity.

Suddenly the figures for her heart rhythm increased by a factor of three and her breathing shot up. She rose from the bed and tried to pull off the wiring. She got out of bed, walked around looking upset, and then the attack began. Osborne turned down the sound as she started to scream.

'What's going on there?'

'Wait a bit,' said Osborne.

It was quite clear, even though nothing was said. Suddenly it seemed as if something took over the girl and filled her with an energy that was clearly not her own. She took hold of the bedstead and heaved and tugged at the iron bars. Then she suddenly lifted the whole bed up off the floor.

Annika felt Osborne looking expectantly at her.

She shook her head.

Lucas Henry looked at her.

'The bed weighs more than fifty kilos. And . . . oops.' He paused, while Osborne wound on. 'She hit the camera on the wall,' said Lucas Henry.

'I've seen something similar from other sleep laboratories. In REM sleep. REM Behaviour Disorder. Something is activated in these people.'

'I think it's as clear to you as it is to us that something is happening. Normally adrenalin is released at precisely the second when a person needs it in a crisis situation. I am sure you noticed that here the transformation took place before the girl got hold of the bed. It is quite obvious that she . . . that she turns into someone else. Suddenly.'

'What is your own explanation?'

'We do not have one. Actually we don't have an adequate clinical description of Maria Johnson at all. She exhibits momentary schizo-phrenic behaviour and also reacts to medicaments for psychosis. In other situations without medicine she functions normally. Her activity in dreaming sleep is totally chaotic. She has violent attacks of fear, but can also become extremely aggressive.'

Osborne rewound the tape. He went over to the video player, removed the tape and inserted a new one.

Lucas Henry looked at Annika.

'You know the conditions for the Ganzfeld test? The medium is placed in a soundproof room, with halved table tennis balls attached to their eyes, is flooded in red light, white noise in the ears. The sender sits in an adjoining room. On a monitor a computer programmed for completely random choice from among a number of stored pictures shows the selected picture that the sender will attempt to send to the medium. In Honorton's test the computer has to draw lots from among forty video shots, four different ones with ten copies of each. Based entirely on the law of probability, which says the result will be twenty-five per cent. Afterwards the four shots are shown to the receiver, who must select the picture he or she thinks corresponds to the one the person concerned has seen during the 'telepathic' transmission. In Spinelli's experiment they operated with five pictures, otherwise the principles were more or less the same. Apart from two things: all checking was dropped, because they wanted to investigate a suspicion that it could in fact influence the results negatively. And another significant and interesting difference: the tested subjects were children, and the younger they were the better. Thousands of children were tested. The best ones were three-year-olds. In almost half the experiments they scored bull's-eyes. That's unheard of statistically. With five pictures, according to statistic probability, they should get twenty per cent right. But the three-year-olds got forty-six per cent, the five-year-olds thirty-five per cent, the six- to eight-year-olds twenty-six per cent. We didn't bother making that kind of test on Maria.'

'Don't your dinner guests ever complain about the bent cutlery?'

With a tight little grin Lucas Henry registered Annika's affront, but otherwise remained unmoved.

'Given the knowledge we have today of the development of the brain, it's an interesting result. We know the total capability of the brain culminates when we are quite small. Does the brain try out this form of communication? And why does it do that? Could we use the brain quite differently from the way we do? What are the potentialities for that? And – have we done it before? Consciousness? No one has any idea of what it is, but we all agree that it is there. But now we can look inside. In earnest. Dream. In their time Freud and Jung worked on these things. The sinking of the *Titanic* was foreseen in a dream. Churchill had a vision of the German bombing of Downing Street. Emanuel Swedenborg had visions. Thousands of dream visions have been recorded through the ages. Thousands were never written down. Now finally we have the possibility of learning the way it works. We have the apparatus for looking in. For understanding.'

Annika thought of the PET scans she had been sent. With all the secrecy surrounding Maria Johnson it was unlikely they had taken the scans at a hospital. They must have the apparatus in their own premises.

'There are theories about everything,' said Annika drily. 'What caused the dinosaurs to die out? A meteor? A virus? Earthquake? Climate change? Infertility? Changes in the water level? A combination of several possibilities? Did they die out as a natural process of evolution over a long, long period? Did they never wholly die out?'

Lucas Henry put a new tape into the video player. Osborne set it going and stopped it when images started to appear on the screen.

'Chungsiang, China. A factory in the area produces components for the Chinese rocket programme. From those satellite photos you see now on the screen,' he said, passing Annika three coarse-grained photos of the factory from the air, 'and the co-ordinates of the factory, Maria Johnson drew this picture for us. From this we have been able to make this 3D simulation.' He passed Annika another piece of paper showing the factory from the front. 'As these jet engines can only be ramjet engines, because they have no turbines, we know they are either to be used for air-to-air or ground-to-air missiles, or for something we do not know about. The ASIO reports describe several violent supersonic explosions in the region, and seismographic measurements we have had smuggled out and collocated indicate the same directions and speeds. Directions pointing at an airbase. It looks as if the Chinese are ahead of the Americans with a wholly new type of supersonic plane that can go up to over thirty kilometers' height.'

Osborne fast-forwarded the tape. Stopped at pictures of a hall containing military equipment. A board showing 'AWA Defence Industries' could be glimpsed.

'Nulka. Anti-ship missile. Able, for example, to lead the French-designed Exocet away from its target. Devised by the Australian Defence Science and Technology Organisation. Orders for the Royal Australian Navy, USA and Canada. The girl got the factory co-ordinates. At this time no officially available photographs of the missile existed. And here is,' said Osborne, waiting for the next picture, 'a shy and embarrassed Maria Johnson showing off her drawing, which showed to a T what she had been set to find out . . . pretty convincing, isn't it?'

Annika sat looking at the girl as Osborne froze the picture. There was a glaring contrast between this innocent girl and the reality, these apparent powers whose extent or significance she herself did not comprehend, and Annika felt a strange tender warmth spreading through her. She felt a desire to take the girl in her arms and hug her tight and rescue her from these machines, these drawings, these co-ordinates and figures.

'How can she make such accurate drawings? In such detail?'

'We don't know. But apparently she does it like autistics do. She photographs, and in autistics, of course, we also see that the limi-tations in their latent creative powers are apparently going against nature, transcended by the precision in what they produce.'

'What do the computations of her brain tell us?'

'As you can see on the screen, she moves almost entirely in theta rhythms. As we see in dreamers. Four to seven cycles per second. It should make her incapable of functioning normally. But apparently it has no effect on her.'

'Does it not worry you at all that you don't know how it affects her?'

'In essence that is probably the difference between science and intelligence services. Science desires to know how things work before it will say that they do actually work; intelligence desires to see it work first and then find out how. And then, moreover, preferably say nothing. This girl works. We just don't know how.'

Osborne activated the play button and let the tape run, without sound.

'That doesn't mean anything,' said Annika.

'Have you ever tried to follow the obvious logic that led Heisenberg to his uncertainty principle? His grounds for the mathematical steps he took are quite simply incomprehensible. If you asked your father he would undoubtedly say I am right. Even today the physicists cannot follow his reasoning. But the result was revolutionary. Max Planck's theory of thermal radiation? Einstein's photon theory of 1905? The same principle. Physics has its own magic. The greatest discoveries in physics have been made by the power of intuition. By the power of thought, of force. Maxwell spoke of a force outside himself that wrote his equations.'

'When a wide-awake brain rejects reduction and emphasises intuition, the same brain forgets that it is the reductionist who is working at that moment.'

'You're not easy to convince, are you?'

Annika rose and shook her head. Lucas Henry started to leaf through his papers.

'It just doesn't make any sense,' said Annika.

'You know Bell's theorem? It invites ideas of correlated phenomena, if I'm right?'

Annika looked at him and nodded.

'But correlations between electrons are one thing. Thoughts, brain signals, are another. Meaning that a signal should superimpose itself on the correlation. But the moment you interfere with the correlation, you destroy it. It is such a fragile entity.'

Lucas Henry passed her a little bundle of A4 photocopies. Ten in all.

'What is it?'

'An article in *Scientific American*, August 1993. An experiment with quantum optics. Chiao, Kwiat and Steinberg's attempt to send light through an almost non-transparent glass plate. The light that got through passed at a speed of 1.7 times the speed of light. There are other experiments. The German physicist Günter Nimtz of Cologne University. A microwave through a waveguide; 4.7 times the speed of light. He went still further. It is the quantity of information that is problematic. Nimtz transmitted Mozart's Symphony No. Forty and although Mozart sounded better before than after he had been exposed to these extreme velocities, that doesn't undermine the fact that the most fundamental constant of physics has been undermined.'

'How can a fourteen-year-old girl without any knowledge of military installations be able to describe them in detail?'

'Not everything is as detailed as what you have seen here. In fact the best results we have had were when she had some link with what she was looking for. An emotional correspondence. Simon was working on diverting her powers.'

'But still?'

'Why do you think we are so interested in her brain?'

'This brings me back to my earlier question: is it you who are helping Maria Johnson, or is she helping you?'

'What do you mean?'

'A revolver, Chinese supersonic planes, missiles? Is it by chance that the three examples I have been shown are all military targets?'

Osborne cleared his throat.

'Miss Niebuhr, we are an intelligence service, not a travel bureau.'

Annika looked at the screen and was taken aback. The sound was so low that she should not actually have been able to hear anything, but it was as if the long, mournful screams that came from the girl on the screen penetrated everything, and Osborne made haste to find the remote control.

'What is it?' said Annika.

She stared at the screen, where the pictures suddenly started to jump, and it looked as if there was a fault in the tape. Yet it did not look as though the tape was scrambled, it resembled bursts of transmission, and then the pictures jumped again and became wavy and watery.

'Recording's no good,' said Osborne and stopped the tape.

'What's happening in those pictures?'

'Simon's experiment. He overdid it. This is where the disagreements started. There's nothing to see.'

'There is more, isn't there? There is something you aren't telling me?'

'We want to find the girl. So do the Americans. That's all,' said Osborne.

Lucas Henry put the tapes in their boxes and cleared away the mugs. He offered Annika a cigarette and lit it for her.

'What do you want from me?'

'We don't know where Gaia Jessup is. We are reasonably sure she is looking after the girl. But time is running out. If she doesn't get treatment soon she may become very ill.'

'How ill?'

'You saw the video. You have seen her during an attack. Maria Johnson lives in another world. Gaia Jessup is not trained to take care of that type of problem. Maria Johnson lives in a world of visions all the time. Unless someone who understands her and her problem talks to her, unless she gets her medication, we risk losing her.'

'Is that worse for her or for you?'

'What do you mean?'

'Perhaps it is better for her to be where she is now. I can't help suspecting that this is not the best place for a child to be.'

'What do you know about it?'

'A childless adult is hardly disqualified by knowing what adults are capable of.'

'What precisely do you mean, Miss Niebuhr?'

'How far will you go in your hunt for knowledge?'

'I hate to sound critical, but how far will you go yourself, Miss Niebuhr? Kate Carpenter, Mike Lewis? How far will you go? We are doing what we think is right. Which I am sure you have done yourself.'

'I still don't understand the role I'm supposed to play. Why have you told me all this?'

'We were hoping it would not be necessary.'

'But now it is?'

'We are pretty certain that you formed part of Simon's plans. Gaia Jessup cannot manage on her own. She needs help. We believe Gaia Jessup will make contact with you. We want to be near by if and when that happens.'

'Quite simply, you will shadow me?'

'I don't like the idea of the Americans possibly knowing more than we do at the moment. You shouldn't like it either. We were not the ones who tried to kill you.'

They left towards evening.

Osborne was with her in front of the building when Agent Cooper brought the car out. Annika opened the rear door.

'My revolver? My mobile phone?'

Osborne realised he was holding a plastic bag. He passed it to her.

'I did not have it in the dinghy, Osborne.'

'We are searching. I promise you. We'll keep you informed.'

Then Annika got into the car and closed the door. She opened the window when Cooper put the car in gear and started to move.

'Shouldn't I be blindfolded? I could tell the whole world what goes on here.'

Osborne smiled.

'I trust you, Miss Niebuhr. And besides: who would believe you?'

They drove away from the buildings and into the forest of tall eucalyptus trees surrounding the area. They passed two checkpoints with armed guards, the second by the outermost boundary, and then they were out of the complex. Annika asked Cooper to drive down to The Spit, where her car was parked.

Annika opened the side window. She let the wind play over her torn cheek, where the grazes were rough and felt like a shell on top of her skin. She leaned her head against the edge of the little side window and dozed off.

Cooper watched her in the rear-view mirror.

'I am sorry if I alarmed you, Miss Niebuhr.'

'Sorry?'

'I didn't sniff around your private things. That evening. I apologise for the mess.'

'You were fiddling with my kitchen knives?'

'They were beautiful. I must have been dreaming. You have a lovely home.'

Annika smiled at him. He was a mere boy to look at. So young and already involved in a web of concealment and lies. Undoubtedly the perfect job for a young man like him. Undoubtedly an intolerable job for his sweetheart.

'Cooper, there's something I don't understand.'

He smiled and caught her eyes in the mirror.

'I'm not sure I can give you an answer,' he said.

Annika looked out of the open window.

'I have just been initiated into some of the top-secret military particulars of this country. Particulars that the agents of alien powers take years to dig out. I find it hard to understand why I am not allowed to know what it is the girl has seen.'

His gaze faltered.

'Even if I knew I wouldn't be able to tell you about it, Miss Niebuhr.'

Annika leaned her head back against the seat.

Cooper said no more but gave her a friendly smile in the mirror.

Annika dozed off again. Finally she fell asleep.

Her mother was in the big living room asleep in her chair with a book on her lap and her reading glasses on the end of her nose. The television in the middle of the floor sent clear colours and hectic flashes of light into the room, otherwise lit solely by the reading lamp whose cone of light fell over her shoulder. The only sound came from the ventilator above the television, dutifully sending cool clouds of air into space.

Clouds were gathering outside and making the room seem darker than usual. Annika walked softly over to the window and glanced out. Cooper was waiting outside in the street.

Quietly Annika crossed the room and went upstairs to her father's library. The door was open and through the crack she could see him sitting bent over the table, immersed in his work.

The sight of the atlas and the geodetic maps made Annika think of her school text-book versions of the globe. The distorted models of the continents, the deceptive relationship between the size of Greenland and the size of Africa. The inadequacy of the globe in relation to what it purported to show. Mathematics does not permit the surface of the earth to be covered in one single map. Only the earth itself masters that art. We have no doubt that we know what the earth looks like, that we know its shape. Yet we are forced to give up. We need at least two overlapping maps to re-create the world, and that only in an adaptation. Annika recalled newspaper articles that described how for years the Russians had falsified their international declarations about the length of coastlines and mutual land boundaries.

To a world tortured by paranoid ideas and clear-cut visions of enemies, it was an easy way of perceiving the political climate, but the truth was that for many years geographers were confronted with the problem of every coastline being in principle endless, so that without standardised rules for using scale there was merely confusion where clarification was sought.

Annika went over and stood with her hands on a chair. She looked across the table at her father, who was absorbed in scribbling notes on a pad. He didn't react. Then she pulled out the chair and sat down. Her gaze roamed over the jumble of papers on the desk.

The collective vanity of every civilisation seems to resist having to accept that one is only a single account in the great cosmic reckoning.

It says a lot about the human brain that the first thing young scientists tried to do after the discovery of chaos was to bring order into it. The human brain does not care for disorder. The old guard of physicists, to whom her father belonged, still tirelessly broke matter up into yet smaller pieces, so the number of particles long ago exceeded the number of basic elements in the periodical system. The discouraging thing for physicists is that if there are not a few, easily apprehended formulae for the universe, there is not a shadow of a chance that we shall ever come to understand it.

She looked at her father rummaging through the piles of papers on the table. A tenderness came over her. Others had walked through a hall in Stockholm filled with festively clad people, gathered to applaud their work on the Z particle. Had received the honour and glory that could have been his. She had once said to him that she did not understand the prestige of a prize that had demonstrably been awarded to criminals.

He looked up when she shifted on her chair.

'What have you done to your face?' he said.

'I've been spending a day or two with the intelligence service,' she said. 'They brush their teeth with barbed wire.'

He smiled and dived into the sea of papers.

'I've looked at your things,' he said, holding up one of the two black-and-white photographs. 'It is really interesting. Reference exposures in negative. This one,' he said, and picked up the second apparently identical photograph in his other hand, 'ought to be the exact copy of the other. But it isn't.'

Annika leaned forward and looked from one picture to the other. A picture of far, far distant stars. She pointed to picture number two. 'There's a mistake here. There is a scratch on the picture.'

'Right. And wrong. There is a scratch. But it isn't a mistake. It appears that the exposure was made on 30 December. It also appears that the pictures were taken at the Anglo-Australian Observatory. But when I rang and spoke to Kip Thorne' – he looked at Annika as if to make sure she remembered Kip – 'he said they hadn't taken these pictures on 30 December.'

'Why?'

He smiled at her.

'These,' he said, taking the sheets with the correlated pairs of figures, with the strip of columns and numerous calculations, 'these were strange.'

'Co-ordinates?' asked Annika. Her father nodded while trying to get an overview of the various sheets.

'Co-ordinates, co-ordinates. But co-ordinates of what?' he asked, and looked at her.

'Military installations?'

He looked at her, puzzled. Then he shook his head.

'I thought so at first, I must admit. I assume this has some connection with Simon Rees?'

Annika nodded.

'And one could link Simon Rees with military installations, inland bases, naval stations. But Liverpool?'

'Liverpool, England?'

Her father shook his head. He read out from the paper:

'Spider?'

'Harper Stone.'

'What?'

Annika shook her head.

'Nothing. Explain what you're on to.'

'Co-ordinates, yes. Military installations, no. Look here.' He spread out a map of Australia covered with a number of black crosses, which he himself had added to in red.

'The descriptions are incomplete. Southern latitude, eastern longitude – some of the marked points have complete sets of co-ordinates, others are lacking one or other. In some the locality was given, while others again seem attempts at ordinary navigation measurements. It almost looks as if someone has been playing a guessing game.'

'That's probably not far wrong,' said Annika.

'S 12 24°, Liverpool. Here E 134 3° is missing. Spider S 16 44°, here E 126 5° is missing. Boxhole, Kelly West, Lawn Hill . . .' He looked up from the paper at Annika, who shook her head, but it seemed as if something was slowly beginning to dawn on her.

'Acraman, Henbury.'

Annika shook her head.

'Tookoonooka. Wolf Creek, Teaque . . .'

'Comets?'

Her father smiled. He nodded.

'Impact. By and large all the biggest Australian craters from comet impacts. Connolly Basin, Mount Toondina, Dalgaranga, Piccaninny. They're all here.'

With a pencil he led her eyes round the map from cross to cross.

'Goyder, Gosse's Bluff, Strangeways . . .'

He wrinkled his forehead and pulled a piece of paper towards him. He moved the pen over the paper and the calculations with little jerks.

'But it's slightly odd that while most of the co-ordinates are absolutely precise, there is imprecision in some of them.'

Annika gazed in front of her. She hardly dared follow the thought to its conclusion let alone formulate it. So involuntarily it slipped out: 'She can reverse the process. She doesn't need the co-ordinates.'

'What are you talking about?'

'What about the picture? Why won't Kip verify it?'

'I don't know. But it's not impossible that he's been forbidden to.'

'Why?'

'Because,' he said, leafing through until he found the two photos among the other papers piling up on the table, 'because not everyone agrees about how much people can bear to hear.'

'What do you mean?'

'On 9 April 1993 a comet passed over New South Wales. One week later it happened again. According to every statistical context that can't happen. Nevertheless it did. Without catastrophic results, it's true, but . . .'

'But?'

'The second rock fragmented and exploded at the height of eighteen kilometres with a blast almost as powerful as the Hiroshima bomb. The supersonic charge from the comet's course could be heard a hundred kilometres away. Do you remember the bombardment of Jupiter?'

Annika remembered watching the television film of Shoemaker-Levy's collision with Jupiter in 1994. She remembered how amazed she had been that most of the life of Sydney carried on unmoved and unimpressed as always, and how there were people alive who even with a year's warning, and even though they had access to a television set, would go to their graves without the picture of the meteor shower on their retinas. Without the computer simulations of the gravitation field of Jupiter, which tore Shoemaker-Levy to pieces and thus only activated a chain bombardment but did not hinder the impact. Without a picture of the cloud of fire that surged up from Jupiter, which hung there for a year afterwards, and which was larger than the earth.

'Someone woke up when they saw these pictures. Here. In Washington. Everywhere around the globe when it suddenly became clear to others as well as astronomers and physicists what impact, and what significance these pictures might have.'

'That the same thing could happen here?'

He looked at her and nodded thoughtfully.

'But they knew about it. It seems as if they had to see it before they believed it.'

He opened his desk drawer and vanished in a heroic search of the contents. When he emerged it was with an A4 sheet which had been Sellotaped according to a primitive accordion model together with seven other papers, which made up a large map of the globe and its territories. He struggled a while with the paper, and when he had it under control laid it down over the other maps and papers.

'For a long time the American military kept secret their knowledge of incoming meteorites. Of asteroids and impacts. Let me remind you that it was a physicist who had the surveys declassified, so now we are a little wiser. They have been registering incoming celestial bodies for a period of ten years.'

Annika stared at the map, thunderstruck. All known craters and impact localities were marked for the whole world; a number of them had still not been investigated sufficiently for it to be known precisely what had been hit, and those had interrogation marks beside them. This was not the type of map used for teaching in schools. If this were employed as a starting point it would need more than customary teaching methods to convince children of the relevance of concentrating hard in lessons. The way the map looked with all its marks, crosses and question marks, it was more like an extreme illustration of the adage that every new day is a miracle.

'There's a certain irony in the fact that it was spy satellites on the lookout for atomic firing ramps on the earth that showed us that the most hostile factor in the world is space. We were hit two hundred and fifty times in ten years. On average twenty-five times a year. Once in every other week an atomic bomb is detonated somewhere in our atmosphere. And this map,' he said, looking at her, 'shows only the craters we are certain about. Only those we have discovered up to now. We know very little about what the rainforests hide, and still less about what's hidden in the oceans.

'Micronesia,' he said, fumbling about with the map, upside down. 'Impact, 1994. A TNT charge of five times the Hiroshima bomb. Numerous heads of government were warned, I understand. Tungus, Siberia, as you know, 30 June 1908 – 1.3 megatons or thirteen million tons TNT. The Hiroshima bomb in comparison was thirteen thousand tons TNT. Everything in an area the size of Sydney was levelled. You remember the pictures, don't you? Trees snapped like matchsticks and were flattened like straws in a mat at a distance of fifty-two kilometres from the epicentre. Six hundred and fifty Hiroshima bombs released at once. Seismographs all over the world registered the sound wave, which was so powerful that it travelled around the world twice. Afterwards the explosion triggered an earthquake that measured five on the Richter scale.'

'What about the picture? What does that show?'

'The Tungus impact was probably due to a gigantic block of ice. With an estimated size of fifty metres in diameter. Which apparently exploded 8.5 kilometres up. All in all three lucky factors. But what if it had been a meteorite? What if we should now be exposed to a direct hit? By one that had enough mass to resist the collision with the earth's atmosphere? Which did not detonate before making direct impact with the earth? What if it was large? This,' he said, pointing at the little black scratch on the photograph, 'this is a meteorite. An asteroid. A cliff. A mountain. Which no one will acknowledge.'

'What do you mean?'

'I contacted the Palomar Observatory in California, Cerro Tololo in Chile, Mauna Kea on Hawaii. The Keat Peak sun observatory in Arizona, the radio telescopes VLA in New Mexico, Arecibo in Puerto Rico and Parkes, naturally. No one knew anything about or could remember anything about a picture.'

'Perhaps they haven't seen the picture?'

'Perhaps not. But it's an odd fact that a number of them have put pictures on the Internet which show that several of them in the period in question have actually been interested in that part of the sky.'

'But if the picture is genuine, if this is an observed asteroid, surely it must be registered somewhere?'

'Correct. Every amateur astronomer wants to have their name attached to either a comet or an asteroid. Therefore I contacted both the International Bureau for Astronomical Telegrams and the Minor Planets Centre. An observation report should have been sent in. A registration either in the form of a temporary nomenclature or as a permanent name. It can take some time to evaluate whether it is a new discovery or not, but a temporary name with date and literal description should exist. Something should exist. But nothing had been registered for the evening in question on the date in question.

'The following day I received an anonymous telephone call. The caller was very brief. But gave me a full set of data: period of revolution, perihelium, orbit inclination, diameter and rotation time. I asked him why it had not been registered, when they had all the information. He said: "We are not talking about it, but the man who drew our attention to it had already christened it Maria".'

Annika felt a blanket of cold shivers spread from her neck down her back and along her arms. She recalled the last recordings on the video Osborne and Lucas Henry had played for her. She visualised the girl. Heard her screams. Then she shook her head to clear it again.

'What could be the reason for a person not wanting to register themselves?'

'I can only think of two reasons: either he had some strange reason not to. Or he thought there was no reason.'

'What do you mean?'

'We know the perihelion angle. We know the eccentricity, and we know when its orbit crosses ours. We can generally see comets, although Hyakutake was discovered only a month before its passage. But as a rule they are visible. Asteroids on the other hand are crafty. They have no tail of gas or dust to make them visible. No corona. The asteroid Gehrels found in 1993 was, it's true, only ten metres in diameter, but it was also only a hundred and forty thousand kilometres away from us when it crossed our orbit. 1996A was only seven hours away from hitting us. This one,' he said, picking up the picture, 'this one is three kilometres in diameter.'

'What does it mean?'

'That we can hope something will knock it off course. Gravitational effect, fragmentation, a smaller collision with something else out there. Otherwise we may hope for an error in my calculations. For according to them it's on a course for earth.'

'What?'

'Straight for earth.'

'Where will it strike?'

'It will come in at a very oblique angle, on an elliptic orbit, but where in the atmosphere it will explode, or where an impact will occur, is impossible to say.'

'When?' asked Annika.

She lit the cigarette her fingers had been playing with, and inhaled deeply.

'In three days.'

Black clouds moved in over Sydney. They came from the east carried on the dry winds. Behind them the moon and the nearest stars lit up the sky. Like the faint wake of a boat, reflected palely by the moonlight, the Milky Way drew its mists across the evening darkness.

Annika stood in front of the living-room window of the house at Whale Beach looking out over the sea. She was filled with a singular melancholy, which had come over her following the conversation with her father and had not left her during the drive home. He had stressed the uncertainty in his figures, and he had repeatedly reassured her by making it clear that they would definitely have heard if anyone else had come up with the same figures as his. She knew he had been lying to her. They had embraced. Then she had left.

To the south, in over Sydney, the clouds stood still.

Every August, if the weather was suitable, Annika pulled a deckchair out on the lawn and extinguished all the lights in the house. For hours she lay still in the dark observing the Perseids. The shower of shooting stars is not visible in Sydney, but in a darkened garden away from the city their spores of light can be seen clearly for a few seconds low on the horizon like burning after-images.

Light comes from a long way off. Even today it is difficult to understand: that the image we see does not exist any more. That we are looking back down time, that what we are studying at this very moment is an image of the world that is several millions, perhaps billions, of years old.

Michael Larsen

Similar to the way in which starlight comes back to us is an odd redundancy in the history of man. Einstein's lambda, which he introduced into his relativity theory in order to get it to cohere, which he regretted and reproached himself for having included, is now being dragged out by cosmologists and astrophysicists. The entire Newtonian paradigm has definitively collapsed, and any physicist working today would take into consideration the ancient sense of coherence and wholeness; of fields: Socrates' sense of stratified reality, which has been accentuated by quantum mechanics, Aristotle's teleological view of the cosmos, that there is a meaning, that a blueprint exists that we have merely not yet discovered, and which we may never find, because this meaning is created while it is defining itself. Or because we will not have the necessary time.

Once it was the snakes that united everything. The oldest gods we know about. They were held in awe not only in the old Australian cultures but by more or less all peoples of that era. On earth and in the heavens. The Mayas at the other end of the earth saw in the skies the feather-clad serpent, which was a symbol for tribes from the Mississippi to Panama. The snake which, according to tradition, discovered their calendar and created their hieroglyphs.

Perhaps now we understand what it was they saw, and why this vision inspired such great respect, fear, joy and gratitude. Comets, shooting stars that in their lengthy ellipses came sailing in over the earth like brilliant snakes with tails of fire. During solar eclipses they must have believed, like certain primitive races still do, that the world was coming to an end. And the last thing they saw before the moon passed across the sun and highlighted the strange factor that makes the eclipse possible, that the sun may be four hundred times larger than the moon but is also precisely four hundred times as far away, was a curved shining snake. Then all went dark for a few seconds. And then in the next magical moment came the corona. And a world was born anew. The same theme of rebirth was played for them by the snake on earth, when it sloughed its skin. The snake was the only creature out of all those they encountered which was able to crawl out of its old body and be born again.

The story of the snake is the story of how we see and comprehend the world. How our vision of it changes through years that grow into epochs, that grow into ages and, when we are no more, into aeons. Through erroneous interpretations, misunderstandings and tendentious slips of the pen.

Before the great religions of our time, our forefathers, presumably quite independently of each other, held a different view of the world. Before the great patriarchal creation myths the world had goddesses and gods who were snakes. Before the Jews, the Christians and the Muslims, communities without serpent gods were unthinkable. Before the Hebrews became monotheists they worshipped snakes. From Quetzalcoatl to Buddha's seven-headed serpent, to the cobra that protected Vishnu, from the Egyptian serpent goddess Neith, who created the universe, to three continents of Indian cultures, in North America, in South America and with the Australian Aboriginals, where the Rainbow Serpent was the being who united heaven with earth.

Annika looked at the night sky. Some years ago, in the astrological sign of Sagittarius, well inside our galaxy, close to the centre, radio astronomists discovered a gigantic galactic figure. Great magnetic belts of lightning. A hundred and fifty light-years with an unbroken belt of lightning. Formed like a snake.

Out in the belt between Mars and Jupiter the asteroids hover. A belt of large and small rocks. From a planet that may once have failed to develop. Earth's stillborn sister. We are the first generations in the first race on earth to realise the extent of the catastrophe. To comprehend it. If one should strike.

Annika didn't know what to believe. She had no knowledge of the last hours, the last days, the last weeks of Simon's life. Knew nothing about the experiments he had carried out on Maria.

As for the world, as for another person, there were limits to how much and how quickly she was able to take in something that so obviously conflicted with her common sense. She was the child of a scientist, she had the basic modus operandi of science firmly anchored in her system, despite the fact that she

285

belonged to a generation that had seen the Newtonian system fall and Darwin modified. She knew quantum mechanics had been misused to legitimate the most improbable theories, but also that the molecular biologists rushed into self-contradictions that were just as crude as those of pure holists, when they tried to reduce all biological phenomena to molecular physics. *Pars-pro-toto*. The whole is more than the sum of a system's single parts. As a doctor she knew that was a phrase more significant than vapid and empty, although it was frequently made ridiculous by old-fashioned biologists and evolution theorists.

The molecular biologists brought out the enthusiasm of the accelerator physicists when they discovered DNA. But only to make the same discovery as the physicists in relation to the particles, that there were lesser units, that there were other elements, that DNA did not contain an explanation in itself, that the discoveries are endless. She knew that all reductionist and mechanistic expositions now as always before would be forced to throw in the towel when they had to explain the most obvious and most miraculous circumstance of all, that a child is born as the result of a meeting between two human beings. How in this as in the whole, on all decisive points in our comprehension of ourselves and the universe, we have no certain knowledge of the world we live in. How nobody in this world can explain how morphogenesis functions. How molecules in a living organism take form. How cells can know what they should look like. How the single cell can know precisely what function it has, how cells can change course and repair the damage of potential catastrophes incurred as the result of exterior influences.

Annika felt physically ill at the thought that her father's calculations might be correct. That this was what Osborne would not reveal to her. That this was what the girl had seen. And that it must be kept secret. Her father had told her before that it was not a question of 'if' the earth was hit again, but solely a question of 'when'.

Annika put her hands in her back pocket. She felt something and pulled it out. A card. A business card. 'Dr Lucas Henry.' And his telephone numbers.

She had been in his presence for days, without sensing anything. He had not said anything, and it had never occurred to her to ask. But it was him. He had sent the scans of Maria Johnson.

Annika went into the kitchen. Saw Agent Cooper's car standing at the kerb. It was completely dark now. The first spots on the panes. Soon it was pouring.

She went into the bedroom and pulled out the third drawer. She found the box of cartridges. She filled a couple of magazines and put as many as she could into her pocket. Then she picked up her mobile phone, but just as she was about to dial Lucas Henry's number, the phone rang.

It was Kahn. He informed her briefly that they had found a murdered man at an illegal reptile centre in a basement flat close to Chinatown. He gave her the address.

'I think it's your snake man.'

It was as good as impossible to get into central Sydney. Everywhere the processions surged through the streets, music played, people sang. The rain bucketed down, but no one seemed to notice it. When Annika got out of her car she saw Cooper parked farther down the street.

The road fronting the building had been cordoned off. Two police cars were in front of the taped-off area, preventing the curious from getting any closer. Several fire engines were parked across the street. In spite of the rain their hoses sluiced great fountains of water at the flats above the basement where the fire had taken hold. The firemen had almost brought it under control. Annika stood just before the cordon, staring into the flames. Beside her a few people were standing wrapped in blankets, undoubtedly residents who had been evacuated from their homes for safety's sake.

Great ideas have been born at the fireside. The German chemist August Kekule discovered the structure of the benzene molecule one evening as he was sitting dozing in front of his stove. It seemed to him that before his eyes the flames suddenly started to dance. He thought he could see the actual atoms of the fire dancing. In snakelike formations. And suddenly one of the snakes seized hold of its own tail and formed a ring. What he had felt was that a hugely intractable and almost insoluble problem had been solved for him by the fire. All that remained was to show the consequences of this discovery and prove that the ring was the molecule structure he was searching for.

Annika went up to one of the policemen. She introduced herself and asked for Detective Superintendent Kahn. The officer went inside and shortly afterwards came out with Kahn, who waved her over to him.

'I thought you ought to see this,' he said.

He put his hand on her arm and led her down the basement steps through a small unlit passageway at the end of which was a flat.

'They are very peaceful. But I gather that's quite normal, isn't it?'

Annika looked down the room. Along the whole of one wall on a long table was a row of glass cages furnished with humidity meters. There were also mounted light fixtures and thermostats that automatically regulated the temperature. Annika walked slowly through the room inspecting every cage. The snake's name was labelled on each one, its Latin description, the word 'Danger' and a skull-and-crossbones sign. Annika put her face close to the plexiglass of a cage containing a taipan. She met the snake's eye in the glass and in the reflection caught sight of her own face.

'Snakes don't understand fire,' said Annika.

Right at the end, the room gave on to another one at right angles to the first and almost as large. Police technicians were working in front of the body. Their photographers took shots from various angles.

'Robert Beacham. Unemployed. Now more than ever before. One or two sentences for theft, one violent, otherwise nothing. Shot in the back of the head, as you can see, and we have also found bite marks on one arm with attendant swelling, so we assume someone tortured him with a live snake first, but this will emerge from the post-mortem.'

'Illegal trading with reptiles?'

'You don't know him?'

Annika shook her head.

'Sure to be illegal export. But something indicates that he knew what he was about.'

Kahn went over and opened a freezer in the corner of the room. On the shelves stood various glass and plastic containers. All were neatly date-marked and supplied with detailed information on which snake had been milked.

'Pretty lucrative, I gather? Keys to the brain?'

'M4. From the mamba. The value per gram is higher than gold. Yes, it's lucrative.'

'The million-year-long evolutionary development of methods for decoding the brain's complicated codes. How does it work?'

'Receptors. Now we invert it. Decode how nature decodes.'

'Means to combat pain?'

'We use pain – and turn it around.'

'Hard to tell what pain is, isn't it? Hard to tell what poison is, isn't it? Salt. Sodium chloride. Simple kitchen salt, which we eat every day. In sufficiently large quantities – lethal.'

'Hard to tell anything at all.'

Kahn consulted a piece of paper which turned out to be a tally of the contents of all the cages and diverse details from this cave of vice.

'Various lizards, pythons, three Collett's snakes, two tiger snakes, four death adders, one black whip snake, three taipans. Also two nine-millimetre pistols complete with silencers, a .223 rifle, a sawn-off shotgun, tear gas cartridges, a couple of hand grenades. Oh, yes, and a single king brown' – he looked at Annika – 'or mulga, as it is also called.'

She looked at him. He smiled ironically back at her.

'A whole little one-man army.'

Annika went back to the taipan cage. She had learned from snakes. Learned to study a system thoroughly. Harper Stone took casts of old skulls with him on his expeditions. On the outside are deposited the brain's convolutions, which are almost as good as the annual rings of dendrochronology that biologists and taxonomists use to observe injured fins and tails for identification, and the genes tests with which the courts can determine paternity cases with considerable accuracy. Herpetologists and doctors with an extensive interest in snakes study scales. Almost identical species can be separated out from each other by scale patterns and diagonal counts of the scale courses, and Annika was one of the few who could describe in her sleep the microscopic difference between a roughscaled snake and the harmless keelback.

When you study a system thoroughly like this, you learn something fundamental, about other systems as well, and you learn that the only thing these systems really have in common, despite a mass of apparent similarities, is that that neither separately nor together can they explain everything.

Annika gazed intently at the glass.

Kahn looked at her.

'Do you recognise anything, Miss Niebuhr?'

'I should have to pick it up to be quite certain.'

'You don't need to do that. It is the one.'

'Is this how you catch your criminals, Kahn?'

'What do you mean?'

'I thought Harper Stone delivered the taipan to Taronga Zoo.'

Kahn smiled.

'You are very observant, Miss Niebuhr.'

'Where snakes are concerned. Otherwise I can be terribly naïve. It is a weakness. Simon warned me against it.'

Kahn clicked his tongue thoughtfully. Then he pulled out his cigarettes. He knocked out a cigarette and lit it.

'Why did you send me to Brisbane, Kahn? You work for them, don't you? For the ASIO?'

Kahn smiled cunningly and beckoned her out as he left. Annika followed him. He turned round when he was at the entrance, and with a friendly gesture invited her to share his umbrella.

They walked a little way down the street.

'What's going on, Kahn?'

'You really do know a snake when you see one, don't you? How do you do it?'

Annika looked at him.

'Many years' experience. How did it end up here?'

Kahn smiled.

'We all dream of simple answers, don't we? Even you. We all think we have them, don't we? All the answers. When we are young. Then come all the questions.

'Have you never imagined, Miss Niebuhr, being there in Paris, in the Pantheon that day in 1851, when Foucault's pendulum swung like a globe through the room? You almost get shivers down your spine imagining it, don't you? One thing is knowing it. Another is seeing it. That Copernicus was right. That it's the *earth* that moves.

'Or Einstein's demonstration of Newton's tiny inaccuracy in his calculation of Mercury's orbit, which caused Newton's theory of gravity to fail in favour of Einstein's general theory of relativity? Penzias's and Wilson's astonishment at the detector noise that came into their receiver in 1965? They had no idea themselves that what they were measuring were microwaves, a light so red-shifted that it could only come from the Big Bang.'

'What are you trying to say?'

'Someone thought wrongly that you had a part in Simon's great plan. I must admit I was sceptical about that. But there were some who knew better. There were some who thought that if only you saw what had happened to Gaia Jessup you would panic. Make a mistake. You did not. For you didn't know what sort of mistake you might make. There were some who thought that if only Simon got to know what had happened to Gaia Jessup, he would send the girl back and give up his plan. He would not. There were some who were sure the girl was with Gaia Jessup. She *was*. But not when they came. There were some who thought I exaggerated when I said they should not underestimate Simon Rees. You must know the feeling, Miss Niebuhr. Don't you sometimes feel you're surrounded by complete idiots?'

Stunned, Annika looked at Kahn. She pulled away from him but had the surreal feeling that he would suddenly start to laugh. For a fraction of a second that feeling grew into a vain hope.

'I don't know what to say . . .'

Kahn smiled crookedly. The rain drummed on his black umbrella. He tossed it back slightly, braced himself against the water beating down on his face with closed eyes and a broad, satisfied smile. He put out his tongue and tasted the raindrops.

'Do you know, Miss Niebuhr, that there are people who don't care for the scent of sun-dried washing. That's the scent of ozone. Personally I've always liked that scent. It is like rain. Everything smells so clean.'

Then he turned his face to Annika and took her by the arm.

'Come,' he said, starting to pull her into the alleyway.

'I think I'd rather stay here . . .'

He pushed her jacket aside and pulled her gun from her belt.

'What's this? Do you have a permit for it?' he asked. 'We've become rather careful after that psychopath in Tasmania.'

'I have a permit.'

'It is temporarily suspended,' said Kahn, and threw the gun into the alleyway.

He made an exaggeratedly elegant gesture as an invitation to accompany him.

Annika stayed where she was.

'I could scream,' said Annika. 'Shout for help.'

'Is it young Cooper you're thinking of? Why should he think you are in danger? You're with me, after all.'

For a second she was looking out at the street, and hardly noticed it. Didn't realise what had happened before she was on the asphalt on all fours. This must be what it was like when Mike had his asthma attacks. She struggled for breath, but in those seconds she existed solely on the air already in her lungs. Everything went black and she felt a speckled warmth in her eye sockets before at last she gasped in some air. The pain in her diaphragm was intense. Where a few days ago had been a vague tenderness there was now a raw pain, sharp and round and intolerable.

Then she felt Kahn seize her by the hair and pull her after him into the alleyway.

'You're absolutely right, Miss Niebuhr. You *could* have screamed.'

He pulled her alongside him, and she was forced to go with him on all fours as best she could. She was frightened and paralysed at the unexpected strength of his grasp. Her knees bumped on the asphalt and she felt one start to bleed. Her hands splashed in the puddles in front of her. Then he got hold of her waistband, dragged her forward and at last let go of her so she tumbled into some cardboard boxes jumbled up against the wall of a building.

Dazed, Annika tried to get hold of herself. One leg would not support her, and when she managed to get her knees off the asphalt and tried to stand up it was only a second before she found herself lying on the contents spilt from a metal dustbin, some cartons of discarded lettuces and a small box of empty bottles. This time as well it was a few moments before she realised she had been hit. This time on the back of the head. By a blow or a kick.

'I don't think Osborne . . .'

Kahn kneeled down in front of her and pulled her face up to his.

'I don't work for Osborne, Miss Niebuhr. Hasn't that dawned on you yet? I work for whoever pays best.'

Annika tried to think clearly. She threw a sidelong glance towards the street, trying to locate Cooper, but there was nothing to be seen, and the rain splashing down on them, on the alleyway and the street, muffled all sound.

'You knew I'd be aware there was something wrong about Simon's suicide?'

Kahn did not reply.

Whether it was his fist landing straight on her jaw or the blow to the back of her head when he dropped her, so she fell limply back on to the asphalt with nothing to lessen the impact that knocked her out for a brief moment, she did not know, but when she came to again and could focus on the shafts of falling rain high above among the rooftops, here and there lit up, she realised she must win time by talking to him.

'What are you going to do with me?' she asked Kahn, who was smoothing his clothes and trying to straighten his hair.

'Kiesworik thinks I should kill you. Osborne says it is essential you should survive. So what's to be done? It isn't always easy to have two employers who want different things.'

Annika looked at him. She managed to pull herself into a sitting position. She tried to stand up but could feel it was no good. Not yet. With difficulty she pushed a rotten and stinking cardboard box behind her back.

'Simon couldn't be bribed?'

'Simon lost his focus. So I heard. It wasn't his job.'

'How much do the Americans pay you, Kahn?'

He laughed scornfully.

'Oh, Miss Niebuhr. We're all turning into some sort of American, don't you think? Why not accept something for it, then? In the true American spirit?'

'You have children yourself, Kahn. Don't you give any thought at all to the poor girl?'

'You ... you are so fucking self-righteous. Wasn't it your precious Denmark that was perfecting its project involving experiments on the retarded long before Hitler and Himmler? Didn't your politicians lie about Thule and the American atom bases? Everyone has something to accuse others of. It was the German Heisenberg who had problems in the German laboratories, so that the German development of the atom bomb was rendered impossible, but it was Einstein the Jew who by his paltry little equation $E = mc^2$ made its development possible at all.'

'These experiments on the girl. She is ill. And you couldn't give a damn?'

'What do I care if one girl feels a bit off colour? I couldn't care less whether her mother and father were bad drivers or were murdered.'

'I'm sorry to have to remind you, but don't you in fact represent the law?'

'Haven't you ever had a patient admitted to your hospital you told yourself you didn't feel like treating?'

'Yes, but there was nothing wrong with you.'

Kahn smiled. He made no comment on Annika's insult, but merely looked around him, and when his jacket slipped open slightly she caught sight of the gun in his shoulder holster. Somehow she must lure him closer. She cautiously tested how weak she was and concluded that she must get hold of a weapon to dispense with him.

Kahn stood with his face lifted to the rain drumming down around him. He put his hands to his ears and shook the lobes as if to get rid of a ringing tone.

'All these amateurs around one. Everything one has to put up with. All the dilettantism.'

He stood there staring at Annika.

'Did you have a very strict father, Kahn?' she asked ironically. 'If you feel like crying you may as well do so here.'

He took a step forward and squatted down in front of her. He wiped off the rain that had flattened his hair and run down his face. Then he stared at her.

He grabbed the neck of her T-shirt and pulled her face up. Then he slapped her head from side to side, mechanically and almost gently, with the back of his hand. When Annika tried to shield her face with her hands the blows grew harder, but she tried to unbutton his shoulder holster without letting him realise her intent.

'Osborne still thinks you know where Gaia Jessup is, doesn't he? But we both know you do not. We know there was no reason whatsoever for sending you out on that odyssey, don't we?'

'So what was the idea of my going to see Kate Carpenter? Why did you lure me up there? Why kill her?'

Kahn smiled. And stopped his battering for a moment.

'Intelligence chiefs are like the hysterical old cows on the stock exchange. Kiesworik was paranoid about Osborne's suspicion that you knew something. That you were involved. Some of the conversations between Kate Carpenter and Simon were not recorded. Suddenly there was some doubt about her role. I personally saw no reason to keep you alive.'

'If you kill me you won't find the girl, Kahn. Think again. I can be useful to you.'

Kahn smiled and shook his head.

'We know where she is, Miss Niebuhr. Kiesworik and his people have known for some days. Why do you think it really got serious in Brisbane?'

'Why don't you just pick her up, then?'

'I think they want to be sure Gaia Jessup won't mess them around this time. They've put their foot in it by shooting people a tad too fast. This time they are certain.'

He pushed his sleeve back and looked at his watch.

'I think they're actually on their way down to get her now.'

He looked at her. And Annika saw he was about to hit her yet again.

The blow struck her on the jaw, but she saw it coming and went with it, pulled her leg up under her, and at the same moment kicked out with all her might at his jaw, and Kahn fell aside as if every signal in his body short-circuited at once. As fast as she could she jumped down over him and quickly tried to get his gun free of the shoulder holster. But she fumbled with the stock and couldn't get it up, and Kahn recovered himself enough to register what she was trying to do, and seized the hand struggling to tear the gun out of its holster.

There was a loud crack when the gun went off. Kahn seemed to stiffen before her. His face took on an expression of incredulity. Only then did Annika realise he had been hit.

She looked towards the street. Even in the rain the crack of the gun had travelled along the shaft of the alleyway, along the walls, from wall to wall, and Annika expected people would hurry in any moment. Show up at the end. But no one came.

Kahn lay before her. He moved.

Annika pulled him up by the hair. She put the pistol to his head.

'Who shot Simon? Who killed him?'

Kahn coughed up blood. His throat rattled. She couldn't disentangle his syllables into intelligible sentences. But the last thing he said was unmistakable.

'Fucking cow . . .'

Breathless and bruised, Annika stood at the crossing of Elizabeth Street and Liverpool Street, gasping for breath. She felt blood running from the wound on her cheek which had been ripped open, and she had blood in her mouth.

The sounds of the numerous processions thumped through the town. Above her the monorail hummed. Packed with people. Annika fixed her gun firmly in her belt and pulled out her mobile phone. With her left hand, swollen and almost numb, she carefully drew the card with Lucas Henry's telephone number out of her pocket. She tried his private number first but there was no answer. Not until she tried the mobile number did she get through.

Lucas Henry announced himself. It was a bad line, but in a clear moment Annika gave him her name.

'I need some information. About the girl.'

'Why don't you just overtake?'

The signal blurred and a word or two vanished. Annika turned round but that didn't help. For a time the phone went quite dead, then the signal returned.

'Are you there?'

'Yes. Where on earth are you?'

'First I must tell you something, Miss Niebuhr. Osborne lied to you.'

'What do you mean?'

'The girl is ill. Osborne. It was Osborne who forced Simon into doing the last sessions.'

'Are you quite sure, Dr Henry?'

'She can't take any more. That was why Simon wanted to get her away.'

'The last sessions, the videos I wasn't allowed to see. Do you know what went on?'

'I was not there. It was Simon himself who . . . but he said he was under orders from Osborne.'

'I need to know where the girl is.'

'Why?'

'Because they know where she is.'

'How do you know that?'

'I just know it. Tell me where she is. Are you on the way to her this moment?'

'Do you know the newspaper kiosk by Heart Bells? The first white building after that. Just opposite Hinkles. Second floor. I'm on my way there myself. Meet me down there.'

'Ring Gaia and say she must get away.'

'How do you know someone is on the way? Just over . . . take.' Annika heard oaths and cursing, broken up by the poor connection clicking and scratching. Pressing the phone hard to her ear, she tried to extract a sensible context from the incomprehensible noise, but it was impossible to get any meaning from the chopped-up sentences and constantly recurring gaps.

'Kahn,' she said, when the connection was at last clear again. 'Detective Superintendent Kahn. I have shot him. Kahn was working for the Americans.'

'Oh, no.'

'I had no choice. He was going to kill me.'

'I am not thinking of that, Miss Neibuhr. I have not contacted you again because they all became so suspicious. When I spoke to you I said nothing that could give me away. How did you get hold of me? What betrayed me?'

'What do you mean?'

'I must have said something that made you suspect me of all people.'

'Your card. You gave it to me . . . it was in my pocket.'

299

'Oh, no. It's a trap, Miss Niebuhr.'

'What are you talking about?'

'They know. Now they know. I did not give you my card, Miss Niebuhr.'

That was the last thing Annika could make out. Then there was only Lucas Henry shouting in terror, and some loud reports in the background.

Annika held the mobile phone in her hand, thunderstruck. She listened, but for seconds that felt like minutes there was nothing but silence at the other end. Suddenly she felt a presence, a face close to hers. Instinctively she took the phone away from her ear and stared at it. Then she switched off.

According to Newton's theories, in principle you could, if it was possible to calculate the movements of all the atoms, predetermine everything. In practice we already have a problem when we have to evaluate three quantities in relation to each other – a situation that becomes painfully clear when human beings are involved.

Annika felt she had been seen through and foreseen to a sinister degree. Lucas Henry was the man it was all about. He was the leak who had to be found and eliminated. Cooper had found the scans and the drawing in her drawer and had reported to Osborne. Osborne had naturally kept watch on Simon to the very end. Shadowed him night and day. He must have known that Simon could not have sent her the envelope. He had known there must have been someone else they had not kept watch over, who had helped him.

Kiesworik and his men were on their way. They had been a step ahead all the time because of Kahn. Osborne had reckoned that something was wrong, and in his homing search he had made use of Annika. Now he had both Lucas Henry and the address. She cursed inwardly at not having seen through it, that she hadn't foreseen the traps laid for her.

She thought of Kahn's bluff about the switchover of Simon and June's mobiles. How could she have foreseen that? No one could have foreseen it. No one would have seen through that.

Kahn, who had known her reaction patterns the whole time. Had known how she would reason and react. Had told Kiesworik about her suspicion. Had shown her the article from the *Courier-Mail*. That whole play. As if there were a written script for the whole sequence of it.

And Osborne. Osborne who had gambled, placed his bet, suspected Lucas Henry of being the leak. Sensed he was the man who was hiding Gaia Jessup.

It was like standing face to face with a machine. An automaton calculating without restraint not only episodes but the whole sequence, limitless combinations of episodes that mercilessly led on to a catastrophic fate. In Brisbane. Kiesworik and his whole show. Carpenter. The escape and the aeroplane.

One or two police cars were still in the street, but Cooper's car had gone. Annika ran to hers, let herself in, turned the ignition and drove off.

She parked some way from the building. Sat there for a while orientating herself to the street picture. She kept her hands on the wheel because each time she lifted them or let go she saw how much they shook.

Spectators and people in costume were still making their way into the city centre and towards the big processions. In a gap between the buildings, Sydney Tower rose up with its illuminated cylinder. The numerous steel cables stretching from the summit of the Centrepoint building and right up to the top of the tower resembled a gigantic spider's web.

On the corner in front of the Heart Bells kiosk a solitary girl stood peering up and down the street. She held an opened umbrella which partly hid her, but even in the dark it was easy to see she was in costume. She had been spray-painted from head to toe in blue, and on her legs flecked tinsel sparkled. Her hair was combed back and painted a deep violet colour, her face was painted in the same blue as her body, her lips were dark violet, almost black.

Groups of unpainted young people on their way to see the

processions passed her, moving in the direction of Darlinghurst and King's Cross. Without taking any special notice of the girl, who resembled one of the many participants in the festivities.

Normally in our world colours and dressing up are used to emphasise and display. But on an evening like Mardi Gras they can be used for concealment.

There is a snake with an evasion technique that it would be quite insulting to call reflex behaviour. It is the American *Heterodon nasicus*. It is not at all dangerous, but when it is threatened it inflates its head and by grating its scales along the sides of its body imitates the sound of the rattlesnake. If that doesn't work it plays dead. It lies on its back with its mouth right open, completely lifeless. It is able to turn the whole of its naked-looking cloacal region inside out, as if it has been ejected by the gases emanating from putrefaction inside the body. Even the stink from the exposed mucous membranes at both ends is the stench of death, and it is extremely rare for this impressive performance to be punished by killing.

Annika was witnessing a similar performance. And not until one or two cars drove past, stopped in the middle of the street and started to reverse, and the girl with the umbrella began to draw back, did Annika realise that it was Gaia Jessup.

Cautiously, Annika got out of the car. She saw men in jackets leaving their vehicles farther along, then the cars speeded up again and vanished. Annika saw the men making for the steps to the flat without haste. None of them approached Gaia Jessup, whose retreat beneath the umbrella Annika watched from her side of the pavement.

Annika followed her, and when she rounded the corner she broke into a run and crossed the street between hooting cars.

She ran round the corner and found she had lost sight of the girl. She walked slowly down the street, peering to left and right, convinced that Gaia Jessup could not have managed to run down to the next crossing, but must be hidden in a basement entrance or inside leading to one of the stairway doors.

Almost without a sound she suddenly stepped out from a hiding place behind a staircase and pointed a gun at Annika.

'Dr Niebuhr? Have you been sent by Osborne?'

'Where is Maria?' said Annika.

'Why?'

'Because she is in danger. Because you are in danger.'

'Why do you think I'm running away? How do you explain that you've come with all those bloody men?'

'I know all about Lucas Henry, Gaia. You were waiting for him here, but he didn't come because they've got him now. It's my fault. They have used me. Gaia, they know.'

It was impossible to interpret Gaia's expression on her heavily made up face, but for a moment it seemed as if she was irresolute. At both ends of the street people streamed past on their way to the centre. In the side street behind Gaia there was loud shouting and song and the sound of clinking bottles. Behind Annika there were fewer people and not so much din, and when she heard the sound of a car braking, doors being opened and footsteps on their way to the corner of the building, she knew they had not come to watch the carnival. Annika saw that there was no possibility of getting down to the bottom of the street and merging with the sea of people. She turned and decided there was no way back either. Heard the person slacken speed close to the corner. Gaia turned her eyes from Annika to the building and from the building back to Annika.

'Put your gun away,' said Annika, putting her hand decisively on Gaia's and moving it down her body. Gaia did not protest, perhaps because the movement was so natural, perhaps because doubt and indecision had taken the upper hand in her. Nor did she move back or protest when Annika took a step closer to her and put an arm round her neck, bringing Gaia's face up to her own.

'Kiss me.'

Someone stood at the end of the street watching them. The same person whistled a typically male tune. Then he turned away, but only when Annika was quite sure he had gone did she take her face away from Gaia, who stood still with closed eyes and half-opened mouth.

'Hey,' said Annika, clapping her hands in front of Gaia's face. 'Wake up. And no silly remarks.'

'You kiss quite a treat,' said Gaia.

'I know that,' said Annika, rolling her eyes. 'Now tell me where she is.'

'I've moved her. I've borrowed a friend's flat. It's this way.'

Gaia let herself into the flat and Annika followed her down a little narrow passage, passing a surfboard hung with a lemon-yellow T-shirt from Shark Attack. At the end of the passage was a small toilet with the light on. Over the door hung a stolen Exit notice.

Maria Johnson sat on a chair by the window facing the street, gazing stonily into space. At intervals a neon sign on the façade of the house by the window cast a red strip on the underside of the blind.

Annika stiffened at the sight of the girl. Gaia had spray-painted her from head to toe too. Only she had reversed the colours, so body and face were violet while lips and eyes had deep blue shades. Gaia had laboriously plaited her long black hair, put it up and rubbed in some kind of resinous substance, and in the furrows between these plaited sausages of hair she had painted blue shadows that made the hair look almost alive.

Annika went over and bent down before her. She did not look like a girl of fourteen. She was like a baby. A baby and an old woman at the same time. There was a lost melancholy expression in her eyes, the distant gaze you see in very young babies who still can't focus sharply, or like the oculars on an astronomical telescope searching a distant night sky.

'What have they done to Dr Henry?' asked Gaia.

'I don't know,' said Annika. She placed her hands carefully on Maria's arms, which hung loosely at her sides. 'Has she had any medication recently?'

'Dr Henry usually does that. I just move her around.'

'Doesn't she communicate at all?'

'Hardly at all. Sometimes she doesn't sleep either. I have some sleeping pills to give her.'

'Gaia, did Simon ever tell you about the sessions Maria went through?'

'Simon relied on me. He said it was important to get her away. But the clients hardly ever discussed our experiences. We were also there to get help, you know.'

'You suffered from ophiophobia?'

Gaia nodded.

'I had actually got over it. But when I got into the car it came back. Maybe it was the shock. I don't know. Simon and I had arranged for there to be money in the car. It was as if a spiral flew right up into my face when I opened the glove compartment.'

'You died in hospital, Gaia. You died in our hands.'

Gaia looked at Annika with an unfathomable expression.

'It didn't feel like that.'

Annika turned her attention to Maria again. She laid her hand on the girl's forehead. She did not react. She didn't even blink when Annika passed her hand across her face.

Gaia looked at her.

'What do you think is wrong with her?'

'I don't know. I'm not even sure she is the one something is wrong with.'

Annika started to stand up, but as she let go of Maria's hands the girl grabbed Annika's wrist as if in a reflex action. Smiling, Annika squatted down again with the girl's hands in hers. She felt warmth go through her. She was going to try to catch the girl's eye again, but that proved unnecessary now, for she was looking directly at Annika.

'Mother,' she said.

Annika looked enquiringly at Gaia, who merely shook her head resignedly.

'She does that sometimes,' said Gaia. 'She talks about her mother now and then.'

Annika smiled, and when she tried to give Maria a hug she felt the girl's body turn quite stiff at first, then cling to her almost desperately, and only reluctantly let go of Annika when she drew away again. Annika stood up, and her fingers slid out of Maria's.

Annika stood observing her for a while.

'When did she start to be like this?'

Gaia considered.

'At Christmas-time.'

'Perhaps she is catatonic. Maybe she has chosen this mental state herself. Maybe she has seen something she didn't want to see.'

Annika looked at Gaia.

'Doesn't she ever say anything?'

Gaia shook her head, but then seemed to think of something.

'She says the earth is burning.'

People were up in the trees, standing on balconies and fire escapes to watch the Mardi Gras parade. Through the streets they streamed in thousands, shouting, hooting and whistling, up to the districts around Liverpool Street, Darlinghurst and Moore Park Road, to see the drag queens, the gays with their provocative bananas, and Asiatic and Aboriginal gays and their inflatable dolls and and gigantic papier-mâché figures of the most extreme right-wing politicians.

Annika watched from the window of the flat while she studied the grazes on her hands and the bruises on her elbows. She bent her head and tried to force a few clear thoughts out of it. Her bent head said it all.

'You don't know what we should do, do you?' asked Gaia behind her.

Annika made no reply. She looked out into the dusk, lit by the artificial streetlights, by the neon advertisements on the house gables, and she looked up at Sydney Tower, proudly illuminated, with the subdued light at the summit where people were eating and enjoying the view.

She turned to Gaia.

'Did Lucas Henry say anything? Didn't he know anything?'

Gaia shook her head.

'Don't we know anything at all? Where he wanted her to go? Or his contacts?'

Again Gaia shook her head.

'You don't even know why she had to be moved?'

'I only know it was important.'

Michael Larsen

Annika turned to the window again. She saw a black car roll up
and stop just outside the entrance. Out stepped four persons. They
aimed straight for the entrance.

'Oh, shit,' she said, drawing back from the window. She glanced
down. One of the men stood looking up at the house. It was Frank
Kiesworik.

'What is it?' asked Gaia, straightening up in her chair.

'Is there a back way out?' asked Annika. 'A kitchen staircase?'
Gaia nodded.

'You can get out through the back yard.'

Annika crossed the floor swiftly, making for the hall.

'Take the girl. Meet me at Centrepoint.'

Gaia stood up and took hold of Maria. She made her stand up, but
as they crept past Annika in the hall, Maria grabbed hold of her.

'Come on now,' Gaia whispered, and pulled Maria, but she
wouldn't let go. She pressed herself against Annika's back and
wound her arms tightly around her body.

'I'll take her,' whispered Annika. 'Run, Gaia. We'll come in a
moment. I hope. If not . . .'

'What then?'

'Nothing. Run now.'

Gaia hesitated a brief moment. Then she vanished into the
kitchen. Annika took Maria's hands to make her let go. She turned
round to her and made a sign that she must be quiet.

'No matter what happens.'

Annika went cautiously to the door and put her eye to the spyhole.
There was nothing to see, but she took a half-step backwards in a
reflex action when the intercom rang. She let it ring.

She fumbled on the wall for the switch and when she found it
turned off the light. A lamp in the living room was still switched
on. She found the electricity cupboard hidden under a temporary
curtain just beside the front door. She switched off all three meters
and the flat was plunged into darkness.

When the intercom stopped ringing her mobile phone started.
She took the call but said nothing.

'Miss Niebuhr, we know you are in there. Let the girl go.'

Annika did not reply.

'Give us the girl and let's get it over with, Dr Niebuhr. I promise we'll let you go.'

'Do you really expect me to believe you, Kiesworik?'

While Kiesworik was speaking, Annika went into the kitchen to orientate herself. She went cautiously to the door, eased it open, made sure there was no one on the stairs, then picked up a bread knife that lay beside the sink and put it in the opening so the door could not slam.

Next, still holding the mobile, she went over to a telephone on the wall and rang the fire service to give the address. Then she searched on the table and in the wall cupboards. Pans, plates, bowls. Colander, cake tins, sieves. She tore things out of cupboards and drawers. A stone remover, an ice-cream spoon, forks and knives, ladles, palette knives, boning knives, butter pats, sharpening steels, a garlic press.

Annika cursed inwardly at the thought that they might be in a home that contained nothing combustible apart from the flat itself. Where is civilisation when you need it? At last she found what she sought in a tall cupboard beside the door. Methylated spirits. One can was full, another half full. And behind these was a row of other explosive fluids. Acetic acid, caustic soda, turpentine, and two bottles of Basta Pronto spray. She picked up an armful and carried them into the passage in front of the door.

'What have you got in mind, Miss Niebuhr? Are you going to publish what you know?'

'If no one else will.'

'Who would want to hear that message?'

'D'you know what, Kiesworik? Simon thought the USA and American culture had a disease that's slowly spreading. He was wrong. It does not spread slowly.'

'Open that door now. We haven't got time for all this.'

'No, I realise our time is limited.'

'Fascinating, isn't it, Miss Niebuhr? You and I and a small

exclusive circle will know about it. One second before it happens we shall know it. Sixty-five million years of evolution behind us, and the only advantage the most highly developed being this planet has known possesses over dinosaurs is that we know it. That we know we are going to be hit.'

'And you consider this knowledge to be restricted?'

'How would you have us explain it? That God can find it in his heart to do it? I am sure you nurture noble motives on behalf of this world. I think Simon did too. But look at the girl beside you. What do you think made her brain short-circuit? A few harmless ideas on geographical co-ordinates or the vision of a gigantic rock rumbling through space? We take responsibility for people. People have elected us to do that. Or appointed us to do it. And we stand by our responsibility. We take decisions. We arrange things.'

'I think all those responsible people seem a bit paralysed at the moment.'

'All we have, Miss Niebuhr, are calculations. What if we are wrong? Remember Swift-Tuttle? The comet? Periodic. Like Halley's. God's snowball? Remember the astronomers' predictions? It would hit us in 2126. In the seventh or eighth month. Blow us into dust. Annihilate all life. Fortunately they were wrong. Astronomers at the Minor Planets Centre recalculated the figures. Gravitational disturbances had taken it slightly off course. According to the updated figures we were no longer on a collision course.'

'I don't recall there being any great excitement over it.'

'It was too unreal. Too far away. But imagine the panic if we made it public that a celestial body was on course directly towards us and would strike within a few days.'

'But you have had weeks, haven't you? Months?'

'Wouldn't make any difference. Nothing could be done. Imagine Ragnarok. The numbers of dead. And then imagine we had been wrong.'

'And opportunist to the last, you gamble on an error in the calculations, or at least that it won't hit America?'

'You know that makes no difference.'

'What do you mean?'

'That a celestial body of this immensity will obliterate all kinds of class distinction and national disparities. That it will make not a jot of difference being a great VIP on some list that secures entrance to an underground bunker in case of war or global catastrophe. That the impact, regardless of where it occurs, will be all-encompassingly destructive.

'Calculations have been made that show if an asteroid of only five hundred metres diameter falls into the Pacific close to New Zealand, it will not only immediately wipe out New Zealand. It will raise a tidal wave that will be three hundred metres high in Japan, ten thousand kilometres away. Tsunami. The one that strikes Australia will be several kilometres high. We were not aware of that until recently. That asteroids can release tidal waves. Tales of the Flood in all the creation stories begin to make sense, don't they? An impact on land will create the same flood – only of earth. Right on the other side of the world where the surface waves and the inner waves will be focused, the effect will be almost exactly the same.'

'And no one does anything but sit and gape?'

'What would you do? Shoot it down? Risk fragmentation and a greater probability of being hit? Or hope for an error in the calculations? Or a deviation from the orbit?'

'I don't know.'

Annika could hear noise out on the staircase. She could guess from Kiesworik's breathing, which had quickened and affected his speech, that they were on their way in and up the stairs.

'The speed will probably be thirty to forty kilometres per second at the moment of impact. Imagine the earth being carpet-bombed continually with atom bombs of the Hiroshima size for a year and you have a picture of the extent of the catastrophe. Following that will come all the natural disasters one can think of. The rocks that are thrown up will fall and strike again. The seismic activity will release volcanic eruptions all over the world, the temperatures will be enormous, up to ten thousand degrees, everything on this earth that can burn, will burn. Then will come the darkness. No

311

light for years, the temperature will drop, there'll be radio active fall-out, atomic winter, followed by acid rain – plants, animals, human beings will have long since been wiped out – and then finally the greenhouse effect.'

'So if it strikes, nothing matters. And if not, you have Maria and can expect a pay-off from Uncle Tubby?'

She heard Kiesworik's voice through the door and cut off the telephone.

'Are you near the door, Miss Niebuhr?'

Annika hesitated. She looked through the spyhole and could make out several faces in the darkness of the stairs. She bent down and screwed the lid off one can.

'The girl is standing in front of me.'

'Dr Niebuhr, you know her brain is important. That it may be of decisive importance to decode the processes taking place in her head?'

Annika took the lid off the other can. She poured the contents over the little heap of cans and spray bottles. Then she stepped back a few paces and lit a cigarette.

'As Simon tried to do?'

'Look at the girl. Do you think he made a good job of it? Do you think Simon had the right to do what he did to her?'

'He was forced into it.'

'You are wrong, Miss Niebuhr. But if that's the picture of Simon you wish to maintain, I won't destroy your illusions. Besides, I don't have the time. Last chance, Miss Niebuhr. Give us the girl.'

'In what way am I wrong?'

'Are you still by the door, Miss Niebuhr?'

'Yes.'

'Then if I were you I would move away. We're coming in now. You can still open it. You have a count of three.'

She shouted:

'Tell me in what way I'm wrong.'

'One . . .'

Annika ran to Maria, who was sitting on the kitchen floor. She had her hands over her ears.

'Come along, love. We must be off.'

Annika took her hand and pulled her up. She could hear someone tugging at the door down the back stairs.

Just before a salvo of shots splintered the front door, Annika threw her cigarette stub on the floor, where the trail of methylated spirits leading to the cans and sprays caught fire. Whether it was this that ignited parts of the little heap of incendiaries or the shots coming through the door it was hard to tell, but when Annika, with Maria in tow, was on her way out of the door, something burst like a projectile through the wall of the passage to the kitchen and on over their heads. There was the hollow boom of an explosion accompanied by yells and screams. Almost at the same time shots could be heard from the back yard and there was the thunder of heavy steps on the stairs.

Annika emptied a magazine down the shaft when she and Maria had reached the first landing. She took out the empty magazine, dropped it on the floor, pulled a new one out of her pocket and inserted it. Then they ran up to the next floor.

Annika kicked the door just by the lock. Something gave way and the door cracked a few millimetres from the frame. And the second time she kicked, it opened. There was no one in the flat, which was in darkness. Annika pulled Maria after her and went through to the front door.

She tore open the door and ran out to the staircase. Just managing to make out a shadow farther down, she pulled Maria in front of her.

Down the stairs Frank Kiesworik stood aiming a gun at her.

She walked slowly down towards him with the girl in front of her.

'I know it's not very gallant of me,' said Annika. 'But . . . I am a woman. Throw down your gun, Kiesworik.'

'Let go of the girl, Miss Niebuhr.'

313

Michael Larsen

At the very second Annika saw him lowering his gun, he vanished from view a few steps down the staircase, so she could no longer hit him even if she tried.

Annika knew that in Frank Kiesworik's eyes she ranked no higher than a pair of bellows, an automatic lung, to be terminated if necessary. She knew he would not hesitate for a second to shoot her if he got the chance. But she also knew that under no circumstances would he risk hitting Maria.

With the girl pulled in close Annika crouched behind her head and started to walk down the stairs.

'Be sensible, Miss Niebuhr. You'll never get away from here.'

'Sensible? After Brisbane? You seem to have recovered miraculously fast, Kiesworik. What will you actually say to Osborne when he turns up?'

'He doesn't know where we are.'

'Yes, he does.'

She went on down the stairs cautiously.

'Thanks to you I have lost two people I loved. And now you ask me to be sensible? Is that how I'm to understand you? You killed Mike Lewis.'

'I only mean . . . Brisbane was a mistake, we just wanted to frighten you.'

'Why don't I believe you, Kiesworik?'

Annika descended step by step with Maria in front of her. Below them, farther down the staircase, Kiesworik moved backwards, keeping out of her range all the time. She glanced nervously behind her in case of a sudden surprise.

'Who shot Simon?'

'Is that what you want to know? Is that all? Kessler. Kessler shot him.'

Kessler. She had completely forgotten about him. He had brought Gaia in, he had circled around the Swedish couple when she was in the hospital reception area. He had stolen Gaia's bag. Not to conceal who she was. It was Kahn who had revealed that to her of course, when he turned up with all his questions and selective glimpses of the modest progress of the investigation. Kessler had been searching for Gaia's hideout. An address. How to find Maria.

'Now listen here, Miss Niebuhr. I'm putting my gun away now. So you can see I don't wish you any harm.'

'Out, so I can see you, Kiesworik.'

Hesitantly he took a step or two up the stairs. With a casual movement he threw down his gun on the landing in front of her and Maria.

Annika walked quickly down and pulled it towards her with her foot.

She hesitated a moment on the landing, and then made a sign with her revolver that she wanted Kiesworik up where there was more room for them to get past him. He stepped up on the landing and stood with his back against a door.

With her gun aimed at him and Maria as protection, Annika edged along the banister, but just as they were passing him he hit out hard at her gun, it flew out of her hand and down the stairs, she let go of Maria and kicked out at him, but he threw himself over her and together they tumbled down the stairs. Before Annika struck her head against the wall she had a confused glimpse, which rocked up and down like a merry-go-round ride, of Maria bending down and picking up her revolver. After the blow on her head her eyes turned into a camera in a frantic search of the surroundings, trying to focus sharply on Kiesworik, who was attempting to struggle upwards to reach his own gun, on Maria, who slowly raised the gun and aimed it at him, on her own hand stretching out in an effort to stop Maria from shooting.

Maria, still galvanised, stood pulling at the trigger when Annika's head cleared. But the sound of shots had turned into clicks. Maria had emptied a magazine into Kiesworik, who lay unmoving with a hand on the rail and his body spread over several steps.

Annika got up. She went to Maria and put her hand on the gun.

She twisted it carefully out of the girl's hand and pulled the last magazine out of her pocket. Then she put her arm round Maria and led her down to the exit. Behind her, heavy steps could be heard on the stairs.

'Come on, love. We must get away from here.'

The world was once very different. The Amazon river did not exist, and the Brazilian jungle and most of north-eastern Australia were covered by great oceans.

On the west coast of Australia near Pilbara are the stromatolites – 3.5-billion-year-old ancient forests of low algae trees. Sculptures like weird brain-like memorials to the first known life on earth.

The parts of the stromatolites that rise above the water are as hard as granite boulders; below the water they are soft and spongy. Here the primeval soup once bubbled. Here were the amino acids, the building stones of the proteins, the simplest substances in a living cell. Here carpets of algae with their deposit of carbonates left the first preserved traces of living cells.

In 1955 two scientists from the University of Chicago re-created a laboratory version of the earliest period of the world, and by exposing a mixture of methane, hydrogen, ammonia and carbon dioxide, which made up the probable atmosphere of the time, to electrical sparks that passed for lightning, produced amino acids within a few hours.

To Annika the Miller-Urey experiment had always seemed one of the most absurd endeavours in the history of man, for while you can rejoice in a weak moment at human insight into physics and chemistry, and at the fact that intellectually we are able to straddle billions of years, all this in reality serves as a powerful illustration of the relative strength we so often forget – that it will take over five billion years to verify that this attempt will lead to the human being.

The same feeling of hopelessness seized Annika when she stood outside the building, holding Maria's hand. Never had it seemed more fruitless to get herself moving, and she felt convinced that if she sensed the least inertia in Maria, the smallest mental block, she herself would come to a halt and be unable to move any more.

She ran away from the street, where the fire engines snailed their way among the costumed and excited people, with Maria's hand in hers. Never before had she felt so greatly distanced from the world and the human beings she moved among. They did not know it. Never before had people seemed to her so beautiful. Never before had they seemed so close. And never before had she felt them so far away.

While they ran through the streets, past the coffee bars, past Real Ale and the Café Cup with its black-and-white blinds, up alongside Hyde Park with its avenue of jacaranda trees and waratah bushes behind the wrought-iron railings, and through the human sea towards the Town Hall, she veered between envy at their innocence and a strange, indefinable indignation at it.

She looked up at the sky but there was nothing to be seen. The lights of the city lay like a delicate belt of photons above the buildings. Even if you screamed or shouted aloud no one would listen. You wouldn't be able to explain it to anyone. You would run into the same tolerant head-shaking and disbelief you met when trying to explain to visitors that Australia is a world where the cars drive on the left, where the steering wheel is on the right, where it is summer when it is winter in the north, where the swans are black and not white, where the water runs the wrong way down the drain, where the ocean currents run the opposite way to those in the northern hemisphere, where the sun stands highest when it is in the north, and where Cassiopeia's W in the sky is an M.

The amino acids are everywhere in space. In the enormous clouds of the Milky Way and in the asteroids that at intervals strike the earth. It is possible that once at the dawn of time, they provided the conditions of life. It is also possible that in themselves they are the recipe for how it could be annihilated again. It is possible that they act as regulators on our planet, according to laws and principles we do not know of. Everything is possible.

Annika looked at Maria, running along beside her. Something had been released in her. Something had brought her back. And something was driving her on. And it was with the aid of this indefinable energy she herself could move. As if by the faint friction of warmth that burned gently in her small hands, as if borne on by a strange love impossible to isolate and explain.

It is said that at the moment of death people experience an unleashed rush of images and fragments from their lives. Relive seconds, minutes, hours, see and participate in whole days and weeks and years of moving episodes in an otherwise lost time.

Another kind of picture, like the cyclone that suddenly revealed thousands of hidden dinosaur remains in north-western Australia, came helter-skelter into her head as she ran through the streets with Maria.

It was like stepping into a mental maelstrom, like sinking down into an internal time tunnel. And when it happened she felt goose-pimples on her arms, and waves of heat broke out all over her body.

She saw the sacrificial offerings beside the statue of Artemis, glass and ivory figures from Phoenicia and the small amber pomegranates from the shores of the Baltic. She travelled to Alexandria and saw the library burning and the ancient Egyptian lore and Greek papyrus rolls curl together in flames. And she saw Cleopatra put out her hand for the cobra that had protected Egyptian queens and kings for three thousand years. She saw the last pharaoh die.

She saw sabre-toothed tigers and mammoths perish in seas of flame and roaring floods and collapsing mountains, clouds of fire, rivers of rain. She saw nations she had never heard of, saw clothes unfamiliar to her, temples and sacrificial sites that did not exist, and animals that had never been described.

She saw the death struggle of a *Stenonychosaurus*, a swan lizard making for the depths of a blue ocean, she saw the looming walls of Knossos falling.

When she came out of her vision she realised that no time had passed. It had been like seeing with the eyes of a blind person, hearing with the ears of one deaf, travelling like ball lightning, pressed flat by gravity, like absorbing and consuming everything and yet devouring nothing. She had felt like this once before in her life. It was up in the Northern Territory when she was with Kookillo Dhamarandji, and they had experienced the 'Morning Glory,' the enormously strong sea winds that form over the Cape York peninsula every spring and roll in overland as a hundred-kilometre-long, three-kilometre-wide, dark bar of clouds at over a hundred kilometres an hour. Nature can be so vast and powerful that no words can give meaning to it. Beauty can swell up around this kernel of meaning. But no words can enclose it. No poem set it free. No painting can reproduce it, no music release it and no mathematical model express it. Even the word 'nothing' is impoverished. It is too small. And yet too much.

It is found by the sea, on the horizon, in the sky. It is found in all the places where the horizon extends beyond man's realm. It has nothing to do with God. It is far greater.

She thought of Simon as she ran. She looked at Maria. She thought of Simon. Of greatness that falls.

She ran over to the lifts that lead up from Market Street to the Gallery Level at Centrepoint. She looked around her but could see no pursuers. But nor could she see Gaia anywhere. She decided to try one of the other entrances to Centrepoint. She pushed Maria along in front of her, always holding her firmly so she did not vanish in another direction. Out in the street they ran and elbowed their way through the crowd and on to the next entrance. No Gaia. Then they ran back round the block. She wasn't there. Annika waited for a short while with the girl in front of her. She looked at her watch. Gaia should have arrived long ago. She looked around, her eyes roaming from one fast-food restaurant to the next. They went just inside the building and under the escalator that went up to the Gallery Level. There was no Gaia. She must have gone to the lifts that went up to the tower. Annika took Maria by the hand and led her on to the long moving staircase that rose to the first floor and the lifts.

They walked along on the soft carpets of the first floor, past fashionable Gucci and opal shops. From the tables, where guests in evening dress sat on comfortable chairs drinking cocktails while waiting for the lifts, they heard muffled conversation from beneath green plants like parasols.

'Welcome to Sydney Tower,' said a woman in uniform. 'Have you booked a table?'

'I'm just looking for a friend,' said Annika. 'Can I have a look around?'

The woman stepped in front of Annika, looked her up and down, looked at her torn and ragged trousers, the blood on her clothes and her face, and raised an eyebrow at the sight of Maria in all her colours.

'I don't think . . .'

Annika fished out her gun and stuck it under the woman's nose.

'I don't give a toss what you think. Will you kindly get out of my way?'

The terrified woman stepped aside, and Annika and Maria went over to the lift where they heard the operator's 'Sir and madam' as he invited a new group of guests to follow him to the open door. Annika took a quick look around the hall, in which she and Maria, like two exhausted and scruffy castaways, seemed likely to arouse as much attention as the revolver she was discreetly trying to hide behind her back.

Annika went up to the lift operator and shoved the gun in his side.

'You can do it discreetly. Or squeal like a pig. But get all those people out. Now.'

The man stood as stiff as a post. He opened his mouth but no sound came out.

'You've had your chance,' said Annika, and stepped into the lift, with Maria in front of her, pointing the gun from person to person.

'Out. All of you.'

A woman screamed. And the scream reached the people waiting at the tables, who fled in all directions. When the last person had left the lift and Annika and Maria were alone, Annika leaned out and looked around for a last time, but Gaia wasn't there. She must have gone up.

'Take us up to the first restaurant. If the lift stops at any time, or any other untoward thing happens, the girl will die. Immediately.'

The man looked at her, shaken. He nodded. Then the door slid shut.

Annika felt them being pressed against the floor as the cabin shot up through the shaft. At seven metres a second it would take them slightly more than half a minute to get up to the restaurant, which was 250 metres up. With Maria in front of her, she pinched her nose to neutralise the pressure in her ears. She was worried about what had happened to Gaia, but consoled herself with the thought that Gaia must have misunderstood her, or perhaps had been followed and forced to alter the plan.

She looked up at the monitor in the corner. The three double-decker lifts in Sydney Tower each have a monitor in the corner where one of the other lifts can be followed on black-and-white film. Annika had never discovered which of the others you were looking at. But she wondered why the one she was looking into was almost empty. In fact, as far as she could see, only one person was in it, a man with his back turned. A security guard, maybe. But she found it hard to believe they would dare to send a guard to arrest her after her threat to kill Maria. She knew there was constant radio contact with the tower, and the staff at the Gallery Level must undoubtedly be raising the alarm. No, she and Maria would be safe until the time came when they would have to go down again. The tower would be sure to have emergency plans. Against terrorists and hysterical women. They would have to go down again before the guards were organised, or Osborne and his men arrived. But then it occurred to her how close they were to the police stations.

In Liverpool Street and in Bathurst. And at that moment she knew that it would all come to an end here.

Annika stroked Maria's hair. Strange emotions washed over her. She so much wanted to do something for her, but it all seemed hopeless. She knew this ascent led to their journey's end. In one way or another. When they had found Gaia, what then? Where could they escape to? She wondered whether the girl could understand what she had seen. She hugged her close and felt Maria take hold of her hand.

Suddenly she tightened her grip. And Annika followed her gaze, which was directed at the monitor. The man with his back to them had turned round. It was the man with the scar, the man in the hospital – it was Kessler. He had Gaia in front of him.

Annika saw Kessler smile as he raised his gun.

She let go of Maria and started to hit the inside of the lift. She struck the control panel and the emergency button, but nothing happened, and she remembered she herself had commanded them not to stop the lift under any circumstances. She looked at the monitor again. She looked at her watch. Another twenty seconds and they would be up.

Annika moved behind Maria again. She laid a hand over her eyes.

It happened quite soundlessly. She saw the shot go off and Gaia's head thrown to one side. She put up her hand to prevent it, but she saw how Gaia just collapsed like a rag doll in Kessler's arm, which was still holding her up. Then he let go of her. She felt a violent tremor pass through Maria's body; she twisted free of Annika's grasp, slumped down in the corner of the lift and screamed.

Annika knelt in front of Maria, who hit out kicking and screaming. Annika tried to comfort her while keeping an anxious eye on the time and the door.

'Maria, love. Look at me. She may be alive. It's not certain she is dead.'

But Maria only screamed and kicked. Ten seconds. If she did not get the girl under control they were lost.

'Maria, love,' she said, 'look at me.'

Then Annika took hold of her and shook her. When she continued howling and screaming, Annika finally slapped her hard. Then she fell quiet. Shocked, she took her hands from her face and looked at Annika.

'I'm sorry, love. But if you don't pull yourself together, we'll die. Both of us.'

When the door opened they heard an almost celestial rushing sound. Cool air whispered over the thick carpets and soft muzak oozed gently from the loudspeakers on the little platform in the tower.

Annika stood with Maria in front of her. She crouched down behind her and whispered in her ear: 'He won't shoot at you.' Maria nodded, and Annika started to push her towards the lift entrance.

'I've got the girl, Kessler. In front of me.'

No one answered. Nothing but silence. Annika slid up behind Maria with her gun in her hand. Together they moved cautiously out of the lift, while Annika checked in both directions as thoroughly as she could. When they came to the corner of the wall, a uniformed waiter put his head round it and Annika started to give him orders.

'Ring for an ambulance. And see that the lift goes down. There's a wounded girl in it.'

It takes an hour and ten minutes for the cupola to revolve around the tower. From up here Annika had once seen the Southern Lights undulating on the horizon around the Pole, and in clear weather you could see the Blue Mountains over a hundred kilometres away. She reasoned that she and Maria must not only concentrate on not being hit, but also watch out for ricocheting bullets, as a shot striking the windows of the cupola would probably rebound from the two layers of glass.

Annika walked with Maria in front of her into the restaurant full of customers dining. The black table lamps sent out only a subdued light, so the reflections from the windows did not prevent the customers from seeing the view of Sydney, far below and flickering with lights.

A waiter balancing a tray of red and green drinks stopped at the sight of Annika and Maria.

'Ssh. There's a madman on the loose up here,' said Annika. 'Get the customers out.'

The waiter nodded, staring at the gun in Annika's hand and the colourful Maria.

At that moment the tray flew out of his hand and he grabbed his arm with a scream. When he fell to the floor Annika saw Kessler down at the end of the oval bar. She threw Maria to the floor, and as total panic broke out among the diners, crawled towards the bar with Maria at her side. People shouted and screamed. Some ran towards the exit, others threw themselves under the tables. Tables and chairs fell over, glass splintered, bottles fell and rolled across the floor.

She heard noise from the lifts. And saw policemen in combat uniform come running like a wall towards the first fleeing customer. Annika pulled Maria farther on in the direction of Kessler, so they would not be hit from behind.

The police yelled commands out into the room but Kessler responded by shooting at them. Then they threw the first tear gas cannister. It struck the thick glass of the cupola on the far side of the bar and continued on diagonally towards Kessler. The fire alarm was activated and the cupola sprinkler system immediately started to send down thin streams of water.

Annika glanced nervously at the curved wall from where she feared Kessler would come crawling at any moment.

The gas started to make her eyes smart, and she heard Maria whimper beside her. She put her arm around her, but at that moment Maria went stiff all over and put a hand on Annika's arm.

'The evil is going away,' she said, and directly after her words Annika rose above the bar counter and, turning, saw Kessler running towards the exit, saw him turn his face towards her, saw the gun in his hand, and then she quickly shot three times in a row, and Kessler fell.

There was silence. And then came yet another gas cannister.

Annika tore a cloth from a table and poured mineral water over it. She put the cloth to Maria's face and crawled farther out into the cupola. She barricaded herself with Maria behind an overturned table. Then came total silence. Water was falling around them.

Osborne appeared by the entrance. He walked, apparently unaffected, past the officers with their shields, stepped with a disapproving glance over Kessler and came towards Annika and Maria.

'Give me the girl, Miss Niebuhr.'

'What if I say no?'

'What do you mean?'

'If I think that would be wrong?'

'I would not like to be cheated out of the great reunion.'

She held the soaking cloth pressed hard to Maria's face so she could breathe. The gas and the lump in her throat brought tears to her own eyes. She carefully raised her head over the edge of the table and tried to focus on Osborne, who grew more and more blurred. Her eyes stung.

'I have only just received the information. As far as I understand it we have picked up a man who may be Mike Lewis. Alive.'

Annika felt there were real tears in her eyes now. Saliva gathered at the corners of her mouth and her nose was running.

'Are there no limits to what you can do?'

Osborne smiled at her.

'I'm not joking. It *is* Mike Lewis. And he is alive.'

Annika put her hand up to her face. She concentrated on not starting to weep and hesitated slightly before speaking, to stop her voice from breaking.

'Can I speak to him?'

'You must trust me. For the moment.'

'Where is he?' she asked.

'With our people in Brisbane. It is not official yet ... that he has survived.'

Annika rubbed her eyes. She looked at Maria beside her.

'How long have you known this?'

Osborne ordered everyone out of the place. Little by little Annika could hear his men leading the customers out to the lifts. Finally all sounds ceased. And she heard him sending his own people down. Now only Osborne was left.

'Two hundred and fifty metres up. You can't get any higher in Sydney, Miss Niebuhr. Has the view brought you some clarity as well?'

Annika drew the girl close. She turned round and tried to get a view over the place. The bar in the middle made it impossible to see if he had posted any men there while she hadn't been watching. She rubbed her eyes with the back of her hand.

'Are you alone now, Osborne?'

'Yes, I'm alone.'

'I could shoot you.'

'You could,' said Osborne, and Annika heard a match being struck as he lit a cigar. 'But you won't. You still have some questions, haven't you?'

'I don't know what to believe any more.'

'Isn't that a basic condition we all share, Miss Niebuhr?'

'You lied to me. Why did you lie to me?'

'I wasn't sure how you would react. I knew that you thought a lot of Simon, as I did. But I also had the feeling that you didn't realise what finally happened to him.'

'What do you mean?'

'Always problematic when man forgets how small he is, isn't it? Always problematic when man wants to play God. I have always thought that cynical idealists are worse than idealistic cynics. I have China to keep an eye on. It is my job. But Simon wanted to save the world. Miss Niebuhr, you and I know that we have no right to that kind of thing.'

'Why didn't you tell me about those sessions? What if those visions were not fortuitous?'

'I have seen the exposures. I don't know. Her screams. Unarticulated outbursts. One can recognise certain words and expressions. Most of it is incomprehensible.'

'I know his interpretations were correct, Osborne. I know he telephoned his information. I know the meteorite is on its way.'

'I have been in contact with NASA's JET Propulsion Laboratory as well as Caltech this evening, Miss Niebuhr. According to the new calculations, which have been confirmed by the Anglo-Australian Observatory, we have a margin of a couple of hours. It will not hit us, Miss Niebuhr. No one will ever hear about it.'

Annika said nothing. She pressed Maria's hand and laid her head back.

'You used me, Osborne. I could have been killed.'

'I made a mistake about Kahn. I am sorry about that. Now let the girl go. Then you will get Mike Lewis.'

'What have you done with Lucas Henry?'

'Dr Henry is going through a crisis of loyalty at present. He will get over that all right. He took a different view of the whole course of events. It can happen.'

'What will happen to me?'

'Nothing that diplomatic contacts can't handle. We are accustomed to sorting out these . . . controversies quite amicably. You are free, Miss Niebuhr.'

'What will happen to Maria?'

'I shall take her back with me. Believe me, Miss Niebuhr, that is the best thing for her. We have doctors who know her and can treat her.'

'I want to have access. I must have access to her.'

He hesitated for a long time before replying. And when he finally did, she was not sure he meant it.

'I can't see that being a problem,' he said. 'Can I have the girl, then, Miss Niebuhr?'

*   *   *

Annika slowly stood up. Maria stayed on the floor beside her. When Annika was standing, Maria looked at her, and Annika smiled and put out her hand.

When they had reached the middle of the room, the sky was illuminated by a great white light followed by an ear-splitting crash. Annika felt a shock go through her, but then realised that the flash of light and the crash came from Sydney Showground.

'Fireworks,' said Maria to Annika, 'it's only fireworks.'